An
Undiscovered
Life

by

Nancy Moser

Overland Park, KS

The Books of Nancy Moser

www.nancymoser.com

Contemporary Books

An Undiscovered Life
Eyes of Our Heart
The Invitation (Book 1 Mustard Seed)
The Quest (Book 2 Mustard Seed)
The Temptation (Book 3 Mustard Seed)
Crossroads
The Seat Beside Me (Book 1 Steadfast)
A Steadfast Surrender (Book 2 Steadfast)
The Ultimatum (Book 3 Steadfast)
The Sister Circle (Book 1 Sister Circle)
Round the Corner (Book 2 Sister Circle)
An Undivided Heart (Book 3 Sister Circle)
A Place to Belong (Book 4 Sister Circle)
The Sister Circle Handbook (Book 5 Sister Circle)
Time Lottery (Book 1 Time Lottery)
Second Time Around (Book 2 Time Lottery)
John 3:16
The Good Nearby
Solemnly Swear
Save Me, God! I Fell in the Carpool (Inspirational humor)
100 Verses of Encouragement—Books 1&2 (illustrated gift books)
Maybe Later (picture book)
I Feel Amazing: the ABCs of Emotion (picture book)

Historical Books

Where Time Will Take Me (Book 1 Past Times)
Where Life Will Lead Me (Book 2 Past Times)
Pin's Promise (novella prequel to Pattern Artist)
The Pattern Artist (Book 1 Pattern Artist)
The Fashion Designer (Book 2 Pattern Artist)
The Shop Keepers (Book 3 Pattern Artist)
Love of the Summerfields (Book 1 Manor House)
Bride of the Summerfields (Book 2 Manor House)
Rise of the Summerfields (Book 3 Manor House)
Mozart's Sister (biographical novel of Nannerl Mozart)
Just Jane (biographical novel of Jane Austen)
Washington's Lady (bio-novel of Martha Washington)
How Do I Love Thee? (bio-novel of Elizabeth Barrett Browning)
Masquerade (Book 1 Gilded Age)
An Unlikely Suitor (Book 2 Gilded Age)
A Bridal Quilt (Gilded Age novella)
The Journey of Josephine Cain
A Basket Brigade Christmas (novella collection)
When I Saw His Face (Regency novella)

An Undiscovered Life

ISBN 13: 978-1-7368108-3-5

Published by:
Mustard Seed Press
Overland Park, KS

This story is a work of fiction. Any resemblances to actual people, places, or events are purely coincidental.

All Scripture quotations are taken from The Holy Bible, New International Version.

Front cover design by Mustard Seed Press
Models: Marguerite Young & Nancy Young Moser

Printed and bound in the United States of America

Dedication

To my lovely mother,
Marguerite Young.
I am who I am because
you were who you were.
1921-2020

1942

1953

1971

2020: 99ᵗʰ birthday

1990s

Chapter 1

Elsie

"Come to me,
all you who are weary and burdened,
and I will give you rest."
Matthew 11: 28

I tucked my husband into bed, shoving the edges of the covers between the mattress and box springs.

"Gracious, Elsie. Ease up a bit. I need to be able to move."

"Sorry." I pulled the sheet and blanket loose and let them hang free. "I guess I want you to feel safe."

He extended a wrinkled hand that had an IV taped to its back. He touched my arm. "I am safe. I'm here with you. At home." His smile was wistful and kind. "I can't think of any place I'd rather be during my final days."

I didn't want to think about any *final* anything, couldn't avoid thinking about it, and didn't want him seeing me thinking about it, so I took the glass from the bedside table and filled it with fresh water. Then I moved a golfing magazine an inch closer to the bed.

"Sit," he said. "Now." His voice was stern.

I stopped my fluttering and sat on the dining room chair I'd had moved to the side of the bed. "There. I'm sitting."

"Your body may be sitting, but your mind is running a marathon."

"I can't help that."

"Yes, you can. You *have* to accept the situation, Els. We've had a good run, but I'm nearing the finish line." He smirked. "'Away from the body and at home with the Lord.'"

His faith was stronger than mine. I'd already argued with the Almighty that I wasn't done with Willis yet, had even argued with my husband, telling him he should *not* give up no matter what the doctors said. But neither argument had done any good. Willis was dying and there wasn't a single cotton-pickin' thing I could do about it.

He touched my hand, knowing what I was thinking. "Come on now, wifey. Stop trying to figure a way out of it. I've accepted my fate — long ago accepted it." He let his head sink deeper into the pillow. "Here I am, Lord. Take me."

Whether he liked it or not, it was my job to challenge his words. "Miracles happen every day. Don't begrudge me asking for one."

He gave me a sideways look. "Pray away. I'll not stand in the way of God surprising us, but . . . it's not like *this* is a surprise. Two years of fighting, Els." He held out his arms. "Look at me. I'm a living skeleton. My body's up and done, about to say over and out — and it's okay."

I slapped the side of the bed. "It is not okay! What will I do without you?" It was a question I asked myself multiple times a day.

"You'll live. Carry on."

I shook my head, feeling the threat of hot tears. "We've been married 69 years. I don't remember life without you."

He grinned. "You were a pretty young thing." His face softened. "Still are."

I moved onto the edge of the bed and crossed my hands over my chest. "See how you still melt my heart, old man?"

He drew my hand to his lips, then set it aside. "Now then. Plans. You must remember everything we've talked about."

I remembered. "Call Pastor Miller first thing."

He nodded. "Instead of flowers have people give memorials to our charities."

I shook my head. "You said I could have one arrangement."

He shrugged. "For you sake, not mine." His gaze was strong. "And you know the music I want."

"I do. Golden oldies like 'Amazing Grace' and 'I Surrender All.'"

He nodded. "And then, after I'm tucked away?"

Tucked away? Buried. Even he couldn't say the word.

He was waiting for me to finish going through his instructions. "I'm to call our financial planner. He knows where all the money and investments are." Willis had gone over it so many times I had a checklist in my head. "The other important papers — including the will and your life insurance policy — are in the safe deposit box at the bank." I sighed. "I've got it."

"You've got *that*. But I thought of something else that I really, really want you to do."

I was surprised there was something new. "You know I'll do anything for you."

"I know you will. That's why I'm asking."

He was making me nervous. "What is it?"

"I want you to make sure the family remembers."

Was that all? "They'll always remember you, my love. Don't worry about that."

He shook his head against the pillow. "Not me. I want you to make sure they remember *you*. Get to know you."

"Get to know me? I'll be right here."

"I want them to learn about you as you were in your *before* years. Before you were a wife, mother, grandmother, and great-grandmother."

"Ancient history."

He pointed a weak finger at me. "*Your* history. There's a lot they could learn from you."

It was ridiculous. "I never did anything important."

"Pish-posh."

I would miss him saying those two words. They were *his* words, the ones he said whenever I was overly concerned about something that didn't deserve my worry. Sometimes I'd found them annoyingly dismissive, but most of the time, those two nonsensical words helped me recapture some perspective.

But enough of him talking about me. "Right now we need to focus on you."

"For the moment perhaps, but I'm talking about after the boo-hooing, burying, and bundt cake." He nodded once. "Then it will be your turn."

I sat back. The idea of talking about myself made me uncomfortable. Perhaps I could have done so when I was younger, but as an eighty-nine-year-old woman? With old age had come an acceptance for who I was *now*, not who I was a lifetime ago.

Willis closed his eyes, but the conversation wasn't over. "Because of you, our family knows all about *my* life. You made sure of it, always bragging me up like I was God's gift."

"You are God's gift. To me. You deserve all the accolades I give you."

He shrugged. "Truth is, I liked the attention. But you, Elsie. It's time for you to let them know about the woman you are — the woman you were."

"How do I do that?"

He smiled a conspiratorial smile. "You'll come up with something."

I gently whapped him on the shoulder. "You're up to something."

"Maybe."

"Willis . . ."

His sheepish smile and shrug told me he wasn't going to explain. "Here's the reason I'm so adamant about this," he said, "and obviously, I've had time to think about it. The big problem with getting old is that our age becomes all anybody sees. They don't remember how vibrant we were or all the ups and downs that got us to where we ended up." Willis touched my arm. "The family has a lot to learn about living and you're the one to teach them. Share your life, Elsie. Share moments that changed you. If there's a lesson in it for them, it's a bonus. It's the sharing that's important."

I hadn't thought about the details of my past in a long time. It just *was*. As for our family . . . "Sometimes I do think they've forgotten us. They come and visit. They call. They're polite. But it's —"

"It's not enough." His brow furrowed — from emotion or pain?

"I understand they're busy," I said. "They often tell us as much. But sometimes they act like we're here, but not here. We're nonessential, like an old mantel clock you hear occasionally, but usually ignore. We've outlived our usefulness."

He smoothed the sheet over his chest. "I agree with everything you're saying, but don't be too hard on them. As good parents we encouraged them to live their own lives. I don't want to guilt them into being interested."

Maybe. But . . . I felt a spark ignite. "Guilt can serve a purpose. I'm not above using it, if need be."

He chuckled. "Do what you have to do, but . . ." His face turned serious. He nodded to a photograph of our 1952 wedding that had sat on the dresser forever. "Remember, above everything else, it's just you and me, kid."

I touched his cheek. "Everything we have and everything we are is because we were two people who fell in love."

"Actually, it started before we were a couple. Even though our youth was eons ago, those early years shaped us too."

That Elsie was a stranger to me now. She only came to me in fleeting flashes of memory or in the occasional old photo that captured a slice of time, a glimpse of her. Me.

The hospice nurse came in. "It's time for your medicine, Mr. Masterson."

I moved aside and the nurse added a med to his IV drip. Willis took a few deep breaths, and I watched the furrows of his face soften. More than anything I hated seeing him in pain. In the past few months his blue eyes had paled as if the colors of life were draining away from him. The lips that I'd love to kiss had grown thinner and tight.

As the medicine began to take effect he said, "You don't need to sit here, watching me sleep, sweetheart. Go on now."

I stood. "If I must."

"You must."

I gave him a parting smile. "Love you."

He winked as he always did. "Love you back."

I kissed his cheek and left him.

"Mrs. Masterson? Elsie?"

I drew in a deep breath and opened my eyes. The night nurse stood before me. I pushed myself upright in my chair. "Sorry. I dozed off. I'll go to bed."

"Yes, well . . ." Her face was solemn. "I'm sorry, but your husband is gone."

"Gone?" *Gone where?*

"I left the room to get a cup of coffee and when I went back in he had passed."

I pushed myself to standing, feeling wobbly. "Let me see him!"

The nurse handed me my cane and I took her arm for more support. We hurried to the bedroom, though there was no reason to hurry anymore. I stood beside the bed and looked down at my beloved.

He looked so peaceful.

Although I longed to throw my arms around him and sob into his chest, I knew he wouldn't want that. Willis had never been demonstrative with high and low emotions. *Keep an even keel on it, Els.* So instead I sat beside him and cupped his hand in mine. His skin was paper thin, a far cry from the strong hands that had held me, worked for me, and prayed with me.

I reached out and touched his cheek. "I wanted to be with you when you reached the finish line, my love."

The nurse stood nearby, but gave me room. "There have been signs he was passing soon, but even I didn't think it would be tonight."

My eyes brimmed with tears and I swallowed a lump in my throat. "He was all alone." I hated the thought of it.

"Don't fret about that one minute," she said. "The dying often wait until they're alone. Even if they have visitors who are perfectly silent. Even if they haven't opened their eyes or responded in days, they sense if someone's there. Many like to make the final journey alone."

"But I was his wife for nearly 70 years!"

The nurse put a hand on my shoulder. "There's no right way to die. It was between him and God."

I didn't like being left out.

"I have to make some calls, Mrs. Masterson. You're welcome to spend some time with him."

Time. We were out of time.

After she left the room I forced myself to breathe in and out. Then I stroked his cheek. "I should have stayed with you while you slept, old man."

"You don't need to sit here, watching me sleep, sweetheart. Go on now."

On. Going *on*. What did that mean?

It was over. He was over. God had him and I didn't.

A wave of anger collided with a downpour of grief, to be washed away by the surge of another emotion that was overwhelming, all-encompassing . . .

Love.

I let the tears have their way with me in deep, wracking sobs. I didn't think Willis would mind.

Finally, they retreated and I could say, "Love you, dear man."

I closed my eyes and imagined his usual wink and his *Love you back*. Then I smiled and tucked our endearments away in a special place where I would remember them forever.

Chapter 2

Elsie

"The world and its desires pass away,
but whoever does the will of God lives forever."
1 John 2: 17

They took him away. Took my love away. I cringed when I heard the front door shut. Then click. I heard their footsteps receding.

I would never hear Willis' footsteps again. Never see him. Hear him laugh. Or snore. Or get annoyed when he tapped his pen against the crossword puzzle magazine.

I would never feel his hand holding mine or feel his heartbeat as I snuggled against his shoulder. Or smell the Old Spice aftershave that I gave him every Father's Day.

I sat in my chair and closed my eyes in order to see him. I tried to push away the image of the shell of a man who'd inhabited the sick bed. I searched for the memories of a strong man digging a hole for the new maple in the front yard; the powerful man who spoke at bank conventions with authority and wisdom; and the charming man who sat across the kitchen table from me, letting me know with a look what he truly thought of my newest culinary experiment. For the record, I didn't like ratatouille either. Slimy, limp vegetables. The texture made me cringe.

I looked across the living room at his recliner which mirrored the angle of mine as they both faced the television. I wouldn't have to watch World War II documentaries anymore. Or endless, boring baseball games. But "American Pickers"? There was a chance I'd watch that on my own. And actually, I'd watch a thousand baseball games if he was here again.

It came to me that I could watch all the sappy romances I wanted and he couldn't stop me. It didn't give me comfort. Watching movies about love found, lost, and found again? My love was lost. Forever.

I heard movement in the bedroom. Vicki was here. Faithful Vicki, one of our favorite homecare ladies. A friend. The hospice nurse had called her, just as Willis had arranged. He'd known I would need Vicki's tender care. She'd come right over, and was cleaning up the room — bless her heart.

She appeared in the hallway, holding a rumple of sheets and towels in her arms. "I'm done in there, Elsie. Let me get this in the washer. I'll be back in a minute."

I listened to her movements: the sound of the detergent bottle being set on top of the washer, the closing metal door, the beep of buttons pushed. Then the whirr of water pouring in to wash away death so life could be made fresh again.

Willis had been made fresh again. I smiled when I thought of him in heaven, saying how-de-do to our Savior and reuniting with our parents and friends who'd gone before. If there were committees in heaven, Willis would surely be assigned a leadership role.

Vicki returned and sat on the ottoman at my feet. She touched my knee. "What can I do to help?"

I appreciated her not asking how I was, for *that* question was unanswerable. "You've done so much already. You're like a daughter to us."

She squeezed my hand. "The feeling is mutual. Willis was a delightful man, always full of surprises. He could always make me smile with his knock-knock jokes."

"His horrible, cheesy knock-knock jokes."

"Yes, they were." She glanced toward the door. "Do you want me to call the family for you?"

The thought of the family descending upon the house with *their* tears, *their* fears, *their* well wishes . . . Although Willis and I only had one daughter, the family had expanded two generations beyond. Six people would descend upon the house, saying all the right things, hugging, asking for details. I wasn't up to that. "Not yet," I said. "I need a little time." I thought of another excuse. "It's the middle of the night."

"That doesn't matter. They'd rush right over."

"I know."

Vicki nodded with understanding. Then she smiled and fished an envelope from her pocket. "Since we have some time . . . Willis wanted me to give you this as soon as he was gone."

I took the envelope from her, turning it over in my hand before opening the flap. My name was printed on the outside. Inside the envelope was a small notecard with an M embossed on the front. I'd given Willis a box of the cards ten years ago, and we still had half a box left. I opened the card, held it toward the lamplight, and read aloud. "'My dearest Elsie. I miss you already. Don't miss me too much, as I'm already having great discussions with Jesus about how things should be run up here.'" I laughed, imagining it was true.

"He always was an organizer," Vicki said. "A doer."

"Always." I looked back at the note. "'Through the years you always put our family first and made life interesting and enjoyable. You created treasure hunts for us every chance you got. I pretended to be annoyed, but actually I loved them because they let me know you were thinking of me. We always felt so loved. And so, because I'm thinking of you, I have created a treasure hunt for you, dearest wife. Follow the clues. All my love, Willis.'" I looked up at Vicki. "A treasure hunt?"

"He told me about all the hunts you put together for him and the family. Sometimes Easter baskets or for birthdays?"

"Or just because." I touched the words on the note. His handwriting had gotten so shaky, yet I appreciated his effort. "The rest of the family seemed to like the hunts, but Willis got annoyed when I'd set him off with a few clues, just to have the treasure be a love note, or a plate of cookies, or a new pair of shoes at the end. He'd act all peeved and say, 'Why do you make it so complicated, Els? Just give me the prize.'" I shook my head. "I'd always say, 'What's the fun in that?'"

"It took a lot of work for you to do that. They sound delightful."

"That was my intent." I looked at his words. "'Follow the clues'? What clues?"

Vicki pulled a slip of paper from her pocket, but held it close to her chest. "We don't have to do this now. It can wait."

I shook my head. "The one thing Willis hated was procrastination. He made me a treasure hunt, I shall take his treasure hunt. Now."

Vicki smiled. "I think he'd like that."

I held out my hand.

"Clue number 1." Vicki gave me the paper.

I read two words on the page, "'Best movie ever.'"

"Do you know which movie he meant?"

I thought a minute. "If it was *my* best movie ever it would be *It's a Wonderful Life*, but I have to think like him." The image of Steve McQueen came to mind. "*The Great Escape*."

"Do you have a copy of it?"

"Of course." I pointed toward the TV cabinet.

"I'll get it."

"No, I need to fully follow the clues." She helped me up and I rummaged through the old VHS tapes. "Here it is." And there *it* was — another clue taped to the side of it.

"How did he get all these clues set?"

"DeEtte told me she set them out for him the last time she worked."

"You ladies have been so good to us." DeEtte had worked two days ago. It touched me that Willis was thinking of me till the end.

The next clue . . . "'What we eat watching movies.'"

"Popcorn?" Vicki asked.

I shook my head. "Ice cream." We went into the kitchen and I opened the freezer. There were two cartons inside, his and mine. "Indulging in two flavors was a recent development. I finally tired of his French vanilla — with no toppings. A woman can only take boring so long."

"Sixty-nine years?"

Very funny. The other carton was definitely mine: Peanut Butter Party. "Willis hated peanut butter. How can anyone hate peanut butter?"

"Tis a mystery." Vicki pointed at the Vanilla. "I see another clue." She reached it for me.

It read, "Turquoise.'"

"The color or gemstone?"

"Gemstone I think." I headed to the bedroom, to a wood box on his dresser where Willis kept his cuff links and tie clips. "Willis wasn't a flashy man, but he really loved the intense blue color of that stone. He always wore the turquoise for important meetings." I lifted the lid on the box. Another clue waited. "'Hebrews 4: 16.'"

"I don't know that one."

Neither did I. Willis' Bible was on the nightstand and I handed it to Vicki. "Can you read for me? My eyes don't work on the small print without my magnifying glass."

She took the Bible, found the verse, and read, "'Let us then approach God's throne of grace with confidence, so that we may receive mercy and find grace to help us in our time of need.'"

"That's a nice one." It reinforced my image of Willis being confident in heaven. Plus the knowledge that God was with me now, as I dealt with it.

Vicki glanced at something else in the Bible then handed it to me. "This photo . . . is this a picture of you?"

Indeed it was. I sat on the bed to take a longer look. The photo showed me smiling on a swing as I held baby Rosemary on my lap. I was wearing a navy checked skirt and a peach blouse. My petticoat showed beyond the hem. Rosemary wore the cutest yellow jacket and coveralls that I'd made from a fine-wale corduroy. "Rosemary's about nine months here, so this has to be from 1956. Willis always said it was one of his favorite pictures."

Vicki sat beside me to look closer. "You look completely happy."

The memory of the day came back, fresh and new. "Isn't it odd how some memories are more vivid than others? I remember this exact day, looking up at the sky and pointing at the cloud formations to show Rosemary. After the park the three of us had ice cream at the dairy store. It was Rosemary's first cone." I smiled at the memory being played out in my mind. "The first time she tasted it her eyes got so wide. She grabbed for it and insisted on holding it, getting it all over herself. Willis had laughed and laughed." The contentment of that day oozed into *this* day, making me sigh. "Willis chose this photo because he knew it would make me feel better."

"How thoughtful of him." Vicki glanced at the picture again. "You were a beautiful woman — you still are."

"I was never beautiful, but I was pretty."

"You should show it to Rosemary. Share the day with her."

"She was just a baby. She won't remember."

"It's still a nice moment to share. It would be nice for her to see you two together, way back when."

Willis' words came back to me. *I want them to remember you.*

Vicki stood. "Speaking of Rosemary . . . do you want me to call the family now? Or would you like to rest a bit?"

The family. They needed to know Willis was gone.

I set the photo aside. "I'll make the calls."

"Do you want me to stay until they get here?"

She was such a dear friend. "That would be nice."

I tucked the photograph in the Bible and braced myself for the love and condolences of my family.

Chapter 3

Elsie

"For as in Adam all die,
so in Christ all will be made alive."
1 Corinthians 15: 22

How dare he die on me.

I sat near my husband's grave, seeing but not seeing the flag-draped casket; hearing but not hearing the pastor pray for Willis' soul and the peace of his family. I acknowledged but didn't acknowledge our family and friends that were gathered around me.

The wailing strains of a bagpipe playing "Amazing Grace" brought me back to the moment. Willis loved that song. Was he hearing it now from a front seat in heaven? Did God allow people to glimpse their funeral gatherings? Or was Willis too busy enjoying a reunion with everyone who'd gone before? Had he met Jesus yet? If so, I hoped Willis behaved himself. He'd gotten a bit brusque in his old age. He figured being 91-years-old had earned him the right to see who he wanted to see, and talk — or not talk — about things that suited him. And if the visit or the conversation bored or annoyed him, he would simply stand up and say, "Well that's that, then" and leave the room. Even when the ability to leave a room left him, he hadn't been shy about telling others to do the leaving.

I smiled at the thought, nodded at his grave, and whispered, *Well that's that, then. Isn't it, my love?*

Sitting next to me, our daughter Rosemary must have noticed my smile and deemed it inappropriate, for she took my hand and gave it a squeeze. I had employed the same gesture during countless church services when the child Rosemary would squirm or elseways not pay attention properly. What goes around comes around.

The last note of the bagpipe was blown away by the fall breeze. A smattering of leaves chased after it. The flag was properly folded and was handed to me by a man in uniform. "On behalf of the President of the United States, the United States Army, and a grateful nation, please accept this flag as a symbol of our appreciation for your loved one's honorable and faithful service."

"Thank you." Willis would have loved being honored like this. Being appreciated had been important to him and I'd done my best to fill that need. Being appreciated was important to me too, though I'd long ago realized the cup of my need had remained mostly empty.

I'd made a huge effort to sing Willis' praises — not that he wasn't deserving of every brag and boast. He was a veteran of the Korean War, had been a successful banker through high times and low, and was active in various clubs and church activities. When people in the community said they were coming to pay their last respects, they meant it. The funeral was well-attended.

Our family knew all about his life because I had told them. The day he died, he'd instructed me to share my life with them — make them remember *me*.

Easier said than done. Our conversation and the treasure hunt he'd made for me had already grown faded and shady. Could I blame age or grief for my reluctance to follow through? I'd tried to do as he'd asked, but my attempts to pinpoint important moments to share seemed inconsequential amid the funeral preparations. And now, when I tried to remember what I had come up with, my mind was a blank. And I had no idea where my notes were. Perhaps they'd been thrown—

"Mom?"

I looked up at my daughter. The service was over. Everyone was standing.

Rosemary took my arm, helped me up, and gave me a fresh tissue. Only then did I realize I was crying fresh tears.

"It will be all right, Mom. I promise."

I hugged the flag to my chest and said, "Thanks, honey. I know."

Even though I didn't.

I was glad to be home. It had been a long day at the church, at the reception, then at the graveside. Although I would have liked to go to bed, there was one more to-do on the schedule: a family dinner.

"Have a seat, Mom. We'll do all the work," Rosemary said.

Don't mind if I do.

I sat in my favorite chair in the living room and let the six members of my family take over in the kitchen and dining room nearby. Luckily, kind neighbors had brought over casseroles and produce during the last weeks of Willis' illness, so the freezer and fridge were over-stocked. It would be good to get rid of it all. It was too much. Especially since I hadn't been hungry. Still wasn't.

I loved how my family never wanted for conversation. Rosemary and Everett had plenty to talk about with Everett's recent retirement. Their daughter Holly shared her latest adventures in real estate, while *her* husband, Vernon, talked Chiefs' football. Their oldest — my great-granddaughter, Paige — shared her excitement about living on her own, the goings-on at the Comfy Café where she was the cook, and her chef's classes at the local college. And Baylor, my sixteen-year-old great-grandson — last but never least — sat at the island, swiping things left and right on his phone so he could share videos with those around him.

Although their camaraderie gave me pleasure, at this moment it also irked me. There was no reverent talk of their father, grandfather, and great-grandfather. It was as though they'd cried a few tears, buried him, and were off to the next life event — without him.

Without me?

I was not one to take offense easily, but after 45 minutes of conversation that completely excluded me, I felt the seed of outrage grow. Not a single person had asked me how *I* was doing. Not a single one had thought to ask me if I *wanted* to be in the kitchen where I could share a Willis story — something to make them think beyond their own busyness. Nope. They'd dropped me off in my chair in the living room, to sit, be still, and stay out of the way. Good dog.

It was obvious Willis' time in the limelight was over. Dead. And. Gone.

I closed my eyes and willed the anger away. What good would it do to make a scene, showcase their selfishness, and demand the attention I deserved as a new widow and the matriarch of the Masterson brood. I could imagine the scene, but chose another way.

I stood, took up my cane, and slipped away to the master bedroom. I closed the door with a subtle click, sat on my side of the bed, then lay down, turning onto my side, shoes and all. I drew Willis' pillow out from under the bedspread, hugged it close, and took in the scent of him.

I dozed.

I wasn't sure how long, but was awakened by Paige touching my shoulder. "Nana? You want to come eat something?"

My eyes shot open. I felt a bit embarrassed to be caught napping. This was my house. I was the hostess. I had guests. "I'm coming. Give me a minute."

Paige kissed my cheek and left me alone.

I lay on my back and drew in a deep breath, forcing reality into my lungs. I looked heavenwards. "Help me get through a few more hours, Lord."

I'd worry about the rest of my life later.

"A few hours more" was accomplished.

I nibbled on some food to appease my family and the rest was tucked away in Tupperware and dispersed to other freezers. Soon after, they took turns saying their goodbyes. Unwittingly, the farewells played out from youngest to oldest. Baylor gave me a peck on my cheek, Paige hugged me long and hard, Holly's hug was a quick touch and release, Vernon put his arm around my shoulders, Everett — a big bulk of a man with a lumberjack beard — gave me a bear hug that tickled my neck, and Rosemary embraced me cautiously as if she feared I would break.

She paused at the door. "Do you want me to stay?"

Yes. No. Maybe.

No won out. I gave her the same answer I'd given her the past four nights. "I'll be all right. I guess I'd better get used to it."

She gave me a plaintive look as if my truth offended her. "I'll call you in the morning."

I stood in the doorway and waved as they drove away. I lingered there until the street grew quiet again. I missed the drone of cicadas that accompanied the heat of the summer, but I loved the smells and sights of autumn. A carpet of maple and elm leaves covered my yard and the air smelled of spice and pumpkin pie and naps. Willis and I had loved the season. Would I continue to love it now that it was the season of his death?

A breeze shuffled the leaves and made me shiver, so I went inside. I stood in the foyer and let the silence wrap around me like...like...

A warm blanket? Or a shroud?

It was too soon to tell.

Out of habit I went into the kitchen to finish cleaning up, but everything had been done. It was almost disappointing. I refolded the kitchen towel that hung from the dishwasher handle and patted it twice.

Now what?

I returned to the living room and glanced at the small TV. Our family always teased us about it. "We need to get you some binoculars to see it." Willis and I had never upgraded our 1980s television because TV wasn't that important to us. We had a few favorite shows, but we never just had it *on*. We were too busy.

Before he retired Willis had worked all day at the bank and often had to schmooze customers in the evenings. For much of the twenty-six years since then, he'd met his cronies at a local café for lunch once a week to talk politics and football.

He liked to dabble with his woodworking, and he'd taken up golf, but had never gotten good at it. I had taken it up too, just to be with him, even though I found no joy in it and would have rather been doing laundry. Willis never forgave me for getting a hole in one when he'd never shot one himself.

I had spent our retirement years playing bridge—I'd tried bunko but found it too silly. I was involved with church and neighborhood meetings as well as numerous Bible studies. Since most women worked outside the home, many of the gatherings had to take place after dinner. So when did we have time to watch TV? During the week I had coffee with my best friend, Neda; sewed patchwork blankets for charity, cooked great meals for Willis, and read. A lot.

All of which meant I was used to spending time alone in this house. Yet tonight . . . tonight was different. Everything was *over*.

I heard Willis's voice in my head. *Get on with it, Elsie. Don't dwell.*

As usually, he was right. So I checked to make sure the front door was locked, turned off all the lights but the one by my chair, and walked toward the bedrooms.

But in the hallway I paused. I looked toward the room we'd shared for sixty-nine years.

The room where he'd died.

I glanced at the guest room at the other end of the hall. When he'd gotten sick I'd slept in there to make him—both of us—more comfortable. After he died I'd continued the habit.

I looked from one room to the other. It felt like a defining moment. *Don't be ridiculous, Elsie. You napped in the master. It's your room too.*

But napping wasn't sleeping. Somehow the master had changed ownership. It now fully belonged to Willis, the master of the house. And since he was gone . . .

"Love you," I called out.

The silence was heavy. Willis wasn't there to wink and tell me "Love you back." And so I walked toward the guest room.

Chapter 4

Elsie

"Anyone who does not provide for their relatives,
and especially for their own household,
has denied the faith and is worse than an unbeliever."
1 Timothy 5: 8

I opened my eyes and glanced at the clock. 7:32. I immediately sat up in bed, glad it was finally a reasonable time to get up. My awakenings at 11:52, 1:14, 2:35 — and at least three other times — were frustrating because common sense had won out, telling me I *had* to stay in bed, fitful or not.

My muscles objected to my first steps. They hadn't gotten enough rest either. My cane received a strenuous workout as I went to the master bedroom to get dressed.

I paused beside the bed. The empty bed. A dining room chair still held vigil at its side. How many hours — how many days — had I sat in that chair, talking to Willis, trying to cheer him up by chatting about the family, reading to him, praying over him.

A lot of good it had done.

During the final weeks the hospice ladies were amazing — I was in awe of their compassion and calm. They'd been completely knowledgeable and had gently explained what was happening — and what would happen. Their words had played out exactly as they'd said, which gave me a certain sense of comfort. Dying was natural. It's what people . . . did. Willis and I felt peace in knowing where we were going and that we'd see each other again. How did people who didn't have that reassurance of faith handle death?

Faith or no faith, it still galled me that Willis chose to die when I wasn't in the room. I had seen many movies where the family was at the bedside during the last breath. In some ways, I felt cheated.

Yet I should have expected it. Willis had always been an independent sort. Periodically he longed for solitude and would often be blatant about it. "I need my time, Elsie." I'd learned to take the hint and would leave him be, for if he *didn't* get such time I'd suffer under one of his bad moods.

The phone on the bedside table jarred me out of my memories.

"Morning, Mom. I hope I didn't wake you."

Rosemary was also an early riser. "You didn't."

"How did you sleep?"

I didn't want to go into it. "Well enough."

"Would you like me to bring over breakfast?"

Breakfast.

"Mom?"

I blinked slowly with a new realization. "I made breakfast every morning for 69 years."

"I don't know if that's inspiring or depressing. But today I'll do it for you. What would you like? I could make eggs or oatmeal or — "

"No!" I hadn't meant for my response to be so intense. "No eggs. No oatmeal. No toast. That's all your father wanted to eat."

"Why?"

"Because when he turned fifty he decided to eat healthy." *Forty-one years ago?*

"You can eat healthy tomorrow," Rosemary said. "What *would* you like? The sky's the limit."

My mind went blank. "I'm not really hungry."

"Nonsense. I'll surprise you. Would you like coffee?"

Coffee. I couldn't remember the last time I'd had coffee because Willis's health kick had included changing his drink-of-choice to tea. Earl Gray. *Don't mess up good tea with any of those fancy flavors, Els.*

"Coffee might be good." I used to love coffee.

"Cappuccino? Mocha latte?"

"I have no idea what you're talking about."

Rosemary laughed. "Leave it to me. See you in thirty."

I hung up the phone and sighed. I had thirty minutes to make myself social.

Rosemary swept into my kitchen on a wave of autumn air and the intoxicating smell of coffee.

"I come bearing gifts!"

She set a grocery sack and a drink tray on the kitchen table.

"What did you get?" I asked — for now I *was* hungry.

"Be patient. And have a seat. I'm not through yet." She went outside again and came back carrying a box that held a Mr. Coffee machine. "For you."

"You didn't have to do that."

"Do you have a coffee maker?"

I had to think. "I might have an old percolator somewhere."

"Case closed." She put it on the counter. "I'll set it up later." Then she stood over the bag with a mischievous smile, as if it contained treasure. "Firstly . . . voila!" She pulled out a small can of coffee. "French vanilla. Do you like French vanilla?"

"I have no idea."

"If you don't like it I'll take it home and get you something else."

"Rosemary, you're too good to me."

"You ain't seen nothing yet." She pulled a box of cereal from the bag. "Frosted Flakes."

I had to laugh. "Those were your childhood favorite."

"Still are." Next she took out some bananas and blueberries. "To top off the cereal."

"Sounds great."

Rosemary mimicked Tony Tiger. "They're gr-e-e-e-at!"

It felt good to laugh.

"And finally . . ." Rosemary removed a white bag. She unfolded the top and took out two chocolate sprinkle donuts and one white frosted one. "I already ate my other white one. The two chocolate ones are for you." She set them on a napkin in front of me.

All I could say was, "Oooh." And I meant it. They looked delicious. Decadent.

Rosemary put a hand on my shoulder. "It's rather pathetic that you *oooh* donuts."

I huffed at her. "I am not pathetic. Don't call me that."

"I didn't meant to offend." She handed me a coffee. "It's a pumpkin-spiced latte — meaning it has milk in it."

I put my hand around the paper cup. "Do I take the lid off or not?"

"Your choice. What would you prefer?"

"Off, I think. In fact, could you pour it into a mug please?"

Rosemary gave a little groan of disgust. "You're so old-fashioned."

"Yes, I am. And I'm also old. Indulge me."

She went to the cupboard, got out a china mug with wildflowers on the sides, and transferred the coffee. "There you go." She sat in Willis' chair. "Now eat. Savor. Enjoy."

I looked at the donuts.

"You have to pick them up to eat them." As if demonstrating how to do it, Rosemary took a bite of the white-frosted donut. "Mmm-mmm."

I took a bite of a chocolate one. A sprinkling of sprinkles fell onto my lap. Yet its deliciousness trumped the mess.

"Yeah?"

"Mmm."

"Told ya. Now try the coffee."

I blew on it, then took a sip. Again, the flavor was delightful. I dabbed at my mouth with a napkin. "You spoil me."

"Wow. You're easy."

Suddenly, I felt a wave of sadness wash over me. I pushed the donut away.

"What's wrong?"

I wrapped a hand around my mug, letting it warm me. "What am I going to do now? He's *gone*, Rosemary. The man who was my life is gone."

Rosemary bought herself a moment by taking another bite. "I can only imagine how hard this is for you. Unfortunately, I don't have any specific answers. I don't think there *are* any specific answers."

"I like having answers."

"I know you do, but —"

The doorbell rang, but before either of us could stand to answer it, we heard the door open. "Hello? Nana? Mom?"

"Back here," Rosemary said.

Holly entered the kitchen dressed for work, her shoulder-length hair smoothed into a neat bob. She'd recently had some reddish highlights applied to her usual dark brunette. She looked pretty and put together.

Holly did a quick scan and pointed at the box on the counter. "Hey! You got a coffee maker. I hated when Grandpa wanted us to have tea with him. Tea is not my cup of tea."

"Nice to see you too, Holly," her mother said. "You could say hello first." Rosemary nodded toward me.

"Sorry." Holly kissed my cheek. Then her attention veered away. "Donuts?" She peeked inside the empty white bag. "None for me?"

"You can have my second one," I said.

"No, you can not," Rosemary said.

27

Holly sat at the table and squished a wayward sprinkle with her forefinger. "How you doing, Nana?"

"Fine. I'm fine." I realized this might be a oft-used word in the next few weeks or months. It was easier than explaining what was hard to explain.

"She *will* be fine," Rosemary said. "We were just discussing what Nana should do next."

Holly's dark eyes brightened. "Are you going to sell this place?" She popped out of her chair and walked around the small kitchen. "These Mid-Century Modern houses go for a mint—even though we're twenty miles from Kansas City."

I was appalled by the idea of selling. "Where would I go? We've lived here forever."

"There are all sorts of nice retirement places around, and—"

I shook my head. "I am not leaving."

Rosemary intervened. "Of course you aren't. You still have Vicki and DeEtte coming to help, right?"

"Of course. They're like family."

"Good. As far as you wanting to stay put? That's not something we have to talk about now." Rosemary leveled her daughter with a look. "What's on *your* agenda today, Holly? Do you have a showing?"

"I had one last night, but this morning I realized I didn't lock up the pool house in back so I have to run over and do that—luckily, the house is empty." She sighed as if the day had already been long. "My head is *not* on straight lately. Baylor just called to remind me that he needs a ride to something-or-other, so I have to get him first, and . . ." She took a breath. "I also want to go to two realtor open houses in the city this weekend, and will be closing on a house that sold for $400,000. It's been a busy week."

"Indeed it has," I said. *Remember your grandfather's death and funeral?*

Holly seemed to catch her mistake and tried to placate me with another peck on the cheek. "Sorry for rambling on, but I gotta run. Just wanted to stop by." She paused at the doorway leading from the kitchen to the dining room. "Can I get you anything before I go, Nana?"

More than three minutes of your time perhaps? But I said, "Not right now. Have a good day."

"Ta ta." And she was gone.

Rosemary sighed. "Sorry, Mom. I apologize for my daughter. You should take as much time as you need to figure out your next steps."

She glanced toward the front door. "I've talked to Holly about being self-absorbed, but . . . I thought once she hit forty she'd mellow."

I chuckled. "I don't think that's possible. I just wish she wasn't so tightly wound."

Rosemary's face turned pensive. "Actually, I fear it's hurting . . . things."

"What sort of things?"

Rosemary popped the last of her donut in her mouth and talked while chewing. "Nothing. Don't worry about Holly and her family."

Holly and her family were having trouble? Paige was off on her own, but Baylor was still at home. I had a soft spot for him. I was always drawn to the underdog—a term that suited Baylor perfectly. Nerdy, nice, and neglected.

Thinking about my granddaughter's family made me think of my daughter's family. "How are you and Everett doing since he's retired and home all the time?"

"Okay. I guess."

I raised my eyebrows.

"You know I'm busy with all my meetings." Rosemary's face lit up with a fresh smile. "The state board of Beautify Kansas is nominating me for president."

This wasn't surprising. "That's nice," I said. I hesitated to say the next, but said it anyway, "Do you need another time-consuming responsibility like that?"

"How can I refuse? The other woman who's in the running—you may know her? Sandra Carhart?"

I shook my head.

"She's pretty worthless. She tries and tries to worm her way to the top, but never wins."

"So it's a question of winning?"

Rosemary threw away the bakery bag then folded the grocery sack and put it between the fridge and the lower cabinet where a dozen of its mates hung out. "I serve where I am asked to serve."

"Even though you have a retired husband at home now?"

"Everett's okay with it."

"Is he?"

Rosemary opened a drawer. "Want me to put your extra donut in a Baggie?"

"Sure."

I watched Rosemary's busyness as she tidied and got the coffee machine set up. For some reason it exhausted me.

"There," she finally said. "You are ready for tomorrow. The coffee filter and ground coffee go here. Pour the water in the back, push ON, and you're set."

I knew I wouldn't remember any of it.

Rosemary looked around the kitchen. "Now that breakfast is finished . . . what would you like to do today? Do you have any tasks you put off while Dad was sick? I'm game for anything."

Surprisingly, the thought of her staying for any length of time didn't thrill me. I wanted people's attention, but didn't? "I think I'd like to rest a bit — if you don't mind."

Rosemary cocked her head. "You just got up."

"I didn't sleep well." I pushed on my cane and stood. "If you don't mind."

Rosemary's eyebrows spoke for her. "I'll leave you be then." She gathered her coffee and the empty appliance box and headed to the door. "Call me if you want some company. Or . . . you *could* watch some TV."

It was interesting how she equated the company of companionship with the company of TV people. We exchanged a hug and she left.

I walked into the living room and sank into my chair. I enjoyed the silence a few minutes, then realized it would be too easy for it to swallow me whole.

Remembering Rosemary's suggestion, I took up the remote and turned the television on. A local news anchor detailed two shootings before awkwardly segueing to an announcement about some beer fest this weekend.

Next. A shopping channel showed a woman with too much makeup and scary-long fingernails trying to sell me skin cream that would minimize my wrinkles in three weeks. "Not these wrinkles," I told the screen.

I switched to a game show, but the canned noise was intrusive. People clapped and cheered for washing machines and a four-day trip to Vegas. Didn't they know that *things* were of little consequence?

All the shows seemed completely insignificant.

Yet they were better than the significance of silence.

Chapter 5

Holly

"Pride goes before destruction,
a haughty spirit before a fall."
Proverbs 16:18

I awakened with a bolt and immediately looked at the clock on my bedside table. And burst out of bed.

My sudden movements roused Vernon. "What's wrong?" He looked at me with one eye open.

"I overslept!"

He raised his head enough to see the clock. "Don't be stupid, Holly. It's five-fifteen."

"You know I need to get up at five."

He grumbled and turned over. "Nobody needs to get up at five."

I ignored him and went through my morning routine—which was extensive on workdays. My forties had hit me hard physically. No more pastries for breakfast or three pieces of pepperoni pizza for lunch. My expanding waistline made me choose yogurt with granola and two pieces of gluten free veggie pizza. Yuck.

My skin had betrayed me too. Even though I had a lighted magnifying mirror attached to the bathroom wall, I leaned toward the regular-strength wall mirror to put on my makeup. Whoever invented the magnifying mirror was a masochist, for it was far too honest about my wrinkles. Scary honest.

Once I was ready I passed Baylor's room on the way out. His light was on—which was unusual. I knocked softly.

"Yeah?"

I opened the door and found him sitting at his computer. "Why are you up so early?"

"Trying to keep up with Momsie."

"Don't be rude." I noticed an opened book nearby. "Homework?"

"Math test." He didn't turn around to look at me.

"You'll do great. I'm off now. See you at dinner."

"Maybe."

"Maybe?" Was Baylor actually going to be *out* around other people and socialize?

"I'll be here. You and Dad might not be, but I'll be here."

I couldn't argue with the truth. "Ace your test."

"I always do."

I closed his door with a soft click. Of course he would do well. Baylor was thriving in advanced classes at Carson Creek's only high school. I'd always struggled to get good grades. Taking the exam to get my real estate license was a challenge, even after I had Baylor and Paige quiz me. The fact that both my kids were brilliant academically was a mystery. That they obviously took after their father was annoying.

In the kitchen I poured coffee in my travel mug, grabbed a banana and a protein bar, and headed to the office to conquer the world. Or Kansas City. Whichever came first.

Even after waking up late I was at work by six. My colleagues came in at seven. Which was, of course, the plan. And there *was* a plan, a carefully detailed masterplan to be the most successful real estate agent in the metro area.

"Morning, Holly." My boss, Charles, passed my cubicle — one of twelve in the main room of Dream Chasers Realty. "Hard at work — as usual."

"Yes, sir." I stood. "Actually, I wanted to let you know that I think I'm getting a new listing. The Barrett place in Prairie Village. $525,000."

He nodded approvingly. "Excellent. List it *and* sell it."

"I'll do my best, sir."

He moved on to his office and I returned to my computer. I couldn't help but feel a little deflated. I wanted Charles' approval — ached for it — yet every time I shared a victory, he diluted his praise with another challenge. Yes, it was true that I could double my commission if I sold the house as well as listed it, but in some ways that was harder. It involved finding buyers who wanted to hire me to take them around to dozens of houses — some, multiple times. The whole agenting process was the old Catch 22 — without a distinguished reputation no one would hire me, and I couldn't gain a distinguished reputation *until* people hired me.

Toward that end, I checked my calendar. The monthly Chamber of Commerce Meet & Greet was today at ten. I'd be there with my business cards, my best spiel, and a beaming smile. *That* was the way to be a success.

I entered the reception at the Chamber and immediately sized up the room.

I saw a coworker but could talk to him later. And there was a woman who owned an insurance company, but she'd shunned me last time, so I wouldn't give her the time of day. I returned the wave of a woman who ran a clothing store, but didn't move toward her. I'd heard it wasn't doing very well. I didn't want to align myself with losers.

Finally, I saw Anna Thompson who owned the Timberstone Steak House. I'd heard she might be selling her house — a rumor that was reinforced when I saw two agents from a competing company taking turns, shaking her hand.

There would be none of that.

I inserted myself in the group. "Hi there. Nice to see you, Anna. How's business?"

"Very fine, thank you." Anna turned to the other agents. "You know Bob and Bridget?"

I gave them a nod, then turned back to Anna. "I heard you might be selling your house?"

Bob and Bridget's eyebrows rose as they exchanged a look. So be it. It wasn't my fault they were timid.

"Yes, you heard right," Anna said. "But it's still a bit early. We're just starting to do some fix-ups here and there. We're going to paint the dining room this weekend."

"What color?" I asked.

"I've always liked burgundy."

I crinkled up my nose. "Actually, that's so . . . nineties. If you want to appeal to buyers you need to go neutral. Everywhere."

"But neutral is boring."

Bob chimed in. "It doesn't have to be. You can add color with accessories."

I was going to say that. Instead I said, "You'll also need to declutter. Take down all your family pictures because they make it hard for buyers to imagine themselves in the home."

Anna looked worried. "I love my family pictures."

Bridget put a hand on her arm. "And what a lovely family you have. You can keep some of them up. I like seeing who lives in a home. It makes it feel like a home."

I was incensed. Everything I'd said, they added to or negated. I wasn't getting anywhere. I handed Anna a card and smiled. "When you're ready I'd love to list it." I gave a look to the other two. "And I'd sell it. Guaranteed. Nice seeing you."

I strolled away but immediately noticed the trio putting their heads together in gossip mode.

Whatever.

I spotted someone I didn't recognize. He was an average-looking man in his fifties, dressed in business casual but looking anything but because he kept shifting his weight from foot to foot. Was he worth my time? I didn't want to get stuck making small-talk with someone who had no influence.

Yet out of the blue the business-me mentally stepped down as I remembered standing alone at such events not that long ago. I'd wanted to be anywhere else, even as I'd known that I should step up and make connections. When I saw the man take too much interest in stirring his coffee my compassion won out.

I approached him. "Hi there." I extended my hand. "I'm Holly Lindstrom. I haven't seen you here before."

The man's smile was bathed in relief. His handshake was eager. "I'm new. Just moved to town. I opened the Picture Perfect Photo Studio."

"In the old vacuum shop?"

He laughed. "That's the one. We've cleaned it up a *lot*."

"I'm sure you have . . . ?"

"Oh. Sorry. The name's Meier Stopmeier."

"Now that's an interesting name."

He shook his head. "I don't know what my parents were thinking."

I chuckled. "It's certainly memorable."

Meier sipped his coffee and made a face. "Ooof. I haven't found a locally-owned coffee shop yet. Any suggestions?"

I immediately had an answer. "I'll tell you where *not* to go. Howard's Coffee."

"That bad?"

I shrugged. "My son worked there but the owner fired him for no reason."

"Did you complain?"

"I—" I suddenly noticed Howard standing nearby. He glared at me. I felt my face go red. "Hi there, Howard. Have you met Meier?"

Howard strode toward us. "Nice to meet you, Meier." He turned his attention to me. "I don't appreciate you bad-mouthing me, Holly."

I wasn't sure what to say. "I'm not bad-mouthing you." Not exactly. "But Baylor really liked that job."

"We liked having him. We were forced to fire him when he skipped out on work for three times without calling, and never made any effort to fully learn the process. I was losing money on his re-dos— *when* he decided to show up."

This was not the story Baylor had told me. "That surprises me because Baylor excels at everything he does."

"Not this time."

I looked toward the exit, desperately wanting to leave. I felt like a fool. Meier was stirring his coffee again. I needed the conversation to be over. "I'm sorry, Howard. I didn't know."

"Now you do." Howard turned his attention to Meier. "You run the portrait studio, right?"

I let the two men talk, wishing I could fade away, but nodding in all the right places, trying to save face.

I was relieved when someone from the Chamber stepped up to make announcements.

I heard none of them.

It was only noon but I felt done in. And beat up. Not only had I alienated a seller about their paint choice and family photos at the Chamber meeting, I'd publicly made an enemy of an established businessman in front of a new one—neither of which was the right way to make friends and influence people.

I'd gone from that meeting to our weekly office meeting where I'd had to endure Charles singing the praises of the office's top-seller, Andrea Maddox. He'd mentioned my recent sale, but my success paled when held to the bright light of Andrea's. The woman even had her face on her own for-sale signs. I couldn't go anywhere without being reminded of how far I had to go.

When the meetings were finally over, I sat in my cubicle and pretended to work.

"Holly?"

I looked up to see the receptionist. "Yes, Brianna?"

"A couple just walked in, wanting to look for a house. Everyone else is busy. Could you take care of them?"

Yes! My mood brightened. "Show them into the conference room. I'll be there in a minute."

After she left I took a few deep breaths to calm my nerves. As much as I longed to be Andrea Maddox, I wasn't her, which meant I still felt pangs of uncertainty when meeting possible clients. To boost my confidence I put on some fresh lipstick, smoothed my blouse, and entered the conference room wearing my best smile.

Matt and Margaret Livermore were in their mid-twenties. They had a sleeping baby in a car seat, wrapped in a pink blanket. They were looking for their first house. They needed two bedrooms, one bath, at least a one-car garage, and wanted to keep it under $175,000.

That little? Joy. I quickly did the math. My part of the commission would be about $5k, minus paying Charles 50%. I knew $2500 was better than nothing but it didn't seem like it.

To make matters more complicated, they were only in town today and tomorrow. Could they see some houses now?

It was short notice but I did my job. I showed them some listings on the computer, made some calls, and we left to see three houses.

I had to use GPS to find them as they were far beyond my normal stomping ground. As I drove, the couple told me about Matt's new job as a mechanic, and how they were a little apprehensive about moving from Council Grove, Kansas to the big city. I lost track of how many relatives they had and thought the baby's name was Alyssa. Or was it Melissa?

The front yard of the first house was mostly weeds, but the door had been freshly painted. Within minutes they declared the house a no. There was a pet smell that made new carpet a necessity. Baylor and Paige had always wanted a dog, but the thought of cleaning up accidents had made my answer a constant no.

Next.

House number two was a bit better. The kitchen was tiny but cute in a grandma sort of way.

Margaret ran a hand over the yellow Formica counters. "I was hoping for granite."

"And these appliances are ancient," Matt said.

They were delusional. "You can't expect granite and new appliances in this price range." I saw the couple exchange a look. Did they want me to lie to them?

The third house was small but had charm and a nicely shaded backyard. It was a contender but was on a busy street.

The baby started to fuss and needed feeding, so that was the end of it. Which was fine by me. "I'll keep looking," I said after returning them to the office. "I'll call you tomorrow morning."

They exchanged a few nervous glances and were both frowning. "We're a little confused right now. And disappointed," the wife said. "We need to pray about it."

Really? "Pray all you want, but I assure you even God doesn't know more about real estate than I do."

They were quiet as they walked to their car and drove away.

They were confused and disappointed? Join the club.

I decided to go home. If I was lucky, I could make it there in time for dinner.

When I came in the door, both of the men in my life were eating at the kitchen table. They looked shocked.

"Sheesh, guys. You look like you've just sighted the Loch Ness monster."

"A Holly-sighting is just as rare." Vernon said. "There's lasagna on the stove. Grab a plate."

I spotted a sack from Gribaldi's, which meant great breadsticks. I served myself a square of the pasta, got one lonely breadstick out of a foil-lined bag, and sat at my place.

"This looks great," I said, digging in. I knew I should eat something green. "Isn't there a bag of romaine in the fridge?"

"It's wilted," Baylor said. He was nearly done eating, which meant he would be heading to his room for the evening.

There was something I'd been wanting to ask him. "I had an interesting conversation today. I was at a Chamber event and saw Howard, your old boss."

"Mmm."

"He gave a slightly different story about why you no longer work there."

Baylor picked up his plate and stood. "Good for him."

I wasn't in the mood for his flippant answers. "Sit!" I pointed to his chair. I lowered my voice. "Please."

He slid the plate across the table, making the fork skitter away. "What did Howard say?"

I looked at Vernon for reinforcement, but he was busy sopping up marinara with his bread.

I chose one of Howard's complaints. "He said you made so many mistakes that it cost him a lot of money."

"That's not my fault. Guys from school would come in and say I did it wrong. But I didn't. Howard always believed *them*."

Vernon nodded. "The customer is always right."

"Even when they're trying to get me in trouble?"

That *was* a new take on it. "Why would they do that?" I asked.

"Because they like to embarrass me."

Even Vernon looked up, putting down the remainder of his breadstick. "Why?"

Baylor shrugged. "Why not?"

"That's not an answer," I said.

"It's all I got."

I moved on to Howard's second complaint. "Why didn't you show up for work---without calling?"

He stood again, picked up his dish, and looked down at me. "Because I don't like being humiliated. Do you?"

I felt my face flush but made sure to keep my tone gentle. "No, I suppose not. And if it wasn't a good fit, fine, but you could have handled it better. Give notice and quit, but don't let it get so bad you get fired."

"Whatever."

I had no idea if he'd gotten my point but I moved on. "And now, you should get another job. You have more than enough free time."

"I'm looking, okay?"

"Watch your tone," Vernon said.

Baylor repeated the words with less attitude. "I'm looking." Then he rinsed off his plate, put it in the dishwasher, and left.

I sighed. "Did you know about all this?"

Vernon licked a finger. "I didn't, but I believe him about the wrong orders. Kids can be mean."

It was too pat an answer. "He should have told us the truth."

Vernon bit the tip off another breadstick. "Maybe." He stopped eating. "Speaking of the truth, I need to talk to you about finances."

That had come out of the blue. "You're the accountant. That's your department." I feigned ignorance, but I guessed what he was going to say.

"The money's not coming in like we need it to, Hol. I'm not sure how much longer we can afford this house."

And there it was. "I'm working as hard as I can. You know that."

"I know that. And you *are* working your tail off. I'm just stating a fact." His eyes strayed to the beamed family room nearby. "When you get down to it, we really don't need a place this fancy."

Need had nothing to do with it. "Living in an impressive house is good for business."

He shrugged. "Maybe. The trouble is that my income is steady, but yours isn't." He was quick to add, "We're okay at the moment, but keep the idea of selling this house in mind."

I would *not* keep it in mind. I would shove it *out* of my mind.

He took a sip of water. "By the way, Paige checked in. I asked her to come over for dinner, but she and Drew had other plans."

I rolled my eyes. "They always have other plans." I supported our daughter being independent, and should have been happy that she'd found a guy she really liked, but that didn't mean *I* had to like it. Or him. "He's far too possessive."

"Paige told me she loves him."

Told Vernon. Not me. I said, "I know," to Vernon, even though I didn't. It wasn't unusual for Paige to confide in her dad. They'd always had a special bond. Yet it *was* kind of embarrassing. And it hurt.

He took the last breadstick. "Elsie called too."

"What did Nana want?"

"She said she's lonely and would like a visit."

I pushed my plate away. "I'm working long days and don't have time for you, Paige, Baylor, or myself, and now Nana needs me? I was there yesterday."

"She just lost her husband, Hol. Where's your compassion?"

"*I* just lost my grandfather."

He looked down. "No one would know it."

Low blow. "That's not fair. Am I supposed to wear black and go into mourning for a year?"

He gave me a dismissive look. "Just don't forget about him — or them — too quickly."

I pushed back from the table. I put my lasagna back in the foil pan. "I'm doing the best I can, Vernon."

He finished eating. "I thought it might be nice if we sent Elsie some flowers."

Huh? "She didn't want flowers at the funeral, she wanted money sent to their charities."

"They wouldn't be for the funeral, they'd be for her. Now."

I hated when he thought of things I probably should have thought about. "You're right. That would be nice."

"I'll make the call. But when *are* you going to visit her again?"

My phone rang.

"Saved by the bell," Vernon said under his breath.

I ignored him and saw the caller ID. "It's Charles. I have to take this."

"Of course you do."

I leaned against the counter. "Hi, Charles. I'm glad you called. I wanted to let you know that I have a new client. They're looking for their first house. Their budget is only $175,000 but they seemed pleased with what I showed them today."

"Are you sure about that?" he said.

What was he talking about? "Of course I'm sure. They haven't found the perfect one, but I'm going to take them out tomorrow to see more."

"No, you're not."

"I'm pretty sure I am. I'm calling them in the morning."

"Actually, you're not. I just got a message that a dissatisfied couple wants to change agents. The Livermores."

My stomach dropped. "That's my couple."

"Not anymore. I assigned them to Steven."

"But—"

"They said you made them feel cheap and told them they don't deserve granite and nice appliances."

My stomach tightened. "I never said they don't deserve them, I said they probably wouldn't get them at their price range."

"Which is pitifully small in your eyes."

I turned my back to Vernon, wishing he wasn't in the room. "In anybody's eyes, Charles."

"Regardless, Holly. Also . . . did you say you knew more about real estate than God?"

My stomach clenched. It had been a regrettable overstatement. "I just meant that I'm knowledgeable. Besides, God has more important things to do than worry about houses."

"Be that as it may, you're not going to get very far if you can't keep a customer for more than one afternoon. Sorry, Holly. Better luck next time."

He hung up, but I pretended he was still on the line. "Thanks for the heads up, Charles. And thanks for the new client. I'll meet with them tomorrow."

When I turned around, Vernon was staring at me. "What was that about?"

"Real estate dramatics." I hesitated just a moment, then added, "I have a new client."

He cocked his head, clearly not believing me. He brought his dishes to the counter. "You want to fill the dishwasher or put the food away?"

I took his plate and rinsed it, needing the sound of the rushing water to cover up the screaming in my head.

Chapter 6

Paige

"Blessed are those who listen to me,
watching daily at my doors,
waiting at my doorway.
For those who find me find life
and receive favor from the Lord."
Proverbs 8: 34-35

I stood at my station in pastry class and carefully folded almond flour into the whipped egg whites. I glanced at the other students who seemed to be doing it like they'd done it a million times.

Panic threatened to take hold, but I shook my head, forcing it away. I could do this. Unlike some other types of cooking, baking desserts required careful measurements and following directions precisely. I was good at both. Thanks to Grandma Dudley and Nana I had the skills.

I had *not* learned to cook from Mom. Her idea of homemade cookies was buying a log of Slice & Bakes. Dinners were often ala Stouffers or take out. I didn't hold it against her. Cooking wasn't her thing.

But it was mine. My dream was to be a chef. I was a proud cooking nerd and couldn't wait to come to class every day. But today . . . I knew macarons were finicky and could be ruined if I folded too hard, and would be grainy if I didn't fold them enough. Argh.

When Chef Roberts stopped at my station, I concentrated doubly hard on doing it just right.

"Fully scrape the bowl with every fold," he said.

"Yes, Chef."

"But ease up, Miss Lindstrom. You're supposed to enjoy the process."

"I'm trying to, Chef."

He smiled. "Try harder."

I took a deep breath and tried to relax. Nana often told me I was too intense. Cooking was about joy. I knew it could be. Would be. I knew it was the one thing I could do that made me *and* other people happy.

Unfortunately, everybody in my life needed a hefty dose of happiness. Since I moved out Baylor was going through some moody, teenage angst stuff. Mom was fixated on real estate and was too busy for the rest of us. As an accountant, Dad was better with numbers than people, and seemed clueless about how to handle either of them without me around. My boyfriend, Drew, never seemed to be in a good mood for long, no matter how hard I tried. And now that Papa was gone, Nana was all alone. There was nothing I hated more than thinking about an old person alone.

My thoughts were interrupted when I noticed that my classmates were piping the batter onto their silicone mats. *Concentrate, Paige.*

I found a small corner of my thoughts available for macarons and finished the work.

A perk of my cooking classes was bringing food home. As usual, Drew would be over for dinner and would stay long into the evening. I hoped he'd like the macarons— they'd turned out perfectly. One point for Paige.

I hung my keys on a hook by the door, then sorted the mail—I didn't get that much yet, as I'd only moved into my apartment two months earlier. Ads mostly. And utility bills.

I hated bills. I'd been naïve about how much things would cost— and that *everything* would cost. Whose budget took into account the expense of soaps, trash bags, can openers, paper towels, bowls, spatulas, and food staples like sugar, flour, and spices? Mom let me take the mixer with me, but I'd bought my own cookie sheets and a good skillet and saucepan.

It wasn't easy to afford everything by being a cook at the Cozy Cafe. But a job was a job. My schedule was packed. On weekdays I worked the morning shift and had school every afternoon. On Sunday mornings I went to church with the family. Drew worked at an insurance company all day and didn't like to get up early on weekends so we spent every evening together and Saturday and Sunday afternoons. Some days I needed a reminder to breathe. But I was only twenty-one. I could handle it.

My kitty, George, rubbed against my leg. I scooped him up, nuzzled my cheek into his white fur, and felt myself relax. I was just getting him dinner when the phone rang.

"Hi, Paige, this is Chef Bernard from Rolly's."

My heart skipped a beat. "Yes. Hello, Chef. How are you?"

"Good. But I'll be even better after you take the job as our new *commis chef.*"

I was glad I'd looked up what that was before applying for the position last week. It was an assistant to the *chefs de partie* who manned the various food stations. It was a great way to learn everything from salads, to grilling, to pastries.

I put a hand to my chest. I couldn't believe he was offering me the job. "Are you sure?"

He chuckled. "Yes, I'm sure. Your application was thorough and you had a glowing recommendation from Chef Roberts. What do you say?"

Working at a high-end restaurant was my dream. "Yes, of course I accept. Thank you, Chef! You made my day. "

"Glad to hear it. Can you start Friday night?"

"Of course. What time?"

"Would five work? We'll be showing you the ropes for a few nights, but I'm sure you'll catch on quickly."

I thought of my classes. "I go to culinary school until five but I could get there right after that."

"That would work. By the way, I commend your pursuit of a degree—your instructor spoke highly of you—yet I also promise you'll learn just as much by working."

"I'm looking forward to it—and thank you for adjusting the hours."

"You're welcome. See you Friday."

I hung up and did a little happy dance, which caused George to look up from his dinner. "I got it!" I told him. "Rolly's is fine dining and they took *me.*"

The cat went back to eating. His indifference didn't matter. I was ecstatic. This was a victory, a huge step toward becoming a real chef.

I called Dad. He was always the first person I thought of when sharing good news.

"I'm so proud of you Paigey-girl. Pretty soon we're going to have to call you, Chef Lindstrom."

"Oh Dad, stop." I loved the sound of it, but the title was still a long way off.

As usual Dad went on to tell me how great and talented I was. I absorbed every word. He was definitely the number one encourager in my life. When I hung up I thought of someone else I needed to tell.

Drew.

My conversation with Drew would be very different from the one with my dad. Drew wasn't keen on me applying for the job. I'd tried to explain how important it was to work at a place like Rolly's, but I hadn't won him over. But now that it was real . . . surely he'd be happy for me.

To get the reaction I hoped for I decided to reach Drew through his stomach. I'd make his favorite chocolate mousse.

I checked to make sure I had everything I needed, but was missing cocoa powder. No big deal, my neighbors were always willing to lend me a few ingredients here and there. I walked across the hall and knocked on Carlos and Camille's door.

Carlos answered. "Hi, Paige. What's cooking?"

It was his usual greeting. "Chocolate mousse. But I need cocoa powder. Do you have any?"

His twin sister called out from the kitchen. "That depends on whether you make enough for us."

I smiled. "No problem."

"Come get what you need. My hands are sudsy." Camille was washing dishes.

I opened the spice cabinet. I loved being familiar enough to feel at home. "Got it." I paused. "You might like the recipe. It's only three ingredients."

She turned off the water. "Really? I have to make something for a family dinner next week . . ."

"I'll write it down for you."

Camille shook her head. "I learn best by seeing. Can I come over and watch?"

"Of course."

"Let me finish here and we'll be over."

I headed back across the hall and got out the heavy cream, powdered sugar, and cocoa. I gathered a bowl, a hand mixer, and four parfait glasses. Carlos and Camille walked right in and sat on the two stools at the counter.

"Look at you," Carlos said. "All set up like a video star."

I gave a little bow. "I learned to get organized in my cooking class."

"Have at it," Camille said. "Make us fat and happy."

I chuckled. "This recipe is really easy," I said. "I usually like to chill my bowl, but I don't have time today, and —"

Carlos popped out of his seat. "Wait! Let me make a video."

I wasn't against the idea. I swept a hand through my hair, which I'd hastily pulled back in a bun. "But I look horrible."

"You look great. Hold on a minute." He set aside his stool, got out his phone, and moved back to the right distance. "When I say action you need to introduce yourself and tell us what you're making."

I could do that.

I *did* that, and within a few minutes I'd whipped up the ingredients and snipped off the corner of a plastic bag to pipe the mousse into the serving glasses.

"And there you are," I said. "You can garnish it with butterscotch chips, a crushed Heath bar, strawberries, or even a drizzle of caramel sauce." At the last second I realized I needed to sign off. "Thanks for watching. Eat happy."

Camille clapped enthusiastically. "That was awesome. It's like you've been doing it for years."

Carlos agreed. "You are definitely a natural. Where should I post it?"

An online video of myself for all the world to see? Other people did it but I'd never . . .

"How about posting it on your blog?" he asked.

I was surprised he even knew about that. "I only have twelve followers. I started it for myself, as a place to store recipes."

"Do you have other videos posted?" he asked.

"Not a one."

"Give me the info and I'll get it posted for you."

I wrote down the web info and my password. I looked at the time. "You two need to scoot. Drew will be here any minute and I haven't even started the Alfredo."

"Fettuccine Alfredo?" Carlos said it with awe in his voice.

"From scratch. It's a special occasion." I quickly told them about my job.

They both hugged me. "No one deserves it more," Camille said.

"Drew is one lucky man," Carlos said. "Maybe I can video you making the fettucine too?"

Camille pushed him toward the door. "Maybe next time. Move on, brother."

I picked up two parfaits. "Don't forget your mousse."

Drew came into my apartment without knocking. I rushed to greet him with a kiss.

He patted my back then sank onto the couch.

"Hard day?" I asked.

"The hardest. I lost a big customer, and the boss wasn't happy." He glanced toward the kitchen. "Is something burning?"

"The garlic bread!" I ran to the oven and took the pan out from under the broiler. Only one piece was ruined. I transferred the rest to a breadbasket and put it on the small table for two that was set with a Caesar salad, the pasta, and lit candles. The mousse would be the final surprise. "Come eat. I've made a special dinner because — "

He looked for the TV remote. "Can we eat out here? The game is starting."

I glanced at my nice dinner. I'd gone to a lot of trouble to make it nice to celebrate my job.

But Drew was already sitting on the couch and had the remote in his hand.

I gathered the plates and set them on TV trays.

"Thanks, hon," he said. "This looks great."

I sat on the couch nearby. "Who's playing?"

"The Chiefs of course."

Of course. With Kansas City being a stone's throw away we were Chiefs' fans. While growing up I'd loved to watch football with my dad. But since moving out I hadn't watched a game with him. I'd need to fix that. Soon.

I turned toward the TV and watched a few plays. A flag was thrown on the Chiefs. "Come on, ref," I said. "That was *not* pass interference."

I knew all the players and the intricacies of the game. Dad had taught me everything I knew. He'd been proud of me for learning. Baylor didn't like football, which was another reason I needed to go back and watch a game with Dad.

Drew focused on the game and ate. I'd lost my appetite. Things weren't going as I'd planned. I needed to tell him my good news.

I waited for a commercial break. "So Drew, this is a celebratory dinner because I have something I want to talk to you about — something good."

He took a bite of pasta. "*This* is really good. Can I get seconds?"

I took his plate to the kitchen and filled it.

"More garlic bread too, please."

Whatever you want, master.

I brought him his plate and sat. "My news is that —"

He held up a hand, stopping my words. "Can the news wait? The game's back on and they're about to score."

"Sure."

As if I had a choice.

"Woo hoo! Touchdown!" Drew held up a hand, waiting for my high-five.

I slapped his hand but I was having a hard time concentrating on the game.

I was fuming inside. Early on I'd resigned myself to telling him about the job during a commercial, but Drew filled each break with phone calls, checking his email, or going to the bathroom. It's almost like he was trying *not* to hear the news.

As the last minute of the half played out I said, "Want to go on a walk at halftime? I really want to talk —"

"I would, but I need to make a few more calls for work." He gave me his best smile. "Did I see a plate of cookies on the counter?"

"Macarons. And I have some chocolate mousse in the fridge."

"Nah. The cookies are fine." He flashed his best smile, which usually made me weak in the knees. Tonight it just annoyed me.

I carried the plate of cookies to him. He took a bite and closed his eyes. "Mmm. Crunchy yet creamy. They're great, hon."

His words could have filled up my near-empty tank but it was emptied again when he stood and said, "I'd better make those calls."

He stepped onto the tiny balcony, took a seat, and dialed. I imagined myself whipping the door open, grabbing his phone, and tossing into the parking lot where it would shatter in a hundred pieces.

The thought gave me a smidgen of satisfaction, but I knew such behavior would just make him mad and I'd end up saying I was sorry, and he wouldn't take any responsibility for the *reason* I threw his phone, and life would be miserable for two or three days. And so . . .

I sank onto the couch and stuffed a whole cookie into my mouth. It *was* good. I wondered if Nana would like them.

I picked up my phone. Nana took a while to answer and I started to worry. Finally, she picked up.

"Hi, Nana. How are you doing?"

"Hi, sweet girl. So good to hear your voice. Truth be, the house is too quiet."

Of course it is. "We all miss Papa."

"Do you?"

I was surprised by her tone. "Of course we do."

Nana's voice softened. "Of course you do. Sorry. I'm just feeling a bit sorry for myself."

I looked at the clock. It was already eight-thirty, the second half of the game was about to start, and I hadn't talked to Drew about my new job.

But right was right. "If you want, I can come over for a little while. I've made some macarons. Would you like me to bring you some?"

"I'd love that. You're a dear."

I hung up and took a deep breath. I did *not* need this task added to my day but I couldn't bear to think of Nana feeling lonely.

I slid the balcony door open. "Drew?"

"Hold on." He put a hand over his phone. "Is the second half starting?"

I shrugged. "I have to go to Nana's."

"She okay?"

"She's lonely. I may be awhile. Lock up when you leave."

"Tell her I'm thinking about her."

If only it were true.

Nana's face beamed when I opened the door. "Hello, sweet girl."

I gently hugged her as I balanced a Tupperware container of macarons. "I brought treats."

"How delightful. Just set them in the kitchen for now."

I walked through the living room. Everything looked as if nothing had changed. Papa's crossword puzzle book was still next to his recliner. And in the kitchen, I spotted a World's Best Grandpa mug on the rack and a Royal's ball cap hung by the kitchen door. With little effort I could imagine Papa walking in the room with a big grin on his face. "Come to play a little gin rummy, girl? Penny a point."

I paused a moment to let the wave of memories subside. It wouldn't do Nana any good to see me cry.

When I went back to the living room, I noticed her face was drawn. "How are you doing, Nana? Really."

"I'm fine. I'm good." She fiddled with her cane.

I shot her a concerned look. "Nana . . ."

She shook her head. "I'd say I'm fair to partly cloudy but it's a fact there are a few more clouds lately." She pointed her cane at the couch. "But this evening, you are my sunshine." We sat next to each other. "Do you remember me singing that to you?"

Images of snuggles and nap times came to mind. I softly began to sing, "'You are my sunshine —'"

Nana joined in. "My only sunshine, you make me happy when skies are gray...'" She patted my knee. "You even remember the harmony."

"Of course." I felt a pang of deep devotion. "I remember everything, Nana." Or I tried to.

She slipped a hand around my arm and leaned her head toward my shoulder. "I know you do. You are a dear girl and I appreciate your visit immensely." She sat upright. "So. Tell me what's going on in your life."

I finally had someone's ear. It didn't surprise me that it was Nana's. I always talked to Dad first, but with Mom trying to establish herself these past few years, and Grandma Rosemary being so busy with her committees, I often talked to Nana. "I just got offered a job as an assistant to the chefs at Rolly's."

Nana's eyebrows rose. "Fancy. Especially compared to cooking at the cafe."

I didn't want to disparage Cozy's. "The two are completely different. I love the home cooking at Cozy'a, but I need to learn how to do more."

"Smart girl. Never stop learning. That's why Papa and I took all those adult-ed classes."

I smiled. "Because you never know when you'll need information about the Russian Revolution?"

"Because it's interesting, that's why. Did you know there were two different dates for the revolution? The first one was on March 8, 1917, but in Russia they say it happened on February 28."

"Why?"

Nana took a breath as though she was going to recite a fact in school. "Back then, Russians used the Julian calendar and the West used the Gregorian calendar — which is what we use today. Hence, the difference."

"That *is* kind of interesting."

"Told ya."

I chuckled.

"When do you start your job?"

"Friday. Yes. Friday."

Nana's eyebrows dipped. "Why does your answer sound tentative?"

My words *had* sounded iffy. "I haven't told Drew yet. I was going to this evening, but the game was on and then he had to make some calls for work." The loss of my happy celebration weighed on me more heavily than I liked.

I felt Nana's gaze but was afraid I'd get emotional if I met her eyes.

"How *are* you and your man?"

"We're fine. We're good."

Nana shook her head. "I reject your words of false happiness as much as I reject your lukewarm 'Friday.' What aren't you telling me?"

I was tempted to share my frustration with Drew yet remembered Papa. Nana had just lost her husband. She didn't need to be burdened with my boy problems. I put on my best smile. "I'm just tired from work and school. Truly, everything is good."

Nana's hazel eyes drilled through my lie but she didn't call me on it. "You work too hard." She quoted a verse, "'In vain you rise early and stay up late, toiling for food to eat — for he grants sleep to those he loves.'"

I thought of another verse Nana had made me memorize years earlier. "But what about 'Be strong and do the work?'"

Nana smiled. "I'm impressed."

"Don't be. I'm not good at reciting verses like you are. I just know a few."

"I've had seventy more years of practice. To your point, yes, God approves of hard work. But if I'm understanding correctly, you have two jobs *and* school. And a boyfriend. And me. And family." She took a deep breath and let it out slowly. "Even Jesus rested. Something's gotta give, sweet girl."

I looked at my lap and nodded. As usual she spoke the truth.

Nana yawned and covered it with a hand. "Sorry about that. I haven't been sleeping well."

I looked at the clock and realized it was getting late. "Let me help you get ready for bed."

"No, you don't. You were kind enough to call and stop over. I don't want you to waste the rest of your evening."

I helped her up. "Spending time with you is never a waste. And I promise I'll come back soon. We didn't even talk about you."

"As it should be. Life's been too much about me lately."

"As it should be. Come now. Let me help you."

We walked arm and arm toward the master bedroom, but in the hallway Nana paused and pointed toward the guest room. "I'm sleeping in there right now."

I was surprised. "Why?"

"Because Papa's still in there." Nana gazed toward the master and I saw pain in her eyes. "One of these days I'll go back. Just not yet."

It was hard to imagine what she was going through. Suddenly becoming a "me" after being a "we" most of her life? "Nana, you do whatever you need to do."

"Thank you for not judging me."

My throat tightened. "Never."

I helped her get in her nightgown but saw Papa's clothes in the dresser and closet. When was the right time to clear them out? Once again I doubted there was a right answer, but I vowed to help when the time came.

When Nana was ready, she sat on the bed and pivoted to get her feet under the covers. I tucked her in.

She touched my face. "Thank you, sweet girl. Now go home. Kiss your honey. Rest. And as far as your new job and your busyness? Ask God for His take on it. The Good Book says to turn your ear to wisdom and apply your heart to understanding."

Easier said than done.

I locked up as I left, then drove home. Drew had left his dishes in the sink.

I heard my phone ping and checked my texts.

But it wasn't Drew, it was a text from Carlos. *Just posted your video, superstar!* He texted a link.

I clicked on it and had to admit it looked good. I was concise and personable. And — just as Carlos had told me — I looked fine with my bedraggled end-of-the-day hair and makeup.

Yet something struck me beyond the logistics of the cooking lesson. Something about the essence of the video grabbed my attention.

I was happy as I cooked. I was at ease.

I fell into bed feeling neither.

Chapter 7

Elsie

"We all, like sheep, have gone astray,
each of us has turned to our own way;
and the Lord has laid on him
the iniquity of us all."
Isaiah 53: 6

I opened my eyes and tossed the covers off. I needed to check on Willis.

My feet were touching the floor before I realized that wouldn't be necessary.

I sat motionless on the bed and let a new wave of sorrow pass over me. Through me. My chest tightened and heaved with the raw pain of it.

He. Was. Gone. I would never ever see him again in this world.

I was alone.

I gasped. The sudden intake of air turned into a weak moan. Tears filled my eyes, but didn't fall.

Maybe that was progress.

Father, help me get through this. With a few deep breaths in and out, the wave passed by—until the next time when the tide would roar over me again.

I distracted myself by going through the motions of the day. I got dressed, made coffee in my new coffee pot—half a pot—and ate the leftover chocolate donut that I'd forgotten about. But then I made some oatmeal. Old habits . . .

I washed the dishes by hand, as it had quickly become clear that the dishwasher would rarely be full enough to run. I didn't mind. The smell of Ivory dish soap always reminded me of my mother. Funny how smells did that.

I had just finished up when the doorbell rang. "Coming!" I called loudly. I walked as fast as I could to answer it.

I opened the door to a floral delivery man holding not one, but two arrangements. "Hi, Mrs. Masterson."

I recognized him from church. "Hi, Stan. For me?"

"For you. Want me to bring them inside for you?"

"Please." I pointed to the coffee table. "There, so I can see them all day."

He began to leave, then said, "Sorry about Mr. Masterson. We're going to miss him in the choir."

I chuckled. "Actually, you probably won't. We all know his voice was loud, but not necessarily in tune."

Stan smiled. "We'll still miss him. Enjoy the flowers."

There was one plant of red mums, and another arrangement of yellow roses. I plucked out the note on the mums. *Some flowers to brighten your day. Holly and Vernon.* How sweet. I loved the colors of autumn.

Now, to read the note on the roses . . .

Brianna: Beautiful flowers for a beautiful person. Vernon.

Brianna? I looked at the outside of the envelope where my name was clearly printed.

"Oh dear," I said. "Somebody made a big boo-boo." Huge. My grandson-in-law was sending flowers to someone named Brianna.

And not just any flowers. Roses. Those weren't the flower-of-choice to send to a mere friend.

I hated to embrace the obvious: there was something going on. Something . . . elicit.

Yet that couldn't be. Vernon was a solid, stable, good man. He didn't go out drinking with the guys. He wasn't flashy and flirty. He was polite and kind. Even a bit boring. He wasn't the sort to have an affair.

Yet I knew that people could hold deep secrets in their hearts.

I looked down at the roses, briefly remembering another bouquet, in another time.

I shook the memory away and concentrated on the here and now. What should I do with them?

The doorbell rang again. Maybe it was Stan, returning to fix his mistake. I carried the notecards with me to the door and opened it. It wasn't Stan.

"Holly."

"Hi, Nana. Just thought I'd stop by again."

I slipped the note cards into the pocket of my cardigan. "Come in."

Holly immediately saw the flowers. "They came."

"They were just delivered. Mums are a favorite. Thank you. And tell Vernon thank you too."

Holly glanced at the roses. "Who are those from?"

You don't want to know. "Just a friend."

"Quite the friend. Roses are expensive." She leaned down to take in the fragrance.

"Have a seat, dear," I said.

"I will, though I can't stay long."

She sat on the couch and sighed deeply and dramatically, as though she wanted me to ask about it. I complied. "How is work?"

She sat forward. "I'm having some issues."

"I thought you just got a big sale."

"I did, but . . ." Holly took a throw pillow onto her lap. "A couple came in, looking for a house—a tiny house—and they were really picky, expecting granite and such when they should have known they would only get a fixer upper, and—"

"Everybody has to start small. Papa and I could vacuum our first place from one outlet, and had to choose between ice cream and meat in the freezer because it couldn't fit both."

"That is tiny."

"It was small but our love was huge."

Holly hugged the pillow like a shield. "*Anyway*, apparently the couple didn't appreciate my honesty and asked for a new agent. To which I say good riddance. I doubt they will ever be satisfied, so I wish the new agent good luck."

I didn't like her attitude but wasn't surprised by it.

"*Anyway* again, the whole thing isn't going over well with my boss."

"I wouldn't think so." How could she expect otherwise?

Holly looked shocked. "Nana! You're supposed to be on my side."

I shook my head. "That is *not* in the grandmother's handbook. I will give you unconditional love but not unconditional validation."

"Sorry to hear that."

Holly had never taken criticism well. "My advice is to eat crow, apologize for being too blunt, and learn from it."

She tossed the pillow aside and stood. "We'll see. As I said, I can't stay long." She kissed my cheek. "I just wanted to check up on you. You okay?"

Her concern was an afterthought. I held back the truth. "I'm fine." Horrible word, *fine*.

"Good. I'm glad you liked the flowers. I'll check back soon. Bye."

After she left the air vibrated to a stop and I felt oddly deflated. I loved my granddaughter, but her visits were like adding potatoes to a boiling stew and then removing them before they were cooked. Nothing ever got fully cooked with Holly. She never lingered long enough to let any of the flavors of her life blossom. "Father, I love her, but I fear she's in for a hard fall." I looked at the flowers and took the cards out of my pocket.

Make that two hard falls.

I stirred a pan of soup and turned it to low. I was just putting some bread into the toaster when there was a tap-tap-tap at the kitchen door.

There was only one person who came around back.

I waved at Baylor through the glass and motioned him in.

"Hi, Nana." He gave me an awkward hug. As a little boy he'd always wrapped his arms around my waist, but as he grew taller than me his hugs had turned tentative, as if he wasn't sure how to go about it.

"Hi, yourself. Glad to see you."

He shrugged and looked at the soup. "Broccoli cheese?"

Good timing. I knew it was his favorite. "There's plenty for two. And toast with sourdough bread."

"Yum." He pushed the handle so the bread dropped into the toaster, opened the cabinet, and got out the peanut butter.

I loved how at ease he was in my kitchen. Not many women got to spend time with their great-grandkids, but from the time he and Paige could ride their bikes, they'd come to visit — most often without their parents. Baylor once called my house "my home home." And more recently, having been in Holly and Vernon's latest house, I understood what he meant. The Lindstrom house was huge and sported the bells and whistles of success, but it was cold. Everything was assigned a proper place to the point that it didn't look lived in. My house was a home, completely outdated, and delightfully stuck in the sixties. Willis had told me I could remodel, but I'd never taken him up on it. I'd been afraid I'd mess up the homey-home feel.

I dished up the soup while Baylor made the toast. He poured two glasses of milk and we sat at the kitchen table.

He extended his hand for grace — what a good boy — and we both took a bite of toast. Peanut butter was on my top-ten list of favorite foods.

"So, Bay. What brings you to my house at dinnertime? Not that I object . . ."

"No one's home," he said. "They rarely are. Not that I really mind that much and Dad's home more than Mom but . . ." He sighed. "I miss Paige."

And there it was, the core of his pain said with the brevity of a male teenager. If I'd asked the same question of Paige, I would have received a lengthy and detailed monologue. I almost liked Baylor's way of it better.

"I know you miss her, bud. Your sister stopped by last evening. She's all excited about a new job."

"She called to tell me. I'm happy for her. She cancelled on me for my concert Friday night because of it."

"You have a concert?"

He blew on a spoonful of soup and smiled "Wanna come?"

"Of course. If you'll pick me up."

"I can't. I have to be there early and I'm hitching a ride with another guy from orchestra. But Mom and Dad should be able to take you. Give Mom a call."

"I'll do that."

He brushed a crumb off his chin. "What's it like with Papa gone?"

Right to the point. What should I say? I smoothed my napkin against my leg, trying not to cry. "It's odd and scary and quiet and . . . it is what it is." My voice steadied. "I'm doing okay with it. Him being sick for so long gave me time to dip my toe in the water of being alone. I kind of got used to it a little at a time."

"I'm sure it still hurts bad. You two were together forever."

"Pretty much."

He licked some peanut butter off his finger. "I miss him. I mean Papa was always here for me. You both were. And I liked helping him with his crossword puzzles."

I got an idea. "Would you like to have his crossword magazines?"

His forehead dipped with emotion. "Yeah. I would."

I pointed to the living room. "Go get them. They're where they always were."

Baylor got the magazines and came back to the kitchen. He set them on the table and pressed his hand against them. His forehead was furrowed. "Thanks, Nana."

"You're welcome, bud." I touched his hand. "I want you to know how proud Papa was of you, of your good grades and your good character. Me too."

His face reddened. "I know."

"Speaking of . . . how *is* school?"

He shrugged. "I got an A on my last pre-cal test."

I shook my head. "I'm lucky to add two plus two."

"Four, right?"

I laughed, then touched on a more delicate subject. "Have you made any friends this semester?"

He concentrated on his toast. "Not really. Most of them are either jocks, pot-heads, or jerks. So not yet."

"Jerks? You mean bullies?"

"A few. I can handle 'em."

Although I loved Baylor dearly, I wasn't naive. He was a scrawny 16-year-old who played the bassoon in the orchestra. He was more interested in reading and video games than girls or sports. It wasn't surprising he was a target.

"Have you told your parents?"

He scoffed. "It's not that bad. And what would they do about it? What *could* they do about it?"

"Contact the school. Contact the parents of the boys."

He shook his head vehemently. "Paige knows. She says to ignore 'em, cuz they like attention. So that's what I try to do."

"Successfully?"

He hesitated. "Pretty much." He offered a wry smile and flexed his bicep. "I'm not as scrawny as I look. See?"

I smiled. "King David was a scrawny shepherd when he defeated Goliath."

"I'll keep that in mind."

I added Baylor's needs to my prayer list.

Chapter 8

Rosemary & Everett

"Religion that God our Father accepts as pure and faultless is this:
to look after orphans and widows in their distress
and to keep oneself from being polluted by the world."
James 1: 27

"Rosemary? Phone!"

Everett called out to me just as I was walking out the door. The only people who ever phoned our landline were car warranty salesmen and my mother. At that moment I wasn't sure which one I would rather talk to.

"It's Elsie," he said.

I backtracked and picked up the phone. "Hi, Mom."

"Don't sound so enthused."

I checked myself. "I'm just tired."

"Paige is tired, Holly is tired. Now you? What have you been doing?"

My mother, ever the inquisitor. I didn't like having to defend my weariness, but did. "I had a church deacons' meeting last night and was made head of the fall dinner."

"You always get that job."

"I like that job. I'm good at it."

"Mmm. Go on."

She wanted more, I'd give her more. "I'm off to a meeting of women voters. I'm giving a presentation on ex-Senator Nancy Kassebaum. Did you know her father Alfred Landon was a two-time governor and ran against Roosevelt in 1936 — losing, but he ran."

"Yes, dear. I believe I did know all that. She's a year older than I am."

Of course Mom knew all that. Mom and Dad had often talked politics at the dinner table, a topic that I used to think was extremely boring. It was ironic I found myself involved now.

I fiddled with my keys, eager to get out the door. "Anyway, later this afternoon I have an Art Guild meeting. I'm the head of the silent auction in November."

"Of course you are. If there's a chairmanship to be filled, you will fill it."

The way she said it . . . I felt wounded. What would it take for her to be proud of me? "You could be happy for me."

"Of course I'm happy for you. It's merely an observation. Are you going to offer something to auction off?"

"I was thinking of getting back to painting scarves. It's been a few years."

"That's a wonderful idea. I love the green one you gave me."

So she *was* proud of me?

I was disgusted with myself for caring one way or the other. Surely at age sixty-five I didn't need my mommy's approval. I glanced at the clock. "What can I do for you, Mom? I really need to get going."

"It can wait. I just need my summer flowerbeds cleaned out."

Everett walked by on the way to the stairs and I got an idea. "Hold on." I put the phone to my chest and whispered to him. "Everett? Would you clean out Mom's flower beds today?"

He only hesitated a second. "I can do that. I'll go over right away." The fact he hadn't balked made me feel guilty. I was an expert *balker.*

I spoke into the phone. "Everett can come now, if that's okay."

"Tell him I'll pay him with oatmeal raisin cookies."

I smiled slightly. "He'll love it. Gotta go. I'll call you later."

I reached over and gave my husband's beard a tug. "You're a good man, Everett Dudley."

He rolled his eyes. "I'm as good as a puppy who sits when you tell him to." He grabbed the keys to his truck. "When will you be home?"

"I'm not sure. After my meetings I need to talk to the church's food supplier and see if I can get a better deal on kitchen supplies."

He made a face. "Since when are you in charge of the kitchen?"

"I'm not. Not really. When Pastor mentioned it, I volunteered. I think I can get a better price on supplies than they got last year."

"That's my Rosie, always going after good, better, best."

I scowled at him. . It didn't seem like a compliment. "Is there something wrong with that?"

He nudged me to the door. "Weren't you late for something?"

While Everett gathered garden tools and compost bags from the garage, I drove away feeling a chip settle on my shoulder. No one appreciated my hard work, in fact, they all made fun of it, even disparaged it. Every one of my positions were volunteer. I didn't get paid a penny. Was it too much to ask for an occasional atta-girl?

This wasn't the first time I'd felt this way. I recited a familiar verse aloud. "'From everyone who has been given much, much will be demanded; and from the one who has been entrusted with much, much more will be asked.' I've been given a lot of talents so I'm using them. What's wrong with that?"

Since the car gave me no answer, I gripped the steering wheel harder and fumed in silence.

After leaving Rosie to her busyness, I drove to Elsie's. I took a shovel with me to the front door and held it upside down like the farmer with the pitchfork in the American Gothic painting. I rang the doorbell.

I heard the three-point progress of two feet and a cane but was taken aback when Elsie opened the door. Had she lost weight since the funeral? Not a good idea when she was a bitty thing to begin with. But I hid my concern behind a stoic face and stiff pose.

She giggled. "Everett. You're right out of a painting."

"Yes, ma'am. At your service."

"Before you start, come in for a bit and keep me company. I just finished mixing the cookie dough."

I left my supplies outside and offered her my arm as we walked to the kitchen. Her skin was papery thin and she seemed more slumped forward than usual.

She looked up at me. "Such a gentleman. Such a gentle man."

I liked the compliment. "Aww shucks, ma'am. You flatter me."

"Not nearly enough, Everett." She sat at the kitchen table next to a cookie sheet and a mixing bowl full of dough. "I used to stand to work but now . . . sitting is best."

I sat nearby. "Whatever works." I drug a finger along the rim of the bowl and licked it. "Mmm. I can taste the cinnamon."

"It's my grandmother's recipe." Elsie used a fancy cookie scoop to drop the dough onto the pan, but squeezing the handle to make it drop seemed to hurt her hands. Her arthritis?

Even though I knew it could be a ploy like Tom Sawyer painting the fence, I took the bait. "That looks like fun. Can I do it?"

She let out a breath as if she'd been holding it during the exertion. She handed the scoop to me. "I used to use two spoons, but that's hard to do sitting down, so Paige bought me this fancy scooper." She rubbed her right hand. "It's nifty, but my joints object."

"No problem." I tried a few scoops, then stood. "It *is* hard when you're sitting." I finished the tray and put them in the oven. "How long?"

"Ten."

I set the timer.

"I didn't realize you knew your way around a kitchen. Do you cook much?"

"Never did when Holly was growing up, but when she left, Rosie got busy with her committees, so I stepped in to cook once in a while. And now that I'm retired . . ."

"She expects you to do more?"

If that wasn't the understatement of the year. I decided to be kind. "I don't mind. I like her to be involved."

"Do you?"

Elsie had a talent for seeing through horse mucky. I moved to the sink to wash my hands, not because I had to but because I needed to create a distraction.

Elsie spoke over the sound of the water. "Do you like her to be so involved, Everett?"

I knew I couldn't escape a true answer so I turned the water off and faced her. "I used to. But now that I'm around all day I thought..." I didn't like sounding needy so I shrugged.

"You thought you'd spend more time together?"

Bingo. "I always thought retirement was about traveling, going to concerts, taking long walks, and doing projects together." So far Rosie and I were zero for four.

"That's not Rosemary's view of retirement?"

I turned on the oven light and peered inside even though it was way too soon for the cookies to be close to done. "She reminds me that *she's* not retired."

"That's true."

But it was more than that. "I think I annoy her. I'm in the way." I sounded like a grumpy child.

Elsie leaned forward in her chair and put both hands on her cane. "You are in the way."

"Thanks a lot."

She waved a hand. "Think about it. Rosemary has had her days and the house to herself for forty-some years while she took care of Holly and you worked from dawn to dusk on jobsites. When Holly was grown Rosemary immersed herself in volunteering. You both created unique daytime lives. Now that you're home all day she doesn't want to give up what she's created. At least not easily."

I'd never thought of it that way.

"Flip the scenarios. Let's say you were still working and she quit all her committees and plopped herself at your jobsites all day."

It was a good analogy. "I'd hate it." The problem was now properly identified. "So how do we handle it?"

"You both need to be patient. You didn't learn how to be a roofer in a month, did you?"

"No, ma'am."

She spread her hands.

I grinned at her. "How'd you get to be so smart?"

"Trial and error. Many errors." She raised a finger. "'If any of you lacks wisdom, you should ask God, who gives generously to all without finding fault, and it will be given to you.' *Will* be given. Not *might*."

The verses always came so easily to Elsie, as if her mind was a Bible computer and she only needed to log in a key phrase for the perfect verse to pop out.

"So?" she asked. "Will you ask for wisdom?"

How could I say no? "Sure." What could it hurt?

"Good," she said.

The timer rang and she got up to peer in the oven. "They look done to me. Take the pan out and I'll do the rest."

The kitchen was filled with the delicious smell of cookies. "Do you want me to fill the pan again?"

"I'll manage. But after the flower beds there's other favor I have to ask of you."

"Name it."

She stood beside the cookie sheet. "For years Willis rented a shop-space at the Woodworker's Guild warehouse."

"He used to love that place."

"He did. I had my sewing and he had his wood projects."

"One of his bowls sits on our coffee table."

Elsie nodded toward the living room. "The house is full of his projects. He thought about giving up the space a few years ago when his eyesight started to fail and his hands shook. But he never got around to it. Actually, I think he liked going there to talk to the other men. It was a good outlet for him. Could you go shut it down for me? Empty it out."

"Of course."

She picked up a spatula to take the cookies off the pan. "Don't you have outside work to do?"

I did. I liked working outside. It gave me a lot of time to think.

After clearing out the flower beds for Elsie, I went to the woodworking warehouse. Might as well get all the to-dos done in one day.

I had only visited Willis's workshop a few times in the forty-five years Rosie and I had been married, but I'd always been impressed by the setup. For a monthly fee people could share some of the largest — most expensive tools like lathes and table saws — while having a personal workbench and lockers for their projects. Plus, any mess was made away from their homes, which was always a perk.

I had no idea how much stuff Willis had in his space, so I'd brought along a half-dozen boxes.

There was only one other person there among the dozen or so spaces. A skinny elderly man with slumped shoulders sat on a stool in the space next to Willis's workbench. He was sanding a table leg. "Morning," he said.

"Morning."

He stopped sanding. "I haven't seen you here before."

I dropped the boxes near Willis's locker. "I'm the son-in-law of Willis Masterson."

"I heard he passed. So sorry for your loss. My loss too. He was an interesting man."

"That, he was." I dug the key to the lock out of my shirt pocket and opened the double-doored locker. It was stuffed full. I would need every box.

"You're Everett, right?"

I was surprised he knew my name. "I am. And you are?"

"Doug." He held out a hand dotted with age-spots. "Nice to meet you."

I shook his hand. "Likewise." I began to fill a box with small pieces of wood. "You been coming here long?"

"Twenty-five years."

I chuckled. "That's long."

"First came when I retired — which was about the same time Willis started coming." He went back to sanding. "He told me about you."

My radar flipped on. Willis wasn't a big fan. "What did he say?"

"He always thought you'd be good at woodworking, you being in construction and all."

Me being in construction was the root of my father-in-law's bad opinion of me. "When my wife and I first married I used to dabble. Made a few boxes and such. My grandpa had a shop. But when Grandpa died and his house sold . . . I let it slide." I straightened the wood in the box. "Willis tried to get me interested again, but . . ."

"You didn't want to do it because *he* wanted you to, right?"

First Elsie saw the core of me, and now Doug? "Why do you say that?"

Doug waved my concern away. "Don't get riled about it. It's just that he and I did a lot of talking. He knew all about my wife's cancer, my daughter's money troubles, and knew too much about the trials and tribulations of my great-grandsons' bad choices. He listened. And so did I."

I felt my walls go up and mentally circled the wagons around our family. "I don't much like the idea of Willis talking about us."

"Don't get your dander up. He liked *you* a lot."

Strike one for Doug. "No, he didn't. He didn't approve of me marrying Rosie at all. Claims I ruined her life."

Doug's eyebrows dipped in the middle. "That doesn't sound right."

I didn't appreciate Doug acting like he knew more about the family than I did. "It's true. Rosie was in college when we met at an Eagles' concert. We fell for each other fast and hard. I never asked her to quit college, but she did. We got married and Willis and Elsie resented me for it. It didn't help that I never went to college and made a living doing manual labor."

Doug thought about this a moment, and I embraced an inner, *So there,* and went back to packing.

"People change," Doug finally said. "You musta grown on him 'cuz he always told me how much he liked you, respected you, and appreciated how happy you made his daughter. *That's* why he wanted to share the woodworking with you. He wanted to find something you could share."

I froze. This was news to me. Yet it sounded like it could be true. But knowing Willis was gone now and it was too late . . . I felt the thud of regret in my innards. "I didn't know."

"Yeah? I'm not too surprised. Willis wasn't good about telling family how he felt about 'em."

"But he told you."

Doug shrugged. "I guess I was safe. Our paths didn't cross outside a'here with him having been a big-shot banker and me being a lifer at the electric company. I think us two getting along so well made him think it might be similar if you came here. Making stuff might splash a little glue on the two of you."

My thoughts flew over a heap of memories of Willis and me. All along I thought the wall between us was my father-in-law's fault. Maybe it'd been that way at first, but for over forty years?

"I wish he would have pushed it," I said.

"No, you don't."

I let the truth sink in. Yup. Doug got a hit to center field with that one. Maybe he did know things.

"You're right that I didn't want to get into woodworking because he wanted me to." I tossed a piece of wood in the box with a clatter. "Willis was always the rich daddy and I was always the working-class schmuck who held it against him. How juvenile was that?"

"Yeah. Well . . . I got a few regrets of my own. Everybody does. Add it to the pile."

I liked this guy. I understood how Willis could have let down his guard and shared stuff with him.

"You still roofing?" Doug asked.

"Just retired."

"Welcome to the club." He nodded toward the locker and workbench. "You want to take up where Willis left off?"

I looked at the tools and supplies. There were parts of a Shaker-style chair on the bottom shelf. "I know next to nothing about making furniture. I'm not very creative."

"But you are good with your hands, right?"

I looked down at my calloused, weathered hands. "I suppose I am."

"I don't mind helping you figure things out. I'm teaching my great-grandsons some of the basics. I could do the same for you."

Grandsons . . . "I have a grandson."

"Bring him along sometime. I'll teach both of you."

The thought of working with Baylor filled me up like a mug of warm milk.

I put the wood back where it belonged.

After a long day of meetings, I was glad to be home. As soon as I opened the door, I smelled a roast. The aroma drew me into the kitchen where I found Everett mashing some potatoes.

"Gracious," I said. "This is a feast."

"I worked up an appetite in Elsie's yard, and I also went to your dad's workshop and was going to clean it out, but ended up talking to this guy who told me—"

I was tired of hearing people talk. "You've had a busy day."

"Very." He nodded toward a plate of cookies. "I'm making dinner and Elsie supplied the dessert. Go ahead and sit." He pointed toward the dining room. "In there."

The dining room was for holidays and family dinners. What had gotten into him? "Very fancy. I'll get the dish—"

"Already done."

I set my purse on the counter and went into the dining room. The table was set with my fall placemats, our pottery plates, water in goblets, and cloth napkins. There was a lettuce in two salad bowls and rolls in a basket. But the goblets were on the left and the silverware was set wrong, so I quickly fixed it. You'd think after over four decades he would have learned the right way. I sat at my place and waited—which made me feel extremely odd. *I* was the one who served the meals.

Everett carried in a plate of meat with potatoes and cooked carrots on the side. "Voila!"

He set the food down, sat, and did a doubletake at the goblets and silverware. Then he held out a hand to say grace. "We've been neglectful of this."

I took his hand. When was the last time we'd formally given thanks? We always did it at big family gatherings, but rarely when it was just the two of us.

He led the prayer, then said, "Amen." The food was passed and we began the meal.

"Yum," I said at the first bite of roast. "So tender."

"I didn't get home until early afternoon, so I wasn't sure it would get done enough. How were your meetings?"

I was glad for his interest and gave him a detailed summary of each one, ending with, "I was right about getting better food prices. The church will save ten percent from our old kitchen costs."

"Good for you. We've both had a busy day."

"The busiest." And I had more to do on the computer as soon as dinner was over.

Everett speared his final carrot. "I met a friend of your dad's at the shop. He said something real interesting about what your dad thought of me."

My mind felt a spark of interest, but not enough to ask more.

But Everett continued. "Did you know Willis grew to like me and wanted me to get into woodworking so we'd have something to do together?"

My dad liked Everett? No way. "I never saw it."

"Me neither. But it makes me sad to think that the chips on *our* shoulders might have been so heavy that we missed it."

Great. Something else to make me feel guilty. I didn't want to think about it. "Who's the man who told you this?"

"Doug. I don't know his last name."

"Kind of gutsy for him to say such a thing, making you feel bad and all."

Everett shook his head. "That wasn't his intent. He's a good guy. I'm going to keep the space and he's going to teach me how to make things. I was thinking Baylor might like to go with me."

"Baylor doesn't work with his hands. He's a techie-type."

"That doesn't mean he can't learn. Maybe he just hasn't had the opportunity. Vernon isn't a hobby guy." He tossed his napkin on the table. "Why are you fighting me on all this by saying Doug doesn't know what he's talking about—that your dad *didn't* like me? And Baylor won't want to spend time with me?"

I was shocked by his reaction. "Don't be so sensitive." I watched his chest heave up and down and knew I'd been too blunt. Again. "I'm not saying that it's untrue about Dad, just that I didn't see it."

"Maybe you could never see that he finally accepted me because you've never accepted me. Maybe you regret quitting school for me. Maybe you're so busy with all these committees because you don't want to spend time with me."

I felt like he'd slapped me. Where had all this come from? "I chose to marry you, Ev. I chose to quit school. We've been married forever. Don't you think you're overreacting? I'm busy because I like helping people. Until recently you worked all day. What was I supposed to do all those years, sit around eating bonbons, ironing sheets?"

Everett ran a hand down his beard. "No. Of course not. I'm just upset I didn't know how he felt. My dad died when I was young and Mom died thirty years ago so your parents were all I've had. And now I find out I could have been closer to Willis? That he wanted that?"

I thought of a tit for tat. "You never acted as if you liked *him*. You called him snooty and bossy."

"He was snooty and bossy. And now he's gone." He put a fist

against his chest. "I'm mad at myself, Rosie. Mad about missed opportunities, regrets, the whole kit and clumsy kaboodle."

I folded my napkin and put it on the table. "I have a few regrets about Dad too. We butted heads a lot. He didn't *get* me. And *I* was the one who quit school." And married a construction worker. This memory lane stuff wasn't doing either of us any good. "We can't do anything to change the past, Ev."

"That doesn't mean I can't feel bad about it."

"I don't suppose it does." I didn't want to talk about it anymore so I stood. "Thank you for the yummy dinner, but I haven't been at the computer all day. I need to check to see if there's any news about the state beautification board."

"So that's that, right?" He began clearing the dishes.

It was odd how Everett often wanted to talk about feelings more than I did. And now he was upset — which was rare. I was the one with a temper. If only I'd listened just a few more minutes, we could have avoided all this.

Too late now.

Even though I didn't want to clean up, I said, "Leave the dishes. You cooked. I'll clean it up in a few minutes."

"No," he said, taking my dish away. "I wouldn't want to put you out."

Didn't want to, but he was. What difference would it make if I cleaned up in a half-hour? "I said I'd help. Just give me a minute to check—"

He walked into the kitchen. "No need. What you're doing takes precedence over everything else."

I hated that my first thought was, *yeah, it kind of does.* I followed him because I knew that's what I was supposed to do. But I also knew it wouldn't help. Everett was slow to anger but when he did get mad he tended to simmer a while. He would never let me help, so this play-acting was a waste of time. Yet it was part of the game.

He turned quickly and nearly ran into me. His eyes were blazing. "I think you liked making me believe your parents didn't approve of me. It kept me away from them so you could have them all to yourself."

That wasn't true. I'd been glad to be out of their house — and their control. Yes, Everett was a means toward that end, but . . . "You're not making sense."

He waved a hand. "You've always made me feel inferior."

I'd also heard this before and I knew it didn't matter what I said or how much I built him up. I had my baggage and Everett had his. "I never meant to — or mean to — make you feel that way." I touched his shoulder but he pulled away. "I love you, Everett Dudley. You're an amazing man."

He made a *pfft* sound and finished clearing the table. "Go on."

"But . . ."

He put the goblets by the sink. "Go on because I'm sure I'll clear the table wrong or clean the kitchen wrong. Just like all the things I got wrong when I set the table."

I kicked myself. Why had I rearranged things when it didn't matter? "I shouldn't have changed it. It's just a habit for me to fix things that are out of place."

"Like me." He turned the water on to fill the sink.

Shoot. He was really hurting. He was overreacting, but I hated seeing him in pain. I touched his back. "Ev . . . I'm sorry."

He shrugged my hand away and faced me. "Did you ever consider that some of your habits need fixing? That your ego is like Nana's gangly rose bushes that needed to be whacked back?"

I noticed he had a bread crumb in his beard, and I almost plucked it away — had my hand poised to pluck it away — before I let my hand drop.

He brushed the crumb aside himself. "Go do your thing and I'll do mine." He reached for the tray of cookies. "Have one. Your mother made them special for us. Isn't that kind and generous of her?"

I took a cookie. The points against me had been made — and made again. I didn't argue because I couldn't. I was in the wrong — partially. But he was wrong too. I was doing important work. And it wasn't my fault my father hadn't made Everett feel wanted.

I left him to the cleanup, escaped to my office, and turned on my computer.

But that's as far as I got. To check my email as if nothing had happened would be the epitome of an overactive ego.

I shut it off and sat before the blank screen. I still held the cookie. I set it on the desk. I didn't deserve a cookie. I didn't deserve to enjoy a home-cooked meal from a husband who'd spent the day helping *my* mother in the garden and cleaning out *my* father's shop space.

I shook the thoughts away. Everett liked helping people, but so did I. Why did he try to make me feel guilty about my activities while I was supposed to bow down in gratitude for his?

It's not about you.

I drew in a breath, knowing the thought was not my own, and also knowing that I'd heard the inner words before. Repeatedly.

And yet . . . "I'm doing good in the community, Father. That's important. Help Everett see that. I'm sorry about the issue with my dad. Wasn't it up to him to make his feelings known to Everett? I had a hard enough time trying to get him to be proud of *me*. The two men should have been able to work it out between them. Right?"

There were no more inner thoughts from the Almighty.

I sent up one final prayer that should make things right. "You're the Fixer of the universe, God. Fix this, please?"

I liked that it was an all-encompassing prayer. God knew everything. I appreciated that He didn't need me to spell it out for Him.

I wish I could have come out of my He and me time feeling whole and new and perfect, but I didn't. It came down to this: I trusted God to do what needed to be done and I'd try to make things good on my end.

I heard the TV in the den.

Everett. The dear, overly-sensitive love of my life.

I had made a mess of the dinner, but maybe I could make this moment better. One moment at a time?

It was worth a shot. I detoured to the kitchen and poured cashews — Everett's favorite — into a bowl. I grabbed two cans of Diet Coke.

I paused in the doorway of the den and held them up. "I come in peace?"

He moved a pillow and patted the cushion beside him. I snuggled in and we watched a documentary on D-Day — something I would never choose to watch. In fact, on more than one occasion I'd taken his interest in the History Channel as a way to grab some alone time in another room.

But not tonight. Tonight I would make this sacrifice.

Actually, the show was kind of interesting. Everett added to the commentary. He knew a lot about the war. His dad had fought in the Pacific.

I actually felt myself softening to the evening, then heard myself ask, "Want to go out Friday? Do something special?"

"A date night?"

I was surprised Everett even knew the term. But yeah. Why not? "Sure. A date night. Dinner? A walk around the square with my favorite man in the whole world?" Look at me being all romantic.

He kissed my hair. "You're on."

Good for me.

Good for us.

Chapter 9

Holly & Paige

"The Lord is close to the brokenhearted
and saves those who are crushed in spirit."
Psalm 34: 18

Since the humiliation with the Livermores, I'd felt as helpless as a singer with a sore throat. I needed to get some new clients — fast. When I went to work at Dreamchasers I rearranged my cubicle so I could see the front door of the office. Maybe if I was the first to see people come in I'd be able to nab them.

Unfortunately it was a slow morning. But then . . . I was surprised to see Vernon walk in. I stood to greet him but paused when he stopped at the receptionist desk and leaned on the counter in front of Brianna. Brianna greeted him with a smile, then a laugh. Vernon leaned toward her in a happy give and take. I kept expecting them to call me over but they continued the conversation as if I didn't even work there. What was going on?

I knew what was going on.

I shook my head. I didn't *know* anything. Call it women's intuition. In the past few months I'd seen subtle changes in their behavior: Brianna would tell me "Vernon called" instead of her previous "Your husband called." And there was Brianna's sudden interest in my schedule — especially my evening appointments. Was that when they were seeing each other? And Vernon hadn't asked me to spend time with him like he usually did — even though I would have declined. The proof was totally circumstantial, but other than finding them together, what else was there? For now at least.

I watched their conversation wind down. I couldn't confront him until I knew for sure. Plus, there loomed the bigger question: did I *want* to confront him? Was it awful that I felt a bit of relief that he was occupied so I didn't have to feel guilty about my long hours?

"Hey there," he said as he reached my desk.

"Hey there yourself. What are you doing here?" Unfortunately, my words had an edge to them. I smiled to soften their effect. "What's up?"

"I don't have an appointment until two so I wondered if you'd like to go to lunch."

We never went to lunch. "Sorry, I can't. I'm meeting a possible client. But thanks."

He looked genuinely disappointed. "Will I see you for dinner?"

Actually. . . "Not tonight. We have a joint agency dinner meeting. Remember?"

He shrugged. "Never mind. I guess I'll use the time to meet with a client about their audit."

"Do what you need to do. Thanks for stopping by." It sounded so formal. "I appreciate it, Vernon."

He put his hands in his pockets, then pointed at my computer. "You switched things around."

"I did." I couldn't explain my reasoning without risking other people hearing how desperate I was to get new clients.

He gave me an awkward nod then turned and left. He gave Brianna a little wave and a smile on his way out.

An awkward nod versus a wave and a smile.

I turned back to my computer. Should-haves and could-haves warred within me.

I was just getting into my car after cooking class when Drew called. "I'm going to be a little late coming over tonight," he said. "I'm meeting a couple buddies for a drink."

He still didn't know I'd accepted the job at Rolly's. I knew it was wrong to keep the news to myself—as if he wouldn't find out—but since he'd never asked, I hadn't wanted to say anything.

Until I had to. Which was right now. "I'm on my way to work."

"Since when do you have the dinner shift?"

"Since I got a job at Rolly's."

Silence.

"You know I don't like that you applied there."

Anger collided with my need to appease. "They don't hire just anyone, Drew. It's a great opportunity."

"To ignore my opinion?"

That was not the point. "I didn't ignore it, but I had to look at the big picture."

"Which doesn't include me."

"What?" The conversation had been hijacked. He was good at that.

"Obviously, you don't want to hang out with me anymore."

It was complicated. "I don't want to be away from you, but those are the hours of the job. It's a great oppor —"

He hung up.

I sucked in a breath as tears swept over me so mightily that I had to pull onto a side street and park. I gripped the steering wheel and leaned my forehead against my hands. "What am I supposed to do? Why doesn't he understand how important this is to me?"

My phone pinged.

I looked at a text from Drew. *Thanks for showing me where I rate.*

I wrote back: *Don't do this. Be happy for me.*

No can do.

I didn't know how to respond.

Then Drew wrote: *Gotta go. You're obviously too busy for me. See you later. Maybe. Sometime.*

"That's not fair!" I screamed at the phone. The tears flowed and my whole body shook in anger, confusion, and sadness. Finally, I took a deep breath. I looked at the time. I had to leave the argument behind or I'd be late for my new job—the great opportunity that was interfering with my relationship.

I wanted to call Drew back and talk this over, make him understand how lucky I was to have the job, but also let him know how important he was to me. Yet I had no idea how I could convince him. He *knew* how important the job was. And certainly he *knew* how important *he* was. Any discussion would end up back where it started.

I felt like going home, climbing into bed, and snuggling up with George. My kitty loved me, no matter what.

But no. I couldn't do that. Couldn't retreat and hide away. It was time to act like a grownup.

I wiped away my tears, fixed my smudgy mascara, then drove to work. I parked behind the restaurant and looked at my reflection in the rearview mirror. I pressed a finger against the crease between my eyes. "You can do this."

Time would tell.

I stood beside Chef Hart, the salad chef, and listened as he explained the finer points of each menu item. I took notes.

My phone pinged — for the fifth time.

The chef gave me a look. "I thought you muted your phone after you got that call."

"I thought I did. Excuse me." When I turned on my phone I saw the messages — and call — were from Drew. He'd be furious I wasn't answering. I turned the volume down. "There. Sorry. I'm listening."

"I hope so," he said. "This may be the least complicated food station, but you can't move you on until you master it. Understood?"

"Yes, Chef."

It took my full will power to concentrate on salads — or to appear to concentrate on salads.

Two hours after my shift started I got a break. I stepped outside Rolly's and looked through all Drew's missed calls and texts, which had grown more and more snarky and confrontational. I texted him back with a simple, "Hi. I'm on break now. Work is going good."

When I got no response, I called him. He didn't answer. His silence was worse than his texts.

I felt an overwhelming need to get home so I would be there when he *did* come over.

I was texting one last time when Chef Hart came outside. "Fifteen minutes for break. Not twenty."

"Sorry." I started to head inside, phone still in hand.

He glanced at it. "Is there a problem, Miss Lindstrom?"

"I . . ." I didn't want to tell him about my boyfriend troubles.

"If you don't want this job, there are plenty of others who do."

In a millisecond I saw my future as a parade of tense evenings at work and home, dealing with Drew. I knew what I had to do. I had to choose right now between him and work.

I heard myself making the impossible choice. "I'm afraid I can't take the job."

His eyes grew large. "Why not?"

"Personal issues."

He shook his head and flipped a hand at me. "Go on then. Get outta here."

I was shocked by his tone. "I should tell Chef Bernard —"

He turned toward the door. "I'll give him your regrets." He went inside. The door slammed behind him.

It was surreal. I stood beside the dumpster, replaying the last few minutes. The last few hours. I'd headed to work, excited about my future. Then Drew had objected. Drew had pulled away. Then Drew had reached out—snarky or not— and I hadn't been there to reach back. And now I'd been forced to choose between a job I desperately wanted and the man who might be my lifelong mate. I'd had no choice but to choose our relationship over my career.

Then why did it hurt so bad?

I removed my black apron with the Rolly's logo on the front. I folded it carefully and set it on a pile of pallets near the door. When I felt tears coming, I hurried toward my car.

Home. I needed to get home to be there for Drew.

I rushed into my apartment.

But Drew wasn't there.

My anger was replaced with logic as I realized he had no reason to come over since he thought I was working. And now . . . he didn't even know I'd quit.

I pulled up our texts, including the long string of my unanswered messages. I added another. *Call me.* There was no response.

I waited a few minutes and tried again.

Nothing.

So I called him—and was surprised when he answered.

"What?" he snapped.

"I quit my job. I'm home."

"Good."

That's it? I heard loud music in the background. "Come over."

There was a pause and I heard laughter. "I just got a fresh drink."

"But—"

"I'll see you tomorrow." He hung up.

I stared at my phone. My thoughts ricocheted between relief that the tension would be over, regret that I'd given up a great job, and anger that I'd been forced to make the choice.

George appeared at my ankles. I swooped him up and nuzzled him against my neck. "At least I'll be home more for you."

I changed from my black pants and white shirt into jeans and a sweatshirt. I went into the living room and switched on the TV.

And waited for Drew to come home?
But he wasn't coming.
What had I done?

I wouldn't have had to stop home before my evening real estate meeting, but the fact that Vernon had said he'd be gone, gave me the incentive to do a little sleuthing about his relationship with Brianna. Ever since he'd stopped by the office and I'd seen them all chummy the awful possibility had grown in my gut like a flu bug threatening to do something nasty.

I had another reason to stop home. It would give me a chance to check in with Baylor. He'd had an attitude lately, and I knew we were neglecting him. Yet in our defense, he wasn't a kid anymore. Most teenagers loved to have time away from their parents. It was a blessing we could trust him to not take advantage.

But as I turned onto our street, I saw him riding in a car with a friend, Justin, driving in the opposite direction. I waved. He waved.

So much for checking in.

Yet having the house fully to myself was perfect. Once inside I went into our bedroom to change clothes for the dinner tonight. Although I could get by dressing in business casual during the day, I liked to dress to impress for these inter-agency meetings.

I tossed my blouse in the laundry, then decided to start a load. I plucked the whites out of the basket but paused as I picked up one of Vernon's shirts. There was an odd smell . . . I put it to my nose and inhaled the scent of him. But also something else.

A perfume. A familiar perfume. One I smelled every day.

Brianna's perfume?

I stared at the shirt and tried to remember when Vernon had worn it but found I was clueless. I didn't pay that much attention to what he wore, and when.

My heart beat double time. The shirt was proof they'd been together. They'd been in close enough proximity to merge her scent with his.

Gone was any nonsense about not caring. I cared. He was not going to get away with this.

I grabbed some scissors from the junk drawer and stabbed into the shirt fabric, gnawing and slicing it into dozens of ragged pieces.

My heart beat in my throat. I seethed with anger, my breathing heavy. When I was done I stared at the shreds on the floor around me. Let Vernon find it. Let him know that I knew. I smiled as I imagined it. I saw his shock and surprise in my mind's eye.

I started to laugh, but suddenly stopped myself. My laughter sounded a bit insane, like the maniacal laugh of a villain.

I wasn't the villain. I was the victim.

Wasn't I?

I realized I couldn't leave the shirt pieces on the floor. Vernon would think I was crazy. *You cut up my shirt because I was nice to Brianna? Because you think you smelled her perfume on it? That's all you've got?*

I definitely needed more concrete proof.

I turned on the washer, then gathered up the pieces and put them in a drawer for another time. I quickly dressed in a navy suit, and continued to carry out my sleuthing in Vernon's office.

I sat at his computer and logged on. He'd given me the password years ago. Most likely he'd forgotten and thought his computer was safe from my prying eyes.

Dream on, lover boy.

I looked at his email account and was disappointed to find nothing from or to Brianna. I even checked his Trash box.

So they didn't email. They probably texted or phoned. I would have to check his phone later.

I scoured his social media accounts, but he rarely posted anything, and if he did it was about sports. If there was a private account, I didn't know how to access it.

I was about to sign out when I thought about checking his virtual calendar. There were a lot of entries about meetings, a dentist appointment, a notation about Papa's funeral. Nothing interesting at all.

Except for . . . a single letter on Monday of this week.

The letter B.

I gasped.

I opened the search box for the calendar and put in a "B-space". Six events popped up, spanning six Mondays.

I felt my heart break into six pieces. This was real. This was proof. I'd wanted proof and now I had it.

How could he betray me like this? What did he see in Brianna that he didn't see in me? Where were they —?

The ring of my phone startled me. It was Nana. Again. I'd had three missed calls from her but had been busy. This time I answered. "Hi, Nana."

"Are you coming to get me?"

"What?"

"For Baylor's concert."

I sucked in a breath, nearly choking on my guilt. I'd completely forgotten. I remembered seeing him and Justin driving away. Justin, his orchestra friend. They'd been heading in the direction of the school.

I looked at the time and felt my heart sink. The concert had already started.

"I've been calling you," Nana said. "I left messages."

"I know. It's been a busy day and I . . ." There was only one acceptable excuse. "I haven't felt well. So, I'm not going. I'm sorry, I should have called you back."

"Yes, you should have. I really wanted to go."

"Again, I'm sorry."

"Baylor was expecting me."

"I'll take the blame." So much blame.

There was heavy silence.

"I hope you feel better. Tell Baylor to call me after." Nana hung up and I leaned back in Vernon's office chair. What a mess. I remembered Baylor telling me about the concert, but I'd made no effort to remember it. *It* had not been logged onto my calendar.

I glanced at my husband's calendar—which also showed no mention of the concert.

I groaned. "We're awful parents."

So what else was new? Add it to our list of offenses.

I turned off Vernon's computer and went to my meeting.

It was after ten when I got home. Vernon had his feet on the ottoman and was watching TV. Just the sight of him made me fume, yet I had other issues to deal with

"Is Baylor in his room?" I asked him.

"Haven't seen him."

I stepped between Vernon and the TV. "You did know he had a concert tonight, right?"

Vernon blinked, then put his feet on the floor. "That was tonight?"

"That was tonight."

"How was it?"

The gotcha-moment was marred by my own guilt. "I didn't go either. I had a meeting."

"Wow. Neither of us? That's bad."

"I know. Nana called me repeatedly but honestly, I ignored her calls because I didn't want her to ask me to come over."

"That's rude," he said.

That was rude? I sat on the couch. "Nana wanted a ride, but by the time she got a hold of me, the concert had started" I glanced toward Baylor's room. "I tried to get out of the meeting early, but, as you see, that didn't happen."

Vernon shut off the TV. "Hopefully your mom and dad went. Or Paige."

I rubbed my hands over my face. "Mom didn't say anything to me about going."

He sighed. "And Paige is starting a new job tonight."

Great. The whole family had failed him.

I called Baylor's phone. I got voice mail and left a message, "Hi, honey. We're just wondering when you'll be home from the concert. So sorry we missed it. Talk to you soon."

Vernon rolled his eyes, "Lame."

My mind raced ahead. "How long have you been home?"

"Twenty minutes."

"Did you check to see if he left a note?" I asked. "Maybe he slipped home and left again to go to an after-party or something."

Vernon shook his head. "Baylor? Party? That doesn't sound like him. But no, I didn't look."

I went into the kitchen and checked the counters and dinette.

Nothing.

We weren't note-leavers, usually choosing to check in on our phones. I felt a seed of desperation plant itself in the pit of my stomach.

"Let's check his room." Vernon followed me in. I flipped on the light. As usual, his room was neat and organized—a far cry from how I'd kept my room as a teenager.

But there it was. A sheet of paper taped to his TV. I snatched it off and read aloud. "'To whom it may concern—though you *aren't* concerned, so you'll probably not miss me. I'm done. Nobody ever notices me so I'm outta here.'"

"Out of here?" Vernon asked. "He's run away?"

I looked on his desk. "His laptop is gone." I turned toward the bed. "His backpack too. He always hangs it on the bedpost." I opened the closet. "He's taken clothes with him."

"How can you tell?"

I pointed at a row of six empty hangers. "He always hangs his favorite shirts together on the left. They're gone. But his bassoon is here." I turned to my husband. "What do we do?"

"We don't panic. He's a smart kid. He can take care — "

"He's our baby! He can't take care of himself out in the world! He's a homebody. He didn't even want us to buy him his own car because he said he had no place he wanted to go."

Vernon peered through the slats of the window blinds. "Which means wherever he is, he's walking."

"A skinny kid, alone with a backpack? Tasty bait for a mugger."

"In Carson Creek?"

"Small towns have crime too."

"Why would he leave? Just because we missed the concert?" Vernon asked.

To a kid that might be enough. But it wasn't just the concert and I knew it.

Vernon knew it too and shook his head. "It's got to be more than that. I know you and I work a lot. We give him his space. I thought he liked that."

"Me too." Or maybe I only wanted him to like that.

"Call his friends," he said.

"I . . . the only friend I know of is Justin." Then I had a horrific thought. "What's Justin's last name?" My mind was blank.

We both stared at the air between us. Then Vernon said, "Calloway. Justin Calloway."

Thank God he knew it.

Vernon did a search on his phone for the Calloways who lived nearby. "It's gotta be this one." He dialed.

"Put it on speaker," I said.

A boy answered.

"Is this Justin?"

"Yeah."

Vernon held his phone between us. "This is Baylor's dad. Have you seen him since the concert?"

Silence.

"Do you know where he went?"

"So he really left?"

"Do you know where he is? He left a note."

"That's nuts. I saw him after, but he didn't want a ride home."

"Was he upset?"

"He was quiet, but that's normal. I never thought he'd really run off."

"So he talked about it?"

"A little. But . . ."

There was a lot riding on that *but*. "What?" I asked.

"I don't know. He said he's alone a lot."

Vernon and I shared a guilty look.

"Do you know where he might go?" Vernon asked.

"Not a clue. I never see him *out*."

Justin didn't know a lot for being a friend. "Can you give us the numbers of his other friends?" I asked.

"Uh . . . he doesn't have friends — at least that I know of."

"He doesn't?" Vernon said.

"Not really. He and I have gone our separate ways 'cept for orchestra. You know people make fun of him, right? He's nice enough but . . . well, you know how he is."

Obviously I didn't. "He's been bullied?"

"I don't think it's anything drastic. I've stuck with him in orchestra cuz we've known each other since first grade. I've told him not to act so geeky. And when they do get on him? Laugh it off — in their faces. But he always puts his head down and scurries away, which makes it worse." He took a breath. "But I guess . . . yeah maybe it has been kinda rough."

A thought came to me, and I hated to ask, but had to. "Do you think he would hurt himself?"

Justin's hesitation spoke more than his words. "I don't think so. He's just . . . moody."

Moody equals . . . ?

"Thanks for the help, Justin. Let us know if you hear anything." Vernon hung up.

I felt tears threaten.

"I'm calling Paige," Vernon said as he dialed. Again, he put it on speakerphone.

"She's probably still at work," I said.

"Maybe she'll pick — Paige. I'm so glad you answered. Baylor's run away."

"What? Why?"

Vernon explained the situation. "Do you think he'd go to your apartment while you're gone?"

"I'm at the apartment. He's not here."

"I thought you were working."

"Not anymore. I'm coming over."

We stood in Baylor's room, looking at each other. "Who else do we call? Where would he go? Do we call the police?" I began to spiral, pacing back and forth.

Vernon sat on the bed, looking deflated. "I don't know what to do." But then he made another call. "Everett . . ." Vernon told him what was going on, then shook his head for my benefit. Then he stopped and listened. "You two want to come over?" He looked at me for my opinion.

I nodded. I needed my parents here.

"That's nice of you. See you soon." He hung up.

"Should we call Nana?" I asked.

Vernon glanced at the clock. "It's nearly eleven. She'll be asleep."

"They have a special bond. I *can* imagine him going over there."

"But wouldn't she call if he was?"

I was weary of would-haves and could-haves. "I'm calling." I knew Baylor wasn't at Nana's when her voice sounded groggy. "Sorry to wake you. We're looking for Baylor."

"Because . . . ?"

"He ran away."

She made a huff sound. "*Now* you pay attention to him?"

"What are you saying?"

"I'm not surprised he's run off considering the way the lot of you ignore him. Regardless, what can I do to help?"

I could only think of one thing — *the* thing that my grandma always did: "Pray, Nana. Pray a lot."

Chapter 10

Everett & Holly

"Be joyful in hope,
patient in affliction, faithful in prayer."
Romans 12: 12

Rosie and I arrived at our daughter's home and got an update —
on nothing. There was no word. Baylor wasn't answering his phone.
Paige had offered to pick up Nana. I didn't know whether to pray,
panic, or be mad at the boy. I'd never thought my grandson was the
runaway type. He was more stable than any kid I'd ever known.

I found myself standing next to Vernon while Holly and Rosie
commiserated and worried aloud. I leaned toward my son-in-law.
"You feel as helpless as I do?"

He nodded. "I can't just sit here. Want to go drive around and look
for him?"

"I'm game." At least it was something.

Vernon got his keys and told the women we were leaving. They
didn't object.

We got in Vernon's SUV and sighed heavily at the same time.
"Where should we look?" I asked.

"The school. Church. He's on foot so he can't have gone too far."
He pulled away and we drove a few blocks in silence.

Vernon was the first to speak. "This is entirely our fault. Ever since
Paige moved out the family seems disconnected. At least that's how
I've felt. She and Baylor were inseparable. Plus, she and I have always
been real close."

"I know. Paige is definitely a daddy's girl."

"Her leaving left a hole in the house."

I could imagine that too. Paige was the social one. Vibrant. Talky.
Baylor . . . wasn't. A memory popped into my head that illustrated just
that. "One time when the kids stayed overnight with us, Rosie and

Paige spent the evening baking cookies. I wanted to do something with Baylor but I couldn't find him."

"He hadn't run away, had he?"

"No, no. I found him playing Legos in our closet. Alone. Happy as a clam."

"He's always liked small spaces. He doesn't mind being by himself. He's an easy kid. Maybe too easy."

"It's not a bad thing to be content in your own company," I said.

"I suppose not. I'm not particularly outgoing either. Holly and Paige are the go-getters."

And Rosie. I had a thought, but I wasn't sure Vernon would take kindly to it. Yet I couldn't worry about that right now. "If I can make an observation?"

"Shoot."

"You've always been close to Paige, but you're not close to Baylor."

Vernon didn't answer right away. But then he said, "Don't get me wrong, I love the kid deeply. Completely. But you're right. He and I aren't close. Not at all. And again, that's my fault. My expectations."

"Expectations?"

"This is going to sound awful, but when we had a boy I figured he'd share my interest in sports. I love football, and played baseball in high school. I wasn't very good, but I loved it. I thought Baylor might take up where I left off. Or at least we'd watch games together."

"That's not Baylor."

"That's not Baylor."

I'd known there was a disconnect between them. I'd never had a son, but I'd been a son. And I'd experienced a disconnect with my own father. I hadn't thought about it in years, but maybe what I went through would help Vernon now. "I thought about running away when I was Baylor's age."

"Really? Why?"

I let my thoughts jump into my past. "My dad was a brilliant man who expected me to go to college. I didn't like school. Even though it was never my thing, I could have done better, tried harder. Who knows? Maybe I was a mediocre student *because* my dad wanted me to be good at it." I realized I'd recently had a similar revelation at the shop: I hadn't tried woodworking because Willis wanted me to. Was I really that stubborn?

"Baylor *does* excel. He pressures himself—too much sometimes. We've never had to tell him to study. Paige was smart but she had a social life, so we often had to push her. But not Baylor."

We parked at the school and walked the perimeter. Vernon tried the doors, but they were all locked.

We got back in the car. "Why did you want to run away?" he asked me.

I put my seatbelt back on. "The summer I was fifteen I got a job as a roofer. The owner was a great guy who was patient with me as I learned."

"Fifteen? You've been doing it that long?"

"Pretty much forever, right? I stayed on with him, worked my way up to project manager, and bought the business from him when he retired." I looked out the window onto the dark streets. There was no movement. No Baylor. "Ever since I started I loved being outside, building something, helping people get a new home, or making their home better. My dad didn't understand how that could fill me up. He made me feel like a failure. I remember one argument at dinner when I was bragging up the job and my boss, Dad told me in no uncertain terms what he thought. He said no son of his was going to work a grunt job all his life." I shook my head. "Grunt job."

"That's harsh."

His words still stung. "After dinner Mama came to my room and told me not to quit because Dad wanted me to. She wanted me to be happy. That was a big thing for her to do—to go against him like that."

"She really cared about you."

"She did. Without her words I might have quit."

"Did he keep hounding you?"

"He did, all through high school." I hated those memories. "It got harder and harder to not give in."

"But obviously, you didn't."

"I didn't, but . . . I remember the moment when I realized I would always be a disappointment to him. I thought it would be best if I ran away so neither one of us would have to deal with it anymore."

"*Did* you run away?"

"I didn't because of my mom and little sister. Dad would have made their lives hell." I took a deep breath. "A week later he died."

Vernon tapped on the brake. "Whoa."

"So I know all about feeling guilty."

"You think the tension between you . . . ?"

"Killed him?" I shrugged. "He had a bad heart. Mama didn't blame me. She said Dad was driven and demanding. I suppose now we'd call him a Type-A personality. But back then she just called him 'Difficult with a capital D.'"

"I'm sorry."

"Thanks." We drove a few more blocks in silence. "Baylor will be all right," I said, even though there were no guarantees.

We drove through the small downtown of Carson Creek. Many of the buildings were empty as businesses had moved to Kansas City. "Surely, he wouldn't go into one of those," I said.

"Who knows?"

"Let's get out and check all the doors," I said.

Vernon pulled into an alley behind the main drag. We got out and tried a few back entrances, but they were locked. As we got back in the car the whole search seemed pretty hopeless.

Vernon sat in the car without starting it. "I wish I'd paid more attention to his life, knew where he liked to go, knew his friends. I'm home more than Holly, but obviously not enough."

I had an odd thought. "You, Baylor, and even me . . . we're all abandoned men. Since I'm retired I'm not sure Rosie has noticed I'm around. She's away from the house ninety-percent of the time."

"She's a doer."

"Over-doer," I said.

"It's what she's used to."

"That's what Elsie said."

Vernon sighed. "Holly takes after her mom."

"As I said, the women in our family have left us to our own devices."

Vernon gripped the steering wheel, staring out into the night. "This sounds pitiful, but with Paige moved out I miss not having anyone to talk to."

"You're talking to me. I'll listen."

Vernon chuckled. "Don't get sappy on me, Everett."

I liked Vernon—always had. "I'm serious. We should go out sometime. To a game or something."

"You don't like sports."

"I don't dislike them. It would be something to do."

Vernon laughed. "I'm better than nothing, huh?"

"Well . . . yeah." I thought of another man in the family. "A few days ago I went over to Willis's shop."

"I forgot about that."

"I was going to clean it out, but I think I'm going to keep it for myself."

"Hey, why not? You're good with your hands." Vernon drove down the alley onto a side street. "Speaking of Willis . . . I miss that guy. I mean, I'm the grandson-in-law, so I didn't spend tons of time with either him or Elsie, but me being an accountant and him being a banker, he and I talked about business and investments, that sort of thing."

"That's more than he and I had to talk about. I never thought he approved of me. Even though I'm one-generation older than you, I was the blue-collar guy who steered his only daughter away from college. Déjà vu to my own father's attitude."

"How long have you been married?"

"Forty-five years next month."

"Surely Willis wasn't holding onto that grudge for forty-five years."

"Actually, I just found out he wasn't." I told him about my conversation with Doug at the shop. "I wasted a lot of time holding a grudge."

"Willis could have tried harder."

Maybe. "I can't do anything about what didn't happen between him and me, but I was thinking of asking Baylor to join me at the shop. We could learn together." I thought of something. "You could come too."

"Huh. I've never thought about woodworking."

"Think about it."

"I will." He pulled away and we drove toward the church.

We took a stroll around the grounds and checked the doors but Baylor was nowhere around.

"I'm going to run past the hospital, then go home."

"Hospital? That seems drastic."

"At least we'll be able to rule it out."

I called Rosie to fill her in but her phone was busy. "I hope they've heard something."

I stood at the front window, peering out into the darkness. Where was my son? "I feel so helpless."

"He's a smart kid, Holly," Mom said.

"If he was smart he wouldn't have run away."

"He's still a kid."

I perked up when I saw the headlights of a car turn into the driveway.

"The men?" Mom asked.

"Paige and Nana." More to commiserate with.

The two women came inside and Paige helped Nana to a chair. "Any news?" she asked.

"Nothing," I said.

"The men are out looking."

"Can I see the note he left?" Paige asked.

I gave it to her to read.

"I was afraid of that."

"Him leaving?"

She handed the note back to me. "Not *that*. But I knew he was feeling alone since I moved out." She slumped onto the couch. "Probably before that. We used to be close, but when Drew and I got more serious . . ." She pulled a pillow to her chest. "I pretty much abandoned Baylor."

"Join the club."

Nana shook her head. "God tells us to 'Listen to my instruction and be wise.'"

I sat on the window seat. I wasn't up to hearing Nana's words of wisdom because they often made me feel dumb. "God didn't give Vernon and me any instructions."

"Nonsense," Nana said. "'Start children off on the way they should go, and even when they are old they will not turn from it.'"

I felt my pulse quicken. "You're saying we're bad parents? We *did* bring him up in the way he should go. *He* made the choice to leave. We didn't push him out."

Mom leaned forward in her chair. "It's not just you, Holly. Everett and I have ignored him too. He is—this will sound awful—but he's easy to ignore. He's a good kid and doesn't make waves."

"Until now," Nana said.

I didn't want to psychoanalyze Baylor—or our family. I returned to the window. I agonized over our last conversations, trying to pick out any small detail that might be helpful. I ended up remembering what Justin had said. I shared it with the others. "His orchestra friend said Baylor's been bullied."

Paige nodded.

"What?" I asked. "You knew about it?"

"A little. I remember a few times when I still lived at home I found him sitting on his bed with his laptop but when I came in he closed it. I thought he might be emailing a girl or something personal, but I also thought it might be another kind of personal. Online troll junk." She stood so she could take her phone out of her back pocket. "Let me check his Facebook page."

Baylor had a Facebook page?

We waited while she found it. "Not much here. Just a few videos of guys on skateboards. Dog videos. Kind of lame stuff and nothing to worry about." She looked at her phone more intently. "Wait." She read more. "Some of the comments are mean."

"Mean, how?" Nana asked.

Paige shook her head. "Making fun of what he posts. Nothing horrible, but if he was already feeling bad about himself . . ." She set her phone aside.

I felt horrible that I didn't know any of it. I wasn't a touchy-feeling mother. I was never huggy, and never offered to play dress up or Battleship with my kids like perfect TV parents did. But I should have at least been *aware*.

Nana said, "Well then. Did anyone go to his concert?"

The silence spoke volumes.

"When I got the job I told him I wouldn't be there," Paige said.

Mom put her hands at her temple. "Dad and I forgot about it completely. We had a date-night."

"Vernon forgot too," I said. "And I . . . I had a meeting."

Nana shook her head. "You forgot about it too. When I called to get a ride, you said you were sick, but you weren't."

There was no way around it. "I forgot too."

"Poor Bay," Paige said. "I just assumed *someone* was going. No wonder he left."

My phone rang. My heart jumped. But it was Vernon. I put him on speaker so everyone could hear. "Yes?"

"No sign of him. We even stopped at the hospital and he's not there. Stopped at the police station too but they say it's too early to file a report."

"We can't put out an Amber alert?" Mom asked.

My dad answered. "We asked—but we can't. That's for an abduction, for a child in danger. We'll keep looking if you want us to."

I looked at the others. "Yes, please. We're going to stay together here."

I hung up and sat on the edge of Vernon's oversized leather chair. I wanted to grab an afghan and curl up in a ball. I felt so useless.

Then Nana spoke up. "I ran away once."

"*You* ran away?" Paige asked. "When?"

"When I was forty."

We all chuckled.

"Don't laugh," she said. "It was real. I was in a situation very much like Baylor's."

"People ignored you?"

90

She considered this a moment. "You could say that."

Interesting. Because we needed a distraction, I said, "Tell us what happened, Nana."

"It all started with wanting breakfast in bed."

"What did that—?"

Nana raised a hand. "Do you want to hear the story or not?"

We sat back and listened.

Chapter 11

Elsie – 1973

> "For in the day of trouble
> he will keep me safe in his dwelling;
> he will hide me in the shelter of his sacred tent
> and set me high upon a rock."
> Psalm 27: 5

I'm forty today!

I turned on my side to cuddle with my husband. But Willis wasn't there.

Was he was making me breakfast in bed? He'd never done such a thing, but this *was* a big birthday.

I wasn't sure what to do. Should I pretend to be asleep?

I managed to do so for ten minutes, but when the clock on the nightstand showed five-after-seven, I had to get up. It was a school day and Rosemary occasionally overslept.

I quickly got dressed and ran a comb through my hair and once again noticed how boring it was. Maybe I should get it cut in a poofy shag like Goldie Hawn wore in *Butterflies are Free*?

But I was not Goldie Hawn. I was the mother of a teenager.

I was forty.

I heard kitchen sounds and walked down the short hall to join my family. I smiled at the thought of seeing Rosemary making pancakes and Willis warming up the syrup.

They both looked up when I came in the room and were most definitely not making pancakes. Rosemary put her empty cereal bowl in the sink. "Gotta go, Mom. Mandy's picking me up. I have student council after school, and we're going out for pizza after. See you later."

And *poof*, she was gone.

Willis sat at the kitchen table, reading the newspaper. "Can you make the coffee? I don't know how."

He couldn't fill the percolator with water and coffee? He couldn't plug it in?

For some reason it incensed me that he hadn't made any effort to learn this daily task. Yet as I went through the steps I conceded that I'd never asked him to learn, nor offered to teach him.

Resigned to a normal morning, I asked, "Would you like some toast?"

"No thanks. I had cereal."

I put a piece of bread into the toaster for myself. "What's on your agenda today?" I asked as I always asked. But then I added, "Anything special?"

"I have a dinner meeting with a developer in Kansas City. We're trying to pull his business our way—not an easy task in Carson Creek, but I'll do—"

"Your best," I said. It was an oft-heard statement. Willis always offered his best—to the world.

He folded the newspaper neatly, stood, and put on his suit coat. We went through our goodbye ritual: I straightened his tie, kissed his cheek, and said, "Love you."

Willis winked and replied, "Love you back."

And *he* was gone.

I stared at the door. Had my family really forgotten me? I buttered the toast while imagining another way this morning could have gone. There'd been no breakfast in bed, but what if Willis had said, "Happy fortieth birthday, Elsie! For dinner I thought the three of us would eat at Frederico's. How does that sound?"

Like a pipe dream.

I spent three hours puttering around the house, accomplishing little—physically. Mentally and emotionally I'd done ten Jack LaLanne workouts.

My conclusion? No one appreciated me. No one noticed I even existed unless their laundry wasn't done or dinner wasn't on the table. They didn't know how I spent my days—and didn't care to know. Neither of them had asked me what *I* was doing today.

As a last attempt to jar myself out of my mood I turned on the soap "All My Children." Maybe if I let myself be absorbed into the drama of Pine Valley I'd feel better about my own situation.

It didn't work. Watching Erica Kane, her mother Mona, Phoebe Wallingford, Jeff Martin and the rest, I felt exhausted, and totally unable to tolerate their problems on top of my own.

I felt an intense urge to flee. Run. Escape.

Without planning it I pulled a suitcase from under our bed and filled it with clothes and toiletries.

Even as I packed I fought a battle between *Go* and *Stay*.

Why should I stay? They didn't appreciate me. They didn't care what I did or thought. And they were rude. They forgot my birthday! Why should I stay and endure more of their abuse?

I closed the suitcase and carried it into the living room where I grabbed the book I'd been reading and a photograph of Willis and Rosemary — that *I'd* taken. I was rarely in family photos because I was the designated photographer. No one had ever asked me if I wanted the job, they just assumed.

They assumed a lot of things.

I detoured to the kitchen and got some money out of a casserole dish that I kept on a high shelf. I'd been saving a little every week from the household allowance Willis gave me — saving for what, I wasn't certain. Obviously, saving for *now*.

I gathered my purse and keys. I was ready to go. Should I leave a note? Probably. I tore off a fresh sheet of paper from my shopping list pad, the one with the cartoony illustration of fruits and veggies at the top. I sat at the kitchen table and wrote: *"It's my birthday but no one cares so I'm leaving."* It was rather blunt, but I felt blunt. I even added two more lines: *"I have no idea when I'll come home – if ever. Make your own dinner. Mom."*

My heart beat wildly as I read it over. Was I really doing this?

I pressed a hand to my chest, and even managed a weak, "Lord?" But I didn't wait for His answer. I *was* doing this.

The two-car garage always seemed so much bigger after Willis left for the day. He drove the good car, his beloved black Ford Galaxie 500. I had made the mistake of calling it a Chevy once and he'd been incensed. My car — that I shared with Rosemary — was a 1961 VW bug. Willis had bought it second-hand from a friend without ever thinking that I might not know how to use a clutch and stick-shift. "I guess you'd better learn," I was told. I was proud of myself for doing just that. Rosemary learned too. He hadn't given us much choice.

I put my suitcase in the front trunk and was glad it fit just above the spare tire. As I backed out of the garage I spotted my eyes in the rearview mirror and pressed a finger against the crease between my brows. Being upset was a wrinkle-maker.

Once on the street I drove north — because I always drove north — but I had no clue where I should go.

I pulled to the curb to think this through. It was my birthday. I could go anywhere and do anything. What did *I* want to do?"

A car drove by and the driver honked. A friend waved.

What I didn't want to do was drive around Carson Creek where everyone recognized my car. I needed to drive to Kansas City where I could fade into the traffic and be anonymous.

And so I did.

My mind had to concentrate on driving in city traffic, but when I saw a sign for the Nelson-Atkins' Art Museum, I suddenly had a destination. I'd been wanting to go for years, but Willis thought looking at art was a waste of time.

Today I had the time — and the inclination.

I followed the signs to the museum and went inside. I hadn't been there since coming on a field trip as a teenager. Twenty-some years between then and now. The visit was most definitely overdue.

I was welcomed by a dapper looking man in a suit. "May I direct you to any specific type of art, ma'am?"

I knew exactly what I wanted to see. "The portraits, please."

He gave me directions and soon I was looking at paintings of people. I knew nothing about art but knew that I wasn't keen on statues and artifacts — no matter how old they were. Landscapes were pretty, but didn't move me. But portraits? I felt a connection in seeing a person who'd actually lived. Looking into their eyes made the gap between their time and mine slip away.

I strolled past many faces and scenes, but stopped when I saw one particular painting of a woman dressed in a gorgeous white and gold silk gown from the 1880s. She held an ivory fan in her lap and was staring across the room, pensive, unsmiling, non-committal. In the background was a shadowy glimpse of a grand piano set in front of opened windows where the sheer curtains were billowing from a breeze.

"She's waiting for something to happen," I whispered.

Just like me.

I looked at the plaque: *Mrs. Cecil Wade, 1886, John Singer Sargent.*

I'd seen Sargent's work before and was always impressed with how he could paint fabric to look so real you wanted to touch it.

But it was the name of the woman that made the deepest impression: she was Mrs. Cecil Wade, as if marriage had made her lose the right to have her own first name.

Just like me. I was known as Mrs. Willis Masterson more than Elsie.

Suddenly it just seemed so . . . wrong.

I felt hot tears and dug a Kleenex out of my purse.

"Are you all right, ma'am?" asked a female docent standing unobtrusively at the back of the room.

"It moves me."

The woman stood nearby and looked at the painting, as if for the first time. "It was called the Gilded Age for good reason," she said. "Can you imagine wearing such a fancy gown, with a corset and bustle?"

She was missing the heart of the painting. "She's all dressed up like a perfect doll, waiting for her husband to take her somewhere." I pointed to the plaque. "We don't even know her first name. Shouldn't we know her first name?"

"I've never thought about that." She pointed toward the doorway. "I could probably find out for you."

I waved a hand at her. Again, she was missing the point. "No need. Thank you."

The woman stepped away, leaving us waiting wives alone.

After spending a little more time with Mrs. Cecil Wade, I left the museum to go . . . where?

I was in the same state of mind as I was when I left home — if not worse. I needed something to lift my spirits and make me feel better about myself. About my life.

Within moments, I knew just the place.

I entered Jeanne's Sewing Emporium and drank in the familiar aisles of colorful fabrics. The store was busy so I simply nodded at my favorite clerk who was helping another customer.

I perused the bolts, my eyes grazing over the colors and patterns. They fueled me. Occasionally, I touched one, letting it drape over my hand. I made my choices through sight *and* feel.

I stopped at a lightweight yellow wool that had tiny flecks of gray. I immediately knew what it could become. I'd seen a pattern for a long-sleeved dress with pintucks on the bodice. It would be the perfect outfit to wear for bank-customer dinners.

I paused with a hand on the bolt. If I didn't go home there wouldn't be any more bank-customer dinners.

There wouldn't be a lot of things.

The consequences of future choices overwhelmed me: Willis, Rosemary, the house, finances, friends, holidays . . . ?

I shook my head vigorously. I couldn't let my thoughts linger on frightening what-ifs.

To get back in the moment I stroked the fabric. I loved the feel of it, the color, and the design in my head. I would make the dress for me—no strings attached.

I took the bolt with me to the pattern tables, where I found the Vogue pattern. I pulled the right-sized pattern from a drawer nearby.

A woman who sat across the table from me noticed my choice. "Vogue. Aren't those hard to sew?"

I couldn't lie. "They can be challenging because they have special details like bound buttonholes and flat felled seams."

The woman shook her head. "You must be a good seamstress."

"I guess I am." I checked the back of the pattern envelope for yardage. "I was going to be a fashion designer—in another life."

The woman nodded knowingly. "Ah yes. The regrets of 'another life.'" She flipped the pages of the Simplicity book.

The pensive look on her face made me ask, "What did you want to be?"

Her smile was bittersweet. "I wanted to pursue musical theatre. In college I was the lead in 'My Fair Lady' and 'Oklahoma.'"

"I love those shows." I repeated the phrase the woman had used on me. "You must be a good singer."

She smiled. "I guess I was. Am." She stopped at a page, studied it, then turned it around for me to see. "Do you like this caftan? Do you think it would be hard to make?"

It was a very easy design with a zipper up the front. Pretty shapeless but comfortable. "Not hard at all. Have you put in a zipper before?"

She nodded.

"Then you'll have no problem."

"Thanks for the encouragement. I needed that today."

Join the club.

"If you have time, would you help me choose a fabric? You seem to know so much about sewing. I'm new at it."

I could think of nothing I'd like better.

Patty and I—for we exchanged names—spent the next hour shopping together. I helped her pick out a printed knit that had enough body to be easy to sew, yet had a nice drape to it. We stood side by side at the cutting tables.

Our shopping done, we checked out. The owner of the store came over to chat, then waved good-bye. "Have a good day, ladies. Mrs. Masterson."

He said it as though I didn't have a first name. I needed to rectify that. "Call me Elsie," I said.

Mrs. Cecil Wade would approve.

My mood had changed from depressed to delighted. Helping Patty had filled me up in a way the painting's inscription had brought me down. I smiled as I drove and found myself thanking God for the blue sky, the sack of yellow wool on the seat beside me, and the gorgeous rows of trees lining Ward Parkway. It was my dream to live on this street. The houses were built in the 1920s and 30s on enormous lots. Gardeners trimmed roses along the long tree-shaded drives, and the sunlight caught the reflection of leaded glass windowpanes.

At a stoplight I saw a sign: *Open House!* There was an arrow pointing right.

Why not? Maybe God would lead me to *our* new house. Now *that* would be an amazing birthday present.

I parked up front and tried to dissect my thoughts. *Our* new house? Willis's bank dinners? I kept flipping between making things better in my current life and leaving that life. How fickle was that? Obviously, I didn't know my own mind.

A real estate agent met me at the door and welcomed me inside. I entered a world of grand staircases, crown moldings, furniture *not* bought on sale, and real paintings in gilded frames.

A couple came in, drawing the attention of the agent away from me. "Don't forget to look at the pool house," she said.

A pool? Such luxury. I went outside and strolled around the blue lagoon. The door to the pool house was open and —

Chapter 12

Elsie & Baylor

"Do not exasperate your children; instead,
bring them up in the training
and instruction of the Lord."
Ephesians 6: 4

" . . . the door to the pool house was open and — "

Holly jumped out of her chair. "I know where Baylor is!"

I was taken aback. I'd been telling the women about my fortieth birthday and how I'd run away, hoping it would help. That it *had* helped was a surprise.

"Where is he?" Rosemary asked.

"At the pool house. There's one at a house I listed." Holly paced in a tight path in front of the couch. "He knows about it because he went with me to lock it up. He saw where the key was kept."

"Why would he go there?" Paige asked. "Wouldn't he bother the homeowners?"

"The house is empty." Holly grabbed her purse. "I have to go."

"Do you want us to go with you?" Rosemary asked.

"No. Thanks. I don't want to gang up on him." She was out the door.

I put a hand to my chest. "That was unexpected. Let's hope she finds him."

Paige checked her phone again. "I wish he'd answer."

Rosemary returned to her chair. "I guess there's nothing else we can do but wait."

"I hate waiting," Paige said.

"Patience has never been my virtue either," I added.

"Meanwhile," Rosemary said with a sigh, "continue your story, Mom. What happened at the pool house in your story?"

I pressed a hand to my forehead, trying to return my focus to the past. "The pool house was unremarkable. It was just one room and a bath, and smelled of chlorine and musty towels. I don't remember many other details. Except one."

"Which was . . . ?"

"A life-changer. As I was walking out I saw a sign above the door that said, *Pool Sweet Pool*." I shrugged. "It was an awkward phrase, which obviously was a play on *Home Sweet Home. But it* made me realize home *was* sweet and I wanted to go back."

"Were you really going to stay away?" Rosemary asked.

I'd asked myself that question many times. "I don't really know. Every bit of logic told me I had a good life, a nice home, a great family. But something big was missing."

"Freedom?" Paige asked.

An interesting word coming from Paige. "Not freedom. Something almost more important. Affirmation."

My daughter and great-granddaughter exchanged a look.

"Meaning . . . ?" Rosemary asked.

"Meaning my life lacked support and encouragement. I needed to feel affirmed. Worthwhile."

"Noticed?" Paige asked.

She was such an insightful girl. "Yes," I said. "Noticed and appreciated." I saw Rosemary rub a hand against the armrest of the chair, staring at nothing. "Is something wrong?"

She stilled her hand and blinked a few times. "I'm so sorry about that day. I was so clueless. I was all wrapped up in my own little world."

"You were a teenager."

"That shouldn't be an excuse."

I didn't want her to feel bad about it at this late date. "At least now you understand."

She nodded. "Offering each other encouragement and affirmation . . . those are wise words."

I thought of my conversation with Everett. If my story could help them appreciate each other . . .

Rosemary sat forward. "But we *did* remember it was your fortieth birthday." Her voice sounded younger, like her memories of being a teenager had changed her tone. "At lunchtime that day I remembered and called the house but you didn't answer. Then I called Dad at work. He felt so bad that he went home to take you to lunch, but you weren't there. He saw your note. I came home straight after school and saw it too. We both felt awful. That's when we made plans to have a party for you. I never knew you thought about leaving forever, Mom." Rosemary's eyebrows dipped. "And I don't remember seeing you bring in a suitcase."

"I snuck it inside. We'll never know what would have happened if I would have stayed away. But I know I had to leave as though I meant it. I had to mentally give myself the option to leave."

My daughter reached out and squeezed my hand. "I'm really sorry, Mom. We never forgot again."

"No, you didn't. And I never left like that again either." Not exactly.

"It does sound like you had a fun day out on your own," Paige said.

"A day of lessons." I thought of a verse to share. "'What I tell you in the dark, speak in the daylight; what is whispered in your ear, proclaim from the roofs.'"

Rosemary shook her head, amazed. "You can find a lesson in grape jelly."

I didn't take offense. "Finding the lesson makes the pain bearable."

"So what did you learn?" Paige asked.

I hadn't thought about that day in a long time, yet the lesson *had* lingered. "I learned to appreciate that I lived in 1973 and not a hundred years earlier when women had fewer rights and their days were filled with tasks of survival, with little or no free time. On the flip side I appreciated that I wasn't like Mrs. Cecil Wade with too much free time and little purpose. I learned that joy comes from helping others, I learned that *our* home was very sweet. And . . . I learned to forgive."

"Even back then I realized Dad and I took you for granted."

"I took both of you for granted too. After that day I tried to show my appreciation more often. Yet the most important lesson was . . ." I held up a finger.

"Was?" Rosemary asked.

"I stopped keeping score."

Paige gazed at the door. "I hope Bay doesn't keep score."

I stretched out on the couch in the pool house but couldn't get comfortable. It was old and lumpy, but better than sleeping on the ground somewhere. Running away was more complicated than I thought it would be.

I lay on my back and put an arm under my head but had to change positions because of the lump on my forehead where the rock had hit me. I didn't like to think about how close it had come to my eyes. The thrower realized it too, which is why his buddy had yelled, "Let's get out of here!" and they'd run off.

I knew the creeps who'd done this. I wasn't their only victim. Nor was this the first time they'd come after me. Cousins Clark and Colton Mowry should have had BULLY as the caption under their yearbook picture. They were thick, dumb losers who tried to make themselves important by hurting people — which only made them dumber. Pitiful.

But powerful.

I'd tried standing up to them once, but it hadn't worked, and they'd hassled me twice as often for the week after that.

I touched the bump. They'd never thrown rocks before. And I didn't get why they made fun of me for being in orchestra. I knew a couple cool kids who were in it and they never had trouble.

Though I'd hitched a ride to the concert with Justin, I'd planned to ride home with Mom and Dad. Or Grandpa and Grandma. Somebody. But no one had come. I'd scanned the audience for them, then assumed they'd show up backstage where other families came to congratulate their kids.

When I realized they truly weren't there, I started to walk home. Crossing paths with the Mowrys had just been bad timing. Being dressed in black pants, a white shirt, wearing a bow-tie, and carrying my bassoon, gave them plenty to tease me about — though it's not like they needed a reason. Just seeing me set them off. I didn't get it.

They called my bassoon a baboon and made "ooh-ooh, ahh-ahh" noises and scratched under their armpits like a chimpanzee. I made the mistake of saying, "That's not a baboon gesture, that's a chimp."

Dumb move. They'd both stopped and stared at me. That's when Clark threw a rock — that missed.

Running from them had been a bad idea. They chased me into backyards and side streets. I heard them panting and when they couldn't catch up, Clark threw *the* rock.

It was a direct hit that took me to my knees and brought tears to my eyes. I'm glad they ran off because my tears would've made things worse. But who wouldn't cry? It hurt bad.

I'd run home, expecting to find Mom and Dad there. I hoped that my bump would get their attention and make them feel doubly bad. Maybe the pain would be worth it.

But no one was home. So much for them feeling sorry for me or apologizing. No guilt trips in this family.

Not yet anyway . . .

That's when I made the decision to run away. Maybe then they'd feel *really* bad. The thought of them panicking and blaming each other and even fighting over it was awesome. I packed a bag fast. I certainly didn't want them coming home before I'd left because that would have sliced their guilt-trip in half. I wanted them to suffer like they made me suffer.

It would serve 'em right.

As soon as I left and got out of the neighborhood, I had to decide where to go. I didn't want to be where there were people who could tell my parents they'd seen me — that's if Mom and Dad actually went out to look for me.

I thought about slipping behind some bushes near the library for awhile, but sitting on the cold ground wasn't appealing. And I hated crawly bugs.

And then my head started to throb and I felt the lump swell up. It was really tender. Did I have a concussion? I'd heard about football players getting those all the time. Even though that would add to my family's guilt, I wasn't self-destructive. I didn't want to make things worse by ignoring it.

I needed to lie down.

That's when I remembered Mom had a house for sale nearby.

An empty house.

With a pool house.

And I knew where the key was.

I'd never done anything like this before — I mean I was virtually breaking in — but I meant no harm and wouldn't hurt anything. And now, stretched out on the couch I liked the idea of being hidden away. No one in the entire world knew where I was.

I wanted to turn on a light but didn't dare. Even though no one lived in the house right now, there were neighbors close by. The last thing I wanted was to get arrested for trespassing — though *that* would certainly get my family's attention. Yet that kind of rebellion wasn't my style.

Neither was running away.

Or revenge.

I started thinking of ways to get back at the Mowrys. Since they had me beat in the brawn department I had to think of another angle. Egging their house or trashing their lockers wasn't enough. Trolling them on social media was an option, but it was so *done.* I needed something that would really hurt them.

I closed my eyes, feeling the weight of the day, and the softness of the couch . . .

I hadn't planned to fall asleep. And never for three hours.

I woke up to moonlight streaming in the windows, lighting up a poster of a swimmer on the wall, and an odd *Pool Sweet Pool* sign over the door. *Pool sweet pool . . . home sweet home?* Should I go home?

As I sat up my vision started to spin. My head really hurt so I looked in the bathroom cabinet and found some Tylenol. My bump was impressive but the skin wasn't broken. A little blood would have been kinda cool. A real wound.

I went outside to the pool and stretched out on a chaise, leaning it back so I could look at the stars. They weren't as brilliant as I expected they'd be. The moon was too bright.

I looked at my phone to check the time and saw a ton of texts and missed calls. I'd turned the sound off during the concert and had never turned it back on.

The latest was from Paige: *Where are you? We're worried.*

Well, what do you know? My plan was working. They'd found my note and Mom and Dad had called Paige. Mission accomplished.

I went through the other texts, emails, and voicemails from my family. Paige, my parents, grandparents, and even Nana. Very cool.

Yet . . . a question loomed: did I want to go home? If I hadn't left the note would they have noticed I was gone? Their concern was too little too late.

Too late for what?

What did I really want?

I let the question hang. Unfortunately the moon didn't have an answer.

But then it came to me: I wanted attention.

How lame was that? I mean, I was allowed to think such a thing because I was only sixteen, but I was a smart sixteen. I got great grades, was coasting through school, had my head on straight, and —

Somehow having my head on straight didn't fit with running away. I suppose some psycho-babble doctor would say I was acting out.

Was I?

I didn't like the term at all. My parents were lucky I wasn't like Keith Brennen who was expelled for breaking into the school and trashing the science lab because the teacher gave him an F. Or Thad Greene who crashed the car he'd gotten as a birthday-present while he was high. Or tons of other kids in my class who got girls pregnant, took drugs, cheated on tests, or bragged about shoplifting or screaming at their parents.

"I'm a good kid," I told the sky.

Didn't I deserve some attention?

Nobody noticed me. Or cared. I spent tons of time trying to make things as perfect as possible so they'd notice. But it didn't matter.

My family . . . *they* were far from perfect.

Grandma Rosemary tried to be the perfect grandma. She and Grandpa used to ask Paige and me to stay overnight once in a while when we were growing up, but lots of times she had some meeting to go to so she was gone most of the evening. Grandpa Everett would play Monopoly with us and we'd watch a movie until Grandma got home and gave us ice cream before bed.

I needed to quit watching old TV shows like "The Waltons" and "The Andy Griffith Show" where all the grandmas gave big hugs and baked pies, and all the grandpas shared their hobbies and down-home wisdom. I wasn't really surprised they hadn't come to my concert. Them coming to stuff like that was hit and miss.

But my parents . . . they had no excuse. They expected me to be a perfect son but they didn't even try to be perfect parents. Mom was obsessed with proving she was some super-agent. I had no idea if she was good at it or not, but I didn't like how totally consumed she was. She was as jumpy as our neighbor's cat who'd sit on our porch railing staring at the door, but as soon as we opened it, she'd run off. Once I put a bowl of milk out there and watched her from inside. She'd walk toward it like it would bite, take a sip, then another, but when I made a sound, she'd bolt away. Both Mom and the cat wanted something but were suspicious of everybody, and probably were afraid of getting it.

I wanted the old Mom back—the one who worked part time at Hobby Lobby, was home after school, and who bought us all sorts of craft stuff that we'd make together. Once she'd gotten it in her head to be a "professional" and work toward her license, she'd changed. She'd told us that her hours would be flexible and she'd be home more. I hadn't seen it. The difference now was that even when she was home she was thinking about real estate.

Not thinking about us.

Not thinking about me.

I missed Paige. She was the jelly to my peanut butter. She was popular in school, was good at art, was on student council, and could talk with anybody about anything. People liked her. I liked her. I loved her and she loved me. But when she moved out it was like we'd gotten divorced. Even if she left on good terms, things weren't the same and they never would be. I was plain old peanut butter without her.

But again, no one noticed my pain.

Actually . . . Dad was hurting too. He and Paige had always been close. When Paige came in the room his face changed: he smiled and his eyes got all bright.

When I came in the room he usually didn't look up from his phone or the TV. One time I sat in the family room with him for over an hour and he didn't notice. I got up to get something to eat and asked if he wanted anything. He looked up and said, "Oh. Baylor. When did you get here?"

No wonder I ran away. I'd virtually lost both my parents and my sister.

And Papa.

I closed my eyes and wrapped my arms around myself feeling my own guilt rise up. Did I miss him?

Actually . . . not really. I didn't know him very well other than helping him with his crossword puzzles. He was always a presence at family gatherings, a hawk hovering in the rafters — watching for prey? Once in a while he'd swoop down and interrupt a conversation with his opinions — which were usually different from everybody else's — but then he'd fly back to the rafters until next time. He was the patriarch. Not ever a "papa".

"At least it wasn't Nana who died."

I couldn't believe I'd said the words out loud, yet they were true. I adored my great-grandma more than anyone in the entire world — even more than Paige. It wasn't that I even saw her that often, but when I did, it was like wading into a heated pool where I could cover myself in warmth up to my neck. My body would relax and my mind would clear. I could just *be* with Nana. She was the one person who accepted me as I was. She knew about my quest to be perfect and appreciated it, even as she assured me I didn't need to try so hard. God loved me unconditionally — and so did she. I didn't like the thought of Nana worrying about me.

I looked at the time. Two-thirty in the morning. Was she with the others? She needed to be home in bed.

Enough was enough. I'd made my point. It was time to go —

"Baylor?"

I saw my mom coming out of the house. I got off the chair, nearly toppling it. My body twitched, wanting to run back into hiding, but I held my ground. "Hi."

"Baylor!" She ran down the deck stairs. "That's all you can say? Hi?"

I shrugged.

She came next to me and I noticed she was two inches shorter than I was. When had that happened? I braced myself for her yelling.

Instead, she pulled me into a hug. "I'm so glad I found you. We were so worried."

I was shocked. She really cared? I wrapped my arms around her and nodded against her hair. It felt good to be hugged. "Sorry mom."

She took a step back, rubbing tears away. "This is not who you are, Baylor. You're too good for this. You're my perfect child." She took a breath. "And we're sorry. We should have been at your concert."

I was relieved they got it. They felt bad. Victory was mine. But then I heard myself saying, "It's okay —"

"It's not okay." She stared at me, then touched my head. "What happened?"

"Some kids threw rocks at me."

She gasped. "Paige said you've been bullied. She saw mean comments on your Facebook."

"She was on my Facebook?"

I winced as Mom touched my hairline. "We were trying to find you, trying to understand. Where were you going?"

I wished I had a great answer, but I had nothing. "Just away. For now."

"Well let's go home. We'll talk about it there."

Even though I'd already made the decision to go back on my own, a big part of me wanted to stay away. To go home and have all those people ask questions, wanting to talk about it. It made me nervous.

It was easier to be alone.

My family was waiting for me — even at three in the morning. Even Nana.

I received hugs all around. It was nice, but awkward. I'd left because I wanted to take control of things and get the attention I deserved, make them feel bad and all that. But coming back . . . it was like they thought I was weaker than before.

When I bent down to hug Nana she whispered in my ear, "Home sweet home, bud. Home sweet home."

My throat grew tight because I wanted it to be like that.

She looked at the bump on my head. "You're hurt."

"It'll be fine. Don't worry about it."

Mom went into the kitchen. "I'm getting some ice. Some boys threw rocks at him."

"Who?" Dad asked.

No way would I tell them. "Just let it be, okay? They were shocked it hit me. They ran away." I sat on the couch and hugged a pillow to my chest.

"They'd better run, far and fast," Dad said. "I'm going to call their parents."

It was kinda cool he wanted to defend me, but as far as him actually doing it? I wasn't ten. "Leave it alone, Dad. Please."

Paige sat beside me and leaned close. "Do I know them?"

I shook my head, though there was a chance she did.

Mom brought out an ice pack. I dutifully held it to my head. The cold stung.

They all sat around the living room, staring at me. What did they want me to say? I thought about apologizing, but didn't. Not this time. Let them do it first.

"I'm ashamed we all missed your concert." Dad shook his head adamantly. "No excuses."

Mom nodded. "No excuses — for that, or for leaving you on your own so much." She traced the piping on a chair cushion. "I guess I thought you liked being alone."

"I do, but —"

Nana piped up. "Him liking to be alone doesn't mean he doesn't need people. Doesn't need to be appreciated. Acknowledged. Encouraged. Right, Baylor?"

She'd said it well. But there was more to it. "Alone is okay. But I was more than alone." I tried to think of a good way to explain it. "I felt . . . invisible."

Paige touched my arm. "Ah, Bay. I feel bad about moving out and leaving you here."

Our eyes connected as she gave me a look that implied *with them.* "I know you couldn't live at home forever," I said.

"Yeah, but . . ."

Dad sat forward in his chair. "Are you being bullied a lot?"

They were hung up on the bullying. "That's not the problem."

They all looked confused.

Grandma pointed at my head. "The bump on your head says it is a problem."

They *didn't* get it. "This bump isn't why I ran away."

Mom nodded. "The concert."

I tossed the pillow into Paige's lap and stood. "Yeah, the concert, and me feeling invisible, and . . ." I thought of something Mom had said at the pool. "You called me your perfect son."

"You are my perfect son," Mom said.

I dropped the ice pack on the couch. "What good has it done me? I do everything I'm supposed to do, but you still don't notice me."

Dad ran a hand through his hair. "Wow. I guess in a way you're right. I'm so sorry."

I looked at Mom. Would *she* get it?

She saw me looking, but looked away. Then she nodded. "Me too," she said. "I can see how it could seem like we've totally taken you for granted."

Really? "It was more than just *seeming* like it, Mom. You did."

Dad flashed her a look. "We did, Hol. Admit it."

She swept her hair behind her ears. Then she nodded — more to herself than anyone else. "Yeah. You're right. I admit it." With a final nod she stood. "No more. I promise." She walked over to me and pulled me into her arms. "I love you, Baylor."

Even in my anger I was embarrassed by how much I needed to hear those words. One by one I let my family hug me again and say they loved me. It was just like in the movies and I felt my anger flow away. Yet I wasn't sure I wanted it to go away so soon.

Then Nana said, "We all need to go home and get some sleep."

Agreed. I was done.

Yet I had one question. "How did you find me?"

The women turned to Nana but Paige answered. "Nana told us a story about when *she* ran away. She ended up at a pool house where she saw —" She nodded to Nana. "You finish it."

"I saw a sign above the door that said, 'Pool Sweet Pool' and it made me think of 'Home Sweet Home', which sent me home again and —"

Mom interrupted. "Which made me think of the pool house of the listing I have — that *you* saw, and —"

I couldn't believe it. "I saw that same sign in *my* pool house."

"What a coincidence," Grandpa said.

Nana shook her head, adamantly. "There's no such thing as coincidence. God sent both of us signs."

Dad looked incredulous. "So Baylor's pool house sign is the exactly the same on as yours, Elsie?"

"No, it wasn't," Nana said. "Mine was in Kansas City. But it doesn't matter. The sign then and the sign now were God's clues of where to go next."

Leave it to Nana to find the core of it.

Grandma put on her jacket. "The mention of clues reminds me of the treasure hunt clues you've give us in the past, Mom. You always liked to send us on a hunt for a prize."

Nana stared ahead. She blinked a few times. Had she heard?

"Are you okay?" I asked her.

Nana shook her head, scattering the moment. Then she kissed my cheek. "You are the best prize ever, young man. Don't you forget it."

Paige drove me home and offered to help me get in bed.

I was quite capable, though I couldn't remember the last time I'd stayed up all night. The clock on my nightstand read 4:10.

I smoothed the covers over my chest and sighed. It was times like tonight that reminded me how important family was. I was glad my story had helped the situation, providing the final clue. At eighty-nine I had a lifetime of stories. A lifetime of lessons learned. The details between then and now may have changed but the essence of my experiences . . .

A lifetime of clues.

And treasure hunts.

When Rosemary had said those words, I suddenly remembered what Willis had told me before he died and in the treasure hunt he'd made for me. He wanted me to share the before-moments of my life, the moments that had changed me. Maybe I had a few treasures left to share.

I smiled in the dark and fell asleep. Tomorrow would be a busy day.

Chapter 13

Elsie

"Do nothing out of selfish ambition or vain conceit.
Rather, in humility value others above yourselves,
not looking to your own interests
but each of you to the interests of the others."
Philippians 2: 3-4

I wasn't one to sleep late. Even though I'd gone to bed after four, I was up by eight.

I had work to do. Treasure hunts to create.

But first . . . After getting dressed and making my bed, I sat on its edge and bowed my head. "Lord, I've felt so rudderless since Willis passed. My identity was linked to his for nearly seventy years. I've never felt so alone."

I opened my eyes and saw a family picture on the wall, taken right before Willis found out he had cancer. It was odd how the cancer had created a before-and-after moment in our lives. The before time was filled with blissful ignorance, almost like the years when teenagers fly through life believing they are invincible. Of course Willis and I had known that one of us would get sick one day, and someday after that one of us would die. It was inevitable.

But even knowing didn't prepare us for the moment when a doctor's words sliced our lives into two with *before* ending and *after* helplessly being forced front and center. A newborn situation where everything had to be learned.

I found myself standing before the photograph though I didn't remember getting from there to here. I looked at each smiling face. Three new generations existed because of me and Willis. All because two people fell in love. It was such a miracle.

I touched his face. "I wish you were here with me. The family needs you."

The family needs you.

Tears sprang to my eyes but didn't spill over. I pulled my hand back, letting the inner words resonate in my mind. "The family needs *me.*"

I looked upward. "The family needs You, Lord."

I smiled when I remembered my attitude just moments before. I was rudderless no more. It was time for my family to climb into the boat with me. To share the journey.

I nodded when I remembered one of the most important verses of my life. I repeated it out loud. "'Trust in the Lord with all your heart and lean not on your own understanding; in all your ways submit to him, and he will make your paths straight.' Let's do this, Lord. I'm counting on You."

When I entered the kitchen the need to hold onto my thoughts of Willis spurred me to make a bowl of oatmeal to go with my coffee. When it was cooked I poured milk into the bowl and sprinkled it with raisins and brown sugar. My eyes closed as the first bite brought me back to other mornings when we'd sat together at such a meal. Not hundreds of mornings or even thousands. Over twenty-five thousand mornings. And though my husband's chair was empty, I felt his presence there.

When I was finished eating I found a pad of paper and a pen in the telephone drawer and brought them to the table. At the top I wrote *Nana's Treasure Hunts.* But that didn't seem quite right.

What did I want from my family?

One purpose of the hunts was to get them to see the whole of me as an individual, not just as the role I played in their lives. I wanted them to see me as a young woman, a bride, an entrepreneur, a wife, an explorer, a person beyond the Nana-title. So I changed the heading to *Elsie's Treasure Hunts.*

The rest of the page stared back at me. "Now what?"

Willis's words returned to me: *Choose moments that changed you.*

I sipped my coffee, trying to mentally relive my life in search of those moments.

Nothing stood out. I'd led a pretty ordinary life. But Willis had said the moments didn't have to be big, they just had to be significant—to me.

Most of my memories revolved around family. The fact they'd grown up to be good people with meaningful lives was a victory. But *I* hadn't done anything special to make it happen.

I took my bowl to the sink and refreshed my coffee from the pot. My thoughts strayed to last night when the family had gathered to worry after Baylor—who'd been found. I'd enjoyed sharing *my* running-away story. If not for that story, Holly might not have thought to look in the pool house.

Which was like my pool house. From forty-nine years ago.

The past and the present had merged. Two hurting souls had sought affirmation and connection with their families—a common, universal desire. A snippet from a verse came to me. "'There is nothing new under the sun.'" I knew there was more to it than that and retrieved my Bible from my desk. The words were from King Solomon, the wisest man to ever live.

I needed a little wisdom right now.

I opened to the book of Ecclesiastes. I knew the book contained the greatest piece of wisdom there was: that a life that wasn't centered on God was of little consequence.

I skimmed the first chapter and pegged a finger on verse nine: "'What has been will be again, what has been done will be done again; there is nothing new under the sun.'"

Suddenly, I knew what I had to do. My treasure hunts weren't about rehashing the moments of my life willy-nilly, they were about pinpointing the needs of my family—like I'd done while waiting for Baylor—and sharing life lessons that could help. Lessons that would span the years between us. Connect us.

My first thoughts went to my dear great-grandson. Everyone was thankful he was home safe. A small bit of progress might have been made in the family, but I knew there were more issues at stake.

What ailed Baylor and his family life could not be fixed with just a kiss, a hug, and good intentions. Appreciating each other needed to be sincere and effortless. Not forced. And never demanded.

In a rush of years, memories surfaced of a dinner party for Willis's boss. Even now I felt the anxiety and the desperate need for Willis's appreciation. Even now I felt the weight of the pain that came that night.

I wrote Baylor's name then detailed the story I would share.

Words came to me as if the dinner had happened a month ago, not sixty years. When I was finished reliving the evening, I was faced with the harder task: the clues. In all the treasure hunts I'd planned before, there had been some prize at the end. But this kind of treasure hunt was different. There wasn't a physical prize to be found, but experiences to be shared—in all their glory or folly.

I looked around the house, trying to find inspiration. *Show me how to do this, Father.*

I stopped in front of the hutch and took out a piece of the china I had used that night. It was a gorgeous gold-rimmed plate adorned with pink flowers. "Castleton Rose," I whispered.

The china led to another thought, and another, until I knew what to do for the rest of Baylor's treasure hunt.

One family member down, five to go.

That evening, as I waited for Baylor to answer my summons to come over, I checked the clues.

Since everything was ready, I sat in my chair to wait. And rest. It had been a grueling day mentally and emotionally. For with the memories came the emotions. There were so many thoughts to think and feelings to feel.

The clock struck seven. I closed my eyes, realizing I hadn't taken my usual afternoon nap. Being a matriarch was hard work.

I heard the kitchen door open. "Nana?"

"In here."

He kissed my cheek before sitting on the couch. His shoulders seemed tight. "So, bud. How are you do —?"

"If you're worried about me, don't be," he said. "Things are better today. Dad and I even watched a football game together."

"You don't like football."

He shrugged. "I like Dad." He looked down and bit his fingernail. "It was stupid to run away like that. I won't do it again."

"Glad to hear it. But I didn't ask you to come over because of that — at least not directly."

"Good." He leaned back, the tension falling away.

I beamed at my nerdy great-grandson with the unruly dark hair and the inquisitive brown eyes. "It's time for your very own treasure hunt."

He cocked his head, then straightened it. "It's not my birthday. Or Easter."

"Doesn't need to be." It was best to get on with it. I handed him a slip of paper. "Your first clue."

He read it, looked up, then read it aloud. "Go to the china hutch and count how many pieces of china and crystal are there."

"That's right."

"You want me to take inventory for you? Are you going to sell some of it?"

I hadn't thought of that. "Maybe. Go on now. Follow the directions in the clue. There are three patterns." I gave him their names.

Baylor used his organizational skills to log in dinner, dessert, and salad plates. Plus cups and saucers and the occasional serving bowl or platter.

I watched him as he worked, his face intent on the task, his long fingers counting the stacks and logging them onto a neat list.

I was excited for him to be done because I knew that the list was merely a means to an end—and the next clue. But I let him do the work. I used the time to get him some cookies and a glass of milk.

Finally he closed the doors of the hutch and handed me the list. "There. Done. You have a ton of dishes, Nana."

"Too many. Eventually, I'll let some of them go, but for now, I keep them because they help me remember past dinners and celebrations. And those pink ones help me remember a life lesson."

"How do they do that?"

It was time for clue number two. "Look under the third dinner plate in the Castleton Rose dishes."

He found it and read, "'Go to the guest closet and find an emerald green dress in a garment bag.'"

I followed him into the second bedroom where I kept out-of-season and sentimental clothes. He started looking but came upon Willis's suits first. "My clothes are on the left."

Baylor found a row of garment bags. "You have lots of them. Which bag?"

"I'm not telling." I smiled as I shrugged.

He gave me a boy's look of exasperation. "You can't just tell me which one?"

"What would be the fun in that?"

I'd purposely placed the dress halfway through the row.

"Here's a green one," he said.

"That's sage green, not emerald green."

"Really?"

"Really. Keep looking."

Three bags later he said, "This has to be it." He took out the bag and unzipped it completely.

"Take it out."

He struggled with it, clearly not used to handling garment bags or dresses. It was a jewel-tone green silk with a cinched in waist and a flowing circle skirt. The neckline was adorned with a shawl collar. Just seeing it made me remember that night.

"Did you wear this to a dance or something?"

"Nope. I wore it at a dinner party. At our house."

He looked confused. "Isn't this too fancy to wear at home, just to have people over?"

I touched the bodice and remembered how the silk felt against my skin. "That's what we did in the Fifties. Women dressed up in heels and jewelry and men wore suits."

"Nowadays, you'd be lucky if people put on a clean tee-shirt and wore shoes instead of flip-flops."

The casualness of now made me sad. There was more to life than being comfortable. "It felt good to dress up. In case you haven't noticed, people act differently when they're dressed up than when they're wearing jeans or yoga pants or whatever it is people wear now. Dressing up shows respect for the moment and the company."

"This dress looks uncomfortable."

Comfortable or not I wanted to get back to what was important. "This was my favorite dress, but I never wore it again."

"Why not?"

"Memories."

"What memories make you keep china you don't use and a dress you won't wear?"

"Read the note that's pinned to the bag."

"'Go to my desk and find the small pink notebook.'" He looked up at me. "The desk in the living room?"

"That's the one."

A moment later he stood before the desk. "You're not going to tell me which drawer its in, are you?"

I shook my head.

He found the notebook in the bottom drawer and read the cover: "Dinner Party Diary?"

"That's it."

He leafed through the pages. "You kept a diary of every dinner?"

"Every item served — with notes about what went well and what didn't, every dish and glass used, who came — and who declined our invitation, and what transpired."

He paused at one entry and read silently. "You wrote down dialogue? What people said?"

"The words that stuck with me. People's lives are revealed through conversation."

He read some more. "You talked about politics? I've heard you're not supposed to do that. No politics or religion at the dinner table."

"I do not abide by such restrictions and as you know, neither did Papa."

Baylor continued to look through the diary. "This one says, 'Willis got a promotion with a raise of $1000 a year.'"

"It was a very successful dinner party. We hosted the president of the chamber of commerce. Papa got his account."

"At the bank that he ran?"

"The same one."

He flipped the pages. "This is crazy. There are so many. Years and years' worth. Mom had the head of her office over once, but we grilled chicken and ate outside."

"Turn to April 23, 1955."

"The night of the dress and the dishes?"

"The very same."

He turned the pages toward the front and looked at the entry. "I thought ratatouille was a kids' movie."

I chuckled. "It's also a French dish of stewed vegetables. That night I served it with a crown roast of pork, homemade dinner rolls, a Caesar salad, and pineapple upside down cake for dessert."

Baylor checked the book. "Wow. That's exactly what you served. How do you remember?"

I shrugged. "A lot of thought went into each dinner and I remember that night especially well." It was time. "Read my notes."

He turned the page, searching. "There are none. All the other dinners have a lot of notes and stuff. Why doesn't this one have any of that?"

I sat in my chair and pointed at the ottoman. "Let me tell you a story . . ."

Chapter 14

Elsie - 1955

"Be merciful to me, Lord, for I am in distress;
my eyes grow weak with sorrow,
my soul and body with grief."
Psalm 31: 9

I took the pineapple upside-down cake out of the oven and fanned it with a towel. It would look so pretty with the caramelized top, but the proof would be when I flipped it over. I needed to let it cool a bit before I dared try that. As with all the food of the night — save Grandma's dinner rolls — I was using new recipes. I knew it wasn't the smartest thing to do, yet our normal fare of meatloaf, tuna casserole, and spaghetti wouldn't impress anyone.

Willis had told me multiple times that tonight's dinner wasn't just important, it was essential to his future. Our future. Mr. Carlton was the president of the bank where Willis worked. He was getting close to retirement and there had been murmurings among the loan officers that he was looking to make some changes in personnel. Although that had sounded ominous — for "changes" could mean firings as well as hirings — Willis was excited about it. I'd rarely seen him so hopeful.

The fact that Mr. Carlton had a son who worked at the bank made *his* succession a slam-dunk, but if Carlton Junior moved up, it would start a communal ladder-climb that would hopefully lift Willis higher.

That's why tonight's dinner with both Carlton men and their wives was so essential. Everything had to be perfect.

I looked at my list of to-dos and checked off the cake. And the rolls — which were already cooling on the counter.

I went over the other items on the list: the standing pork roast had been tied and the exposed rib bones covered with foil. It went in the oven next, for two-and-a-half hours, resting for thirty minutes beyond that. Scalloped potatoes were ready to cook, and a Caesar salad would be a last-minute task, with the ratatouille put in the oven with the roast when it had an hour to go. I'd already sliced the vegetables and had arranged them prettily in a pan. It was sitting in the fridge, ready to be cooked.

I set the list down and took a deep breath. "You can do this, Elsie." I *had* to do this. And not just for the promotion. This dinner was my big chance to make Willis proud of me. Although we'd been married nearly three years, he'd only been at the bank for two — since he'd come back from the Korean War. Up until now our only dinner guests had been family — and they'd helped with everything. And they loved me. I had never had to put on a party by myself. For important people.

I was startled when the doorbell rang. *No! It's not time yet!* I glanced at the clock and realized there was no probability that the person at the door was one of our dinner guests. I put a hand to the curlers in my hair. Guests or no, I couldn't go to the door looking like this.

The doorbell rang again. But then there was a knock. "Elsie? It's me, Betty."

I breathed easier. Betty was our neighbor, two doors down. I answered the door. "Sorry. I'm a bit frazzled."

Betty smiled at the curlers. "Very cute."

"Hopefully. Eventually."

We went to the kitchen and Betty held out a glass cake plate I'd asked to borrow. "Want help turning the cake out on it?"

I felt the side of the pan. It seemed cool. "Please." We stared at the cake pan. "Have you done this before?" I asked.

"Never. Do you have directions?"

I read the recipe. "'Run a knife carefully around the edges of the cake. Put serving plate on top and quickly flip the pan and plate over.'" I snickered. "Sure. Piece of cake."

Betty put a hand on my shoulder. "We can do it."

We followed directions and flipped the cake over without dropping it on the floor. But what would it look like? The moment of truth . . . I carefully removed the pan and gasped. The red dye of the maraschino cherries had bled into the cake. "It looks like blood!"

"It does not. It looks exactly like it's supposed to. I think."

"Maybe I should have blotted the cherries first."

"Ease up, Elsie." Betty nodded toward the rolls. "*They* look great."

I let out the breath I'd been saving. "Would you check the place settings for me?"

"As if I know how it should look? But sure."

We moved to the dining room. The table was already set with my pink flowered china.

Betty ran a finger along the gilded edge. "Very fancy."

"They were a wedding gift from my parents. I only have six place-settings so I'm glad no one else is coming."

"That's six more than I have of any china." She picked up a fork. "Sterling?"

"I found it at an estate sale."

Betty put it down just-so. "It's really lovely, Elsie."

"It has to be perfect."

Betty gave me a look I'd seen before. Betty was as easy-going as I was tightly wound. "You worry too much. I'm sure Willis will be ecstatic."

He'd better be. Our future depended on it.

I was just putting the vegetables in the oven when I heard the garage door open. Willis was home! He'd be so proud of the dinner I'd made and all of my hard work. He'd come in and see it and say, "Well done, Els. You're amazing."

I wiped my hands on my apron as he came in the back door. "I'm so glad you're home," I said. "Look at what I've cooked for our first fancy dinner party."

"Nice, nice," he said, rushing past me. "I need to change my shirt — did you iron it?"

"I did. And I polished your black shoes."

He stopped at the doorway of the kitchen to look back at me. "Shouldn't you be getting dressed too?"

So much for compliments or even a thank you. I realized how horrible I must look in my chinos, a red gingham shirt tied at my waist, a dirty apron, and my curlers — Willis hated curlers. I'd meant to change before he got home. I took the curlers out of my hair as I hurried to the bedroom.

Luckily, he was in the bathroom, so I stuffed them in a drawer. I ran my fingers through my hair, then quickly put on the green dress I'd bought for the occasion.

I had just zipped up the back when he came out of the bathroom. I swished the wide skirt back and forth. "How do you like it? Don't I look pretty?"

He gave it a glance as he drilled his shirt in the laundry basket. "Is that new?"

"I got it on sale." For $9, which *was* a little more than I usually spent. "The saleslady said the color looked beautiful with my complexion."

He got fresh socks out of a dresser drawer. "Salespeople are paid to say things like that to get the sale."

Had I been played? The clerk had seemed sincere.

He stood at the dresser mirror to tie his tie. Maybe he'd say more after I added my string of cultured pearls and matching earrings.

And makeup! I had no makeup on!

I sat at the vanity and made quick work of it. I hated to rush, but I'd gotten behind with cleaning, cooking, ironing, and setting the table.

"Hurry up, Els. They will be here in thirty minutes." He pinned on his turquoise tie tac that matched his cufflinks. His parents had given him the set when he'd first gotten the job at the bank. I thought they were rather flashy for a banker, but Willis seemed to like that they set him apart.

He took one last look in the mirror, then said, "I'll get the drinks set up. Carlton Senior likes martinis. Are the appetizers ready?"

I sucked in a breath. I'd made the olive cheese spread to pipe onto the celery, and had bought meat and cheese for a cracker tray but I hadn't put any of them together. What was wrong with me?

"Els?"

"It'll be ready in time. I promise."

I quickly brushed my hair and sprayed it with hairspray. I was thankful I found some hose that didn't have runs in them. And finally I slipped on my new black patent heels. All in five-minutes' time.

My heart raced, my thoughts scattered, and panic tapped me on the shoulder. I'd expected Willis to be proud of me and give me all sorts of compliments, but so far all I'd gotten was a blah "nice", and orders to hurry up. Didn't he see how hard I was trying?

The evening felt ruined before it began.

While serving the appetizers, I noticed the pink nail polish on my right hand was chipped. I knew I'd be self-conscious about it the entire evening. If only I could eat left-handed.

Dinner went well. The roast was tender, the potatoes creamy, and the ratatouille done just enough—though I discovered I wasn't a fan, well cooked or not. Both Mrs. Carltons were polite and mentioned how delicious the meal was.

But I didn't taste much of it. As the conversation ebbed and flowed I kept looking at Willis, waiting for him to give me a smile. A wink. A nod. Something that would let me know that *he* thought things were going well. But I got nothing. He was witty and charming to everyone else, but he ignored me. More than once I wanted to raise my hand like a kid in class, begging him to call on me. *Yes, Elsie? Do you have a question?*

As the evening continued my imaginary answers grew more cranky, moving from *How do* you *like the dinner, my love?* To *Do you have any idea how hard I worked to make this evening come together?* To *Do you even care?*

Unfortunately this inner dialogue demanded most of my attention. I could only assume I responded correctly and smiled in all the right places. I knew I wouldn't remember much of it. I took heart in seeing that everybody else was smiling and laughing. Good for them.

As the dinner winded down—they didn't seem to mind the bloody cake—my anger turned into weariness. I longed to send them all home, dump the leftovers in the garbage, turn off the lights, and dive into bed—not into *our* bed, but into the one in the guestroom.

After dessert Willis finally looked at me. But it wasn't with an encouraging expression but a questioning one. I ignored him like he'd ignored me. Let *him* worry for once.

Finally the guests said their goodbyes while gushing about the nice evening.

Nice. I hated that word. It was hardly proportional to all my work and worry.

As soon as Willis closed the door I shucked off my uncomfortable heels and marched toward the dining room where I picked up two cups and saucers and brought them to the kitchen.

To his credit Willis followed my lead and brought two more in, setting them by the sink. I brushed past him to get the final two.

I looked for my apron but it must have been in the bedroom, so I grabbed a new one, shutting the drawer with a loud thud. I turned the water on full blast to fill the sink.

"If you keep pounding around you're going to break something, Els. Is something wrong?"

At least he'd noticed. I squirted Ivory soap in the water and bubbles erupted. "Nothing's wrong, Willis. Not a single thing."

I nudged him to the side so I could scrape the plates into the trash. "Go on. Let me clean up." I reached past him to get the final plate that was on the counter.

"I'll get that for—"

"Don't bother. I've got it. Go to bed."

He grabbed my arm. "Stop it. Tell me what's wrong."

I shook his grip away, stepped back, and said in my most sarcastic voice, "How can anything possibly be wrong?" I shook my head. "At least the *guests* told me it was a perfect evening."

He looked confused. "It was. Except for you being a little detached during dinner conversation, it was great."

"Great." I grabbed onto the word and scoffed. "I guess that's a step up from 'nice'."

"What are you talking about?"

"As I said, nothing. It was a perfect evening."

"Again, I say it. I have a good feeling about the promotion."

I waited for him to add, *Thanks to you, Elsie.*

When he didn't say the words I longed to hear, I turned off the water and started to wash dishes.

He stood beside me at the dish-draining side of the sink. "A promotion a good thing, Els. It's what we wanted."

"What *you* wanted." I rinsed a plate.

Willis reached past me and shut the water off. "Why are you acting so strange?"

I faced him and let my tears fall. He seemed surprised by them and stepped back as if they were acid. "I did everything I was supposed to do, Willis, but you didn't notice any of it."

"Of course I noticed. Everyone loved the food and the evening. They told you so."

I flicked my tears away. "*They* told me so. You didn't say a word about any of it, about the food, the setting, or my dress—except to tell me the saleslady was lying about how nice it looked on me."

His eyes softened. He reached out to touch me, but I stepped away. I wasn't through. "I could have been a hired maid or a cook for all the thanks I got from you." I thought of something else. "Actually, you treated me worse than a maid because I'm pretty sure you would have told a maid thank you—and maids get paid."

His face hardened again. "Now you're being ridiculous."

"Am I? How about this: during dinner you were at your most charming to everyone else, but I couldn't even get you to look at me and smile. A smile, Willis! Would it have hurt you to encourage me with a smile?" I felt the tears return and let them flow. "One measly smile?"

He tossed his arms into the air. "All this because I didn't say thank you and smile? Are you really this needy, Elsie? I thought you were stronger than this." He turned away. "I'm going to bed."

He left me blubbering at the sink. I thought about going after him but I was worn out. There was no argument left in me. It was clear there was nothing I could say to change him.

As I cleaned up, my emotions ran the gamut. I felt sorry for myself, angry at him, frustrated that he seemed incapable of praise, and sad about the thought of spending a lifetime never getting the affirmation I deserved.

Chapter 15

Elsie & Baylor

"Choose my instruction instead of silver,
knowledge rather than choice gold,
for wisdom is more precious than rubies,
and nothing you desire can compare with her."
Proverbs 8: 10-11

Baylor moved to the ottoman. "Did Papa get the promotion?"

"He did, which of course, eventually led to him running the bank. The dinner was a success. *I* was the one who ruined it for myself."

"But I get it, I get how you felt," he said. "Sometimes I think of how I want things to play out, how I want people to act, and when they don't . . . it makes me mad and sad at the same time."

"I understand completely."

He was quiet a moment, then bit his lip. "Did Papa start giving you compliments after that?"

I hated my answer. "Not really."

Baylor sighed deeply. "That's totally unfair."

"Yes, it is."

He stood up. "It makes me mad. If he were here I'd yell at him. Actually, I wouldn't, but I'd want to."

"I appreciate you coming to my defense, bud." I didn't want him thinking badly of Willis. Or his family for not appreciating him like he wanted them to. I patted the ottoman. "There's more to the story."

He sat again. "More?"

"There's always *more.*" I looked toward the kitchen and let my thoughts return to the feelings I'd had that night "What I didn't realize at the time was that *that* particular evening was a turning point in my life."

"How?"

I knew it would be hard to explain, but I let my memories take over. "After cleaning up, I got ready to go to bed."

"In the guestroom?"

"No, in our room. I lay beside Willis with my back to him. I was still mad."

"You had a right to be."

I shrugged. "But then he scooted over and hugged me."

"Good. Did he say he was sorry and he'd do better?"

"No."

Baylor's eyes grew wide. "Why not? You deserved an apology."

"I *was* disappointed that he didn't say anything, so much so that I nearly started another argument about how he wasn't apologizing right—how I needed more from him."

"Nearly started?"

"Nearly. I was lying there in his arms, thinking of all the things I wanted to say to prove he was in the wrong, when a soft voice stopped me."

"What voice?"

I touched my chest. "That still-small voice of God that talks to us from the inside."

He shook his head. "I don't have that."

"Of course you do. You just need to listen harder."

Baylor absently ran his fingers in a small circle against his chest then let his hand drop. "What did the voice say?"

"It said two words: Be quiet."

"As in don't argue?"

I nodded. "From that night on—in a trial and error way—I learned to ask God for the right words during arguments. A lot of the time He told me to be quiet."

"But Papa was wrong."

"Maybe. But that night showed me that I had to make a choice to love him anyway. He was flawed. So was I. So are you. So is your family."

Baylor tucked his legs beneath him. "You're telling me to love them anyway."

I put a hand on his knee. "'Everyone should be quick to listen, slow to speak and slow to anger, because human anger does not produce the righteousness that God desires.' By telling me to be quiet God was telling me to listen more and talk less."

"So we can't argue?"

"We can. And sometimes we should. But the point is, no one is perfect. And no one but God loves us perfectly. Everybody wants to be appreciated, but we often aren't."

"You can say that again."

I went back to the story. "That night as I fell asleep in my husband's arms, I realized that he might never change enough for me. So what was I going to do? He *did* love me. He *did* appreciate me—in his own way. Would he change? Maybe. But the truth of it was that I wanted affirmation from a human being who happened to be flawed. That night I decided to focus on getting encouragement from someone who had no flaws, who loved me unconditionally."

"God again?"

"God again—and always. We need to do our best for ourselves and for God. Live honorably. If other people notice? That's frosting on the cake."

Baylor was not smiling.

"What's wrong, bud?"

"So they treat us bad and get away with it?"

He was taking it wrong. "It's not about them getting away with anything, it's about choosing the hill we want to die on."

"Die on?"

Was he too young to know that phrase? "Is getting attention worth risking your relationship with your family? Are you willing to fight to the death for it?"

"Well, no."

I flicked the end of his nose. "That's what I started to learn that night. It was a turning point between choosing to constantly fight battles in order to get a few compliments from Willis, or looking elsewhere—to God for *His* approval."

Baylor sighed deeply. "People don't change, do they?"

"Of course they do. They change and we change. But we can't wait for them to change. We can't force it. The cost of being disappointed and stressed all the time when they don't measure up is *not* worth losing our peace and joy."

He smiled. "Not worth dying on a hill."

I smiled. "You got it. As I was learning this lesson *I* learned to appreciate Papa. Just because I wasn't getting the kudos from him didn't mean I couldn't give some out." I looked at Baylor sideways. "Do you ever thank your family? Encourage *them*?"

His blank expression answered for him.

"Give it a shot, bud. You know 'it's more blessed to give than to receive.'"

"Yeah. I suppose."

Good boy. "And while we're coming down off that hill you might try to forgive them."

"Did you forgive Papa?"

"I did. As he forgave me for all of my foibles."

He blinked. "What is a foible?"

I laughed. "A foible is a weakness, a quirk on its way to becoming a flaw." I polished my fingernails against my chest. "Believe it or not, I am the proud owner of more than a few foibles." I pointed at him. "So are you. So are your parents."

He unfurled his legs and put his feet on the floor. "Did Papa *ever* change?"

"He did. Some. But not because I got mad at him about it. Not because I demanded it."

"Then what made him change?"

It was a good question. "I don't really know, but I can guess that God had something to do with it. It's important to realize everybody's on a journey, and journeys always involve crises and choices and change."

He sighed dramatically. "Change is hard."

I chuckled. "Absolutely. But in eighty-nine years I've learned an important bottom line. No matter how imperfect our families may be 'these three remain: faith, hope and love. But the greatest of these is love.' Love each other, no matter what."

"I do love them, Nana. Even when I don't like what they do — or don't do."

I clapped my hands. "Bravo! You're further along than most people." I leaned back in my chair and smiled at him. He was such a good kid. "Here's my last piece of advice. Take a chill-pill. Ease up on judging them for their flaws and —"

"Foibles," he said.

"And foibles. Remember that imperfection is the great equalizer."

"Chill-pill, Nana?"

"Isn't that the right phrase?"

He chuckled. "I'll give it a shot."

"That's all anyone can ask." I pulled him into a hug. "I love you, bud. I'm glad you had the first treasure hunt."

"Me too."

"Now go home, hold onto your faith, hope for things to get better, and love your family no matter what." I gave him an encouraging smile. "You won't be alone. 'If God is for us, who can be against us?' Right?"

He scoffed. "Pretty much everybody."

I shook my head. "Not so." I pointed toward heaven then at myself. "You have at *least* two supporters who are always on your side."

"Thanks." He turned toward the door but hesitated. "Can I tell Mom and Dad your story?"

"Of course." I reached over to the end table and gave him an envelope. "Give this to your dad."

Baylor turned it over in his hands. "What is it?"

"An invitation to *his* treasure hunt."

"He gets one too?"

I was surprised by his surprise. "He's family, isn't he?"

Baylor nodded with a smile. "Mom won't like that he gets to go before her."

"As intended, dear boy. As intended."

When I got home I walked into a familiar living room scene. Mom was working on her laptop and Dad was playing solitaire at the desk. What was *un*usual, was that Paige was still there. She'd come to watch football and have dinner, and I was glad she'd stuck around.

She was doing her normal Paige-thing, flipping through channels — which drove me crazy. She looked at me over her shoulder. "How was your time at Nana's?"

"Good."

Dad sipped a mug of coffee as he played cards. "Why did she want to see you?"

I took my usual place on the couch. "She put together a treasure hunt for me."

Mom looked up from her screen. "For you? It's not your birthday or Easter."

Yes, for me. "It wasn't that kind of hunt, and she's going to do it for everybody."

"Cool." Paige muted the TV. "It's nice she made you first, Bay."

Dad turned around in his chair. "What did she make you do?"

"Go through clues."

"What was the prize?" Paige asked.

I shook my head. "It wasn't like her usual hunts. This time the clues led to the prize of her telling me a story about her life in 1955."

"That's a long time ago," Paige said.

I hoped I would do a good job summarizing it. "Nana was giving an important dinner party 'cuz Papa was trying to get a promotion at the bank. It went great. But he didn't notice her hard work and didn't appreciate what she'd done. The other people noticed but he didn't. Nana got real mad about it but he still couldn't bring himself to say thank you, or to say anything nice." Would they get it? Would they figure out the link between Nana's story and mine?

Mom crossed her arms. "Are you saying we're like Papa? Slow to notice? Unappreciative?"

I felt my face go red. She'd certainly gotten the connection. I didn't know what to say. And then . . . I heard a soft voice like Nana had heard. It told me to be quiet.

Dad did the talking for me. "Don't get all testy about it, Hol. It does sound like certain people we know."

Mom shrugged.

Dad continued. "Sorry about how things have been, Bay. We do appreciate you. Like we said, we're sorry we ignored you. You're a great kid. We couldn't ask for better."

Paige huffed and pointed at herself. "What about *moi?*"

Dad laughed. "You're pretty special too, sweetie."

Mom wasn't smiling. I didn't want her to get mad about it.

Then I thought of something. "Nana also told me that I need to appreciate you guys. So . . ." It *was* awkward saying such things. "Thanks for being . . . you, I guess."

"So eloquent," Paige teased.

I felt my face grow hot. "I don't know how to say it, it's just that... I'm glad you're my family, okay?"

Mom raised her eyebrows. "Glad to hear it."

I tried to think of what would make her truly listen. "I'm not perfect either, I know that."

Mom opened her mouth to speak, but Dad interrupted. "None of us are."

Mom didn't say what she was going to say, so I said, "I sometimes focus on what you guys are doing to . . ." I hesitated. It would sound bad.

"Go ahead, Bay," Paige said. "Just say it."

Give me the words, God. "It's just that sometimes when I start noticing things that you guys do that annoy me, or I feel like you're not seeing me, that's all I focus on. Just the bad stuff. I hold a grudge."

"I get that," Dad said. "And then it usually gets worse."

"Yeah." I was so relieved he understood. "Nana says we're supposed to take a chill-pill and not be so hard on each other. Faith, hope, and love stuff."

Dad smiled. "I like that. And I know it's true. But Nana did not say 'take a chill-pill.'"

I smiled back. "She did."

Paige pumped a fist in the air. "Go, Nana!"

I looked at Mom. She hadn't said much. She was just staring at nothing.

"Mom? What do you think?" I wanted her to close her laptop and join in.

But she didn't close it. Or even look up when she said, "I think you've given me a lot to think about."

I was disappointed. She *was* stubborn like Papa.

Paige broke through the moment. "Who gets the next treasure hunt?"

I went to my jacket and got out the invitation. "For you, Dad. It's your turn next."

He opened the envelope and read the invitation out loud. "'Vernon. I request the honor of your presence for your treasure hunt. Tuesday at nine. Elsie.'"

Now Mom looked up, her face incredulous. "You get the next treasure hunt?"

"Apparently."

"Why didn't I get it?"

I laughed. "Nana thought you'd say that."

"So? What's her reason?"

"I have no idea." But I kinda did.

Dad slipped the note back in the envelope. "This should be interesting."

"Can I come along?" Mom asked.

Dad looked at me and I shook my head. "Dad needs to go by himself." Mom's pouty face made me add, "You'll get a turn too, Mom. Everybody will."

She flipped a hand and looked back at her screen, her hands poised above the keyboard. "Whatever. I'm showing houses Tuesday anyway."

I wasn't sure if that was true, but I let Mom get away with it.

Dad gathered his playing cards and tapped the deck on the table. "How about a game of Rummy? Who's in?"

"Me!" Paige said.

"Count me out," Mom said.

"Me," I said. "I'm all in."

Playing cards with my dad and sister was a triple dose of chill-pills.

Chapter 16

Baylor

"Be strong and courageous, and do the work.
Do not be afraid or discouraged,
for the Lord God, my God, is with you."
1 Chronicles 28: 20

I was *not* looking forward to school today. Though the bump on my head had gone down, there was a nasty-looking bruise I couldn't cover up. What would I say to people? And what would happen when I saw the Mowry cousins first period when they sat behind me in American History. Alphabetically, they were always close. Lindstrom . . . Mowry.

I put my jacket in my locker. The halls were filled with kids going to their first class and I kept my head low so no one would notice the bruise. The good thing with being mostly invisible is that most people looked past me. When I did catch the eye of someone, they always looked away real fast like I was going to laser-zap them with x-ray eyes.

I wish.

I went in the class and took my seat. The cousins always came in while the bell was ringing, so hopefully there wouldn't be time for them to notice the bruise or make fun of me running away or whatever spin they'd put on Friday night.

Unfortunately, other kids noticed the bruise. A few pointed and whispered.

I'd thought about telling people that I fell — if they asked — but after standing up for myself with my family I also thought about how it might go if I told the truth. That thought didn't get very far. Being honest with my family was one thing. The Mowrys were another.

Nate, a new kid I'd met at lunch, sat two rows over. He pointed at my head. "What happened?"

Just then the cousins came in.

I made a decision. I nodded in their direction. "Ask them."

The two barreled their way down the row to the two seats behind me. Colton did a double-take when he noticed my forehead, and even Clark paused a second. "Hey there, baboon. We do good work."

Nate said, "You hit Baylor?"

I answered for them. "They threw rocks at me."

"That's not cool," Nate said.

Clark glared at him. "Who are you to know what's cool, new boy?"

He raised both hands, not wanting a fight. But he gave me a look that told me he was on my side.

Some other kids said stuff but it was mostly just blah, blah, blah. No one was going to do anything. There was nothing *to* do. Yet having some of them know how I got hurt felt kinda good. The cousins were the villains. I was the . . .

I wish I could have said *hero*, but the right word was *victim*.

Bummer. I wanted people to feel sorry for me — because it was better than ignoring me — and I wanted them to hate the Mowrys for the creeps they were, yet the whole thing was off. It wasn't satisfying like I'd hoped it would be. It was like almost getting to a higher level in one of my video games, only to have Mom interrupt and tell me to shut it down.

Any further reactions for or against me were interrupted when Mrs. Williams came in. Everyone shushed up because she did *not* tolerate small talk. Extra homework went to those who dared cross her.

While she gave the lesson Clark poked and pushed against my back more than usual. Which kept my nerves pulled tight. Wary. Waiting.

But oddly not fearful.

As we learned about the final battle of the Revolutionary War and the British surrender at Yorktown, I felt like I was one of the victorious American soldiers. They must have been wary, waiting, and even afraid, but they also were brave and courageous. And victorious.

Mrs. Williams held up a piece of paper. "I'm going to read a letter General Washington sent to his wife, Martha, about the event." She adjusted her reading glasses. "I have just witnessed the surrender of eight thousand British troops. They filed through two lines: one of the smartly uniformed French soldiers, and one of our rather bedraggled American forces. The band played 'The World Turned Upside Down.' Very apropos. Some of the king's men were weeping. But our men did not gloat—though they had every right to do so. Before the parade, I rode up and down between the two lines and warned them to be gentlemen. I told them, 'History will huzzah for us.' To their credit, they abided by my wishes.'"

She lowered the letter. "What would the world be like if people honored each other's efforts, no matter which side they were on? Being strong and courageous is about battle, but also about the time after the battle. And the best brand of courage embraces compassion and honor. *That's* a hill to die on. Not vengeance or contempt."

I was dumbstruck. A hill to die on. There were those words again! With my family I'd chosen honor over contempt. But how could I use that with the Mowrys?

Soon after, the bell rang. Books were closed, notebooks were stuffed in backpacks, and kids filed out.

As I neared the door I heard Mrs. Williams call out, "Colton? Clark? A moment, please?"

I left with the rest of the class, but lingered outside the door, wondering if somehow she knew about their bullying.

But her words weren't about me. "As I told the class, we're having a test tomorrow covering the final days of the war. This is a do or die moment for you two. If you fail, you fail the class, and the rules say you won't be able to play ball until your grades are up."

"Not fair," Clark said.

"It's totally fair," she said. "You're here to learn, to succeed in your education first, then on the field. You can't ignore this part of the bargain. Understand?"

"Whatever," Clark said.

"In addition to the class study handout, I've put together a special study outline for you two. Use your book and learn the points on the sheet and you'll do well."

I heard paper rustle. Then I heard footsteps and focused on my open locker.

Once in the hall, Clark snatched the paper from his cousin. "This is what I think of history!" He tore the papers into long strips and dropped them on the floor. Then he whapped Colton on the back and said, "Later, man."

Colton took a few steps away, then looked over his shoulder in the direction his cousin had gone. When Clark was out of sight, he picked up the torn pieces and shoved them in his backpack.

He wanted to do good? Or more likely, he wanted to play ball.

For a moment I felt sorry for him, but then I remembered all the times they'd hurt me. I touched my head, remembering the pain. The fear. The memories still stung.

Suddenly Mrs. Williams's lofty lesson of honor and compassion was overturned by a desire for vengeance — not just for Friday night, but for all the other times the Mowrys had hurt me. I tried to shove the negative thoughts away but couldn't. The hint that Colton was going to study was an opportunity. A weakness. An open door to revenge.

I closed my locker, picked up a stray piece of the ripped paper, and handed it to him. "You want to study together for the test?" Even as I said the words, I wondered what I was doing.

Colton's face showed surprise, but then the tough-guy guise turned on. "Why would I want to do that?"

Because your future depends on it, moron. "It's interesting stuff. I mean, weren't Washington's words cool?"

He looked around as if gauging who was watching him talk to this nerd. "Yeah. They kinda were."

I was shocked. I'd never seen a vulnerable side of him. It offered all sorts of possibilities. "You want me to come to your house or — ?"

He shook his head, adamantly. "No. Yours would be better."

"Seven then."

Colton nodded and walked down the hall.

Our war was far from over. It was time to go on offense.

Mom and Dad were surprised when I said someone was coming over. "Is this a new friend?" Dad asked. It was embarrassing how eager they looked.

"Just a guy." I'd thought about asking Nate to come as a buffer, but since I wasn't sure how things would play out, I'd decided to go it alone.

"There's pop in the fridge," Mom said.

"I know. Thanks."

I don't know why I was nervous. It's not like I wanted to impress the guy and he certainly didn't want to impress me. But I *was* curious to see him without Clark lurking around.

I was still nervous after dinner so I decided to do something while I waited. I stirred up a brownie mix and put it in the oven. Colton might think it was dorky, and might even call me Suzie Homemaker, but wasn't there something about food soothing the savage beast?

Or was that music?

Speaking of . . . while the brownies were baking I looked through my music. My preference for jazz would give Colton more reason to tease me, but it was that or the soundtracks to Star Wars and superhero movies. Talk about nerdy.

Whatever. It was *my* house. My room. I was the good guy, he was the bully. I was the smart guy like Bruce Banner, while Colton was the destructive monster, Hulk.

When the doorbell rang I hurried to get it but Mom beat me to it. Dad wanted to be introduced too. Enough already. Colton wasn't important. They shouldn't ooze over him like that.

"Want a Coke?" I asked, as I led him into the kitchen.

"Sure." He sat on a stool at the island. "Man, this place is huge. Our whole apartment would fit in this kitchen."

"My mom's a real estate agent," I said, as if that explained everything. I got out two cans and saw Colton eying the brownies. "Want one? I just made them."

Colton scoffed. "You? Cooked?"

"Well yeah. I even cook dinner sometimes. I make great spaghetti and garlic bread." I cut the brownies and put four huge squares on a plate.

He took one before I could even get him a napkin, and talked while he was chewing. "We eat a lot of frozen dinners. I tried cooking burgers once, but couldn't get the charcoal hot enough."

I didn't mention our state-of-the-art grill with its instant starter and extra burner.

We took the food into my room where John Williams was playing.

"Star Wars, right?"

"Yup." I'd made the right choice.

I hadn't thought about where we'd sit. There was a beanbag, a desk chair, and the bed.

And the floor. I took that as the best option and leaned back against my dresser while Colton leaned against the bed. I took out our history book and the study guide the teacher had given everyone.

He did the same. "Mrs. Williams told me and Clark that we need to pass the test or we flunk class and lose football. That's harsh."

It sounded logical to me.

"I mean, I'm in class most days. More'n Clark. Doesn't that count for something?"

Not much. "It'll be fine. You can pass it."

Colton snickered.

"Did you bring the study guide she gave us?"

Colton dug in a backpack pocket, and got out the one I had. But then he took out the special one too. I was impressed he'd taped it together. "She gave us two an extra one. But . . . I'm not good at memorizing stuff."

We'd see about that.

"Let me see both of them." I compared them. His special guide had some different questions on it, more basic ones. But it wasn't that different. "Just a minute." I scanned a copy of it and printed it out so we'd each have one.

"Wow. You've got the machines, don't cha?"

Didn't everybody have a printer?

I took a bite out of a brownie, as Colton finished his off. Then I asked the first question: "What did Washington say to his troops about humiliating the British who were surrendering?"

Colton flicked a crumb off his chin. "Something like let history shout hurrah, or something like that."

One point for Colton. "He used the word 'huzzah', but yeah, that's it. You remembered. Number two . . ."

Mrs. Williams hadn't put the answers on the study sheet, just the chapters where to find them. If we looked them all up it would take ages. Besides, finding the *right* answers wasn't part of my plan.

"I'll just tell you what to memorize, all right?"

His face showed his relief. "That'd be great."

I looked at the paper and continued. "What was the name of Washington's son who wanted to join the army at the very end?"

He looked at the ceiling. "George Junior?"

The answer was Jackie. But I said, "That's it."

"Really?"

"Way to go." Next one. "What country sent their ships to help the United States win the battle?"

Correct answer: France.

"Uh . . . Canada?"

"Wow. You're three for three."

And so it went. This was fun.

The entire plate of brownies was eaten and each of us had another Coke.

It had been two hours. Colton stretched his arms over his head with a moan. "I can't believe I remember all this stuff."

"You did good. And you'll do good tomorrow." He'd do a good job at getting himself kicked off the team.

Colton stood and arched his back. "I just might pass. Thanks to you."

I stood too. My body was stiff from sitting on the floor. "I'm glad to help."

Colton folded the study guide where he'd written all the wrong answers. He headed toward the door of my room, but stopped. "You know I'm really sorry about . . ." He nodded toward my bruise.

"Yeah, me too. It still hurts a lot."

Colton looked at the floor. "Clark . . . I won't blame it all on him, but he's one angry dude. I go along because he's my cousin and he lives in the same building as me and . . . well, we get lumped together a lot."

This was an opening to ask, "Why is he so mean?"

Colton scratched the back of his neck, as if buying time while he figured out how to answer. "Most people don't know this cuz we pretty much keep to ourselves, but my family's a mess. And Clark's? His is worse." He shrugged. "All the Mowrys fight a lot. Last month Clark's dad was arrested for nearly killing a guy in a bar fight. I try to get my parents to calm down when they go at it, but that just makes 'em madder."

Yikes. I hadn't known any of this. "My parents fight too."

He scowled and looked right at me. "Does your dad knock your mom's teeth out?"

Really? I felt so bad for him. "No. Nothing like that."

"Yeah, well . . . I keep thinking I'll get used to it, but I never do. My little sister got sent away to live with an aunt. But I didn't have to go."

Didn't *get* to go?

He touched the doorknob, then let it go and put his hand in his pocket. "I wanna do good in football so I can get outta here and play at a college far, far away. My grandpa says that's what I should aim for."

I thought of Colton taking the test, writing down all the wrong answers—which he had proudly memorized—failing, getting kicked out of football, and bringing the news back home to a dad who liked to use his fists.

Suddenly the price of vengeance was way too high.

"I better be going," he said.

I sidestepped and put my hand on the doorknob. "Wait."

He took a step back. "What?"

"Wait. I . . ." How should I say it? "Give me the study guide back."

"But I need it."

I took it over to my desk and started crossing out all the wrong answers and writing in the right ones.

"What are you doing?"

"Just wait." I finished fixing everything and handed the page back to him. "Here. These are the answers to memorize."

Colton stared at the page. "You gave me the wrong answers?"

I let out a breath. "Yeah."

"Why?"

I shrugged. "You hurt me. You guys are jerks, so I . . ."

Colton's eyebrows touched in the middle. His mouth went slack. His eyes looked totally sad. "I thought you were trying to help me."

I wished I could rewind the whole evening. "I was, but then . . . then I wasn't. And now I am. I'm sorry. I just got tired of you always picking on me. This was a way to get back at you."

He kept shaking his head. "But this is major. I'd have lost everything."

Forget me feeling like the genius, Bruce Banner. Now I felt like one of the people in a battle scene who had a car fall on top of them. "You apologized to me, now I'm apologizing to you."

Colton just stood there, his chest heaving, staring at nothing.

Please God. Make it be okay. I'm sorry. I'm really sorry.

Finally, Colton said, "I don't know what to do. I learned everything wrong."

"Wait here." I ran to the kitchen and brought back the rest of the brownies and two more drinks. "Sit. We'll go over it again and I'll give you some tricks to remember the right answers. You'll ace this thing. I promise."

We got to work.

It took another hour, but Colton ended up memorizing all the right answers. We both were wiped out.

"Hey, don't tell Clark we studied," he said as he was leaving.

"I won't. But *you* could. Be proud of it. Don't let him bring you down."

He didn't answer. On the way to the front door we passed Mom and Dad.

"Did you get all educated?" Dad said.

"Hope so," I said. I opened the door for Colton.

Colton waved a hand toward my parents. "Thanks for letting me come over. I know it's hard . . . considering."

Mom looked confused, but said, "Anytime."

As soon as he left, she asked. "What's 'considering' mean?"

I was too tired to not tell them. "Considering he can be a creep, and is one of my bullies."

Dad put his magazine down. "He's the one who hit you with a rock?"

"Actually, his cousin did that, but he was along. Colton's not all bad. I think Clark bullies *him*. "

He looked shocked. "Why would you invite him here?"

It was a complicated question with a really complicated answer I didn't want to share. It was bad enough that *I* knew what I was capable of.

But Dad didn't let up. "There's something going on, Bay. Tell us."

I sighed. Even though I didn't want to, I told them everything about the test answers. "So that's it," I finally said. "I'm not the nice kid you think I am."

"I would have done the same," Mom said.

"Holly!"

She shrugged. "We're not as perfect as you are, Vernon."

"Don't start . . ."

I didn't want them to get into an argument that would veer into subjects I didn't want to think about. "I'm beat. I'm going to bed."

After I got to my room I heard them talking--most likely about me. I was okay with that. Hopefully, in the end they'd forgive me and love me anyway.

I'd do the same for them.

Chapter 17

Vernon

"Have mercy on me, O God,
according to your unfailing love;
according to your great compassion
blot out my transgressions."
Psalm 51: 1

I felt an odd nervousness going to Elsie's alone.

Although Holly and I had been married over twenty-two years, and though I loved Elsie like my own grandmother, I'd rarely spent more than a few minutes with her without family around. The fact I'd been summoned to Elsie's for a treasure hunt before Holly was a point of pride—and fear. I could understand why Baylor had been chosen to go first, but me being second . . . ? What could Elsie want with me?

I parked on the street, went up to the front door, and knocked. I heard a "Come in, Vernon" and found Elsie sitting in her chair. She gave me a good once-over. "You look nice."

I was wearing my usual business casual, though I *had* put on a navy sports coat. After all, I was having a private audience with the queen. That had never happened before.

"Have a seat."

I sat across the room from her, on the couch. "Why do I feel like a kid who's been called in by their parents?"

"I'm not here to scold you, Vernon. Nor judge you."

She used the word *judge*. That couldn't be good. "Baylor said you had a treasure hunt for me?"

"How is Baylor? Did he talk to you and Holly?"

"He did. And I think he's good—better at least. He came home from seeing you and talked like a grownup about appreciating each other."

"And . . . ?"

"And he's right. We don't always notice the good things. We're all trying to take a chill pill—like you suggested—and spend more time together."

"Excellent."

I thought of something that might win me brownie points. "I spent the evening playing Rummy with the kids. Baylor won twice."

"Not surprising. The kids often play Canasta with me. Baylor usually wins at that too."

"He's a smart kid."

"But he's still a kid."

I needed to remember that. "Anyway, thanks for helping him. And us. I think things will improve from now on."

She nodded once. Then she picked up a leather notebook from the end table. "I know you're taking time out of your workday for me—which I greatly appreciate—so let's get on with your hunt. Clue number one."

To the point—the Masterson way.

The notebook had *1985* stamped in gold. I opened it up and saw it was a daily planner. "Yours?"

"It belonged to Willis."

I liked the feel of it in my hands and remembered a few of the datebook I'd owned over the years. "Ah, the days before internet calendars."

"Every year I gave Willis a new day planner on New Year's Day. I have a stack of them. He was a chronicler and logged everything." She pointed toward the book. "See the high and low temperatures for the day at the top?"

Keeping track of the weather seemed a bit excessive. I saw other notations. "What are these numbers?" I turned the book so she could see. "10.5, 8.75, 11.25?"

"Those are the hours he worked at the bank."

I did the math for one week. "Fifty and a half hours."

"Fifty to fifty-five was the norm."

"Sounds like Holly."

"Sounds like trouble."

I felt a twinge. "Since Baylor ran away, Holly says she's going to try to be home more for him."

"And for you?"

My stomach tightened. "And for me. I guess." I got her point. "We need to work less and spend more time with family."

Next clue please.

Elsie raised a hand. "I'm not through with the journal yet. What else is noted there?"

I skimmed the pages. "Luncheons meetings, appointments."

"What else?"

I wasn't sure what she was looking for. And then I noticed that a single initial appeared almost once a week. "What was *D?*"

"I think a better question is who was *D?*"

I felt my face grow red. I had *B* notations on my own calendar. Surely Elsie didn't know . . .

She handed me a note. "Go to this address. Speak to Mrs. Proctor."

"Who's Mrs. Proctor?"

"A friend of mine. Go on now. She's waiting for you."

I stood, wishing I could just go home.

"Come back here when she's done with you."

Done with me?

Mrs. Proctor lived in a ranch-style house from the sixties. A huge maple tree with crimson leaves canopied the front yard.

She met me at the door before I knocked, a pudgy gray-haired woman with a nice smile.

"Hi, I'm Vernon?" Why had I stated my name as a question?

"Glad to meet you, Vernon. Come in. I've made some coffee. Want a cup?"

"Sure." I'm going to be here that long?

I followed her into a cluttered kitchen that obviously needed more counter space. She poured two cups. "You want sugar or milk?"

"Black's fine."

She handed me a mug that was emblazoned with *Maine* and led me to a two-person table by the back door.

She sat with an *ommph,* a sound I'd heard repeated by many people over sixty, and once in a while by me. She looked to be seventy? Even seventy-five.

"So then," she said. "Elsie tells everyone she's doing fine since Willis died, but what do you think?"

I was glad to talk about Elsie versus me. "She's a strong woman. Frankly, she amazes me."

Mrs. Proctor chuckled. "I agree." She changed the subject. "I had never heard about her treasure hunt tradition. Has she done that long?"

"Forever, I think. My wife carried on the tradition with our two kids at Easter. But Elsie did them other times too, sometimes for no special reason."

"How fun. How is Baylor doing?"

I was taken aback. "You know about his . . . situation?"

"Of course. When you found out he was missing, Elsie called and asked me to spread the word that Baylor needed praying after." She spread her hands. "God heard and answered. It's a blessing he's back home again. Is he doing okay?"

"I think so." I took a sip of coffee, and realized how awkward it was to spend time like this with a stranger. "You seem to know our family well."

"Besides the prayer chain, Elsie and I are in a book club together."

"That's nice." But why was I here?

Mrs. Proctor sighed. "I guess I need to get on with it."

"Sounds good."

She put her mug down. "I had an affair with Willis."

The idea that Willis had an affair was hard enough to reconcile, much less with this seventy-something, dowdy woman.

She filled in the silence. "It was a long time ago."

Understood. My insides tightened. The parallel wasn't lost on me but I had to pretend otherwise. "Forgive me for saying this, but why would Elsie send me to the woman who tried to break up her marriage?"

She shook her head. "That's not how it happened." She held her coffee mug in both hands and let the steam veil her face. Then she put it down without taking a sip. "I was a widow. I was still grieving Jerry—he died in a car accident. With him gone I had to make ends meet. I *had* to work."

"I'm so sorry."

"Thank you. I suffered the loss of the love of my life, but our two boys suffered their father's death even more than I did. They were nine and ten and Jerry was their hero. He played ball with them and took them to games and fishing on weekends. They were lost without him."

"I'm so sorry." There wasn't much else I could say except to restate the obvious. "They missed spending time with him."

"And with me. I'd never had a full-time job before. While the boys were little I'd stayed home except for selling Avon in my free time. All of the sudden, I had to work full time and wasn't there when they got home from school. I wasn't there to ask about their day or give them a snack. They had to go to a neighbor's."

I wanted her to think happier thoughts. "Where do they live now?"

She smiled. "One lives in Topeka and the other in Omaha. I remarried and had a daughter who now lives in Atchison."

"Not too far."

"Not too far." She took a sip of coffee and closed her eyes. "Back then there weren't many companies willing to hire someone with little to no experience. Except Willis." Her face softened. "He wasn't the one who interviewed me for the receptionist position, but our paths happened to cross that day and his smile . . . it reminded me of Jerry's smile." She got a faraway look as if she was imagining both.

She shook the memory away. "The details of what happened next don't matter that much to anyone but me. Willis was kind when I needed kindness. He showed compassion when I needed compassion." She rubbed her forehead. "Honestly, I wasn't looking for a new husband at all. He played catch with the boys, and they all enjoyed it. He just had the one daughter and said he missed sharing sports like that. Of course I knew the whole affair was wrong, but I did it anyway."

I could relate. "Did Willis want to leave Elsie?"

I expected to hear a definite "no."

Instead she said, "I don't think so." She sighed. "I didn't want him to." She stood and moved to the window over the sink. The back of her hair needed smoothing. "Our affair was a mistake. Elsie and Willis were meant for each other."

"Did you know Elsie at the time?"

Mrs. Proctor faced me and leaned back against the counter. "We met a few times when she'd come in the bank to see him." Suddenly she turned back to the window. "See those flowers out there?"

I joined her to look outside. The backyard was brimming with bright blooms. "You obviously have the gift of gardening."

"This is a different house from back then, but I've always been good at gardening and Willis liked the flowers. I used to bring bouquets into work to put by my desk. Customers liked them too."

Where was she going with this?

"One time I saw him picking a bouquet of pink peonies before he left my house. I asked where he was taking them. I pressed when he wouldn't answer. Finally, he said he was taking them home. 'Elsie will love them.'"

Ouch. "That was thoughtless."

"Thoughtless towards me. But it got worse. The next day Elsie came in the bank and saw a bouquet of pink peonies on my desk. I remember her commenting on them. Wondering where I got them."

"Uh-oh."

"I said they were from my garden. I will never forget the odd look that fell across her face."

"She figured it out."

"And then some. That night when I came home all the blossoms had been snipped off. Every single one was scattered all over the ground."

I was incredulous. "That doesn't sound like Elsie."

"Who else would it have been?"

There was no other explanation. "Did you break it off with Willis?"

"I did—though I didn't tell him why. I quit my job too. I don't know if *he* ever knew that Elsie knew."

"They stayed married, so she must have forgiven him."

She shrugged. "That was between them. I should have stopped it sooner. Actually, now that I know Elsie I can honestly say I like her more than I ever liked Willis."

"You and her being friends now . . . it's kind of odd."

"God did it." She shrugged. "Over the years God brought us together multiple times. We were often on the same committees, which was awkward, horrible, and humbling. Eventually, I asked Elsie for forgiveness, and she gave it to me."

That sounded like Elsie. "So you really think being on the same committees was God's doing?"

She gave me an incredulous look. "Of course. He wanted us to forgive each other and brought us together to do just that." She nodded as if agreeing to an inner thought. "'For if you forgive other people when they sin against you, your heavenly Father will also forgive you.'"

And there it was. I needed to forgive Holly for ignoring me. And I needed her to forgive me for . . .

Mrs. Proctor looked toward the front of the house. "Well that's it. That's what I was supposed to tell you. Now you're to go back to Elsie's for the final clue."

More like a final judgement. I walked to the front door. "I appreciate you sharing with me like this."

"Elsie didn't say why, but I can guess. What's her name?"

Wow. She knew. Elsie knew. How did Elsie know? "It's not a full affair." Though we'd come dangerously close.

147

She shook her head. "An affair of the heart and mind is still an affair. Unfaithful is unfaithful."

I opened the door, then thought of something. "What's your first name?"

"Dinah."

D.

My thoughts raced as I drove back to Elsie's. If the purpose of my treasure hunt was to make me feel ashamed, it succeeded. Elsie had showed me the consequences of an affair through the eyes of the other woman. Of course I'd always known there was a chance Holly would be hurt — and part of me had even wanted her to be — but I'd never thought much about Brianna's take on it. She'd always been eager to meet for lunch or dinner and was a good listener. Like me, she'd needed to talk to someone as she was recently divorced and —

"She was vulnerable. I was vulnerable."

Those truths had led to rationalization. We met each other's psychological needs. People needing people.

And one evening, when her kids were at her ex's, she'd invited me over.

The memories of the evening did not bring me pleasure. It had been our first fully private time together. We'd kissed — a lot — and it had gotten heated, but I'd pulled away, stopping it. Or at least slowing it down. We'd agreed to take a breath.

"We took advantage of each other's weaknesses."

I was tired of being weak.

It was time to get the last clue. Time to face the full extent of Elsie's lesson.

I didn't knock, but went right in. Elsie wasn't in the living room. "I'm back," I called out.

"Good," she called from the kitchen. "I'm dishing some cookies and iced tea."

My nerves made the thought of eating unappetizing, but I knew I wouldn't be able to say no.

"So," Elsie said as she put cookies on a plate. "How was your time with Dinah?"

I felt like a criminal in an interrogation. "I get the point, Elsie."

Her eyebrows rose. "Do you?"

I still didn't want to fully admit my sin, so turned the conversation to hers. "She told me about the flowers and that you ruined her garden."

Elsie nodded once. "I told her to share that because of *your* flower fiasco."

"My flower fiasco?"

"Who's Brianna?" Elsie asked.

My mouth went dry. How did Elsie know her name? "Nobody. I mean she's the receptionist at Holly's office."

Elsie pointed at me. "Another receptionist."

I put my fingertips against both temples, trying to keep my brain from bursting. All pretense was useless. "What do you know?"

"Too much. Have a seat."

I sat at the kitchen table where Elsie had already placed two glasses of iced tea. She carried the cookies to the table and joined me. "I'm waiting."

"What do you want me to say?"

"The truth."

I straightened the cow and pig salt and pepper shakers. "We didn't mean for it to happen."

"Odd how no adulterer ever means for it to happen."

"We aren't lovers. We haven't . . ."

"What did President Carter say? 'I've committed adultery in my heart.'?"

"What?"

She waved her hand at me. "Gracious. Everybody's too young for my examples. The point is, if you're sending another woman flowers it means you're courting her — by whatever definition you want to use."

I thought of the flowers I'd sent Brianna. "How do you know about the flowers?"

Elsie nodded across the room. "Look in that top drawer there."

I opened it and saw a card from a florist: *Brianna: Beautiful flowers for a beautiful person. Vernon.* How did Elsie have it?

"You sent me flowers on the same day." Elsie didn't say more, but just looked at me.

One plus one . . . "They sent the wrong ones to you?"

"They sent both arrangements to me."

I thought back to the conversation with Brianna at Holly's office. I'd asked if she liked the flowers but she said she hadn't gotten them. I'd meant to call the florist, but then Baylor had run away and I forgot.

"The mums you ordered for me were beautiful. As were the yellow roses."

"Wow." I didn't know what else to say.

"God did it."

"God arranged for me to be caught?"

"Absolutely. Better to be caught now than caught when it's too late."

True. "Can I throw this note away?" I wanted it gone.

"You can, for it has served its purpose."

"In humiliating me?" I tossed it into the trash under the sink.

"In stopping you from ruining your marriage. By the way, why did you get yourself into this mess?"

I returned to the table. "Whatever I say won't justify — "

"Tell me anyway."

Even before I began the explanation I knew it would sound trite. And lame. "Holly is rarely at home and when she is, she's working. Sometimes I want to take her phone and throw it in the fireplace."

Surprisingly, Elsie nodded. "I've seen her obsession. Hopefully after Baylor's crisis, and with your family's new resolve, things will get better."

"I want that too." I ran a finger along the condensation on my glass of tea and wiped it on my pants. "I shouldn't have sent Brianna flowers, or . . . all the rest. But I needed someone to talk to. My parents are gone, Rosemary is super busy, and Everett . . ." I thought back to the nice conversation we'd had while searching for Baylor. "It's nice that he's retired now, but before . . . he was working six days a week."

"You could have talked to me or Willis about Holly."

I'd never though of it, but pretended otherwise. "You were both dealing with the cancer, and then . . ."

"I know talking to an old woman isn't ideal. But I *am* here to listen."

"I appreciate that." I really did.

"What else did Dinah tell you?"

As Dinah had said, the details weren't important. Except for one. "You forgave her."

"I did."

"Did you forgive Willis?"

She took a deep breath. "I did. On our fiftieth wedding anniversary."

I knew they'd been married sixty-nine years. I did the math. "He was unfaithful in 1985 and you waited decades to confront him? To forgive him?"

She rested her arms on the table. "Let me tell you a story . . ."

Chapter 18

Elsie - 1985

> "In your anger do not sin:
> Do not let the sun go down
> while you are still angry,
> and do not give the devil a foothold."
> Ephesians 4: 26-27

Out of breath, I stopped all movement. My heart pounded. My body was bathed in sweat.

Then my eyes focused on the flowers that littered the grass and patio around me.

I did that?

Shame swept over me. I. Did. That.

All those beautiful flowers. Destroyed. I'd just proven *Hell hath no fury like a woman scorned.*

I heard a dog barking in the neighbor's yard. I needed to get out of there.

I dropped the clippers where I stood and hurried around the side yard to my car that was parked a block away. I wanted to run, but forced myself to walk.

Once inside I fumbled the keys to the floorboard — twice. I let them lay. My hands were shaking so I grabbed the steering wheel to still them. I felt nauseous — further proof that I'd gone too far. "Father, why did I do that? It's so . . . impulsive. Juvenile."

You're human.

A cop-out. I was a fifty-two year old, middle-class, God-fearing woman — who'd just destroyed a woman's beautiful garden.

Because she's having an affair with my husband.

My husband. Mine. I realized I should take it out on *him*. Willis was at least twenty years older than Dinah. He should know better.

I had a sudden pull in my gut. Had Willis done this before?

I covered my face with my hands. I couldn't think about that. I'd never suspected anything, but that didn't mean it hadn't happened. Had I been duped? Betrayed for years? Were our marriage vows worth nothing?

I felt a sudden stab in my abdomen — not the first. I hadn't felt well for a few days. The physical exertion of being the scorned-woman didn't help. Although I'd hoped to feel vindication or satisfaction in destroying Dinah's garden, I didn't. Instead I felt defeated. Done-in. Done.

I closed my eyes and prayed. *Forgive me for destroying all those flowers   You created. But I'm hurting so bad. How can Willis betray me like this?*

He's human.

I sat upright. Blaming both of our sins on being human seemed like we were excusing our bad actions too easily. Yes, I was a sinner and God would always forgive me, but that wasn't an excuse to sin.

If there had been other infidelities, if I'd been fooled and lied to . .

.

I needed to leave him.

Suddenly the pain stabbed me again. Worse this time. Shooting. Like a knife.

Its ferocity seemed appropriate. I *should* feel intense pain for the destruction of a marriage. And pain for the destruction of Dinah's garden.

But then it grew vicious like a creature gnawing at my insides. This wasn't indigestion or sore muscles from over-exertion. Something was terribly wrong.

The pain couldn't be ignored.

I looked around for someone to help me. The sidewalks were empty. I was alone in a strange neighborhood.

I only had one choice.

With a moan I leaned down and found my keys, started the car, and drove myself to the hospital.

It was all a blur. Collapsing in the foyer of the ER, being wheeled into a room. Someone asking my name. Saying Willis' name. The bank's name. The pain demanding all my attention. Moaning. Probing. Getting into a gown. The sting of an IV. A warm blanket. Bright lights. An oxygen mask. "Count backwards from 100."

"Ninety-nine. Ninety —"

Blessed oblivion.

"Els? Come on, Elsie. Open your eyes."

I fought between wanting to do what Willis asked and wanting to stay asleep.

I felt him take my hand and stroke my hairline. "Wake up, sweetheart. You can do it."

I did it. And there he was, bending over me, his forehead furrowed. His eyes full of relief.

"That's it! Good girl."

I blinked and took a deep breath. "What's wrong with me? Do I need surgery? "

"You already had it. You're in recovery. You had a ruptured appendix but you're going to be all right."

My groggy mind tried to put everything together. "You're here."

"Of course I'm here. Rosemary and Everett are in the waiting room with Holly. They want to see you."

I tried to sit up but the pain stopped me. Yet maybe the pain was a good thing. Maybe Willis would feel sorry for me and change his mind about . . . her.

He gently pressed me back toward the bed. "Slow there, Els. Rest. You're not going anywhere for a few days."

"Days?"

He kissed my hand. "We almost lost you." His voice cracked. "Don't you ever leave me, you hear?"

He'd had an affair. I needed to leave him.

But Willis wasn't talking about that sort of leaving.

His eyes were heavy with tears, his voice barely a whisper. "Please, Els. Get well. I adore you."

In that moment my mind flipped from thoughts of leaving to the opposite. For I adored him too.

And so I made a choice.

I would never choose to leave Willis.

Chapter 19

Vernon & Baylor

"The LORD is near to all who call on him,
to all who call on him in truth."
Psalm 145: 18

Elsie finished telling the story about Willis and his affair. As she sat at the kitchen table, she seemed to look smaller. Diminished. As if she was worn out by it.

"Sometimes my vow never to leave Willis was tested," she said. "But I stood by it. Him. And us. I forgave him."

I felt a surge of emotion rush through me. "That's generous of you, Elsie. But . . ." Would Holly forgive me? Would I forgive her?

"If you love each other, Vernon, you can forgive each other."

I didn't answer. Our love wasn't even on simmer anymore. It was lukewarm at best.

Elsie sat taller and took a cleansing breath that seemed to reinvigorate her. "Time for your final clue." She pointed her cane at the kitchen counter. "That photograph. Bring it here."

I retrieved an unframed, group photo, similar to the kind a business might post on an "About Us" webpage. But older. Pre-internet.

Elsie put her finger near her husband's image. He was seated front and center. "There he is. Such a handsome man."

It was strange to see Willis so young. I'd been ten years old in 1985 and didn't meet him until the late nineties. I had to admit, the man was handsome. Classy. Powerful.

Elsie pointed at a pretty woman in the back row. She had long permed hair and big bangs. "See there? See that woman not looking at the camera, but looking lovingly at my husband?"

"That's Dinah?"

"That's her."

I looked at the photo closely. It was hard to reconcile the woman I'd seen today with the vibrant, sexy woman in the picture. Her attraction to Willis was undeniable.

"This picture upsets me every time I see it," Elsie said.

"Then why do you keep it?"

"I keep it to remind myself of the dangers outside these walls." She swept her cane across the room. "Your home is your sanctuary, Vernon. Your safe place. Beyond its walls there is danger of losing what you hold sacred *within* its walls."

I felt as low as dust on the floor. "I get what you're saying." More than I wanted to.

"Willis worked too much and I knew it was hurting our marriage, but I never talked to him about it. I didn't do anything to stop it. Not that the affair was inevitable — and actually, *I* could have had an affair during the long hours I was left alone. It's about meeting halfway. Finding time for each other. Nowadays I guess people have date nights." She cocked her head as if imagining it. "Willis and I would have benefited from a few date nights."

I remembered her comment about confronting him on their fiftieth. "Willis was unfaithful in 1985 yet you waited years to tell him you knew about it?"

"Seventeen years. Not until 2002." Elsie put both hands on her cane and leaned forward. "Do you think a victimized spouse should confront the adulterer? Or do you think it's better if the guilty party confesses on their own?"

The question was one I'd thought about. In depth. "I suppose it's better to confess and get it over with."

She chuckled. "That's one way to put it."

"Why did you wait to confront him? And since you waited seventeen years, why tell him at all?"

"Pride. Stubborn pride. A horrible flaw of mine."

I was surprised by her admission. "I didn't expect you to admit *your* faults."

She let out an exasperated sigh. "What all of you need to realize is that the life-treasures and life-lessons I'm sharing aren't necessarily positive high points of my life. Actually, most of them reveal the lesser side of my nature. Know that even the negative times are important — sometimes more important. That's where you see the whole of me. That's where we learn the lessons."

I was learning all right.

"As far as postponing the confrontation? I liked having something to hold over him — if I chose to do so. But 2002 was the year that Dinah and I kept running into each other. It was horribly awkward. I found out she'd remarried and had a daughter in addition to her two sons. I hate to say it, but she was a very nice woman."

"She said she liked you more than she ever liked Willis."

Elsie's eyebrows rose. "Did she now? How interesting." She pulled her tea forward, peered into the glass, then pushed it away. "After one of our church meetings, she sought me out and asked for forgiveness."

"That was admirable."

"It showed her character—which spurred me to deal with a portion of my not-so-admirable character. And so I apologized for her garden and asked *her* forgiveness, and then *I* forgave her, and . . ." She flipped a hand in the air. "That's when I realized I needed to forgive Willis too. The fact we were celebrating our fiftieth made it seem especially appropriate."

"How did you go about it?"

She smiled at the memory. "A few days before we celebrated the anniversary I made him his favorite meatloaf and mashed potatoes. As he was eating I nonchalantly said, 'I saw Dinah today.' He stopped eating a moment, then pretended it wasn't important. Then he said, 'That's nice.'"

"What did you say next?"

"I said, 'I forgive you, Willis.'" Her hands went to her face. "He turned red and stared at his plate. He couldn't deny it after that."

"So he confessed?"

"Reluctantly. At first he kept eating, but I just sat there and waited. Didn't say a thing—God helped me to not say a thing, it was definitely *His* doing, not mine. Finally, Willis put his fork down and asked how long I'd known. It was pretty satisfying to tell him I'd known since 1985."

"I bet he was shocked."

"Completely. Willis was usually unflappable. Nothing fazed him. Until then." She sipped her tea. "I calmly told him about seeing the same flowers he'd give me at the office, and even confessed to ruining Dinah's garden. To her credit, she'd never told him what I'd done." Elsie pointed a finger at me. "It's never too late to confess and come to grips with a bad situation."

I knew she was right. "I have to tell Holly."

She nodded once. "God gives us free will, but yes, from my own experience I do think that would be best. I wasted a lot of years feeling bitter, even spiteful about Willis's affair. If he'd confessed and repented in eighty-five, the next seventeen years might have been better. We'll never know, of course, but God tends to reward truth, repentance, and forgiveness."

"God does, but will Holly?" Why did I fear my wife more than God?

"Err on the side of truth, Vernon. 'The truth will set you free.'"

Maybe. "Do I have to talk to Brianna too? I mean, we never . . ."

Elsie gave me a disgusted look then pointed to her heart. "You did plenty. In here."

The thought of confessing to both women? I'd rather get a root canal.

Elsie must have seen my distress, for she reached over and put her hand on mine. "You'll be better for it, Vernon. And if you do it humbly, from the heart, and are sincerely remorseful, your marriage — and even your faith — will grow from it."

I shook my head. Faith wasn't my thing. "I believe in God and stuff, but . . ." It sounded so immature. "We're not close."

"Whose fault is that?"

It sounded like a trick question. "Mine, I suppose."

"One hundred percent yours. 'Come near to God and he will come near to you.'"

Her ability to quote the Bible amazed me. "How do you know so many verses?"

She shrugged. "Life happened. Troubles. Trials. I needed help. There's no better self-help book than the Bible. And when I started to be open to it, God brought me the right verse at the right time. I've memorized most of them so I can pluck them out of my mind-file when I need them. You can do that too."

"I haven't memorized *anything* since I was in school."

Elsie slapped the table. "No time like the present. The one I just quoted is James 4: 8. 'Come near to God, and he will come near to you.' Short, simple, and full of truth. Repeat it for me."

She looked so eager, so connected with herself, with me, and the world. I would indulge her. "Say it again."

She shook her head. "You heard it twice. What did it say?"

I didn't like being put on the spot but wanted to please her. It took me a few moments to grab the words from the recent past. Surprisingly, I remembered. "Come near to God. And he will get close to you.'"

"'He will come near to you', but yes, that's it. You know a verse. Apply the stickum by saying it a few more times."

I repeated it three more times.

"Bravo!" Elsie said. "Now you'll have it forever and always."

I hated to admit it, but it felt good, like I'd given myself an insurance policy. Wise words to pull up when I needed them.

"So, dear man. Are you going to take care of things at home, as you should?"

"I am." And I was. But . . . "Holly's going to make me pay for it. She probably won't talk to me for days and days. Or . . ." I didn't expand on the "or" out loud because it was a bad alternative. In truth, she might want a divorce.

"Knowing Holly, I know she won't make it easy. But as many times as she pushes you away, you stand your ground."

"And just take it?"

"Part of standing your ground is talking about what's bothering you. Things that are kept bottled up fester and burst." She pointed a finger at me. "Do you love your wife?"

"Oh course." I sighed as I admitted another truth. "But I don't like our life right now."

"Then change it. You're doing that for Baylor anyway, right?"

"We are."

"That's a strong start."

I wasn't sure I should bring it up, but I had one more question. "Do you think Willis cheated again?"

She cocked her head, looking above me. "I think he cheated before Dinah—when I had my blinders on—but I don't think he did so afterwards. I think my brush with death jolted both of us to appreciate 'us'." She smiled. "Want to hear another verse?"

"Do I have to memorize it?"

"You probably can't because I don't know it word for word. It's from Isaiah and says God won't cause pain without allowing something new to be born."

"That's encouraging."

"As intended." She pushed against the edge of the table and stood, then retrieved a note card from the counter. "This is for Holly. I want her to come for her hunt tomorrow at nine. As for you, that's all I've got, Vernon. That's your treasure, from my life to yours."

I hugged her gently and took comfort in the contact. I really needed this amazing woman to approve of me. "I don't know how to thank you."

She pulled back and touched my cheek. "Come near to God, and...'"

"'He will come near to you.'"

Because I owned my own accounting company I could make my own hours and be away from the office. A good thing because Elsie's treasure hunt took all morning, and the afternoon was consumed with thinking about it.

Thinking about what I would say to Holly.

And Brianna.

I went home to the empty house and decided it was best if I dealt with Brianna first so I could honestly tell Holly I'd broken all ties. I didn't want to meet her anywhere, or even go in the office in case Holly was there. A text or email seemed cold. The only other choice was to call.

I sat in my home office and paused with my phone in hand. Then I did something I'd never done before. "God? I need Your help. Brianna's a nice woman who's hurting from her divorce. Please help her forgive me and find someone who can love her. And help me love Holly better. Help me do whatever needs to be done."

I hesitated, hoping I'd get some confirmation that God had heard my prayer. There wasn't anything viable, and yet . . . I did feel slightly stronger, as though I wasn't doing this alone.

"Here goes." It was lunchtime. I dialed and hoped she'd answer.

"Hi, Vernon." She sounded as sweet as ever. She was such a nice person.

"Can you talk?"

There was a pause and I could hear movement and muffled voices, then a door open and close. "I was just going outside to eat my sandwich. So yes, now I can talk."

I'd thought about what to say to her and hoped those words would come out. "I can't do this anymore, Brianna. Can't meet you. Can't text and talk."

A pause. Then, "Why?"

"Because I'm getting too used to it. I enjoy it too much. I need to focus on my family."

"Because Baylor ran away? I'm so sorry you had to go through all that, but at least he's . . . is he doing okay?""

She was always so thoughtful. "He's fine. And that's part of it, but also . . ." My heart was beating too fast. I took a breath to calm it down. "I need to break it off because I love Holly. I can't do this to her anymore—to us anymore."

"Oh."

"And *you* need to find someone who can focus on you and love you like you deserve to be loved."

She didn't respond.

"Bri?" I could imagine her holding a hand to her forehead, a habit when she was thinking hard thoughts.

She finally spoke. "I get it, Vernon. I understand. And honestly? I agree."

"You do?" The relief spread over me like a balm.

"Although I loved our time together because it was just what I needed, I've known all along it couldn't last. Shouldn't last." She laughed softly. "Actually, I think I'm relieved."

I felt the tension flow out of me as if a relief-valve had been opened. "I'm so glad, I mean, I'm glad you're okay with it."

"I want to thank you, Vernon. You helped me through a dark place."

"You helped me too. You're a great person, Brianna." I meant every word.

"Best of everything to you and your family."

"And to you."

I hung up. I just sat there. Was it really over?

I felt my shoulders relax and my mind clear. "I did it."

But then I felt an inner twinge. *We did it.*

I sat up straight, letting the truth take root.

It hadn't been *just* me. I'd come near to God and He'd come near to me.

Wow.

Everything Elsie said was true.

I let the truth of it sink in a minute. I'd told Elsie I wasn't close to God. But in the last few minutes I'd seen that I *could* be. And even more than that, I found that I wanted to be. Again.

Emotions welled up inside me. I felt a stirring, as if my atoms and neurons and cells were being moved around into a new configuration. I felt a certainty that I had never felt before — or at least had never acknowledged before: I was not alone. I would never *be* alone.

My breath left me in a loud expulsion of air. Then it returned as if something old had been expelled and something new had been drawn deep within me. I covered my face with my hands and uttered two words straight from my heart. "Thank You."

Just then I heard the front door open, heard Baylor clomp in, heard the plop of his backpack on the floor, and heard him rummaging in the fridge.

I was reluctant to leave my He-and-me moment, but knew there was more work to be done for my family's sake. And for mine.

I pressed my hands to my chest and took a deep breath. "Please give me the right words." Then I left my office to join my son. "Hey," I said from the kitchen doorway.

Baylor opened a can of Mountain Dew. "I didn't know you were home."

"After Nana's I didn't go back to work."

Baylor nodded to his drink. "Want one?"

"Sure."

He handed me a can and got a new one. "I was going to make popcorn."

"Sounds good to me."

Baylor put a bag in the microwave. As it began to whirr, I tried to make conversation. "How did your history test go today?"

"It went good. We checked them in class and I aced it. Colton passed it too."

"Good for both of you. It was nice you helped him study."

"Yeah. Well." He got out two bowls. "What did Nana make you do on your hunt?"

The hunt seemed like eons ago, and it took a minute for my thoughts to move back to Nana's and her story. I wanted to be honest about it, but didn't want to tarnish Baylor's opinion of his great-grandfather. "Actually, it's kind of hard to talk about."

His eyebrows rose. "Really? What happened?"

Nana had generously shared her story with me. But to share it further? It was so personal — adult personal.

Baylor studied me. "Nana told *me* that I could share my story with *you*. And I did. Tell me what she said. Please."

I sat at the island and raked my hands through my hair.

"Wow. It's that bad?"

I nodded. "One of the clues sent me to a woman who'd had an affair with Papa."

Baylor's dark eyebrows rose. "Papa?"

"A long time ago. Way back in 1985."

"Wow. I never would have thought Papa . . ."

"I know. Me either."

Baylor shuddered. "Talking to the lady musta been weird."

"It was, but she and Elsie have been friends for years."

"That's double weird."

"Yes, it is."

Baylor watched the popcorn bag expand as the room filled with popping sounds. "But . . . why did Nana tell you *that* story?"

Before this moment I'd never considered telling Baylor about Brianna, but there was no way to talk about Nana's and not tell him. He wasn't a child. We'd vowed to be more open with each other.

I sighed deeply. "Let's just say Nana's story hit close to home."

He whipped his head to look at me. "How close?"

Seeing the panicked look on his face made a part of me die inside. I was supposed to be his hero, not this flawed, sinful man. Would he ever look at me that way again?

"Dad? How close?"

If only I could backtrack ten minutes.

But I couldn't. I took a deep breath and chose to tell my son I wasn't who he thought I was. "I hate to admit this, but in the past few months I've gotten close to another woman."

Baylor's silence screamed.

"But I stopped it — before it went too far."

Baylor's eyebrows dipped. His expression showed shock and disgust. "Who is she?"

I wasn't sure what I should say. I didn't want to make it weird when Baylor went to Holly's office. "Just a nice woman who was going through hard times. We both needed someone to talk to." I'd repeated that excuse too many times.

The popping stopped but Baylor made no move to get the bag. "You could have talked to me. Or Paige. You could have talked to Paige."

His words implied the truth, that I was closer to his sister than to him. Yet I was touched he offered to listen. "You're right. I could have talked to one of you. I should have. I will. Both you and I could have saved ourselves a lot of pain by talking to each other." I caught his gaze. "Right?"

Baylor gave me a single nod. "Does Mom know?"

I was going to say no, but realized I wasn't sure if that was the truth. "I don't really know. But I'm going to tell her everything tonight."

Baylor shook his head vigorously. "I do *not* want to be here for that."

"I agree. I don't want you in the middle of our mess. Could you go over to Justin's?"

He shook his head. "Not Justin's. There's a new guy, Nate. I'll call and see if he wants to hang out in the park or something."

A new guy? A friend? "That's sounds great."

Baylor poured the popcorn into bowls. He drizzled liquid butter over the top of his, then handed the butter to me. We both added salt and he sat with me at the island.

"You okay?" I asked.

"Yeah. Probably. When is Mom going to be home?"

"She said she'd be here for dinner. I was going to surprise her and make pork chops."

He nodded. "Pork chops are her favorite."

Exactly.

I was surprised when Holly *did* come home in time for dinner. Experience had given it a 70/30 chance *against*.

The oddest thing was, she seemed happy. Excited. Had she already changed her attitude about spending time with us?

But as we started to eat, my hopes were dashed when all Holly talked about was Holly.

"I saw the most glorious property today at an open house. It has a sweeping staircase, eleven-foot ceilings, a circle drive in front of a columned portico—"

"What's a portico?" Baylor asked.

I answered. "It's a front porch."

Holly huffed. "I guarantee you, this one is more than merely a porch. It's grand in every sense of the word." Her shoulders lifted and fell. "The whole house is grand and I want to buy it."

Her words hung in the air and Baylor gave me a worried look. "We have a house," he said.

"Not like that one."

I did *not* want to move, but had to ask, "How much is it?"

"One-point-seven."

"No way." She couldn't be serious.

"One-point-seven what?" Baylor asked.

"One-point-seven million." Holly sliced her pork chop.

"Million?" Baylor said. "Do we have that kind of money?"

"No," I said. "We don't." And Holly knew we didn't. We'd recently talked about how we couldn't afford *this* house.

"Then why would we move?" Baylor asked.

I tried to calm his fears. "We are not moving."

"We *could* move," Holly said. "We should move. Successful people act successful, dress successful, and live successful. As a real estate agent my home should ooze success." She looked around the dining room as if it disgusted her. "This house is . . . bourgeois."

"Great," Baylor said. "Another word I don't know."

"The word is not a compliment," I said as I buttered a roll. "It means middle-class, which in itself isn't a bad thing. But apparently to your mother, whatever we have isn't good enough."

Holly was silent. But then she shoved her chair back, stood, and drilled her napkin onto the table. "What's wrong with wanting nicer things for my family?"

She could be so blind. "I don't think you're doing it for us, Hol. You admitted you want to show off your success—or the elusive success that's making you work eighty hours a week."

She stabbed her hands on her hips and bobbled her head. "Well excuse me for wanting to improve our lives."

"This house is fancy enough," Baylor said. "I don't care if you call it bouge-y. I like it."

"Me too," I said.

"So you two don't want to better yourselves?"

In usual Holly fashion she'd turned the discussion around so we were the ones at fault. I was not in the mood. "A house does not make *us* better. In fact, it might make our family worse because you know, for a fact, we can't afford it."

"So I'm not working hard enough? Is that what you're saying? *I'm* not enough."

What? I wanted to scream at her. We'd been down this passive-aggressive road before and I knew if there was any hope of having a civil discussion about Brianna I needed to calm things down. So I got up and put an arm around her shoulders. "You work very hard—too hard. Now sit down and let's finish dinner."

But Holly would have none of it and shoved my arm away She was seething. Her face was twisted in disgust. "Don't you dare touch me! You've made it clear that I am *not* enough for you. And I will not have you touch me after you've touched *her.*"

I sucked in a breath. My mind swirled. She knew about Brianna!

Baylor stood and picked up his plate. "I'm outta here."

"No!" Holly yelled. "You will not leave. Since we're a family you deserve to hear about your father's infidelity—with Brianna, no less."

"Brianna. From your office?" Baylor sank back onto his chair and looked at me, his face pained. "You didn't tell me that."

Holly gaped at me. "You talked to our son about this?"

"I never told him her name—on purpose."

"They only talked, Mom. That's all." He stood. "I'm leaving."

Her eyes grew wide. "That is not *all*. And sit." She motioned for Baylor to sit again — which he did. He shoved his plate across the table.

I did not want to go into this with our son in the room, yet I knew Holly wasn't going to let him go. Why would she want to argue in front of him?

"Well?" Holly said.

My heart beat double-time. I took a deep breath, hoping to keep my voice calm. "Brianna and I both needed a listening ear. She's going through a nasty divorce and I . . ."

"So *you* want a divorce?"

"No!" She wasn't listening — which shouldn't have surprised me. "Please sit and we'll talk about it. Actually, I was planning to tell you everything tonight."

"Sure you were." Suddenly, she extended a hand like a stop sign. "Wait right there." She left the room.

"Dad, I don't want to be here," Baylor said.

I sat back down and tried to give him a reassuring look. "Me either, bud. But I think it will make things worse if you try to leave."

Baylor looked miserable.

As was I.

Holly returned, carrying some white strips of fabric. She dropped the pieces on my plate. "Recognize this?"

I saw buttons. And a collar. "Is this one of my shirts?" I started to pick up the pieces, but they had food on them, so I let them be. "Why is it all cut up?"

She took a piece off the top and shoved it toward my face. "Smell it."

I smelled it. It smelled nice. "Gain laundry detergent."

She swiped the piece away from me. "That's not it."

Baylor took a piece and smelled. "Yes, it is."

Holly breathed heavily. Her face was bright red.

"What did you think it smelled like?" I asked her.

A few more breaths, in and out. "Her. Her perfume."

This was ridiculous. "So you sliced up my shirt because you thought it smelled like Brianna?"

Her eyes blinked wildly. Then she said, "You have the letter B on your calendar every Monday for weeks. B equals Brianna."

I thought of the Ds on Willis' calendar. "I don't appreciate you looking at *my* calendar, but yes, you're right."

She put a hand to her chest. "So you admit it! You met with her six times?"

"That sounds about right. We'd meet for coffee on her break, or in the park." And one other time. I raised my right hand, needing to state the truth, but hating to be so blatant in front of Baylor. "We did not sleep together, Holly. I promise. We both simply needed to be heard. We needed comfort."

"You needed comfort . . . ?" She paused, shaking her head as if my reason was ludicrous. "From her?"

"From someone. Our family hasn't been strong lately, Hol. Surely you see that."

"So it's my fault?"

She'd opened the door. . . "Yes. Partly." Her eyes widened. "We're all to blame."

Baylor curled the corner of his placemat. Over. And over.

I stood and took Holly by her upper arms, hoping she wouldn't reject my touch. "I am so sorry for what I've done."

"You'd better be."

I continued. "I need you. I love you. I want to spend time with you. But Holly, you have to admit you're rarely here bodily, mentally, or emotionally." I felt her shoulders slump.

But the fight hadn't left her, and she jerked away from me. "I'm trying to be successful — the best agent in the city. Don't you appreciate that? Don't you want me to succeed?"

She had a one-track mind. What would get through to her?

"Okay, Hol." I pressed my hands downward in the space between us. "Let's say you succeed. You hit it big. At what cost? Baylor ran away. I nearly walked away."

"But Dad didn't leave," Baylor said. "And I came back."

Those were good points. "We want *you* back, Holly." Suddenly I felt the burn of tears. I desperately needed to save *us*. "We want to be around the pre-obsessed-with-success Holly again." I thought of something from our past. "Let's get 'kid and kiddo' back. Can you do that, kiddo? Be that woman again?"

"Kid and kiddo?" Baylor asked.

"Our nicknames for each other before *you* kids came along." I stepped toward her, touched her chin, and realized how seldom I really looked at her. Her dark eyes were brimming with unrest and pain. She had a deep crease between them. From frowning? Worry? Stress? There was no ease or optimism in her expression. All softness was gone and I knew she wasn't going to melt into my arms no matter what I said.

Instead, she took my hands and held them captive between us. "I can't be that person right now. Maybe someday, but not today."

With that she left the room. I was left there, stunned.

"Wow," Baylor said. "That was brutal. She's mad about everything."

"She's miserable," I said. Had I lost her?

"She makes us miserable too."

It was true. "What's even worse is that I'm not sure there's anything we can do to help her. She only sees herself right now."

I looked in the direction of the bedroom hallway and saw Holly carrying her pillow and some clothes toward Paige's old room.

"Uh-oh. That's not good," Baylor said.

Not good at all.

I got in bed but couldn't sleep. Mom and Dad were getting a divorce. I knew plenty of kids whose parents were divorced or on a second marriage, but I'd never thought it would happen to us.

My phone rang, vibrating against the bedside table. I grabbed it fast and answered quietly. "Hello?"

"Baylor? Why are you whispering?"

"Hi, Paige." Should I tell her I was whispering so I didn't wake up Mom—who was next door, sleeping in *her* old bedroom? "It's a long story."

"Something's going on," she said. "I texted Dad to say hi and he wrote back that he was tired and he'd talk to me in the morning. He didn't sound like himself."

"He's not."

"Now you're scaring me, Bay. Tell me what's wrong."

She'd find out anyway. "Just a minute." I took my phone into my closet, which backed up to Paige's closet. Hopefully the clothes would muffle my voice. "Ok. I'm set."

"Set for what?"

I just said it plain. "Mom and Dad are getting a divorce."

It took her a second. "What did you say?"

"Things aren't good, Paige. At all."

"They actually said the D-word?"

"Not exactly. But Mom's sleeping in your old room."

She sighed deeply "Great."

"You don't sound surprised."

"I am. But I'm not. They haven't been getting along for ages."

I knew she was right, but I hadn't paid that much attention to *them*. I'd had my own problems.

"They've argued before, Bay. A lot before. It will probably be fine in the morning."

I couldn't let her brush it off. She hadn't been here. "This is different. Dad had this other woman — but not really — and Mom thinks they're having an affair, and —"

"Whoa! Slow down. What are you talking about?"

I told her about Brianna and how she needed someone to talk to. "As did Dad, and — "

"He could've talked to me." She sounded hurt.

"That's what I told him. He ruined everything just to talk? He *did* tell me they didn't have sex."

"Dad said that? To you?"

"I'm not a kid anymore." They all treated me like I was twelve. "Actually, he said they didn't sleep together, but that's the same thing."

"I hate that you heard so much," she said. "That's not cool."

No. It wasn't. "I tried to leave but Mom wouldn't let me go."

"She does like an audience."

"That's true. But still . . ."

I heard her let a breath out. "Couples argue, Bay. It'll be okay."

She was brushing it off too fast. "I don't know about that. Dad wanted to make up but Mom didn't. She stomped out of the room."

Paige made moaning sounds. "What do you think we should do?"

She was the big sister. Shouldn't she know? "Be there for Dad, I guess."

"For Dad? But he's the one who almost . . . Mom's the victim."

"Mom is *not* a victim." I lowered my voice. "When Dad tried to apologize Mom wouldn't hear it. She made things way worse. You know the way she can be."

"Yeah. I do know. Mom isn't just a drama queen, she's a drama empress. Should I call him?"

I didn't want things to get stirred up again. "Not right now. Plus, Mom's supposed to do the Nana-thing tomorrow, so maybe that'll help."

"If anyone can get through to her, Nana — " She stopped talking and I heard Drew's voice in the background. Then Paige said in a muffled voice. "I'm talking to Baylor. I'll be there in a minute." To me she said, "Sorry. Drew's here."

"Yeah? *I'm* sorry about *that*."

She sighed. "Ease up on him, Bay. He's the man I want to marry."

I made a *pffft* sound. "I have no idea why you'd want to do that with anybody. Especially when Mom and Dad have given you such a great marriage model."

"Marriage is a good thing, Bay. Grandpa and Grandma's marriage is strong. Nana and Papa's—"

"Oh don't get me started on them. Nana told Dad that Papa had an affair."

"No. No way. That's not possible. Dad had to have misunderstood."

"He didn't. I . . . you do need to talk to Dad about it. Call him tomorrow. And call me too if you think of anything we can do."

"I wish I was there to help."

"It's better you're not. I'll keep you posted."

After we hung up I just sat there in the dark closet. It used to be my cubby space, a quiet place I could play with my toys or read and just be alone.

A place to hide.

I pulled a few sweatshirts off the shelves to use as a pillow and curled up to sleep.

As a kid I used to wish things away.

If only that worked.

Chapter 20

Holly & Elsie & Paige

"For if you forgive other people when they sin against you,
your heavenly Father will also forgive you.
But if you do not forgive others their sins,
your Father will not forgive your sins."
Matthew 6:14-15

"Morning, Holly."

I glared at Brianna as she walked by my desk. How could she act like everything was fine?

I got to my cubicle, dropped my things off, then retraced my steps. When I got to the reception area, I leaned on the counter and spit out the words that had to be said. "You leave my husband alone."

Brianna's face reddened. "What? Oh." Brianna looked down. "It wasn't like that."

I pointed at her. "Watch yourself. I have the power to make your life miserable. You can depend on it."

I walked away, not caring if others in the office had heard. I got to my desk and unpacked my bag as if nothing was unusual.

I didn't look up when Brianna rushed to the Ladies'. There was satisfaction in that. She'd made me suffer? It was her turn.

I stared at the clock on the mantel.

Where was Holly? I had instructed Vernon to invite Holly to come for her treasure hunt at nine o'clock this morning. It was fourteen minutes after. Everyone knew I hated tardiness, especially for something as important as the hunt.

I'd wait until the clock chimed the quarter hour.

Which it did.

I dialed Holly's cell.

She picked up on the third ring, "Holly Lindstrom, how can I help you?"

"You can get over to my house for your treasure hunt. You're late."

"What treasure hunt?"

"Didn't Vernon give you the invitation for *your* treasure hunt?"

"No, he did not." She paused. "We were busy. We had other things to talk about."

Interesting. I was glad Vernon followed through. "How did it go?"

"I don't think it's any of your business."

"But it is. After his treasure hunt Vernon said he was going to confess his indiscretion to you."

"You know about that? You're the cause of all this?"

"Watch your tone, Granddaughter. I am not the cause, but I was instrumental in getting him to be honest about it."

"We went through all that because of your silly treasure hunt?"

All this? All that? "If all that includes discussing the situation and having him confess and you forgive, then yes. Starting a clean slate is always good for a couple. For a family. You might give it a go yourself."

"What you've put me through is no treasure. You humiliated me in front of our son, and caused chaos in our family. So much so, that I'm sleeping in Paige's old room."

Oh dear. I thought of the verse about not letting the sun go down on our anger, but didn't dare share it. I too had been guilty of hanging onto my share. "I'm sorry you were hurt. I was hurt too."

"How were you hurt?"

It took me a second to realize Vernon hadn't shared my story. He could have. I'd wanted him to. "Your grandfather had a full-blown affair, so I've been in your shoes. Been in worse shoes actually. I am familiar with your pain."

There was a pause. Then, "Papa?"

She truly didn't know. "It was a long time ago, Holly. My point in sharing was to get Vernon to see the dangers of any type of extracurricular connection."

Holly snickered. "That's a sanitized way to put it."

"It sounds like you didn't forgive him."

"Of course I didn't forgive him. He didn't ask. I have a right to be mad, don't I?"

Mad, she had down. "I want to share a verse that got me through that hard time, it's—"

"I am not in the mood to hear a verse, Nana."

Oh, this child. "You're getting one anyway. 'Be kind and compassionate to one another, forgiving each other, just as in Christ God forgave you.'"

She didn't respond.

"Did you hear me?"

"I heard."

Why was she so difficult? "The point is that Jesus died so all our sins are forgiven. He didn't die so everybody's sins—except Vernon's—are forgiven. Vernon confessed to you and I assume he apologized."

"Whatever."

I'd had enough. "There is no *whatever* to it, Holly." I thought of another verse. "'Do not judge, or you too will be judged.'"

"For what? I didn't have an affair." Disgust dripped from her words.

I wanted to scream into the phone, but took a slow breath instead. I sorely needed a dose of God's patience. "Did Vernon tell you why he spent time with Brianna?"

"Oh I can guess. She got divorced, so she's hot to trot for a replacement."

"Holly! You know that's not true. And don't be crude. What did Vernon tell you about it?"

There was a pause, then Holly said, "He gave some excuse, saying they needed someone to talk to."

"And why might Vernon need someone to talk to?"

Silence. At least she wasn't arguing.

I used my best, soothing grandma-voice. "You work too hard, dear girl, you're gone too much. Your family needs you. They are desperate to have you be a more active participant in their lives."

More silence.

"You are loved, Holly. Come over and we'll go through your treasure hunt."

"I'm tired of people telling me I'm wrong."

"You're not wrong. Just off-track a bit. I'm trying to help things get better."

Holly sighed. "Count me out, Nana. Move onto your next victim. This one's bowing out."

She hung up.

I sat in stunned silence. My own anger rose and I felt my face grow hot. After the success of Baylor's and Vernon's hunts, I was eager to meet with Holly. I expected her to be mad about Vernon's confession, but instead of seeking comfort, or even doing a little soul-searching for the root cause, she'd built her walls thicker and higher, erecting a battlement with a closed drawbridge. And a moat.

I knew a bit about walls. And ambition. And pride. Which only increased my desire that Holly go on her treasure hunt.

But that would have to be another day.

"So now what?" I asked the room.

Dad called me first thing in the morning. He confessed to the Brianna thing — and seemed truly contrite about it. As far as Mom? Not surprisingly she'd gone to work early without saying a word to him. It was her usual M.O. to avoid and deflect.

"Are you sure everything will be okay?" I asked him.

"Paige. Daughter. Dear. Stop your worrying. We'll work it out. But enough about us. Is Drew enjoying having you home every evening? I hope he appreciates you giving up your jobs. That was quite a sacrifice."

"I'm sure he does."

"Sure he . . . ? He hasn't said anything about it?"

Dad wasn't keen on Drew. I didn't want to make his opinion worse. "He likes having me home."

"To cook him great meals."

"Dad. Don't be mean. It's more than that and you know it."

"Sorry. I just want you to be happy, Paigey-girl."

"As happy as you and Mom?" I sucked in a breath. "Oh. Shoot. Sorry. That was really rude."

"Apology accepted," he said. "Every relationship goes through bumps. "

"I know." I knew too well. "I'm glad you called, Dad. Next time you need to talk to someone, call *me*. Okay?"

"Point taken."

"Good luck with Mom."

We hung up. I felt better about the situation. Dad was strong and determined. He'd made a big mistake but had owned up to it. I still wasn't sure Mom would ever acknowledge her part in the problem.

I stretched my legs on the coffee table and accidentally toppled a bowl of pistachio shells. I scrambled to pick up the mess and took the bowl to the kitchen trash—something I'd asked Drew to do before he left last night.

It was a small thing. And yet it wasn't.

Although I'd glossed over our relationship while talking to Dad, Drew hadn't mentioned a thing about me giving up my jobs. I'd quit last Friday. It was now Wednesday. Yes, Friday was the night Baylor went missing, and on the weekend we'd been busy dealing with the family fallout. But that left Monday and Tuesday. We'd had two evenings alone with no mention of my job or a single question about how Baylor was doing after coming home. And I hadn't even thought about telling Drew about my parents' marriage problems.

It's like he and I were together. But not.

I tossed my phone aside. "Did I quit Rolly's for nothing?"

How would I know?

I realized I needed someone to walk me through it—someone different from Dad or Baylor.

My thoughts turned to Nana and her treasure hunts. Baylor and Dad had come through the experience better for it. Baylor had opened up and wasn't being so hard on himself, and it sounded like Dad was trying to make things good even if Mom wasn't cooperating. Everything seemed to be moving in the right direction. Yay, Nana.

Baylor said Mom was next up. Boy, did she need it. When would it be my turn?

And yet . . . even though I wanted someone to give me advice, I wondered what an eighty-nine-year-old woman could share that would be relevant to my life. We were three generations removed from each other. I loved her deeply, but I was skeptical.

My phone rang. I looked at the caller ID. *Speaking of . . .*

"Hi, Nana. How are you doing today?"

"I'll be peachy keen if I can see you. Can you come over this morning?"

It was not lost on me that the only reason I could even consider seeing Nana right now was because I'd quit my jobs. "Sure. I could do that."

"Do you have a few hours? Because if you do, I'd like you to take your treasure hunt."

"I have class later . . ."

"I promise you'll be done in time."

"I thought Mom was going next."

"I choose you, sweet girl. Can you come over now?"

"Give me fifteen minutes."

I kissed Nana's cheek and took a seat on the ottoman at her feet. "You look invigorated. I see color in your cheeks again."

She chuckled. "I feel invigorated. Finding a new purpose has energized me."

I wasn't sure what she was talking about. "New purpose?"

Nana leaned forward as though sharing a secret. "It's the treasure hunts, sweet girl. They've given me a reason to get up every morning."

I squeezed her hand. "I'm happy for you. And I'm glad you called — and glad that I have time enough to come over."

"That's right," she said. "You'd mentioned quitting your new job?"

Finally, someone was interested. "Both jobs actually. I quit the diner in order to work at Rolly's and quit Rolly's because . . ." It would sound weak. Pitiful.

Nana's eyes saw right through me. "You need to finish that sentence."

I didn't want Nana to have bad feelings about Drew. "I quit because it was best. With working in the morning *and* the evenings, plus school in the afternoons, I didn't have time for much else."

"For Drew."

"Well, yeah." I tried to think of something positive to say. "But now I have time for all sorts of things." I gave her my best smile. "Like you."

"You're a dear. But don't you need a job to pay for your apartment?"

"I do. I'll get a morning job again."

"Will the diner take you back?"

I shook my head. "The owner hired his nephew to take my place. That door is closed."

"I'm sorry about that. Doors do close. But other doors open."

"I hope so."

Nana extended her hands, wanting my help to stand. "Let's get this treasure hunt started — for all this proves you need it."

"What 'all this'?"

"You'll see." Nana took my arm and we walked toward the bedrooms. On the bed in the master was a black case in a familiar shape. "You have a violin?"

"It's a viola."

"Sorry. I'm not familiar."

"It's bigger than a violin. Lower in pitch."

I wasn't sure why Nana was showing me this. "Do you play? Did Papa?"

"I played. Past tense. I was first chair in the youth symphony in high school—for a while."

"A while?"

"Until I made a huge mistake."

"What kind of mistake?"

"*That* is what you're going to find out."

My treasure hunt was going to involve music? I was the least musical of anyone in the family. I'd never learned how to play an instrument, and I couldn't sing "Happy Birthday" without making people wince.

Nana touched the black case tenderly. Obviously it brought back good memories. She looked up and blinked a few times, as though coming back to the present. "The symphony gave concerts at an auditorium."

"Which auditorium?"

She smiled. "That's what you need to find out."

"How do I do that?"

Nana pointed at the case. "Open it."

Inside the velvet-lined case was a viola, a bow, and an envelope with my name on it. I pulled out the notecard inside that said, "'There's more to life than being a passenger.'" I looked up. "Is this quote yours?"

"Nope."

"Do I need to know who said it?"

"Yup. Come back to visit when you've found your next clue *at* the auditorium."

I felt overwhelmed. "I don't know where to start."

"You start with the quotation. Now, off with you. I need to get back to the book I'm reading for book club."

It was odd to be ushered out like that. This whole thing was odd.

I got in my car, but before I started it up I searched for the quotation on my phone. Surprisingly, it came up many times. The person who said it was Amelia Earhart. How appropriate. From what I knew about the woman, she was not one to let others control her destiny. She liked to drive the plane—around the world.

Nana had mentioned an auditorium. I searched for Earhart Auditorium.

And there it was, in Kansas City. I set the GPS to take me there.

The Earhart Auditorium was a brick building with ornate stone carvings along its flat roof. There were double doors on either side of an old-time box office booth. A handmade poster for an upcoming singalong was taped to one of the doors.

I'd found it. Now what?

I entered a lobby with red patterned carpet and brass chandeliers. The area was dark except for a few lit sconces on the wall. To the right, I spotted light coming from an office. It was a good place to start.

A woman sat at a desk. I knocked on the doorjamb. "Excuse me?"

The woman looked up and smiled. "Are you Paige?"

I was shocked. "I am. How . . . ?"

"Your great-grandmother is a generous supporter of this auditorium. When she called this morning and asked me for—well, you'll see—I was happy to oblige." She stood. "Come with me."

The woman led me into a small conference room that had two bound books set on the table. She handed me a note. "Mrs. Masterson said you're not to look at the note until you're through."

"Through?"

The woman put a hand on the top book. "She's in here." She left with a smile. "Good luck."

Luck? I needed luck?

I sat at the table and opened the first book that had "1949" embossed on the front. It was a scrapbook of auditorium events. I paged through programs for theatrical shows like "Oklahoma" and "Carousel", lots of choral concerts, and even "An Evening with Lawrence Welk." I wondered if Nana had gone to that concert. I'd bought her and Papa some DVDs of his old TV shows. *Ana one, ana two, ana three . . .*

Then I turned to a page that was captioned *Youth Symphony Spring Concert.* That was Nana's group. There was a group photo and I scanned the faces of the kids in the orchestra, checking out the violinists. But Nana wasn't there.

Then I noticed a much smaller group of violinists next to the cellos. Their instruments were a bit larger . . . "Ah. Violas."

And there she was, in the first chair. I could definitely see the essence of Nana in the young teenager. She was pretty, eager, and confident. It was strange to see her so young. Although the picture was in black and white, I could tell that her hair was a medium brown like mine. It was parted on the side and fell in waves onto her shoulders.

She wore a cardigan set in a light color, with a plaid skirt that was discreetly pulled over her knees. She had on white anklets and dark tie shoes. She sat tall as she balanced the viola on her leg, and was grinning with happiness.

I looked at the list of the musicians. *Elizabeth Swain.* The last name I knew about, but Elizabeth? Elizabeth became Elsie? Why hadn't I known that?

I looked through the rest of the scrapbook but didn't find any more info about the symphony. I closed *1949* and opened the *1950* scrapbook. I skimmed the pages, looking for the symphony again. I found it and immediately looked at the viola section.

But Nana wasn't sitting in the first chair. Out of four groupings of two viola players, Nana was in the last row. Why was she back there? I wasn't musical, but I imagined there was a hierarchy of seating, from best up front to . . . worst?

Nana's physical appearance was similar to the year before, but the difference in her demeanor was striking. Her shoulders were slumped and her frown was a stark contrast to the smiling faces around her. What happened between 1949 and 1950?

It was time to read Nana's note. It contained three words: *Come see me.*

Gladly. I wanted to hear the entire story.

I went into Nana's house without knocking. "I'm back."

She was in the kitchen, warming up some soup. "Since you're here it must mean you made it to the Earhart Auditorium."

"I did. The woman there had everything set up for me. Two scrapbooks. Looking at the pictures I could tell it was you right away."

"I was a cute cookie, wasn't I?"

She made me smile. "You still are." Two soup bowls and spoons were already set. A bowl of oyster crackers sat nearby. I popped one in my mouth. "But Nana, I noticed something. You seemed really happy in the 1949 picture but in the one from 1950? You looked sad and you were sitting way in the back. What happened?"

"I was demoted." She handed me an old photo from the counter. "Clue number three."

It was a photo of Nana at age fifteen or sixteen. She was nestled under the arm of a tow-headed kid with a gorgeous smile. "This doesn't look like Papa."

"Oh no. I hadn't met Willis yet. This was my steady boyfriend, Matthew." She looked over my shoulder. "He was a handsome buck."

"How long did you go out with him?"

"A year. A wasted year."

What an odd way to put it. "How so?"

Nana turned the heat off the burner and pointed to the table. "Have a seat and I'll tell you a story."

Chapter 21

Elsie - 1949

"The Lord watches over you —
the Lord is your shade at your right hand;
the sun will not harm you by day,
nor the moon by night."
Psalm 121: 5-6

The director stopped the orchestra. "We need to go back to measure twenty-five. Trumpets, you were rushing and you're supposed to be in unison. And trombones? You were far too . . ."

Since he wasn't scolding the violas, I let Mr. Staling's words fade into the background. What consumed my thoughts was Matthew. From my front seat in the viola section I faced the door of the music room. I'd seen him stroll past four times already.

And there he was again. I smiled and offered a little wave.

Unfortunately, Mr. Staling saw me and glanced over his shoulder at the door.

My stand-mate Brenda leaned toward me. "Why does he come to every rehearsal?"

I blushed. "He loves me," I whispered.

Brenda shook her head.

I wanted to argue with her. For Matthew did love me. We'd been going steady for almost a year. He gave me presents — virtually anything I asked for. And he wanted to spend as much time with me as he could. That's why he showed up at the symphony's Saturday morning rehearsals. That's why he waited for me after choir practice and at Kresge's whenever I worked.

And yet . . .

He walked by again and pointed at his watch. I glanced at the clock. Yes, we were five minutes past our usual break time.

My heart beat faster. I fidgeted in my chair. *Come on, Mr. Staling, it's time for our break.*

Luckily, others started fidgeting too, which made the director call it. I carefully put my viola on my seat and hurried into the hall. I met Matthew right outside the door. "Hi."

"You're late."

"Not too."

"Too." He put his arm around my shoulders and steered me down the hall of the high school.

"How are you this morning?" I asked. I felt his grip on my shoulder tighten.

"I have something to talk to you about."

I tensed up. The tone of his voice hinted of an argument to come. I hated when he got mad at me — which was often. But then he'd say he was sorry and be so sweet afterward. I didn't have much experience dating. Mom and Dad hadn't let me start until I was sixteen so Matthew was my first real boyfriend. He was a senior. None of my friends had older boyfriends.

We stopped near the school entrance and he faced me. "We need to spend more time together."

"Of course - I'd love to." I gave him my most disarming smile. "You name it."

He leveled me with a look. "Okay, I will. I want us to spend Saturday mornings together. You know I work from three to closing tonight. You have church on Sunday morning, then *you* work, so . . ." He spread his hands. "Saturday mornings are our best chance of having time together."

"But I have rehearsal."

"You wouldn't have to go."

I didn't understand. "I auditioned to get in this group. It's an honor to be in it."

He took my hand and stepped closer, bending it around my back. "Isn't it an honor to be my girlfriend?"

I noticed my friends were looking at us. I tried to step apart. "Not here, Matthew."

He glanced in their direction, then kissed me hard.

I pushed away. I lowered my voice. "You didn't need to do that in front of them."

"No, I suppose you're right. I didn't need to kiss you and get close to you. In fact . . ." His eyes flashed in anger. Then he turned toward the door and noisily opened it as he walked out.

I ran after him. "Matthew! Don't be like this."

He talked over his shoulder while he walked toward his pickup. "You don't want to spend time with me? So be it."

I stood in front of the school, torn about what to do. If I ran after him he would drive away before I got there, making me feel like a fool. If I went back into rehearsal . . . I looked toward the entrance and saw a dozen of my friends pretending not to watch the drama. Unfortunately, they'd seen it before.

A weariness fell on me like a wet blanket on a hot day. I couldn't breathe.

I saw people start to head back to rehearsal. I needed to follow them.

But Matthew was mad. He was still sitting there in his truck. I had to take care of it, make things right.

Maybe I could tell Mr. Staling I wasn't feeling good — which was the truth. My stomach was tied in knots and I felt a headache coming on. As the seconds passed, I felt worse and worse.

With a gesture to Matthew to wait, I hurried inside, wanting to catch the conductor before everyone was back in the room. Luckily, he was still in the hallway.

"Mr. Staling?"

He waited for me. My face must have shown I was upset because he asked, "Are you all right, Elsie?"

The perfect question. "Actually no. I'm not." Suddenly, acting sick wasn't enough. I knew what I had to say. And do. "I . . . I need to leave the symphony."

He looked toward the exit. Had he seen Matthew get mad at me? Did he suspect the reason?

"You're quitting?"

"Uh. Yeah." I was quitting?

"You're first chair. We need you."

"I know, and I'm sorry, but things . . . it's better if I give it up. I can't do this anymore."

He put a hand on my shoulder. "You don't need to give up what you love. Not for anybody."

I knew I shouldn't have to quit, but the thought of going through more Saturday mornings like this one was too much. "I'm sorry. I have to go." I ran into the room and gathered my things as fast as I could. If only I could be invisible.

But Brenda saw. Brenda asked where I was going.

I just shook my head. "I need to leave. See you Monday."

I rushed outside. But Matthew's truck was gone! I'd motioned for him to wait . . .

Now what?

I couldn't be seen standing here when the other kids came out. And home was too far away to walk.

I spotted a payphone by the curb and called Mom. "I'm not feeling good, Mom. Can you come get me?"

As usual, she said she'd come. While I waited I paced up and back on the sidewalk, keeping an eye out for Matthew's pickup in case he came back. But at this point I was glad he wasn't around. I just needed to get home.

I sat on a bench to wait. Doubt peppered down on me. What had I just done? I'd upset Matthew, I'd upset Mr. Stalings, and I'd upset myself. I ran my hands over my face, trying to force the thoughts away. They were too raw. Too dumb.

None too soon I spotted our Nash turning into the drive. What would Mom say when I told her?

Unfortunately, I knew what she'd say.

"Hi," I said, getting in.

"Hi, yourself. How are you doing?"

"Horrible."

"What's wrong?"

"I just don't feel good."

She put a hand on my forehead. "You don't feel feverish. Is it your stomach? Head?"

I shrugged.

She put the car in park and looked at me. "You're not really sick, are you?"

I pointed forward. "Can we just go home?"

She shook her head. "Elizabeth, you tell me what's wrong, right this minute."

I didn't want anyone to see us sitting here. "Drive and I'll tell you."

She pulled away from the school. "Start talking, young lady."

I took a deep breath. "I quit orchestra."

"You what?"

The excuses spilled out. "I'm too busy to have these Saturday rehearsals added to school and family and work. And with the Christmas concert coming up, there are going to be extra rehearsals and—"

Mom abruptly pulled onto a side street and stopped the car. She angled toward me. "You quit because of Matthew, didn't you?"

My defenses kicked in. "You and Dad have never liked him."

"Because he's way too possessive. But that has nothing to do with my question. Did you quit because of Matthew?"

I crossed my arms, then realized I would look like I was pouting, so uncrossed them. "Yes. But he didn't ask me to quit." *Not exactly.* "There's simply too much on my plate, Mom. Something had to give."

"You love symphony."

"I like it, sure. But having my Saturday mornings free sounds really nice."

"You should take time to think about big decisions like that." Mom looked over her shoulder and pulled out into traffic.

"I don't need to think about it. It's done. And I feel good about the decision."

I was lying.

As soon as we got home I called Matthew to tell him the good news. If he came over to the house, Mom would know I made the right decision.

"So," I said after telling him that I'd quit, "since I have time now... do you want to come over?"

There was a pause. "Uh, I can't. Brad asked me to join a game of flag football."

I felt the air go out of me. "But . . . I quit for you."

"Don't go blaming me for that."

"But you—"

"I'll come see you after you're done with work tomorrow. Gotta go. Bye."

I hung up the phone, which unfortunately was in the kitchen where Mom was washing dishes. "Is Matthew coming over?" she asked.

"He's busy." After all I'd done, how could he not come over? I absently straightened the phone book in its slot.

Mom wiped her hands on her apron. I expected her to say "I told you so", but instead she said, "Oh, hon. I'm so sorry."

I ran into her arms.

Two weeks passed and I enjoyed having my Saturdays free for the first time in two years. Matthew and I did spend more time together and he even gave me an antique music box that was on a keychain that had been his grandmother's. It was so sweet of him.

But in between the extra together-time were comments from my friends. "He expects too much of you" and "He's not your boss" and "Why does he show up everywhere? Doesn't he trust you?"

The last one hurt the most because it rang the most true. Matthew didn't trust me. A couple of times when I was leaving choir practice and a boy stopped to talk to me, I'd find Matthew seething by the time I got to his truck. "Who's that?" he'd ask.

"That's Paul." Or Ben. Or whoever.

"You going out with him?"

"Of course not. He's just a friend."

Nothing I said would calm him down until I gave him a lot of kisses and told him I loved him over and over.

But everything changed while I was at work one Thursday evening. Kresge's closed at nine, and as usual I heard Matthew's ancient pickup coming close, and saw its headlights as he pulled out front. He turned the engine and lights off, but I could see his silhouette in the driver's seat. He liked to take me to work and pick me up after. Mom and Dad had said it was okay.

And it usually was.

But on this night, after the last customer paid for some handkerchiefs and shoe polish, the manager locked the front door and flipped the Open/Closed sign. The other clerk and I cleaned up our areas, and my boss asked if I wanted to learn how to close out the cash register.

Usually only clerks who'd been there a long time got to do that. How could I say no?

He let the other clerk out, locked the door again, and he and I stood by the register while he showed me how to count up the money and log it onto a piece of paper. He told me how much to put back in the register for the next day. The rest was put in a bank bag then into a safe in the back office.

I was honored that he trusted me. "I know you're only sixteen, Elsie, but you've shown a lot of promise. It would help immensely to have you learn how to close in case I can't be here. I would up your wage by ten cents an hour too."

"Thank you, sir. I appreciate the chance."

I was thrilled and ran out to Matthew's pickup, on top of the world. "You'll never believe what just happened."

"He kissed you in the back room." Jealousy sliced through his words.

I thought he was kidding. "Of course not. Don't be silly. He — "

Matthew turned toward me in his seat. Even in the dim light of the streetlamp I could see his jaw was set and his eyes were fiery. "You two stood way too close at the register."

"He was showing me how to close. I couldn't stand across the room."

"But then you disappeared in the back. What was that all about?"

He was being ridiculous. "The register money has to go in a safe so he can deposit it tomorrow when the banks open. That's it. Well that, and the fact he gave me a dime an hour raise."

His eyebrows rose as he looked me over. "Which you paid him for."

I was dumbstruck. "Now you're being weird. He's my boss. He just gave me more responsibilities—and a raise."

He snickered. "As I said . . ."

At that moment I thought of doing something I'd never done. I stood up to him. "You're being totally unreasonable, Matthew. Take me home. Now."

He blinked at me, clearly surprised. "I'll leave when I'm done saying what I have to say."

"Take me home, Matthew, or . . ." I saw my boss leaving. "Or I'll get out and ask *him* to take me home."

"Fine!" Matthew squealed his tires as he backed up and drove me toward home.

We didn't talk—which was a blessing. Matthew didn't pull onto the driveway but parked in the street. I couldn't get out of the truck fast enough. I ran in the house and slammed the door, locking it behind me.

Mom and Dad were reading in the living room. Mom stood up. "What happened?"

I just stood there.

Mom set her book aside. "Elizabeth. You're shaking. What's wrong?"

I hugged my arms to make the shaking stop. Then I surprised myself by not making excuses. I told them the truth about what had happened. And not just about tonight, but about other times when Matthew had been mean and controlling. It felt good to let it out.

But as I talked their jaws tightened and Mom kept shaking her head. They were mad.

Oh dear. I'd said too much against him. I backtracked. "But that only happened a few times. He really is a nice guy. I love him and he loves me."

My words didn't even ring true to me.

"That is not love," Dad said. "He's acting like he owns you." He removed his reading glasses and leaned forward. "It's time to be done with him, Elizabeth."

What? Dad wanted me to break up with him?

Mom touched my arm. "You deserve someone who'll love you and respect you."

"I agree," Dad said. "It's time. Past time. You need to do this, Elizabeth. Once and for all."

Their life-changing words made me take a step back. And then . . . it was as if their words caused a page of my life's story to turn, revealing a fresh page.

Fresh. Starting fresh. The idea of it was tempting. Enticing.

Suddenly my defenses fell away and I saw the truth. Mom and Dad were right. I needed to do this. Now.

But how?

I covered my face with my hands. "I guess . . . I do want to end it. But I'm just so tired." I started to sob.

Mom led me over to the couch and sat beside me. She put an arm around my shoulders. "Of course you're tired. But you need to know that true love shouldn't be a struggle. It should be easy and refreshing like . . . like . . ."

"Breathing," Dad said.

Mom smiled at him. "Like breathing."

I took a few deep breaths and my tears began to fade. "So how do I break up with him? It makes me nervous just to think about it."

Mom pointed toward the kitchen. "I understand being nervous. But it's best to not put it off. Call him. Do it now."

I stood and started pacing. I could hear Matthew's voice in my head, hear his anger. "He won't take it well."

"We'll be here for you," Dad said.

Mom nodded.

I believed them. But I was still the one who had to make the call.

Mom looked toward heaven. "God? Give Elizabeth the right words. Replace her weakness with Your strength. "

I liked her words. They gave me an image of shedding a flimsy coat of weakness and God wrapping me with some impenetrable armor. Not only did I have Mom and Dad behind me, but God too. I drew in a deep breath, letting it sink in.

Then I felt a nudge to make the call. Now.

I went into the kitchen, picked up the phone and dialed. At first I wasn't sure if I wanted Matthew to pick up or not. But then I realized I *did* want him to answer. I wanted this over.

While the phone rang I braced myself for his angry words, his accusations, and threats. But then I imagined God's armor protecting me. I could do this.

After the fourth ring he answered. "Hi," I said.

"What do you want?"

Mom and Dad stood in the doorway of the kitchen. Mom smiled and nodded. My resolve strengthened. "I want out, Matthew. I'm done. I'm breaking up with you."

I could hear his breathing over the phone. "You are *not* doing that. I won't allow it."

Mom and Dad moved close and I tilted the phone so they could listen in. "I am doing it, Matthew. I can't take you hounding me, following me around, not letting me talk to guy friends or even my boss without you getting jealous."

Mom mouthed, *It's over.*

"It's over," I said.

"It's not over. It will never be over. I won't allow it to be over."

I shivered. How did I ever love this guy?

Dad took the receiver away. "It is over, Matthew. You will not come near our daughter again." He hung up.

I was stunned by their support. They were so strong and sure. "Thank you—"

The phone rang. My heart rose to my throat.

Mom answered it. "Hello . . . stop calling, Matthew. Elizabeth doesn't want to talk to you anymore." She hung up.

The phone rang again. Dad took it this time. "Stop calling, Matthew." But then, Dad did something odd. Instead of hanging up the phone, he took the receiver and put it in the refrigerator that sat next to the telephone shelf. He shut the door. "There. He can't hear us and he can't call back."

Mom chuckled. "Maybe that will cool him off."

I felt as if the weight of the world had fallen away. I hugged them both, so deeply grateful that my heart hurt. "Thank you for standing by me."

"We're glad you're free of him," Mom said. "And I will be with you all day, every day, and do whatever it takes for him to get the hint." She held my chin in her hand and kissed my forehead. "You're my baby and I will not let anyone harm you."

We shared a three-way hug.

It was hard to get to sleep that night. I kept imagining Matthew outside my window. And maybe he was there.

But somehow it didn't matter because I knew my family and the Almighty would keep me safe.

Chapter 22

Elsie & Paige

"The instructions of the Lord are perfect, reviving the soul.
The decrees of the Lord are trustworthy, making wise the simple.
The commandments of the Lord are right,
bringing joy to the heart.
The commands of the Lord are clear, giving insight for living."
Psalm 19: 7-8

I sat with Nana at the kitchen table, enthralled with her story. I'd never thought of my great-grandma as a teenager—a fact that made me feel rather shallow, as if any life lived before my birth was irrelevant. Not cool at all.

"So what happened?" I asked. "Did he leave you alone? Was quitting the symphony a good thing?"

Nana raised her index finger. "You're getting ahead of me."

"Did Matthew cause more problems?"

"Many. For weeks. Even though Mom drove me everywhere and picked me up afterward, Matthew still turned up—after all, he knew my schedule perfectly."

"What did he say to you?"

"Nothing—thank God. He was just *there,* this foreboding, annoying presence that prevented me from fully moving on."

"So what made him stop?"

"An intervention of sorts."

"That sounds kind of scary."

"It was. But something had to give." Nana put a hand to her chest. "My parents were extremely brave."

I thought about my parents. Would they stick up for me? Dad would. But would Mom even be there to notice?

Nana turned her wedding band around and around on her finger, then clasped her hands on the table. "One evening my dad asked me to take the trash cans out to the curb for collection the next morning. I saw Matthew parked on the street at the far end of our property. He got out and called to me, but I ran inside. Dad asked what was wrong. When I told him, he stood up from his chair and paused there a moment. His face got real serious. I could tell he was struggling with something, thinking real hard. Then he nodded to himself and told me to bring him his jacket. He said, 'Enough is enough.'"

"What did he do?"

"He went out front to face the problem head on. My father wasn't much taller than I was. He taught seventh grade American history. Matthew was over six-foot tall and all beef."

"I *hate* confrontation. Did Matthew hurt him?"

She held up her hand. "Mom and I tried to watch through the front window, but they were out of our line of sight. But then, there they came, walking toward the house."

"Together?"

Nana nodded. "I did *not* want Matthew in the house. I did *not* want to talk to him. I tried to escape to my room, but Mom stopped me. 'It's time to face this, Elizabeth.' she told me."

I pressed a hand to my chest, my nerves feeling the moment. "You must have been so nervous."

"Nervous and scared, but excited too, that maybe, this truly could end it all." Nana's hands flit this way and that, describing the room. "They told him to sit on a chair by the window in the living room. The three of us sat on the couch across from him, me in the middle. That felt good. We were a united front. And for the first time in ages I felt like everything would be all right. They would save me."

I choked up. "Sorry. It's just so incredible that they stood up for you. So bold."

"It was. That's why I felt so safe."

"What did your parents say?"

"Dad did all the talking and basically said, 'We know you're a nice person, but Elizabeth doesn't want to see you anymore. She will *not* see you anymore. It's time for you to move on and let her do the same.'"

"No threats? No harsh words?"

"No threats. Just stern words."

"Did it work? "

"Miraculously, it did. Mom kept driving me around the next week, but Matthew never showed up. I don't think it was just Dad's words that got through to him, but more the fact we were united. 'A cord of three strands is not quickly broken.'"

"Three against one."

"Four." Nana pointed upward. "It was so brave of Dad to go out there like that. They both stepped up and protected me when I needed it. Matthew left me alone, and I was free."

I enjoyed a wave of joy and relief on her behalf. It was an oddly foreign feeling. I fingered the corner of a placemat, needing to share another thought. "You say you were afraid that Matthew was outside, yet you felt safe because of God. If God keeps us safe, then why do people get hurt?"

Nana raised a finger. "A question for the ages, sweet girl."

"Do you have an answer?"

"No. And yes."

"Meaning?"

"No I don't know why bad things happen or why God allows them to happen, but yes, 'We know that in all things God works for the good of those who love him, who have been called according to his purpose.'"

"Meaning?"

"If we love God, we can be sure He will work with every detail of our lives, weaving them into something good."

I liked the sounds of that.

"I bet you're wondering if I went back to orchestra."

"Did you?"

"I thought about it, but at that point I was kind of emotionally spent and — forgive the pun — I wasn't up to facing the music by going back."

"That surprises me."

"It surprised me too. But I was truly starting fresh. I had free time with no orchestra and no boyfriend . . . I felt renewed."

I wanted to feel renewed.

"But then . . ." Nana sat back in her chair and took a fresh breath. "The next semester I heard that the symphony had been invited to travel to Washington D.C. to play for President Truman."

"Ack. Bad timing."

"Very."

"That had to be hard to hear."

"It was a knife to my heart. My parents were big Truman supporters and I admired him too. I think they were as heartbroken as I was."

I remembered the scrapbooks. "I saw the picture from 1950. You *were* there. You did go back."

"Yes, I did. 'Sooner or later everyone sits down to a banquet of consequences.'"

"Amelia Earhart?" I guessed.

"Robert Louis Stevenson."

I scanned my mind but came up blank. "I'm sorry. I don't know who that is."

"He wrote *Treasure Island* and the story about Dr. Jekyll and Mr. Hyde."

"Oh yeah. Impressive."

Nana pressed her hands flat on the table. "The Matthew situation had me dining at that banquet of consequences — and it wouldn't be my last meal." She handed me a letter whose blue ink was a bit smudged.

"Clue number four. It's a carbon copy. That's why it's a little mucky."

I felt childish again. "What's a carbon-copy?"

Nana sighed deeply. "Before copiers, people used carbon paper to make a copy. It had one inky-waxy-side that you put on a fresh piece of paper, then when you wrote or typed your letter, it showed up on the bottom sheet. Think of a group-email you've sent. Did you use 'CC'?"

"Sometimes."

"CC stands for carbon-copy."

"Wow. I didn't know that."

"Your trivia for today." She touched the letter. "Anyway, my mother insisted I make a copy so I wouldn't forget my humiliation."

"That doesn't sound very nice."

"It wasn't. But as you see I *have* kept it all these years. And I *do* remember. Read it."

I held the delicate page and read aloud. "'January 15, 1950. Dear Mr. Staling, I need to apologize for quitting the symphony last November. I have seen the error of my ways, and honestly, the reasoning behind my rash action doesn't make as much sense in hindsight as it did in the moment. I'm so sorry for quitting and was wondering if you'd allow me to come back. Please? I promise I'll work really hard. Yours truly, Elizabeth Swain.' Wow, Nana. That was gutsy."

"Yes, it was."

"And . . . ?"

"A few days later Mr. Staling called and said that yes, I could come back, but . . ."

"But?"

"I'd have to sit last chair. At the back of the violas. In the nosebleed section. Last."

I drew in a breath. "From first to last . . . that must have been hard to take."

"Hard and humiliating. I shared a music stand with an eighth grader who was *not* a very good player." Nana removed her glasses and rubbed her eyes before putting them back on. Her chin quivered.

"You still feel it."

"I do. Even after seventy-one years." She took a deep breath and found her control again. "I had the honor of going to D.C. and playing for the president, but had to humble myself and *be* humbled to do it. It comes down to this: I never should have given up symphony for a boy." She shook her head back and forth repeatedly.

A mental window opened and I thought about my own life: my relationship with Drew, the job I'd just quit for him. I took a deep breath. "I . . . I quit my job for Drew."

"I know." She gave me one of those Nana looks. Of course Nana knew — or she'd guessed. It wasn't a coincidence that my treasure hunt was so perfectly tuned.

"Drew's not possessive like Matthew was," I said. "He doesn't follow me around everywhere."

"Not bodily. But mentally? Emotionally?"

The truth hit like a slap. I pressed my hands against my cheeks — which felt hot. "I don't like this."

Nana touched my arm. "I know that too."

I thought about my impulsive decision to quit. "I can't believe I really quit for a guy. I thought I was smarter than that."

"Sometimes smarts have little to do with relationships. Love is complicated."

I thought back to the night I quit. I'd been in the alley behind Rolly's, on the phone with Drew. I'd been pulled in two directions and felt trapped. I was desperate to make the feelings go away.

"Penny for your thoughts?" Nana asked.

I sighed at the weight of them. "I always base everything I do, every choice I make with what Drew will think or say. Will he approve? Will it make him happy? Or will he make things difficult and make me . . ."

"Pay for it?"

Hot tears threatened, and I pressed them away. "I don't mean to make him sound like he's a bad guy because he's not. I love him. "

"So you've said." Nana sat forward and looked me straight in the eye. "Tell me what happened with the job. It seemed perfect for you."

There was no denying it. "It was perfect. I applied on a whim, never thinking I'd get it. When Drew found out he wasn't happy. He didn't want me to take it because it would cut into our together time."

"That's understandable."

I was surprised. "So you're on his side?"

"I didn't say that. I simply understand his side. But it doesn't change the fact that you still sought the position and accepted it."

"I did. I thought I was so brave and wise to think of the big picture, not just the moment. It was a great career move."

"Yes, it was. Or could have been."

Yes, there was that. "But it turned out I wasn't brave at all. He kept calling while I was in training and I felt like I had to keep answering. I got in trouble with the chef, and then . . ." I was out of breath. "It was just easier to quit."

Nana pressed a hand against her chest. "I know exactly how you felt. It was easier for me to quit the symphony too. Or so I thought."

Or so I thought.

"What about now?" she asked. "Are things good between you now?"

I remembered going home early that night and finding out that Drew wasn't coming over to see me. "It's like it never happened. He seemed—he seems clueless I even quit, much less how much I sacrificed for him."

Nana spread her hands. "I rest my case."

"Are you telling me to break up with Drew?"

I expected Nana to say, "Absolutely not." Instead she said, "That's not for me to say."

The weight of hard choices fell upon me.

Nana must have seen my pain, for she touched my cheek. "Let me take a small detour in my story in an attempt to help you clarify things."

I sighed deeply. "I'd appreciate that."

"When you first told me about your new job, what did I warn you about?"

"I don't remember. I was really busy." I said it flippantly but the words echoed in my brain. "Actually, I do remember. You said, 'Something's gotta give.' And you were right. That's why I quit Rolly's."

"Hmm."

"So what should I have done?"

"Let me ask you a few more questions. Number one: is the following true, yes or no? Do you want to be a chef?"

"I do."

"Can you be a chef without experience?"

"I could get a job somewhere else."

"True. But how will Drew react to that job, which will probably have similar hours?"

There was no hedging my answer. "The same."

"Remember what Amelia Earhart said?"

Surprisingly, I did. "'There's more to life than being a passenger.'"

Nana tapped her own nose. "By letting Drew drive the car of your life, you may see some nice scenery, but you also might miss out on the sideroads that could turn into the main roads leading to your destiny."

Destiny? "I just wanted to please him—and make my life easier. I was tired of all the arguing."

"Weariness is always a threat to courage."

"Earhart?"

"Elsie. But here's something from someone far more wise than I will ever be. King David said, 'The Lord *will* fulfill his purpose in me.' Not *might*, but *will*."

It was heady stuff. *I* had a God-given purpose? What was it? "How do I know if God's will is for me to be with Drew and *not* work at Rolly's or . . . ?" I couldn't finish the sentence.

"That's not for me to say." Nana pointed toward heaven. "It's for Him to say."

"But how will I know which way is His way?"

"I'm betting you won't think my answer is concrete enough—but it is. You'll know if something is His way because it will give you a feeling of peace. Jesus said, 'Peace I leave with you; my peace I give you. I do not give to you as the world gives. Do not let your hearts be troubled and do not be afraid.'"

I put a hand on my gut. "I'm troubled and afraid a lot."

"Of what?"

"Of making the wrong decision."

"Been there. Done that too." Nana put her hands flat on the table. "Here's the deal: sometimes the road of life sends you on detours. If you're sincerely looking to do things God's way and you happen to make the wrong decision, don't you think He's forgiving enough and strong enough to get you back on the right road?"

"Well, yeah, but — "

Nana counted off on her fingers. "Pray about it, listen to your innards, pay attention to the doors that open, and surrender your way to His way." She touched her thumb as the fifth point. "The result is peace."

I was confused. This was too much. I tossed my hands in the air. "I don't even know what I want!"

Nana took my hands in hers. "You are a mighty woman with a loving heart and a budding God-given talent. Don't settle for some mediocre detour that lands you in the mud."

I smiled. "But you said God would get me out."

"He most certainly will, but why waste time with detours at all?"

She had a point.

Nana squeezed my hands. "Don't be a doormat to anyone, sweet girl. You deserve to have a voice in your own life. Stand up for yourself. Be assertive, not aggressive. Compromise when you need to, but don't ignore your own talents and opportunities. Don't close a door that should be kept open, because there *is* a chance it might not open again."

I thought of Rolly's. Could I reopen that door?

Nana pushed against the table and stood. She paused a moment to get her balance with her cane. "I know I've been direct and pushy. But directness is one of the rewards of getting old. I don't have time to beat around any bush." She tapped her cheek with a finger. "Give me a kiss and be on your way. And let me know what you decide."

I considered skipping class that afternoon, but knew that Nana — and the Almighty — would not approve. But that didn't mean my mind wasn't a muddled mess, which culminated when the crepes I made in class looked awful and tasted strange. Turns out I'd used a tablespoon of vanilla rather than a teaspoon.

"You're not with us today, Miss Lindstrom," the instructor said.

"Sorry, Chef Roberts."

"Concentrate."

"Yes, Chef."

When class was over he called me aside. "May I have a minute?"

We waited until all the other students left. "I'm really sorry I flubbed the recipe. It was stupid. I'll do better."

"Forget the recipe."

Huh?

"I heard you quit your position as a *commis chef* at Rolly's. A *chef de partie* in training."

It killed me that he knew. "I did."

"I recommended you for that job and then I find out you quit? I don't get it."

I felt like a fool. Admitting I quit for a guy was embarrassing. "I made a mistake. My life was complicated and something had to give, and —"

"So that *something* is your big chance? *That's* what you gave up?"

"I gave up the diner too — actually, I gave up that job first so I could work at Rolly's and then . . ."

Chef spread his arms to encompass the classroom. "You might as well quit this too then."

"No! I want my degree."

"Why? If you're not going to use it and you're so cavalier with your big break, it would make sense to get a degree in something you'll actually use."

I'd never seen him be hurtful, yet he spoke the truth "I'm really sorry, Chef."

"Don't apologize to me. You're the one who got hurt."

I felt small. And stupid. "I admit it. I made a mistake."

"So . . . ?" he said.

So . . . what? "So . . . what am I going to do about it?"

He nodded.

The notion that there might be a solution was a glimmer of hope. "Do you think if I go to Rolly's this evening I can get my job back?"

"You can't," Chef said. "They hired a replacement."

My dream crashed into a wall all over again. "I...I didn't think..."

"No, you didn't." Chef put his hand on my arm. "Sorry to be so hard on you, and you're not the first person to make wrong choices, but this was a biggie, Miss Lindstrom. The hardest part about achieving your dream is to get other people to believe in it. I believed in you, and so did Chef Bernard." He looked straight into my eyes. "You're the one who didn't believe."

I took a deep breath in an attempt to fend off tears. "You're right. I really blew it."

"Yup."

"What do I do now?"

Chef checked his watch. Another class was starting soon. "I'll tell you something my granddad told me when I had hard choices to make. He told me to find my peace. *That* would tell me which choice was the right choice."

"My great-grandmother just told me the same thing."

"Great minds . . ."

Students started coming in the classroom. "Thank you, Chef. You've given me a lot to think about."

I walked to my car in a daze. The gravity of the last twelve hours hit me in waves. How could one day be so overflowing with truth bombs and life lessons? Maybe I'd have felt better if they'd been spread out over a week's time. Or a month.

As if I had a choice in the matter.

I got in my car and sat there without turning it on. Now what?

There were two big decisions to make. Unfortunately, they were stirred together. It was like trying to separate a bowl of flour and water. There was no simple, clean fix.

Could it be fixed?

I closed my eyes and breathed in and out. In and out.

I hadn't meant to pray, but one word escaped, one all-encompassing word that spoke the thousand words in my heart.

"Lord?"

Then the phrase "first things first" came to mind.

I started the car.

I drove to Rolly's, parked out back, and went in the kitchen door. I spotted Chef Bernard directing work at the meat station.

He looked up and spotted me. I felt the steam in his eyes.

He moved into the walk-in cooler to get supplies. "I'm busy, Paige."

I deserved that. I stood at the door. "I'll make it quick. When I quit I made a mistake and put you in a bind."

"Yes you did." He looked through the refrigerated tenderloins.

"I'm sorry for being unprofessional after you'd given me a chance. If I could . . . I'd like to come back. "

He chose a piece of meat, then paused at the door. "I'm glad you came to your senses but we couldn't wait. I hired someone else to train."

Nana's letter came to mind — and its result. "I'd be willing to work at any station, in any capacity." I looked around at the hustle and bustle of staff. "Please give me another chance."

He studied my face a brief moment and I could almost see his thoughts churning. "Fine," he said. "You're a kitchen porter. Grab a flat of strawberries. They need washing and slicing."

Now?

"You got a coat?"

"My school coat is in the car."

"Get it."

"Thank you, Chef."

He pointed a finger at me. "Don't let me down, Paige."

"I won't."

I hurried out to my car, and called Drew. He didn't answer so I texted him: *I got a job at Rolly's. I won't be home until eleven.*

I turned my phone off so I wouldn't know if he texted back. Then I hurried inside knowing that Drew was just one aspect of my "banquet of consequences."

A triple helping of humble pie was served that night.

It was beyond awkward speaking with Chef Hart at the salad station because my replacement was right *there*. *Hi, I'm the idiot who quit and opened up the slot for you to work here.*

It was embarrassing to be demoted from chef-in-training to kitchen porter where I was at everyone's beck and call, getting supplies, chopping, stirring, cleaning up.

It was also exhausting. I wanted to grumble, but couldn't. Wouldn't. Not when I thought about Nana sitting in the last chair of the viola section. If she could do it so could I. It was comforting to know I wasn't the first person in my family to make this sort of mistake.

I remembered a verse Nana had shared when I'd first told her about the new job. "Be strong and do the work."

Exactly. But oddly this evening the verse played out backwards. For *as* I worked I felt stronger.

I also felt something that was the frosting on the cake.

I felt peace.

I came home to an empty apartment—although I knew that Drew *had* been there.

He'd left a note on the counter: *We need to talk.*

Yes, we did. But not tonight.

Kitty George rubbed against my leg. I scooped him up, holding him against my chest.

His purring added to my peace.

Chapter 23

Paige & Holly

"Listen to advice and accept discipline,
and at the end you will be counted among the wise."
Proverbs 19: 20

I moaned as I got out of bed. My muscles objected to working late at Rolly's. Or maybe it was a combination of the physical, mental, emotional, and spiritual work. Yesterday had been full of all those.

The first thing I did was check to see if there were any texts from Drew.

Nothing. I wasn't sure whether to be worried or relieved. Last night he'd left a note saying we had to talk. I agreed.

But I dreaded it.

I knew where he stood on the subject of my job. Actually, I always knew his opinions about everything, without him saying a word. And when he did talk? He didn't hedge. He never seemed to care about sparing my feelings.

But now things were different: I knew my own mind and had my own opinions. Getting my job back felt good and right. So the discussion already had a line drawn in the sand. I wasn't willing to sacrifice the job a second time.

And so . . . my uneasiness wasn't about work but about Drew.

I ran my hands over my face. "How can I fix *us?*"

George jumped off the bed and looked up at me, stretching his front paws. His look, and the smell of coffee brewing, spurred me to get up. I got dressed, poured myself a cup, and sat on the balcony. The view was marginal—it overlooked the parking lot—but was a great place to people watch.

I saw the couple from a downstairs apartment kiss before getting in their cars to go to work. It was sweet. *Once we're married Drew and I will kiss like that before going to work*

But would we?

I watched a twenty-something jog by, her ponytail swinging wildly. *Drew and I should get healthy together. Take up running or tennis or yoga. Eat more vegetables and fruits.*

But could we?

I saw a mother secure a baby carrier into her car, talking in the sing-song way that mothers talked. *I want to be a mother. Drew and I want to have kids.*

But should we?

I hated that all my dreams seemed iffy. Tentative. They were full of should-dos and could-dos, even as they threatened to be won't-dos.

If Drew came in the door right now, what would I say to him? What was the end goal?

I thought back to Nana's take. She'd been the one to spur me toward seeking a second chance at Rolly's. She'd warned me about consequences.

I knew what Dad and Baylor felt about Drew. But I still needed advice. The logical choice was Mom. Although she was dealing with plenty of her own problems, she was a career woman, juggling work and family. She might know what to do.

When I went to work at the Dreamchasers office on Wednesday I immediately noticed Brianna wasn't there. There was a new girl at the receptionist's desk.

"Who are you?" I asked.

"I'm Angie, a temp. How can I help you this morning?"

This was really strange. "I'm Holly Lindstrom. One of the agents."

"Sorry, Ms. Lindstrom. I see your name here. I'm trying to get acquainted with everyone."

"Where's Brianna?"

"I was told she quit. That's why I'm here." She smiled a sprightly smile. "Let me know if I can do anything for you, Ms. Lindstrom."

I nodded and went to my desk. Had Brianna quit because of me? I saw people looking in my direction and heard them chatting in low tones. This wasn't good.

My boss walked into my cubicle. "May I speak with you, Holly?" He crooked a finger.

"Of course." I walked toward his office as nonchalantly as I could, plucking a stray — invisible — thread off my sleeve. This might get dicey.

"Close the door, please." He sat at his desk.

My heart beat in my throat, but again I tried not to show it. "What can I do for you, Charles?" I asked.

He sighed deeply, clasping his hands on his desk. "For starters, you can keep your private life private. I lost a great employee because of you."

"Because of me?" I wasn't sure whether to act ignorant or fess up.

"Brianna said you threatened her and told her to stay away from your husband."

I felt my face grow hot. There was no denying any of it. "I have a right to protect my marriage from divorcees who play the victim card."

He sat back in his executive chair. "That doesn't sound like Brianna. I am aware of her struggles, but she's been matter-of-fact about it. Resilient."

"To *you* maybe."

He cocked his head and studied me in a way that made me cringe. "You're making serious accusations, Holly."

I did *not* want to discuss this with him. "If you'll excuse me, that's my business."

He shook his head. "You made it my business when you brought it to work and accused a fine woman — threatened her — and caused her to quit."

My world came crashing in. I hadn't meant for it to get this far — actually I'd dreamt about it, but I never thought it would actually happen. "I'm sorry about that. I was upset."

He stood. "Being upset shouldn't involve intimidating another person. I expected more from you, Holly."

I stood, eager to leave. "I know, sir. I understand."

"Now go. Do your job."

Tears welled up in my eyes but I willed them back. The walk from Charles's office to my cubicle felt like I was walking a gauntlet. I liked attention, but not like this.

I was tempted to detour to the Ladies' to cry just like Brianna had done.

But no. I couldn't do that. I had to be strong.

Or pretend to be.

I was surprised when minutes later, Paige walked into my cubicle. "Hey there, daughter."

"Do you have a few minutes to talk about something?"

I hated that my first thought was defensive: *What did Baylor and your Dad say about me?* But I agreed. "Sure. Want to go outside to the bench?"

We sat under a sprawling orange maple tree, and I made some chit-chat about my day and the weather. It sounded totally stupid.

"Mom, stop with the weather report."

"Of course. What did you want to talk about, honey?" *Please don't mention your dad. Or Brianna. Or —*

"Relationship stuff."

I braced myself and decided to beat Paige to the punch. "Hold on. Before you start, I'm sure your dad and brother have bad-mouthed me like they always do, but *he's* the one who had an affair. Not me."

Paige blinked and sighed indignantly. "Dad didn't have an affair."

It was just like her to defend him. "How do you know?"

"I talked to him." She sighed deeply. "And that *isn't* what I wanted to talk about, but since you brought it up . . . the point is, *you* didn't tell me about any of it. Why didn't you? I knew things weren't great between you two but —"

"We are fine." Obviously I wasn't good at hiding anything from anyone.

"You are not *fine*. You barely hang out with anyone anymore. You're always working. You don't even like to be in the same room with Dad." She shrugged as though that was enough evidence to convict.

I leaned close so no passerby would hear. "Your father is the guilty one. Not me."

"There are different kinds of guilt, Mom."

I laughed. "Look at you, Miss Relationship Expert of the World at age twenty-one."

Her face turned red. "I just mean . . ."

I put up a hand. I didn't want to hear it. "I'm sure your dad can find all sorts of reasons to justify his behavior. He says he's sorry but *that* was Nana's doing, not his. After his . . ." I bobbed my head at the stupid term. "Treasure hunt."

"They are amazing, Mom. I just had my hunt with Nana yesterday."

I was stunned. The other three members of my family had seen Nana. "You had one too?"

"You haven't?"

I straightened myself on the bench and crossed my legs. "She invited me, but I had a meeting and . . ."

"You need to go, Mom. Maybe it will help."

I huffed. "I do not need a lecture from my grandmother. She couldn't possibly have anything meaningful to share about *my* life."

"The treasure hunt isn't about you, it's about her, about her life and how it connects to us." Paige pushed an orange leaf aside with the toe of her shoe. "I'm ashamed to admit I never thought of her having a life before us. But she's experienced things that crossover the years. She's done so much. And she made her lesson, my lesson."

"It still sounds like a lecture that will show how she's wise and I'm not."

"It's not like that at all. She shared her mistakes and made me see that I was on the verge of making the same ones."

It sounded dreadful. "I do not want to hear about my mistakes — or hers. She has no right to butt in."

Paige stared at me. "I can't believe your attitude, or . . . maybe I should have expected it."

Low blow. "What are you talking about?"

She stood. "I came here to get my mother's advice about something going on in *my* life and she — you — turned the conversation around to be all about you." She pointed in my face. "Believe it or not, Mother, not everything is about you. Have a nice day."

She walked away.

I wanted to call after her but then people would hear and stare. They would see what was happening and think I was weak. I did not need more people judging me.

And so I sat back on the bench and took a deep breath and even smiled, pretending to enjoy the fall day.

My ruse lasted a whole two minutes before I went back to work — where *they'd* judge me.

It wasn't fair. Not fair at all.

After leaving Mom I got in my car and hit the steering wheel. "Why are you so blind and selfish!"

The person unlocking the next car looked in my direction. I gave her an *I'm okay* smile. Then I forced myself to take deep breaths. Mom's inability to think beyond herself and actually act like a mother reinforced my past decision to move out. But my problem with the Drew-situation remained.

Who else might be able to give me good advice? I was running out of advisors. Then I thought of Grandma Rosemary. Her marriage to Grandpa was strong and had lasted forever.

She might know what to do.

I walked up the front sidewalk to Grandpa and Grandma's house. Since Mom hadn't been any help, I hoped my grandparents would be brilliant and have all the answers.

A few would suffice.

I rang the bell and Grandma opened the door. "Paige! How nice to see you, honey."

"Do you have a few minutes? I need some advice."

"Uh . . . I have a meeting later this morning but —"

Grandma was involved in tons of committees. I turned to go. "Sorry. I'll come back another time."

"No, no," she said, taking my hand and pulling me inside. "My meeting isn't until eleven. I have the time. And you know my advice is always free — and is worth every penny."

I looked around the living room. "Is Grandpa here?"

"He went out for groceries. Do you want him to be here?"

"Actually, just you and me might be best." I nodded toward the back of the house. "Can we sit on the swing? It's gorgeous outside."

"That's a grand idea." Grandma poured two glasses of iced tea and we went out to the swing that overlooked their massive flower gardens.

"It's so pretty here," I said. "I hope I can have flowers like this someday."

"You get the yard and we'll help you plant 'em."

Suddenly the idea of a yard and planting a garden with someone seemed very, very far off. I sighed. Deeply.

"What's going on, Paige?"

I shrugged. "Tons." We swung up and back a few times.

Grandma touched my arm. "You're usually the bubbly one, all words and gestures and energy. But if you don't want to talk, that's okay too."

I wanted to talk, so . . . I just said it. "It's Drew."

"You need to expand on that a little."

"He doesn't like me working at Rolly's."

"I thought you quit that job."

"I did. But then I went back." I didn't tell her I was only a kitchen porter now. "He doesn't like me being gone so much."

Grandma didn't say anything—which was odd.

"Grandma? Did you hear—?"

"I heard." She shook her head. "Similar conversations have occurred in this house once or twice."

I knew Grandma was really busy but I didn't know it was an issue. "So Grandpa doesn't like you being gone so much?"

"He didn't used to mind, but now that *he's* here, he wants *me* here."

"How are you handling it?" I asked. "Are you quitting stuff?"

She scoffed. "Not yet. I'm hoping Grandpa gets involved with his own activities and hobbies. Maybe Drew could—"

I shook my head. "He's not a joiner and he doesn't have any hobbies—that I know of."

"Well then." Grandma smoothed the hem of her shirt against her legs. "As with most relationship-stuff it comes down to this: do you love him?"

I was surprised she'd asked. "Of course."

"'Of course' is not a strong response to the question, honey. You should say 'I love him madly . . . with my entire being . . . I can't live without him.'"

They sounded like lines from a romance novel. "Do you love Grandpa like that?"

She didn't hesitate. "I do. Madly, with my entire being. I can't live without him."

Okay then. "I want that."

"*That* takes a lot of work."

Wasn't I doing a lot of work? I sipped my tea which made me remember sipping my coffee earlier. "This morning I was sitting on my balcony, people watching."

"That's always interesting."

"I saw a couple kissing each other good-bye, someone jogging, and a mom and baby. It's what I want in life: love, health, children, not to mention a job I love."

"Those are admirable goals — and pretty universal. What's stopping you?"

"Nothing. But everything." Maybe if I told her the gist of my treasure hunt she'd understand. "I spent yesterday at Nana's."

"I've been invited for my own audience tomorrow."

I gave her a disgusted look. "Don't say it that way. The hunt was really good. Nana helped me see that it wasn't right for Drew to ask me to quit my job. I know that couples need to compromise, but sometimes . . . in certain situations . . . a person has to make the hard choice."

"What's the hard choice?"

An ice cube clinked as it settled in my glass. "Rolly's is an important step toward me becoming a chef. I can't give up that dream — at least not yet. So yesterday I asked for my job back. That position was gone, so the chef could only give me a lower position. But I took it."

"That's a hard lesson. How did it make you feel?"

I looked at Grandma's expression. It was serious and sincere. Unlike Mom she clearly cared. "I felt awful. It was humiliating to see someone else in *my* job and then end up being a peon in the kitchen. But Nana had warned me there were consequences to quitting."

"That sounds like a lesson my mother would share. What does Drew think about you going back to work there?"

I sighed. "He wants to talk." I quickly added, "I want to talk too, but . . . it's not going to be easy."

"Not easy at all. No man — no person — likes playing second-fiddle. It's . . ." She sighed. "It's a tough lesson I probably need to learn myself."

Suddenly I wanted to know what she thought of him. "Do you like Drew?"

"Does it matter?"

"Yeah. I think it does."

Grandma shrugged.

"That is not an answer. Be honest."

Grandma stopped the swing. "Grandpa and I have accepted Drew as your choice *but* we're not sure we completely trust the guy."

I was shocked. "Why wouldn't you trust him?"

She put a finger to her lips as if she wasn't sure she should let the words out. "It's not because of anything he's done, it's instinct. He reminds us of Eddie Haskell in the old 'Leave it To Beaver' sitcom."

"I don't know that one."

Grandma nodded. "It's way before your time. Like Eddie, Drew always says the right thing with a smile. And he's polite — overly so. But it seems like he's masking his true feelings and as soon as we leave the room he'd say something bad about us."

I wanted to argue with her, but I'd seen Drew's charm in action and I'd heard his snide remarks.

Suddenly I wondered why I loved the guy.

Grandma angled toward me. "Do you think he'll give you an ultimatum: the job or him?"

I nodded. But then I had a radical thought. "Maybe I should give *him* an ultimatum."

Grandma's jaw dropped. "What happened to Paige, the compliant one? The one who never rocks the boat? The person who's first to give in?"

I chuckled. "You certainly know me well."

She touched my cheek. "You're my favorite granddaughter."

"I'm your only granddaughter."

She shrugged. "Are you ready to put it all on the line?"

Was I? "Nana said I shouldn't be a doormat."

"That also sounds like my mother. But there's a difference between being a doormat and willing self-sacrifice. Giving in isn't always a bad choice."

"Have you had to do that, Grandma?"

Her gray eyebrows rose. "Huh." It wasn't a question, but a statement.

"What's *huh* mean?"

She swept her thick gray hair behind an ear. "Grandpa *has* asked me to quit one or two of my committees."

"Have you?"

She started the swing again, and looked out over the flower beds. "Everett planted those purple asters and daisies because they are my favorites."

What did flowers have to do with anything? "That was nice of him."

"Yes, it was." She sighed deeply. "Your grandpa is the essence of nice, always giving me what I need. But as for me being nice?" She traced the chain that held the swing. "Not so much."

I had never seen her down on herself. "I'm sure that's not true. You're plenty nice. And you help tons of people at church and with your charity work."

She nodded but didn't look convinced. Then she sighed. "You come to me for advice, but it turns out I'm not the best role model in give-in-or-don't-give-in situations. I don't want to steer you wrong, Paige, and so . . . I'm sorry, honey. I don't have any clear guidance for you."

"Great." I knew I sounded rude, but I was frustrated. "I was hoping you'd have all the answers for me."

"Sorry. No go. Seems I could use a few answers myself." She squeezed my hand. "Try to remember that your choice with Drew is not just about today but about fifty years from now. It's about forever."

Forever?

Suddenly, in a moment that had a clear before and after, I felt a switch flip in my brain. All those images of the future: love, health, children, a job, and even planting my own flower garden . . . it was all at risk if I didn't make the right decision about Drew.

And that decision was —

Grandma touched my leg. "You got quiet. What's going on?"

I turned to look at her straight on. "I'm breaking up with Drew."

She pulled back. "Where did that come from?"

I stood, needing room for my thoughts to breathe. "I'm not sure. You mentioned forever and suddenly I knew I can't get the forever I want with him."

"So you *are* going to give him an ultimatum?"

I shook my head even though the answer hadn't completely settled. "I don't think so because I don't want *him* to give in and *I* don't want to give in. I just want to close the door on everything. Completely."

Grandma stood and put her hands on my shoulders. "Gracious, girl. Are you sure?"

I nodded once, then nodded again with more certainly. "Nana told me there were consequences to quitting, but I think there are also consequences to staying. And I don't like those consequences. Neither of us will be happy after an ultimatum." I had another revelation. "I think I made this decision a while ago, but couldn't admit it. And today . . . I wasn't really looking for advice from you and Mom but validation — or for someone to tell me Drew was the one for me."

"Your Mom didn't tell you that either?"

I shook my head. "This decision to break up is right. It's good. I'm doing it." My insides were in turmoil, but not in a bad way.

Grandma pulled me into her arms. "Oh, my dear granddaughter. You are one strong woman."

Yes, I was.

At least for the moment.

As soon as I left Grandma's I *had* to get the Drew conversation over with ASAP or I'd be worthless the rest of the day. My stomach was in knots—not because I wasn't certain about my decision, but because I knew it was going to be one of the hardest things I'd ever done.

I called him. "Hi there," I said.

"Hi." His voice was flat.

Out of habit I tried to think of something to tease him out of his anger, then realized I didn't have to do that anymore. What a relief. "Would you meet me for lunch?"

"So you *do* have time for me?"

I didn't take the bait. "Shanahan's at eleven?" It was ten-thirty now.

He sighed deeply. Dramatically. "I suppose."

He hung up.

Since I had a half-hour, I pulled in front of the restaurant and walked across the street to a small park. I sat on the wide rim of a fountain where I could gather my thoughts. I drew in a deep breath and let it out. The cool breeze made the fallen leaves skitter across the ground. I raised my face to a brilliant blue sky. The trees rustled in shades of gold and red. Nature always calmed me. It always made me feel closer to God.

Whom I needed right now. *Help me, Lord.*

Grandma had called me strong. But the strength of my decision-moment had waned a bit. Strength wasn't something I felt very often. In fact, the last time I'd felt strong was the day I moved into my apartment. Everyone had gone home and I was left swimming in a sea of boxes. Mom and Grandma had offered to stay and help me unpack, but I'd shooed them away.

As soon as they left I'd tossed my hands in the air and let out a scream—not too loud a scream, as I now had neighbors, but I'd felt the release of it. I'd felt the sheer strength and happiness of making a big life-decision and following through with it.

Strength and happiness. And freedom.

I'd also felt that way when I went to my first chef's class at the college. I'd been so excited and full of hope for the future. And of course I'd felt a ton of happiness when Rolly's had called. Career stuff made me happy.

I watched a bird peck at a leaf.

But I should feel happy about people too. Relationships. Faith, hope, love. That sort of thing.

It was hard to smile when I thought of my immediate family. They loved me — that was never in question. But Mom and Dad had issues I hadn't even known about. And Baylor had run away because *he* wasn't happy . . . In truth, by moving away I'd abandoned him. And them.

I wrapped my arms around myself, trying to keep the guilt away. Feeling guilty was a strength-killer. I felt a twinge of doubt seep in.

Would I be able to stand up for myself against Drew?

Against Drew?

"Paige?"

I looked up and saw him standing nearby. He had his hands in the pockets of his pea coat. "Hi," I said.

"What are you doing *here*?" He looked toward the restaurant. "We're eating lunch, aren't we?"

"I had some extra time." I patted the place beside me. "Join me."

He sat down, keeping his hands in his pockets.

"Isn't fall amazing?" I asked.

He glanced around, as if just noticing the season. "It's getting cold."

I breathed in the cool air to steady my heart. "I like the cold."

He shook his head. "Not me."

Moments passed.

He let his hands escape his pockets. "What were you thinking, taking that job again after I told you not to?"

And there it was. *The* subject of the day. With a burst of adrenalin my courage returned. My resolve hardened.

"You can't tell me what to do, Drew." I didn't like that I sounded like a petulant child. "My goal is to be a chef. To do that I need experience in an up-scale restaurant. You know that."

"Experience at my expense? "

I thought of Nana's boyfriend making a similar argument. "It's important to me, Drew. It's a necessary step."

"So you don't want to marry me."

"What?" He never talked about marriage. It was on my mind, not his. How did he get from A to Q?

He continued. "It's certainly clear that I'm not your priority anymore."

Now, who was a petulant child?

Yet his words were useful for they had opened the door. I took his hand and angled my knees to touch the side of his legs. My heart beat double time, but each beat pushed the words forward. "You and I are over, Drew."

His head jerked back. "What do you mean *over*?"

This was it. Turn back or stay strong.

I took a cleansing breath that filled me in more ways than one. "Over over," I said. "I don't think we're good for each other anymore."

He stood and faced me. "You're breaking up over a job? That's stupid."

But it wasn't. "It's not just the job it's . . . it's the forever part of a relationship. I can't see us old together. With kids and grandkids."

"That's not true." He paced along the edge of the fountain then pointed a finger at me. "You're the one who talks about getting married. You looked at *dresses*." He spat the word.

"And you're the one who never talks about it." I cocked my head and looked at him with a new boldness. "That is, until a minute ago."

I watched his jaw clench and unclench. "Who put you up to this? Your parents? Your precious Nana?"

I felt my own jaw tighten. "She *is* my precious Nana. But the decision is mine." I moved forward to sit on the edge of the rim. "You know how I'm certain it's the right decision?"

He shook his head.

I put a fist at my midsection. "Because of the peace I feel. I never felt peace when I was with you, Drew. I need peace."

He scoffed. "Sounds exciting."

I smiled. "Yes, it does." I stood. "I need to go."

"Just like that."

"Hardly," I said. His face was pulled and he looked scared. I hated that I'd made him feel that way, but I wouldn't back down. "I did love you, Drew, and I still care for you. I wish you all the best." I leaned close and kissed his cheek, then walked away.

I felt his gaze boring into me, but I didn't look back. Then I experienced a different emotion from the panic I usually felt when he was upset. As I walked I pressed a hand to my chest and felt my heart flutter. Was it fluttering out of anger? Confusion? Fear?

Partly. But there was something else going on, a new emotion had been born.

For the first time after an argument with Drew, I felt like I'd won something. I hadn't given in, surrendered, or been a doormat. I felt strong. Even victorious.

What was this new emotion?

I pegged it. It was joy.

Chapter 24

Rosemary

"So when you give to the needy,
do not announce it with trumpets,
as the hypocrites do in the synagogues and on the streets,
to be honored by others.
Truly I tell you, they have received their reward in full."
Matthew 6: 2

I poured coffee for myself and Everett and put in the right amount of sweetener and cream. I set the mugs on the dinette table next to a basket of bran muffins, then started to make scrambled eggs — his favorite. I would rather have had a yogurt and called it good. But ever since our argument over a week ago, I'd tried to be more caring and patient.

If only it came easy for me.

Oddly, the week's interruptions of Baylor running away, Vernon's affair, and Paige's problems with Drew were a godsend, for their situations had forced me to think about my own priorities and the importance of family. What bothered me the most was realizing that I needed to be reminded. As a woman of faith shouldn't I be naturally caring and loving-to-all?

Fat chance.

I mentally chastised my flippant response. I *could* change — all things being possible with God, and all that. But I knew myself too well. I was one stubborn cookie, and my pride was hard to break. In fact, nothing made me tremble more than knowing that someday God Almighty *would* break me. I shivered at the thought.

At just that moment Everett walked into the kitchen. "You cold?" he asked. "Want me to get a sweater for you?"

"I'm good. Thanks." But I wasn't good. My flaws were too numerous to list. "The eggs are ready."

Everett got tabasco out of the fridge. For me. He didn't do spicy foods. It was a small gesture but screamed loud and clear that he was always thinking about me while I had to force myself to think of him. After forty-five years you would have thought I'd be kinder.

I spooned the eggs onto plates and sat down. We clasped hands and said grace. Amen.

He passed me the salt and pepper first. "What's happening today?"

"I'm going to Mom's for my treasure hunt." I had a thought. "You haven't gone yet, have you?"

"Not yet. As her daughter, Elsie would want you to go first."

I begged to differ. "She didn't do that with Holly. Baylor, Vernon, and Paige have all had their hunts. Holly hasn't."

A crease formed between his bushy gray brows. "That's odd." He took a bite of muffin and chewed. "Do you think I'll even *get* a turn?"

The compassionate thing would have been to say, *"Of course! Mom loves you like a son."* But to be so gushy wasn't my style. "I assume so."

He nodded. "I guess since Vernon went, I'll get a chance too."

I snickered. "I'm not sure going on Mom's treasure hunt can be defined as 'getting a chance.'"

"Don't go there with a chip on your shoulder, Rosie. She's an old woman who's dealing with the loss of her husband, old age, and finding her way alone. Have some compassion."

Lack of compassion. Another fault to add to my list.

After breakfast I was on the way out the door when the phone rang.

"Good morning, Rosemary, this is Monica Larson from the state board."

My heart fluttered. "Hello, Monica. It's so good to hear from you."

Everett looked up from replacing an electrical outlet above the counter. *"What?"* he mouthed.

I covered the receiver with my hand and whispered to him. "Monica Larson. State board."

He nodded, but went back to work, clearly not enthused.

Monica continued. "I am happy to inform you that you have been chosen for the position of state board president."

I did a mental happy dance. "Really? That's wonderful."

"So you'll accept?"

"Of course I'll accept." Yay for me!

Monica went over some of the details and we set up a time for a preliminary meeting.

I hung up and bounced twice on my toes. "Guess who's the new state president of Beautify Kansas?"

I could see disappointment in Everett's eyes. "Good for you." His voice was flat. He turned back to his work.

My excitement and pride slammed into the very real fact that I'd just taken on another activity. My resolution to think of Everett before myself had been disgustingly short-lived. And yet . . . how dare he be so blasé about it? "It's a big deal, Ev. This isn't a local or even a county position. This is for the entire state."

"I know what 'state' means."

I moved to where he was working and grabbed the screwdriver out of his hands. "Aren't you proud of me?"

"Sure. Very proud." His gaze stayed on the outlet.

I didn't believe him. "Then why can't you be happy for me?"

He faced me with a sigh. "Because that position will take you away from home even more than you're already gone. Add it to the rest and I'll be lucky to get fifteen minutes a day instead of thirty." He held out his hand for the screwdriver.

I slapped it against his palm. "I'm off to Mom's. Maybe she'll appreciate my accomplishments."

I grabbed my purse and stormed out. So much for being caring, patient, or kind.

The drive to my mother's house was spent fuming at my own inability to change my ways *and* at Everett's lack of enthusiasm for my new position on the board. I hoped for a better reaction from my mom.

We hugged and sat in the living room. Mom had a shoe box of papers on the table nearby. "How's your day started?" she asked.

I sat on the couch and decided to ignore my argument with Everett. "I just got appointed president of the state board of Beautify Kansas. It's quite an honor."

"If you don't say so yourself."

That was rude. "It *is* an honor."

"I'm sure it is. What does Everett think about this? You're already so busy."

So much for gaining an ally. "He'll be fine."

"Getting overly involved and accepting positions on committees is a pattern with you, Rosemary."

Mom and Everett were in cahoots. My happy day was completely ruined. "It's a talent, not a pattern. Aren't we supposed to use God's gifts?"

"We are. But at what expense?"

My annoyance grew large. "I stayed home when Holly was little. I only started getting involved when she got older. I didn't have a career, which is why I . . . Never mind." I didn't want to bring up my failings and insecurities with my mother.

But she knew them anyway.

"No one is faulting you for not having a career, Rosemary. I didn't have one either."

That didn't make me feel better. Mom was from a different era when most women stayed home. I went back to defending my busyness. "I may not have earned a degree but that didn't stop me from participating and giving back." It sounded good, if not a little needy. "I wish Dad was still alive. The presidency might have impressed *him*."

"Maybe." Mom leaned forward on her cane. "I am sorry your father made you feel inferior about getting a degree. That was wrong of him."

I sat back with an *oomph*. "I can't believe what I'm hearing. Elsie Masterson is admitting her husband wasn't perfect?"

Mom cocked her head. "Why do you say that?"

I was incredulous. "According to you he could do no wrong. You always took his side — ."

"That's not true. Yes, your father could be harsh. Yes, he demanded a lot from you — and me. And yes, sometimes I took his side over yours. But not always." Her face was red with emotion.

We hadn't argued in a long time, and I didn't want to argue now, but I couldn't stop myself. "Name one time. I dare you."

Mom drew her head back. "I don't like being challenged, Rosemary."

"Because you can't meet the challenge?" I immediately felt awful. Mom was newly widowed and I was arguing with her like a teenager. "Sorry. I apologize. I'm in a testy mood."

A few moments of tension-filled silence passed before Mom replied. "Yes, you are, but your apology is accepted." She moved the shoebox to her lap and rummaged through it. "For fun I was going through some old cards and such. I guess it wasn't a coincidence. You need to see something." She handed me a card.

It was a birthday card I'd created when I was little, maybe six or seven. It was made from a piece of blue construction paper folded in half. On the front I'd drawn a picture of my dad next to his black Cadillac. The car was way out of proportion and the black coloring was scribbled. Inside the card I'd written in poorly made letters, *Hape birtday, Dad.* It was signed, *Rosemary.*

Oddly, I could remember sitting at the desk in my room, making the card. "He'd just bought the car and I knew he loved it a lot. But I didn't know how to draw cars very well. Or people." Unfortunately, I also remembered the rest of the day. "I gave it to him and instead of saying thank you he pointed out every little thing I did wrong." His comments still stung. I mimicked my father's voice. "'You can do better than this, Rosemary.'"

"Yes," Mom said. "That was your father, always to the point. But was he right?"

It was an unexpected question. "I don't know. I suppose. I do remember hurrying to get it done so I could go outside to play."

Mom wanted the card back. "The truth is you *could* have done better. You had done better."

I felt the shame anew. "If it's so bad, why did you keep it?"

"To remind me to stand up for you more often."

"What?"

She looked down at the card. "I saw your face after he spoke with you. I could see you were hurt." She put a hand to her chest and her forehead furrowed. "At that moment your pain sparked memories of my own pain when your father would criticize me — despite my good intentions. I knew what you were feeling and it made me bold."

She'd never told me any of this. "Bold? How so?"

"After you went outside I confronted him. I told him he'd been too hard on you. He'd been mean. It *was* a nice card. Was it the best card ever? No, but I saw your effort to draw a picture of his new car."

I was moved. "How did he react?"

Mom ran a hand over the card. "Not well. He pointed out the flaws in the drawing, saying you would have done a better picture and writing if you'd cared about him. I defended you — and myself probably — by insisting that both of us always tried to please him, and *that* needed to count for something. His standards were pretty impossible to meet. Would he rather we didn't try?"

"What did he say?"

"Not much. You know your father. He didn't argue. He just sat there, like he was thinking. I could tell by his expression that my words had hit their mark. Then he nodded once and said, 'Duly noted.'"

"A man of few words. *That* sounds like him."

"He *was* a bit slower to judge after that. For a while. That's why I kept the card—not because it was such a great card, but because it makes me remember a moment when I was brave."

My brave mom. Brave for me. I was touched by her sharing something so personal. "Oh, Mom . . . I've always thought of you as brave."

She shrugged. "I'm glad *you* thought so. This card was the start of me believing it too."

I opened and closed the card without really seeing it. "I didn't know you'd stood up for me."

"There's a lot you don't know about your father. And me. About us."

I knew it was true. "You were my parents but I never stopped to think of you as just people. I'm sorry about that."

Mom put the card in the box and set it aside. "Which is why I've called you here today."

And here we go. "The treasure hunt."

"The treasure hunt. She retrieved a shirt-sized box from the credenza and sat next to me on the couch. "It's time for your first clue."

I opened the box and saw a half dozen pins and ribbons scattered on top of some papers.

She picked one up. "This is for being the president of the art guild."

"Good for you, Mom."

She took control of the box and pointed out a few of the other awards and certificates of achievement.

"So you were a joiner too," I said, fingering a star pin.

"Not just a joiner, a leader."

I felt the guilt of my own leadership choices wane a bit. Like mother, like daughter. "Which one means the most to you?"

Mom looked upward, "Thank You, Lord, for letting her ask the perfect question."

Uh-oh. What did that mean?

"The award that means the most to me is the one I never got."

"That doesn't make sense."

"Yes, it does." She slid an envelope out from under the box and handed it to me.

On the front it said, "Clue #2." Inside was an address.

"Go there," she said.

"Where is there?"

"It's the home of Mildred Delvecchio."

"Who's she?"

"You'll find out. She's expecting you."

Mildred lived in the older part of town in a small white-clapboard home with a wrap-around porch. It was inviting, and made me think of simpler times.

It was awkward to visit a woman I'd never heard of, much less knew.

Mildred opened the door wide. She was less than five-foot tall, and stooped at the shoulders. She seemed younger than my mother by about a decade — in her mid-seventies?

"You must be Rosemary."

"That, I am. My mother sent me to visit you?"

Mildred chuckled and led me inside. "I was so pleased when Elsie called and asked for this favor. I always enjoy a chance to talk about my accomplishments."

Her accomplishments?

Mildred didn't lead me far into the living room. She stopped in front of the largest wall that was covered with all sorts of certificates, awards, and commendations. There were framed pins and ribbons, and even a gavel in a shadow box with a picture of a much-younger Mildred shaking someone's hand.

"My wall of honor," she said. She proceeded to go through at least half the awards, one by one.

I was impressed, but quickly skimmed the wall. *Yes, yes, I see, I see.*

Mildred finally took a breath. "I know it's silly to have them displayed after all these years, but these are the big accomplishments of my life."

"Of course. You have a right to be proud." I thought of all my mother's pins and awards tossed in a box.

Mildred looked at the wall and tapped a finger to her lips. "Oh! I almost forgot. Elsie told me to point out one thing specifically." She stepped to her left and pointed at the gavel piece. "I earned that when I was state president of the Voter's League for Kansas."

"Congratulations."

"Thank you."

Mildred nodded at the gavel. "The interesting is that your mother was up for the position."

"She was?" Mom had said the award that meant the most to her was one she'd never got. I wondered why Mom hadn't been chosen.

"We were both interviewed for the position. I have to say, it meant the world to me." She swept a hand to encompass the wall. "As you see it was *the* highlight of all my accomplishments. Plus, it came at just the right time."

"How so?"

Mildred paused a moment, then nodded at herself, as if remembering something. "That's enough from me. I was supposed to show you my awards, then tell you to go back to your mother's."

Quick in. Quick out. I chuckled. "Well then. Off I go."

Mildred led me to the door. "Tell Elsie hello. I hope I did what she wanted me to do."

"You did fine," I said, though I still wasn't sure what the point of it had been.

On to clue number three — of how many? I had a lunch meeting in a few hours.

I entered my mother's house. "I'm back."

Mom came out of the kitchen. "How was it?"

"I'm not sure what 'it' was exactly. Mildred showed me all her awards. She has them framed and displayed on an entire wall of the living room." I glanced at the shirt box which was back on the credenza. "Why don't you have yours displayed?"

She shrugged. "To each her own, I guess."

We both returned to the couch. Mom had something else to show me. It was a calendar for the year 1967. "I can't believe you've kept your calendars."

"Don't you?"

"I use the one on my phone."

"I wouldn't know where to start with that."

I shouldn't have brought it up. It was enough that Mom had a cell phone at all, though it was an old flip-type she carried with her for emergencies. "So what do you want to show me?"

"Start in April and look through it."

There were various meetings and doctor's appointments, and —
"You went to Maui in April? How nice."

"It was fabulous, very exotic. During the late Sixties the bank had all sorts of junkets at fancy resorts. I made myself the most gorgeous black lace swimsuit with a matching coverup."

"A lace swimsuit? How did that hold up in the pool?"

"I didn't swim, dear. I *lounged* poolside with the other wives while our husbands were in meetings. At night we went to luaus and we even saw Don Ho perform."

"Who?"

Mom sang, "'Mele Kalikimaka is the thing to say on a bright Hawaiian Christmas day. . .'"

"I know that one. It's old."

"I'm old." She pointed at the calendar. "Keep going."

I turned the pages. "Wow. An Alaskan Cruise in August."

"Amazing food and breathtaking scenery. While we were gone you stayed with Grandpa Milton and Grandma Susan."

I remembered staying at my grandparents' farm. "Grandpa took me on a tractor and Grandma showed me how to pluck a chicken." I shuddered. "My first and last time doing *that*. And Grandma got sick. I remember that too."

"She had a heart attack."

"I don't remember the diagnosis but Grandma had to spend a few days in the hospital. Grandpa was so worried and we prayed together."

Mom flipped more pages. "Here's a trip to Vancouver, and . . ." she flipped another page, reaching December. "New York City. The Christmas decorations sparkled on every building and we saw the Rockette's Christmas show."

"You went to a lot of great places in 1967."

"We did." She took the calendar onto her lap. "The thing is, I would never have been able to enjoy any of those places with your father if I'd taken that position as state president of the Voter's League."

I'd heard of that organization before. "Mildred said you were up for the position at the same time she was."

"More than up for it, I'd been asked to serve."

"But you didn't take it?" Suddenly, I could see where this was going.

"I did not."

"Is this a ploy to make me refuse *my* president's position?"

"This isn't about you, Rosemary. I'm just sharing some of my life with you. Let me tell you why I turned it down and you can make your own choices."

Chapter 25

Elsie - 1966

"Greater love has no one than this,
that someone lay down his life for his friends."
John 15: 13

When a Beatles song came on the radio in the living room Rosemary popped up from where she'd been playing Barbies. She held a Barbie and a Ken in each hand and made them dance to the music while she sang along. "'We all live in a yellow submarine . . .'" She stopped long enough to tell me, "Get Midge and Alan to dance, Mom."

I picked up Barbie's friends and made them bop along as I joined Rosemary in singing the final chorus. I held the last note far too long, which made her laugh. Rosemary's giggles made me happy. I knew in a few short years she wouldn't even think of asking me to play with her, and I would get eye-rolls and deep sighs instead of giggles. At age ten she was still my little girl.

As soon as the song was finished, I shut off the radio, sat on the couch, and put on my shoes. "Music time is over. We have errands."

"What kind of errands?"

I knew she wouldn't like my answer. "Fabric store errands."

She fell onto the cushions as if I'd told her we were going to the doctor to get a shot. "I hate that place. You take *forever*."

Very true. Every time I entered Jeanne's Sewing Emporium the creative side of my brain slipped into high gear. Fabric inspired me like a sunset inspired a painter.

"I won't be that long. We have to make it quick so I can get home and make dinner. I'm just picking up some tablecloth fabric I ordered for the church—enough for eighteen tables."

"It sounds boring."

Not boring, overwhelming. But the church wanted to save money, so I'd volunteered to make them. "How about we get some fabric for you — for a new school dress?"

"Ugh. I don't want school to start."

I was eager for it to start. Keeping Rosemary occupied for three months had been a chore. "You're going into fourth grade. You'll be a big kid. That deserves some groovy new clothes."

Now I got the eye roll. "You're too old to say *groovy*, Mom."

I was over the hill at thirty-three? I got my purse and had just taken my car keys out when the phone rang. I considered ignoring it, but what if it was Willis? When he called, I needed to answer. "Hello?"

"Elsie, this is Esther Donovan from the Voter's League."

My heart skipped a beat. Mrs. Donovan was on the executive committee of the state board. She was a woman I looked up to, always so put together and efficient. Respected by all. "Hello, Mrs. Donovan. How are you today?"

While we exchanged chit-chat, Rosemary made an impatient face and I flipped a hand to tell her to go do something for a few minutes. She pointed at the TV. I nodded and she turned it on to *As the World Turns*. I shook my head and she turned the dial to reruns of *Father Knows Best* and sprawled on the floor in front of it.

"Sorry about that," I said, "I had to get my daughter settled. What were you saying?"

"We, on the state board, would like to put your name in play for consideration as our president."

State president? "I . . . I don't know what to say."

"You've served on state committees for three years and we've seen your leadership abilities."

I hadn't expected this. "I'd be honored."

"Very good. Now I'm not saying you're a shoo-in, as another woman has also been nominated."

I didn't like competition. "Can you tell me who?"

"I shouldn't but . . . it's Mildred Delvecchio. Have you worked with her?"

I remembered a slight, raven-haired woman who talked too much. Hardly the sort who would be a good president. Presidents needed to know how to listen. "We've interacted a few times. She's nice." And annoying. Not leadership material at all.

"Very good then. I will warn you that the position requires a strong commitment of time and energy. After all, we are overseeing the League's work in the entire state."

I weaved the phone cord through my fingers as she talked. "I understand that. And I'm willing to do the work."

"Excellent. We want to meet with each of you the day after tomorrow at the board office. Your interview will be at ten, with hers after. Would that work out for you?"

"Of course. Thanks again for considering me." I hung up the phone and awkwardly jumped in the air. "Yay!"

Rosemary sat up. "Yay what?"

I told her about the state board. "Is that good?" she asked.

"It's very good. It proves people appreciate my hard work."

A commercial for Ovaltine came on TV. Rosemary turned on her back. "Do we *still* have to go to the fabric store?"

I felt generous. "How about we go tomorrow?"

It was Rosemary's turn to say "Yay!" I left her in front of the television and went into the kitchen. It *was* best to stay home. It would give me more time to make a celebratory dinner.

Meatloaf, mashed potatoes, and green beans were family favorites. A roast would have been better, but I didn't have time to go to the store.

But I did take time to fluff my hair and put on one of my favorite shirtwaist dresses. I'd made the dress out of a pastel plaid — that I'd matched perfectly at the seams. Store-bought plaid dresses rarely had matched seams. Getting that quality was one reason I loved to sew.

I put on pearl earrings and some pale pink flats. To top it off I sprayed Tabu cologne into the air and stepped into it — a trick I'd read about in *Women's Day*.

Rosemary stood in the doorway. "You look pretty."

"Thank you." We both turned our heads toward the garage as we heard its door open. Willis was home.

My stomach danced excitedly. Rosemary started to run off to greet him. I called after her, "Don't tell him anything. It's my surprise."

She gave me a pouty face, but nodded.

Willis wasn't in a good mood during dinner because he'd had a hard day at the bank. I tried to be supportive as I listened to his complaints, but inside I was bursting with my good news.

" . . . he was totally incompetent and —" Willis stopped his latest tirade and looked at me, at Rosemary, then at me again. "I'm telling you about my hard day and you two are grinning — which is *not* an appropriate response."

Rosemary giggled, "Tell him, Mom."

"Tell me what?"

I set my fork down and smiled. "I'm sorry for the difficulties at work, but tonight there *is* a reason to celebrate."

"Why didn't you tell me? I could use some good news." He nodded at Rosemary. "You know about this?"

She nodded. "Mom got all excited and jumped in the air — sort of."

Willis looked at me, incredulous. "I would have liked to see that."

I felt my cheeks blush. "I tried to jump in the air, because the news made me happy."

"What news?"

Finally. "I was offered a huge honor. Obviously not many people get the chance to do this and I never expected —"

"Elsie! Enough preamble. What happened?"

"I might become state president of the Voter's League!" I told him about the phone call and that I would be interviewed in two days.

"So it's not a sure thing?"

He would point that out. "There's one other woman up for it."

He sat back in his chair, looking at me. "Good. Maybe she'll get it."

I sat back in mine. "Why would you say that? I want the position. They asked *me*."

Willis pushed his chair back an inch and looked at Rosemary. "Would you excuse us, cookie?"

"Can I take my plate into the living room and watch a show?" she asked.

He nodded and she left the dining room. I wished she'd stayed. I wanted her there for support.

Willis pushed his plate toward the middle of the table. "Elsie. dear wife of mine. I want you to turn it down — even before the interview."

"Why would I do that?"

"Because Rosemary and I can't have you away from the house more than you're already away. I assume the position will require a lot of work and meetings — certainly out of town, and perhaps out of state."

Probably. "You go to conferences all the time." Wasn't it my turn?

"I am the breadwinner of this family. I have to attend in order to make a living to support you and Rosemary. You've never complained before."

"I'm not complaining now. I just want to have a chance to . . . to be honored like that. To have some prestige. Some purpose."

He shook his head and fingered the handle of his spoon. "You have prestige and purpose. You're my wife and Rosemary's mother." He pointed his spoon at me. "Beyond today being a bad day, things are going well for me and for the bank, Els. I wasn't going to tell you this, but there's going to be a conference in Maui next year, and of course I want you to go with me."

Hawaii? How exciting. "We could still go."

"It's not just Maui I'm concerned about. I want you to be available to travel wherever we want to travel — whenever I'm free to travel. If you're tied down to the whims of the state board . . . I don't see how that's possible."

I felt myself fuming inside. How dare he ask me to give this up? "I've always supported you in all your endeavors, Willis. Why can't you do the same for me? This isn't just another committee, this is an *honor*."

He extended his hand across the table, wanting me to take it — which I reluctantly did. "Do me the honor of saying no. I need you to say no. For me. For our family."

I pulled my hand free. "You're not fighting fair."

"I didn't know this was a fight."

"You're asking me to throw away my big chance . . . *that's* not fair."

"No, it's probably not." He leaned his elbows on the table and looked down as though contemplating his next words. When he looked up, his eyes were sincere. "I'd like nothing better than to spend all day, every day with you and Rosemary. Travel the world together, hike in the Alps, stroll through the Louvre, or eat pasta in a sidewalk café in Rome."

"That would be lovely."

"It's a pipedream. It will never happen. It can't happen. Real life says that my role is working hard to provide for our family. Real life says Rosemary has to go to school. And real life says that your role as the wife, mother, and homemaker involves being available to nurture our family."

He'd given me no point to argue. "I can do all that *and* be president." But even as I said it Mrs. Donovan's words came back to me: *the position requires a strong commitment of time and energy.*

Willis was studying me and I wondered if he could see my conviction waning. Finally, he said, "Think about this: 'Let each of you look not only to his own interests, but also to the interests of others.' Rosemary and I are your *others.*"

It was so like him to know just the right verse to back up his point.

"Just think about it, Els. Think about it strongly. Think about the repercussions to our lives."

Repercussions . . . it was a powerful word. I nodded.

"Is there any dessert?" he asked.

For the next day-and-a-half I thought about the presidency. Constantly. I prayed about it—not that I'd get the position, but that if God wanted me to have the position, I'd get it. And to his credit, Willis didn't mention it again.

One thing became clear: I needed to try. If they gave it to Mildred Delvecchio, I would accept defeat graciously.

When the day of the interview came, I wore my pink Easter suit with its matching pillbox hat. I felt like Jackie Kennedy.

I dropped Rosemary at a friend's house and arrived at the Voter office thirty minutes early. I was surprised to see Mildred was already there, sitting in the hall. My first instinct was to quickly turn and ignore her, but she saw me and invited me to sit with her.

"Well," she said with a shaky laugh. "I haven't been this nervous since my late husband proposed."

Late husband? "I'm sorry. I didn't know you were a widow."

"Carl died last year. A heart attack. We'd only been married four years."

How horribly tragic. "I'm so sorry. I'm sure it's hard to be a single mother."

She turned her gaze away from me. "We didn't have any children. Actually, I miscarried one time, and then . . ." She drew in a breath from the bottom of her soul. "I've found it's best to keep busy. Of course I've had to take a job. I have the six to one shift at the Sunshine Diner."

"I like that place." I'd only been there one time with my parents. It was a homey greasy spoon with huge helpings of downhome food.

"Next time you come in, I'll get you a free cinnamon roll."

"That's very nice of you."

She plucked a thread from her skirt. "Obviously, this wasn't the life I'd hoped for, but I'm doing okay. I like to get involved with as many organizations as I can. I mean, why not? There's no one waiting for me at home." She let out a breath and tried on a smile that didn't quite fit. "I guess that's why this position is so important to me. I've heard I don't have the years' experience you do but . . . here's hoping." She put a hand to her mouth. "Oops. Sorry. I'm sure you're hoping *you* get it as much as I am."

I nodded and we shared some silence, but inside my thoughts were chattering. Shouting. Crying out.

You can easily beat her. Just emphasize your experience.

You can easily win because you're more well-spoken. And professional. Mildred wears her heart on her sleeve.

Then suddenly, my thoughts changed, as though I'd turned onto a street that took me in the opposite direction.

She needs this position far more than you do.

She has nothing at home. You have a family.

She's seeking a purpose. You have one.

And then the essence of Willis' Bible verse came to me: Don't just think about yourself, think about others.

Think about Mildred.

We both looked up when three ladies approached. "Good morning," said Mrs. Donovan. She turned to the other two women and made introductions. I nodded, smiled, and shook hands, but remembered no one's name.

"Shall we start with you, Mrs. Masterson?" Mrs. Donovan said.

Chapter 26

Rosemary

"Let your light shine before others,
that they may see your good deeds
and glorify your Father in heaven."
Matthew 5:16

I marveled at my mother's story-telling ability. And hearing about the Mildred Delvecchio of 1966 meshed with the Mildred Delvecchio of today. "So what happened in the interview?"

Mom turned her wedding ring around once, then stopped. "Just as I was going in, I prayed that God would help me say whatever *He* wanted me to say."

"I've prayed that prayer."

"It works, doesn't it?"

I scoffed. "Sometimes too much."

"How so?" Mom asked.

"Sometimes He spurs me not to say anything at all — to be silent."

Mom chuckled. "'Be still, and know that I am God.'"

The verse struck home. "I admit that occasionally, I like to hear myself talk. Too much."

"We all do, dear." She got back to her story. "But on the day of the interview I know God wanted me to speak up, to say what He wanted me to say."

"Which was . . . ?"

"I thanked the committee for the nomination, but I withdrew my name from consideration."

I didn't want to hear that. "Why?"

"Because it was best for my family."

The notion that Mom had quit because Dad wanted her to rose up against every forward stride women had made in the last fifty years. "But *was* it best?" I asked. "It was rude of Dad to even ask you to refuse the position. I mean, the gall. He was living a life of atta-boys and significance. It was your turn."

"That's what I thought at first. I was so frustrated. And on the day of the interview I was ready to win myself the position — in spite of his wishes. Only God could stop me."

"I don't understand what changed between sitting in the hall with Mildred and going into the interview."

"God *did* stop me. He opened my eyes."

"I don't get it." But I did get it. I didn't want to, but I did.

"He opened my eyes to a woman who'd not only lost a husband, but had lost her dream of living happily ever after with him and a houseful of kids."

"I get that you felt sorry for her, but everyone has a sad story to tell. That didn't mean you had to give up your chance."

"But it did. Mildred needed the presidency to give herself a feeling of purpose. I had purpose. I had you, your father, and many other activities. It was time to let someone else shine."

I remembered all the awards displayed on Mildred's wall — her proudest accomplishments. I hadn't seen any family pictures at all. "I don't think she remarried or had kids. Did she?"

"She did not. And see? God knew her future, He knew she *needed* to serve on boards and committees. She needed to contribute to society in her own way. I'm sure He used her there, just as He used me that year by staying at home."

I was confused. "So God used you by sending you on luxurious trips?"

She smiled softly. "Actually, yes."

Trips seemed a frivolous reason for the sacrifice. "So you had fun and spent time with Dad. That's great. But it's not . . . God. Honestly, it seems kind of shallow."

"Good thing God is never shallow." Mom placed a hand on my knee. "And it wasn't just Dad and me. You remember spending time with your Grandma and Grandpa while we were gone."

"The tractor and the chickens."

"And Grandma going to the hospital."

"That was really scary."

"Obviously we were all glad she recovered. But do you remember how she got to the hospital?"

I thought back to images of Grandpa carrying Grandma to the backseat of their car. "I got to sit up front while Grandma lay in the back. Grandpa drove real fast."

Mom shook her head. "Who found her?"

The emotions of the day flooded back to me. "I was on the porch coloring when I heard a thud. That's when I ran inside and found her. She was on the floor of the kitchen, groaning and clutching her chest. It was hard for her to breathe. She told me to go find Grandpa but he was out in a field somewhere. That's when I remembered the big bell outside, the one she rang when she wanted him to come inside."

"You rang that bell and he came running. He helped her get to the hospital. She almost died."

The reminder of how close death had come that day made me shiver. "When she was getting better I heard people talking about how she could have died if . . ."

Mom touched her own nose, then pointed at me. "If you hadn't been there to find her and call for help."

I shivered a second time. "I guess so."

"The only reason you were there—at that exact time—was because your dad and I were on a trip."

It all became clear. "A trip you wouldn't have taken if you'd been state president."

"Exactly."

I wrapped my arms around myself. "You always think that way, Mom. You've always been able to see God's hand in most everything."

"I try."

I needed to try harder. "I'm not always good at that, at seeing Him."

"It takes practice. The old saying that everything happens for a reason is true. God doesn't waste anything. 'In *all* things God works for the good of those who love him, who have been called according to his purpose.'"

I knew that. I even knew the verse. But it was like I'd shoved that God-knowledge into a far corner of my brain. Once in a while I dug it out, but eventually it always ended up back where it started. Hidden from view. My view and everyone else's too.

"The memories are still ripe, aren't they?" Mom said. "You look like you're a million miles away."

Just in a corner.

I ran a hand through my hair to spur myself back to the moment. "So the moral of the story is that I'm supposed to give up the presidency of Beautify Kansas so someone else can have it?" I didn't like the sound of that one bit.

Mom moved a stray strand of hair away from my eyes, the way she'd done my entire life. "I don't know, honey. But here's the deal: you and I are capable women who are willing and able to take control of any project or committee we're on. And often—because a lot of people don't want to be in charge—we're given the chance to step up. But sometimes, we need to be aware of the times when God offers us a chance to sacrifice the pride-of-our ability so others get the chance to serve. Just because we can, doesn't mean we should."

I felt defeated. I shuddered when I thought of my rival, Sandra Carhart, running things. "What if you know the other person wouldn't be good in the position?"

"That Sandra-woman you mentioned when you brought me breakfast the day after the funeral?"

I nodded and thought of a verse I'd quoted during the previous discussion with my mother. "Luke twelve, verse forty-eight says, 'From everyone who has been given much, much will be demanded; and from the one who has been entrusted with much, much more will be asked.' See? I can quote verses too."

She laughed and the tension eased. "Well done. But you used that on me before. You can't use a verse twice."

"Says who?"

Mom shrugged. "There are too many great verses out there. Like Proverbs sixteen, two: 'All a person's ways seem pure to them, but motives are weighed by the Lord.'"

I took offense. "My motives aren't impure. Is there something wrong with wanting to serve in high places?"

"Not at all. But *why* do you want to serve in high places?"

"I would do a good job. As you said, I am capable. And they asked *me*."

Mom shook her head. "All I heard was I, I, me."

I huffed. "If I said I wanted to help people it would sound trite, like a beauty contestant saying she wants to feed the hungry and bring about world peace."

"Trite is better than prideful."

I felt my jaw tighten. If I stayed much longer, I'd get upset. Mom meant well. She always did. But I was through.

I stood to leave. "You've given me a lot to think about."

Mom held out a hand, wanting help to stand. "Then I can declare your treasure hunt a success."

I wasn't so sure but thanked her anyway. "I'll call you tomorrow."

"I may be busy."

"With what?"

"With whom. Please ask Everett to come see me tomorrow. At nine perhaps?"

"What life lesson are you going to teach him? How to deal with an overly ambitious wife?" I rolled my eyes.

"Not at all." Mom touched my hand. "I merely want to share another story with him."

"More life lessons?"

She shrugged. "You're free to take them or leave them."

"We'll see." I kissed her cheek and left. I had no idea what I would take or leave.

I was alone when I drove home from my mother's house, yet the car was filled with voices.

"I just want to spend more time with you," came from Everett.

"Step aside and let someone else shine," came from my mother.

"There are consequences to quitting," was heard in Paige's voice.

"Giving in isn't always a bad choice." Those had been my words to Paige.

When the voices began talking at once I drove into the outer perimeter of a Walmart parking lot. I shut off the car and repeatedly slammed my hands against the steering wheel. "Shut up!"

My shout stopped the voices but left me in a cavernous silence. I grabbed the abused steering wheel. "Father," I whispered. "What good will come from me quitting?"

The silence seeped around me again. But more than *seeped*, it embraced me. I fought it at first, but then it held me tighter, supporting me. Reassuring me.

When I stopped fighting the silence I heard a voice say, *You don't see how good can come from it, but I do.*

I gasped. It was God talking to me. That whole "still, small voice" stuff. He'd done so before, often interjecting His opinions whether I wanted them or not. But this time I'd actually asked.

Sometimes His direction was just a feeling. Sometimes there were words. The big question was whether I'd listen. And act.

I leaned my head against the headrest and closed my eyes. "Quitting goes against the core of who I am."

And who are you?

I covered my face with my hands, trying to pinpoint the core of me. My thoughts rushed to a mental listing of my activities. All of them had one thing in common: I liked to lead and serve. I thrived on it.

Yet all the *things* I accomplished were fleeting. Temporary. And if I didn't do them, someone else would. There was always a Mildred waiting in the wings.

But quitting before I'd even got the position? I felt weak by even considering such a thing.

I was startled when someone tapped on the car window.

Everett?

I glanced in the rearview mirror, noticing the red in my eyes and the flush of my cheeks. I rolled down the window. "Hi."

"Hi, yourself. What are you doing here?"

I didn't look at him. "Long story."

He combed his fingers through his beard. "Are you coming from Elsie's?"

"I am."

"How was it?"

I didn't want to get into it. "It was fine. She wants you to come tomorrow at nine."

He smiled. "I'm good with that—but you didn't answer my first question. Why are you parked here?" When I didn't answer he reached in and touched my chin, turning my head to face him. "Your face is red. Your eyes are . . . iffy. You're upset."

"The consequences of a transparent face."

"Can I help?"

He was utterly sweet, fantastically kind. "I'll be all right. I'm just feeling a little weak right now."

"'When I am weak, then I am strong.' Turn it over to Him, Rosie."

I felt tears threaten. "I'm trying."

His burly fingers touched my cheek. "Remember, I'm here too."

"I know you are." I took his hand and kissed it, feeling so blessed that this man was my man.

He motioned toward the store. "Want to go inside and help me pick out light bulbs?"

I chuckled and felt the relief of *normal*. "No thanks. I trust you completely. I'll meet you at home."

He blew me a kiss and walked away. Even at age sixty-seven he had a spring in his step. I watched as he waved at strangers and helped an elderly woman maneuver her cart to the cart corral.

Yes, indeed. I was lucky to have him.

Was he lucky to have me?

That would take some time to answer.

I stood in my closet and got dressed for my DAR lunch meeting. I wound a silk scarf around my neck. But then I remembered . . .

"I'm supposed to make a scarf for the silent auction!" I'd forgotten all about it. I'd promised the Art Guild over a week ago.

I hurried to my studio which was located in the bedroom that used to be Holly's. I paused in the doorway, looking at the stacks of yarn, fabric, and canvases. It had been ages since I'd done anything creative. "I love to paint," I whispered to the room.

"I know you do."

"Everett! I didn't hear you come in."

He stood beside me, staring into the room. "You going to make something?"

"I *have* to make something. I'm donating a scarf for a silent auction, but I completely forgot about it."

"I'm sure it'll be gorgeous. They always are."

"I didn't know you liked them."

"What's not to like? You have an eye for color." He smiled. "Though I don't think they'd go with my jeans and flannel shirts."

I tugged at his beard, once again feeling blessed. "Thank you for the compliment. And for being you." I booped his nose playfully

He shrugged. "Did you get things worked out in the parking lot?"

Not really. "I'm working on it. I'm just spent. You know how exhausted I can get after spending time with my mother."

"So the treasure hunt was a bust?"

"I wouldn't say that."

He ran a finger over a popped-up nail in the door-casing. "What was the treasure? Did she give you something?"

The question had me stumped. "The treasure wasn't material, it's intellectual. Emotional. And — you know Mom — spiritual."

His eyebrows rose. "All that."

"All that."

"But how did your treasure send you to a Walmart parking lot?"

How could I explain it? "I was upset because it made me think about things. Choices."

"Like what?"

I didn't want to get into it now. "Let's wait until after your hunt is over. Then we'll talk."

"If the hunt is 'all that' I'm not sure I want to go."

I hated that I'd spooked him. "Go. It will be worth it."

Everett screwed up his face, making his mustache lift at an odd angle. He scratched his ear. Then the worry left him and he said, "I'm as hungry as a farmer at lunchtime. Want to go out to eat?"

I thought about my DAR lunch meeting. But seeing my husband's pale blue eyes with the laugh-line crinkles at their corners . . . I'd love to."

Chapter 27

Everett

"God's gifts and his call are irrevocable."
Romans 11: 29

I parked my truck in front of Elsie's. I wasn't one to dress up, but today I'd put on khakis. I could blame Rosie for making me change back into jeans. "Mom doesn't want you looking like anyone but yourself, Ev. Wear jeans. But do put on a clean shirt."

That, I could do.

My carpenter jeans with their reinforced pockets and fabric hook for my hammer was the uniform I'd worn for nearly fifty years. It was as comfortable as I got. I didn't own a pair of sweats, and hated seeing men—or women—out in public wearing plaid pajama pants. There was comfortable, and then there was sloppy.

Elsie would accept the former but be offended by the latter.

I paused on my way to the front door to pick a weed in the flower beds I'd recently cleaned out. I set it on top of the mulch. I'd get rid of it after my visit.

After my treasure hunt.

I wished Rosie had told me more about her hunt. Whatever happened had upset her and made her eyes sad. Yet we *had* enjoyed a great lunch together. Orange chicken and crab Rangoon always made her smile.

But I didn't like going in blind. I was used to having the right tools for the job and wasn't sure what tools I would need today, talking with my mother-in-law about . . . whatever it was she wanted to talk about.

The front door opened. "Morning, Everett. Ready for your turn?"

"As I'll ever be."

She waved a hand at me. "Oh, you. It won't be that bad. I promise."

I went inside, and stuck my hands in my pockets. "I'm as nervous as a turkey in November."

She chuckled. "I can always count on you to make me smile."

"Glad to oblige." I looked around the living room for something out of the ordinary. Nothing looked different. "So how do we do this?"

"Have a seat and we'll begin."

I had a favorite place to sit at Elsie's — on the right end of the couch, nearest the fireplace. I began to sit there when she said, "Sit in Willis's chair. It's way more comfortable."

Wow. The place of honor. Willis' chair was like Archie Bunker's chair in "All in the Family."

I sat in the brown leather rocker-recliner. "This *is* way more comfortable."

"Willis loved that chair. When it started to ugly-out I suggested we get a new one but he was already sick by then and he didn't want to waste money replacing it." She used her cane to walk to the credenza against the far wall and took something out of its top drawer.

I recognized it immediately. It was a wooden playing-card box I'd made them for Christmas years ago. "You want to play cards? I'm lethal at Rummy."

"Nope — at least not today." She handed me the box.

I turned it over in my hands. I'd inlaid the initial M in the lid with walnut veneer. "I can't believe you still have this."

"Of course I have it. It's beautiful. You're very talented."

"This is a blast from the past. It's been years since I thought about woodworking — until I went to clean out Willis' space."

"I'm glad you kept the spot. Now that you're retired, you can get back at it."

I shrugged and handed the box back to her. "I'm not sure anybody wants stuff like this anymore. Rosie gave away a lidded box I made for her — granted it wasn't a great box, but . . ."

"Shame on her."

I didn't hold it against her. Too much. "Times have changed. People don't want to pay a premium for handmade knickknacks or custom furniture, not when the furniture marts of the world have 200 tables to choose from, starting at $99."

"Maybe, but those tables are a dime a dozen, and handmade is always special. Create something to please yourself. You don't need to appeal to the masses but to those few who appreciate the art of it." She got something else out of the drawer. "The card box is just a part of your first clue. Take a look at this."

It was a black and white photo of Elsie standing next to a young woman who was wearing a long coat. Elsie had a pincushion on her wrist and a tape measure around her neck. "That's you?"

"It is. Before the war I did my fair share of sewing. I even took some tailoring and fashion design courses."

"Before the war? World War II?"

She laughed. "The Korean War. Don't add ten years on me, mister, I'm old enough already."

I felt sheepish. I was a history buff. I shouldn't have made such a mistake.

Elsie sat in her chair. "The coat the model is wearing was made of wool, had lining, underlining, interfacing, shoulder pads, bound buttonholes, and utilized every tailoring trick they could teach me." She chuckled. "It weighed about ten pounds. It was like wearing an anvil on my shoulders."

I could imagine her weighed down by such a coat. Elsie was barely five foot tall and a hundred pounds. "But I bet it was warm. Did you end up getting your degree?"

"I didn't. The country was going into its second war in ten years. People's priorities changed — my priorities changed. All I wanted was to be home with my family." She sighed and looked around the room as if memories lived in every corner. "Plus, a career in fashion is frivolous."

Is frivolous. Her voice had become harsh when she'd said the last sentence. "Who said fashion *is* frivolous?"

She smiled. "Those were my mother's words."

I looked at the picture again. "I don't know much about sewing but being able to sew a coat . . . that takes real talent — which is hardly frivolous."

"I appreciate you recognizing that. But as I was learning the intricacies of sewing I learned that life has a way of interrupting the best-laid plans."

"What happened?"

"Willis was called up to fight in Korea."

"That would do it."

"We wanted to be married before he left, so we had a simple wedding." She snapped her fingers once. "Then he was gone. While he fought in the war, I lived with his parents."

"His parents? Not yours?"

She looked past me at something specific.

I turned to see a family photograph on the wall. I went to it. "This is them? And Willis?"

"Bring it here please." She gazed at it a moment, then rested the photo on her knees. "This was taken in early 1952. Willis looked so handsome in his uniform. But see how skinny his father was?"

The man had sunken cheeks and his suit seemed far too big for him. "He looks gaunt, though I don't think I've seen many other pictures of him."

"He's gaunt because he was sick and needed help. That's why I went to live with them. He had some kind of cancer and couldn't work anymore. Which meant there was no money coming in. My mother-in-law Susan couldn't try to find a job because she was needed at home to take care of him."

"So *you* had to work?"

"I did. I was nineteen and had only worked at Kresge's. Obviously with the war, there weren't any job openings for fashion designers — or any need for them. So I quit my classes and got a job as a typist at a doctor's office."

Elsie handed me the photograph and I hung it back on the wall. "I guess such sacrifices were the norm back then," I said. "Country came first."

"'All hard work brings a profit, but mere talk leads only to poverty.'" Elsie confirmed the verse with a nod. "We did what we had to do to survive — especially when Willis was risking his life overseas."

"How long was he gone?"

"Fifteen months. The war ended in 1953. He got back just before his father passed. But then his mother was an emotional wreck. Her husband was gone, her son was home from the war — but married. She didn't want to stay in their big house alone, so we found her a smaller place and moved her."

"She eventually remarried, right?"

"She did. When she met Milton years later, we were happy for her. Their farm was the one Rosemary used to visit."

"I remember him. I met him and Grandma Susan a few times."

Mom nodded. "They were good people. So was my father-in-law." She shook her head, as if shaking away memories. "Back to my story... after we helped Susan move into a smaller home, then — and only then — was it our turn to get our own place."

"How long had you been married by then?"

"Just over two years — though Willis was at war for most of that time." Her eyes filled with happy memories, and I saw a hint of what she looked like as a young woman. "I loved our first cottage. It was tiny but it was ours. Willis got a job at a bank. By then my focus had obviously moved far away from fashion design. And Willis was a proud man. He didn't want me working anywhere. *He* was the breadwinner. And I didn't mind. I loved being a housewife, and eventually a mother."

"I'm sorry you had to let your dream die."

She smiled. "Ah, but I didn't . . ." She held out an envelope. "Follow the next clue, Everett."

I opened the envelope and looked at the note. "Sally Strong at the Chronicle?"

Elsie nodded. "She's waiting for you."

I had only been in the Chronicle's office once, to place an ad for my roofing business. Only once because it hadn't paid for itself. After that I'd relied on word-of-mouth, which *had* kept the work steady and strong. For over forty years.

I went to a receptionist up front. "I'm here to speak with Sally Strong?"

"And you are?"

"Everett Dudley."

She smiled. "We were told to expect you, Mr. Dudley. Follow me."

I was led through a maze of cubicles with people focused on computer screens. It seemed slightly odd to have a newspaper rely on computers — their rival.

We stopped at a small office that was brightly lit by a band of windows. The receptionist introduced me and I went inside.

A middle-aged woman with purple readers stood up and shook my hand. "Nice to meet you, Everett."

"Likewise."

"How's the treasure hunt going?" she asked.

"Pretty well, I suppose. You are clue number two."

"Leave it to Elsie to make things interesting." She handed me a piece of paper that had an address written on it. "Elsie said you are to search for this address in our micro-film collection."

"Your what?"

Sally smiled. "Don't worry. I'll help you through it."

She led me to a computer and showed me how to search for the address in some database. "There you go. Box number 100476. The newspaper for July 3, 1972."

We retrieved a small box with that number and she led me to a fancy-looking machine. "Have a seat."

Inside the box was a small movie reel, though the film was wider than the film reels I'd seen. Step by step she showed me how to load the film. Full pages of a newspaper showed up. Sally instructed me how to move the viewing area around and make it bigger and more focused. Even so my eyes strained to read the type.

"That's all there is to it. The address is in this day's newspaper. I could tell you the page number, but Elsie told me not to."

"Why?"

"She said it would mean more if you had to work for it."

"I'm not so sure about that."

"Good luck, Everett. I've got a bit of digging to do myself, so I'll be right over there. Let me know if you need help."

I was left alone with the machine — and July 3, 1972. The headlines lauded Fourth of July celebrations in Washington D.C., in Carson Creek, and Kansas City. I remembered that day. Rosie and I went to a big fireworks display and had a picnic in the grass. It was one of our first real dates. She'd been sixteen and I'd been almost nineteen.

I scanned the articles, some about Nixon and the Watergate scandal, and others about Vietnam. There were blurbs about local floral shows and obituaries. I skimmed an article about *The Mary Tyler Moore Show*. My own mother had loved that show because it was so out of the norm, being about an unmarried career woman.

The minutes slipped by and I got sidetracked looking at ads. What a different time. Hamburger sold for ninety-eight cents a pound, apples for fifteen, Heinz ketchup for nineteen. There was an ad for a Ford Pinto for $2078 and a gallon of gas for thirty-six cents. Those were the days.

I rubbed my eyes. The screen was hard on them. "Focus, Everett. Find the address."

It was then I noticed that every ad had an address at the bottom. Maybe Elsie's address was in an ad? But an ad for what?

I noticed a slew of classified ads. There were sections for help wanted, real estate, items for sale, services . . . Some were only a few lines, but others had their own headlines and were a bit larger. But how could I find a specific address?

I figured Elsie wouldn't have anything to do with a job or property. Maybe the address would be shown in things to sell. But services seemed the most likely. I looked at ads offering handymen services, Tupperware parties, furniture refinishing, and . . .

"There!" I magnified a small ad, not a half-an-inch-high: *Fashion by Elsie. Dressmaking and Tailoring. Affordable fashion for the discriminating woman. 435 Eastridge Drive. 488-3021.*

"Well, I'll be." It looked like Elsie had found a way to use her fashion talents over twenty years after she'd taken classes.

Sally must have heard me. She came over to check on me. "Did you find it?"

"I did. Look."

Sally read the ad. "No wonder Elsie always looks so sharp. She's a seamstress."

"A fashion designer," I said. "Can I print this page?"

Sally showed me how. We rewound the film and put it in its box. "I'm not sure what I'm supposed to do next."

"*I* happen to have another clue for you." We returned to her office and Sally handed me a note with a name and address on it. "Go see Neda."

"She's expecting me too?"

"I'm sure she is."

"Thanks for your help, Sally."

"Anytime. Tell Elsie hello."

I waved goodbye and left. I was enjoying the clues. I'd always loved the Hardy Boys' books where they solved a mystery by following clues. I was on my own Elsie-adventure.

It only took a few minutes to drive to the next address, which was a newer house on the edge of town. I glanced at the name on the clue before I reached the stoop. *Neda Collins.* I wondered about pronunciation. Was it Nee-da, or Ned-a?

I rang the bell. A very tall woman answered. She was about my age, with a swath of gray hair framing her face. She wore large red glasses. "Everett?"

I didn't want to get it wrong so said, "Mrs. Collins?"

"Neda," she said — using the long *e.* "Come in."

The house had all the newest bells and whistles, with an open concept and white quartz counters in a white kitchen. "This is beautiful," I said. "My wife would love to have a kitchen like this."

"Thank you. I'm afraid I splurged. I just retired and wanted a fresh start."

"I just retired too."

"A mixed blessing, isn't it?"

"As mixed as peanut butter on a BLT."

She made a face. "Eww."

I smiled, being used to the reaction. "It's a family staple. Try it."

We sat in the living room in front of a wide fireplace that was only fifteen-inches high. The opening was surrounded by tile, floor to ceiling.

"You cold? I could —" She didn't wait for me to answer but went to the fireplace and flipped a switch. Flames instantly appeared. "Voila!"

"Pretty nifty. I installed the roofs on a few houses down the street, but I never went inside after they were finished."

"If your wife ever wants to see the kitchen to get ideas, she's welcome any time."

I wasn't sure I could afford to have Rosemary see the kitchen. "Do you have a clue for me?"

"I'll get it." She went into another room and came out with a pink wool jacket with matching pants. "I'd model it for you, but I'm not the same size I was fifty years ago."

"Who is?"

"You're sweet." She held the jacket close for my inspection. "Look at the notched lapels, the bound buttonholes."

I knew nothing about tailoring but could tell it was created with a skilled hand. Elsie's skilled hand? "Very nice."

"And look at this." She pointed at the label tacked on the inside of the collar: *Fashion by Elsie.* "She was a pro, that's for certain."

It was impressive. "Did you answer her ad in the paper?"

Neda draped the suit across the back of a chair. "I did. I'd just landed my first job as a secretary in the mayor's office and needed a professional wardrobe." She swept a hand from her toes to her head. "As you probably noticed, I'm tall — nearly six foot. Nothing off the rack fit me. That's where Elsie came in."

"She filled a need."

"She most certainly did. She made me a whole wardrobe — which my parents generously paid for. I felt like a million bucks. I worked my way up from that first job and was active in state and local government for decades because of the clothes Elsie made me."

"I'm sure your own skills had something to do with it."

Neda nodded. "Of course, but the clothes Elsie created gave me the confidence I needed to excel. I truly believe that."

"Elsie is good at getting people to do their best."

"She is, but it wasn't just that . . ." Her face grew pensive. "Elsie changed my life in a way that was even more important than my career."

"How so?"

Neda stood. "Although I've enjoyed talking with you, Everett, it's at this point in the story that I'm supposed to send you back to Elsie for the end of your treasure hunt."

I shook my head and rose. "She's wearing me out."

Neda laughed. "Elsie Masterson wears everybody out."

I was feeling like a ping-pong ball: go to Elsie's, go to the newspaper, go to Neda's, go to Elsie's . . .

It wasn't that I objected to the steps as much as I was curious how many more there would be. I'd called Rosie to check in and to ask how many clues there'd been on her hunt, but the call had gone to voicemail. She was probably at one of her meetings.

I knocked on Elsie's door, then walked in. She was seated in her chair reading a book with a magnifying glass.

"Hi there. I'm back."

She set everything aside. "How was it?"

I sat in Willis's recliner. "Neda is your biggest fan. She credits you for her success in government."

"She overstates."

I shook my head. "Beyond her career, she said you changed her life in some other, more important way. She said I was supposed to ask *you* about that. What did she mean?"

Her eyes sparkled. "When she and I talked the other day, she mentioned that. I'd wanted you to meet her because of the fashion, but for her to bring up *more?* I'm humbled that she thought I should be the one to tell you that part of the story."

I got comfortable. "I'm all ears."

Chapter 28

Elsie – 1974

"If the home is deserving, let your peace rest on it;
if it is not, let your peace return to you.
If anyone will not welcome you or listen to your words,
leave that home or town and shake the dust off your feet."
Matthew 10: 13-14

I entered Jeanne's Sewing Emporium and was greeted by Charity, my favorite clerk.

"Do you have a new project going, Elsie?"

"I'm meeting Neda here."

Charity nodded. "That's always fun."

"Especially fun this time because she's asked me to make her wedding dress."

Charity clapped her hands. "Oooh. Do you know what style she likes?"

"I don't, and I hazard to guess. Styles are all over the place right now. From jumpsuits to ball gowns to—"

Charity made a face. "It's the Seventies. Anything goes." She looked past me toward the doors. "There she is. Good luck."

Neda saw me and waved. "I'm here! Let the designing of the wedding gown commence! Show me the fancies." She leaned down and gave me a hug. "As you see, I'm a bit excited."

"You should be. It's not every day a woman gets married."

"It's not every day a woman who's six-feet tall finds a man who's taller."

"You *could* be taller than your husband."

Neda shook her head vehemently. "Finding a man who wouldn't mind that would be a rarity indeed."

I glanced toward the door. "I thought your mother might come along?"

Her expression changed from joy to disappointment. "Mother wants me to go to a fancy bridal salon in New York. That is so not me. I was adamant that I want you to make my dress."

I felt the weight of her faith in me. "I am honored to do it." Although I'd made a half-dozen wedding dresses, the process was challenging. It stretched me to the full breadth of my skills.

"So," Neda said, wiggling her fingers toward the fabric. "Lead me to the satin and lace."

"Actually," I said, "my experience suggests we start somewhere else. Although you and I usually start with a fabric you like and then choose a pattern, wedding dresses start with the design, which leads to the fabric." I led the way to the pattern books and we sat next to each other. I pulled a Vogue and a McCalls pattern book close and asked *the* question: "What style are we looking for?"

She gave me a wicked smile. "It's a little outside my norm. You probably won't believe it."

"Why?"

"Because I don't want anything tailored like you usually design for my work clothes. I want something just the opposite: playful and flowy, maybe Bohemian?"

"Hippie?"

She nodded enthusiastically. "With a wide-brimmed hat like Farrah Faucett wore when she married Lee Majors."

I vaguely remembered seeing magazine photographs.

Neda fluttered her hands around her head like she was spreading fairy dust. "I want to look totally and utterly feminine."

Girly was *not* her usual style, but I *could* imagine her in such a dress. "We can definitely do that."

We looked through pages and pages of patterns and, as expected, saw everything from poufy skirts to culottes. Many dresses were overly covered with high-necked bodices and long sleeves. We both agreed Neda wanted a skirt that would flow and a neckline that would allow her to breathe.

We looked through half the book before we finally turned a page, both pegged a finger onto a picture, and said in sync, "This one!"

We studied the picture of a dress with an empire waist, short puffed sleeves, and a wide neck and skirt ruffle.

"This is who I want to be on my wedding day," Neda said in a whisper.

"You'll look beautiful in it."

When I looked at her face, her eyes were filled with tears. "Barry's going to love it."

I put my arm around her shoulders. "Yes, he will."

I got the pattern in her size. "*Now*, we look for fabric."

We walked down the rows of white fabric, chatting about this and that. That's when I realized I didn't know the other details of the wedding. "What colors are you wanting for the bridesmaids?"

"Yellow, I think. With a lime green for the flower girl."

I was glad she'd thought about it. "Those are perfect colors for a summer wedding. Where is the ceremony?"

"It's up in the air."

"Don't you need to know that?"

Neda sighed deeply. "My parents want us to be married in their church, Barry wants us to be married in his church. And I'm ready to choose a meadow somewhere."

I'd noticed something odd. "You mentioned your parents' church and Barry's church. Which church is yours?"

She shrugged. "I'm not into church much."

"Why not?"

Neda fingered a bolt of white satin, her eyes downcast. "It's complicated. But I've been doing okay on my own."

"On your own?"

"Without God."

I didn't know what to say. I'd been sewing for Neda for over two years. Although we hadn't talked directly about God or faith, I'd never gotten any indication that she felt an animosity toward Him. "I had no idea you felt this way."

"Yeah. Well." She shrugged. "I understand Barry wanting it— he's an amazing man and believes in all that God-stuff. But my parents?" She scoffed. "They want it in their church for the show of it. They're complete hypocrites."

I didn't know what to say. I'd met Neda's mother a few times and she'd seemed like a lovely woman. "Why do you say that about them?"

Neda looked around the store. We were alone in the bridal corner, with only Charity popping in and out to return cut bolts to their proper place. "I grew up going to church every Sunday. I got attendance ribbons, memorized the verses, and sang in the choir."

"But . . . ?"

"For my entire life I saw my parents put on a holy face in public even after they'd argued all the way to the church and argued all the way home. As a kid it bothered me but it was all I knew. But as I got older I realized they were hypocrites. Playing a part."

I hesitated a moment and considered her situation. "*They* were the hypocrites, not God."

I watched her arms tense up. "They're rich. My dad makes tons of money."

Which was how they could pay for her custom wardrobe. "There's nothing wrong with money."

"There is if you cheat people to get it."

Now *that* was interesting. "What makes you say that?"

She shook her head. "In between their arguments I remember hearing them conspire and even celebrate the extra money Dad made, and the not-so-right ways he made it. Even I knew about 'Thou shalt not steal'."

They stole money?

Neda continued. "In high school I spent a lot of time at my best friend's house. Sydney Burton. Their living room would fit into my parent's bedroom. They didn't even have a dishwasher or a color TV, and Sydney wore the same clothes a lot. I don't remember what her dad did for a living, but I knew they barely got by. Yet her parents didn't argue."

"In front of you."

"No. They didn't argue. I talked to Sydney about it. She said her parents got through hard times by praying together."

"That's commendable."

She sighed. "I know it's awful but I remember praying that *they'd* be my parents."

How sad. "I'm sorry you felt that way."

"I knew it was a dumb prayer, but the contrast of how I felt at their house compared to how I felt in mine was huge. Like living in the light versus the dark."

Sydney's family had been a role model for Neda. But something didn't fit. "You wanted to emulate the Burtons, and they were close to God and went to church, so why are you against Him?"

Neda turned around, leaning against the bolts. She crossed her arms, her face drawn. "When Sydney and I were seniors, Mr. Burton was killed in an accident at work."

"That's horrible."

"Completely. I remember wondering why God would punish that good family while my bad family got all the blessings."

I had no idea what to say. Neda's question was a question for the ages. "God's ways are not our ways."

"No, they aren't."

I hated that I wasn't helping. I changed the direction of the conversation a little. "Have you kept in touch with Sydney?"

"I have."

"How are she and her mother doing?"

"Sydney got married and is a teacher in Rhode Island. And her mom met a great guy and they opened a café in Minnesota."

"So that's good."

"Well, yeah. But they had to go through so much pain. That's why I'm not into God. He hurts good people yet lets my parents ride easy."

I set the dress pattern on top of the bolts and touched her arm. "I don't know why bad things happen to good people. Nobody does. But I do know that people like the Burtons enjoyed a life of faith and love before the father died, and they leaned on that faith afterward."

"I know they did. Sydney talked to me about it. She hates that I don't believe anymore."

"She loves you. *I* love you. And God loves you more than you can fathom. He's brought a great man into your life, yes?"

"Barry's amazing."

"Can you change your parents?"

She huffed. "Believe me, I've tried. I had so many questions about life and God and how unfair things were. I called Dad out on some of his iffy financial stuff too, but he cut me off. They told me it was none of my business. And they certainly didn't like to hear about how wonderful the Burtons were."

I thought of something Jesus said to his disciples. "Jesus and his disciples went from town to town, telling people how radically different their lives could be by believing that Jesus was the Son of God. Sometimes they'd be welcomed and sometimes they'd be bodily thrown out of town."

"That's harsh."

"Your parents were harsh when they wouldn't talk about your questions. And when you tried to tell them how things could be better and they rejected it."

She shrugged. "What did Jesus tell the disciples to do when they were kicked out?"

"He said to shake the dust off their feet and move on."

"Really?"

Her relief was pitiful. "Really. It's not your job to change your parents' minds or actions. You showed your concern, you wanted them to be honest, you wanted to talk about the Burton's genuine faith, and since they rejected you? You're allowed to move on."

"Well good, because that's what I did when I moved out."

"Partially."

"What do you mean?"

"I mean you threw out the baby with the bathwater."

Neda cocked her head and smiled. "You're comparing God to a baby?"

Oh dear. "When you moved out of your parents' home you gave up church and God and faith—which you knew were good things by watching the Burtons. You did that because of your parents."

Neda bit her lip. "Yeah. I guess I did."

"Now you've found a godly man, yes?"

"Barry's the most godly man I've ever met—even counting Mr. Burton. I've been going to church with him, but I'm just not feeling it. I keep remembering my parents."

"Don't. Think of Barry. Think of how God has brought you together. Embrace the fact he wants to marry you in a church with God's blessings. Your married life and your faith life doesn't have to be like your parents'. It can be better and it will be better if you ask God along for the ride."

Neda pressed her hands against her chest. "Why does it have to be so complicated?"

"It isn't. Not really. God loves you and Barry loves you. Focus on that. And love them back."

She nodded but her face was still in pain. "My parents say they love me too."

"I'm sure they do." I rubbed a hand across her back. "They love you imperfectly, as we all are imperfect. This wedding might be a chance to draw everyone together. Start fresh."

I saw the first hint of a smile. "I'd like that." Then Neda drew me into her arms. "Thanks, Elsie. You changed my life today."

I was glad I could help.

We ended up choosing a lovely, embroidered eyelet for Neda's dress and some thick lace to attach to the neck ruffle. Neda proudly paid for the supplies—another indication she was truly an independent woman, free of her parents.

We hugged at the door, but then I realized I'd forgotten to buy thread. As I walked back inside, Charity got my attention, motioning me close.

"I overheard what you said to Neda." She added quickly, "I didn't purposely eavesdrop, but what you said meant a lot to me too. God bless you, Elsie." She gave me an awkward hug. "You got two for one today."

I was overcome with gratitude.

Everyone likes to get two for the price of One.

Chapter 29

Everett

"Let the wise listen and add to their learning,
and let the discerning get guidance."
Proverbs 1: 5

Elsie grinned. "Everyone likes to get two for the price of One."

I felt the full weight of Elsie's story about Neda. And God. And faith. I was in awe of the woman sitting before me. I'd known her for over forty years, yet realized I knew very little about her *before* life.

"You're quiet, Everett," she said.

"I'm soaking it in like a parched garden soaks in rain."

"That's a beautiful way to put it."

I brushed away her compliment. "Now I see why Neda said you'd done more for her than just sewing."

Elsie put a hand to her heart. "What struck me then and still strikes me now, is that the conversation was totally unplanned. We were there to design a wedding dress, not talk about faith and Jesus. And when it started I didn't even know where I wanted the conversation to go. The words just spilled out of me. It was God's doing, plain and simple."

"I don't think there was anything plain and simple about any of it."

Her eyes were intense. "There, you're wrong. If I'd been in charge, if I'd planned this big change-your-life talk to have with Neda, it would have been overly complex, and it would have failed. The Holy Spirit did the talking through me—in spite of me. He gave me the right words at the right time because He knew Neda and knew exactly what she needed to hear."

I was in awe. "You're special that way, Elsie. It's like you and God have each other on speed-dial. That's never happened to me."

She held up a finger. "That you realize."

I shrugged. I truly couldn't think of a time I'd had a Jesus-talk with anyone. "I believe in God, Jesus, the Cross, all of it. But I don't go around talking to people about it. It's not my way."

"Yet. Just like I didn't plan my conversation with Neda, there may come a time when you'll get a chance to share, even if it's not your thing."

I shook my head. "I'm good with a hammer, not with words."

"That's when you let God handle it. Be open to Him working through you, Everett. I know your faith is strong."

I felt a bit uncomfortable calling her on it, but said it anyway. "How do you know that?"

"You've heard of St. Francis of Assisi, haven't you?"

I hoped this wouldn't be a quiz because I didn't know much about bookish things. "I know a little. Is he the one that lived hundreds of years ago in Italy? He was rich and gave it all up to help people?"

She nodded once. "It appears you know a lot. Anyway, these words are often attributed to him: 'Preach the gospel; if necessary use words.'"

"Which means . . . ?"

"We're to tell people about Jesus by our actions *and* our words. I see Him in so many things you do. Your name comes up at church all the time with people mentioned the favors you've done, kindnesses you've shared. Like coming to clean out my flower beds and Willis's shop. Plus, willingly spending time with an old woman like me."

That was sweet. "I like spending time with you, Elsie. And I don't mind helping out."

"Which you do often. I know you shoveled Mrs. Grainger's driveway last winter — without telling her about it."

"She saw me? I thought she was at her daughter's."

"She was, but her neighbor saw you do it and told her it was you."

I remembered talking to the neighbor while he cleared his own driveway. "I asked him not to tell her."

Elsie opened her hands. "You show God's love through humble action."

"But I'm not preaching. I wouldn't be comfortable preaching."

"Your giving attitude can make people wonder what makes you so joyful about life." She grinned at me. "Come on, Everett. What is the source of your joy?"

I rarely said His name out loud. "Jesus?"

"Say it without the question mark."

I nodded. "Jesus."

"Much better."

I shifted in the recliner. "But I don't help people because of Him. I do it because it's the right thing to do. The Golden Rule and all that."

"'And all that' is Matthew chapter seven, verse twelve."

"The Golden Rule is in the Bible? I didn't realize."

"A lot of people don't. You want to know another way I see Jesus in you?"

"Please." She was filling me up.

"The way you tolerate my daughter."

I was taken aback. I had never heard Elsie speak ill of Rosie. "I do more than tolerate her, I love her."

"Which shows. Has Rosie told you about her treasure hunt?"

"Not yet. She wanted to wait until after I had mine."

"Interesting." She cocked her head, thinking. "By the way, the essence of your two stories interconnect."

I ran my fingers through my beard. "Pardon me for saying this, but I'm not sure what lesson came from me talking to Neda except that I need to be open to talking about my faith."

Elsie waved her hands, agitated. "Yes, yes. Of course that, but you need to remember the beginning of the hunt."

I tried to think back a few hours — which seemed like ages ago. "Sometimes my brain is as foggy as a campfire doused with water."

"Clue number one was . . . ?"

The fog cleared. "The coat you made in school. Your dream of being a fashion designer."

Elsie held one hand out, palm up. "That was in 1952." She held out her other hand. "Sewing for Neda was in . . . ?"

I remembered the microfilm. "1972."

"And my Jesus conversation was in seventy-four. The point is, I began sewing for people when Rosemary was in high school. So there was twenty years between the beginning of my dream and living it out — for twenty more years. I sewed for people well into the nineties."

"Why did you stop?"

She shrugged. "Life gave me detours. My parents needed me. My mother had a heart attack in '87, and was never the same robust woman after that. Daddy was worn out, and helping them took a lot of my time. Fifteen years ago I fell on the ice and broke some fingers. After that, the arthritis moved in." She flexed her fingers.

I could tell her joints were swollen. Yet after my meeting with Neda it was easy for me to imagine her hands cutting out fabric and sewing.

"Willis retired and wanted to travel more, and then my eyesight betrayed me. Bit by bit the option to sew was taken away. But boy, did I enjoy it for a good long while. No, I wasn't a fashion designer, but I did use my gift." She smiled. "Just as you can use yours — your woodworking."

I was surprised to feel a surge of excitement. "I do have quite a few tools of my own that I could add to the ones at Willis' space."

"Your space." Elsie wiggled her forefinger in a figure eight. "I can see your mind making all sorts of plans."

"I'm afraid my thoughts are like bumper cars right now."

She laughed. "You don't have to figure it all out at once. Like the Good Book says, 'There is a time for everything, and a season for every activity under the heavens.'"

"Sounds like a song by the Byrds." I knew it well and sang it. "'For every time, there is a season, turn, turn, turn, and a time for every purpose —"

She finished the line with me. "'Under heaven.' That song was based on the first book of Ecclesiastes in the Bible, written by the wisest man to ever live, King Solomon."

"Wisest man, huh? Obviously, not the humblest."

I'd said it as a joke, but Elsie took it seriously. "God proclaimed him the wisest man. He offered Solomon anything he wanted, and because Solomon didn't ask for riches or power, but asked for wisdom, God gave him all three."

"Now *that* was wise."

She pretended to be disgusted with me. "The point, Mr. Wise-cracker, is that a God-given gift should not be wasted. There are detours that can lead to better roads. Remember, it's not just the destination that's important but the journey."

"Woodworking *would* give me something to do. Rosie's not that keen on me being underfoot and with Paige and Baylor growing up on me. . ."

Elsie nodded slowly. "Keep your eyes open and let's see what He does." Then she motioned me close. "Come give me a hug and be off with you. Your treasure hunt is officially over."

"I'm not so sure about that."

She gave me an extra squeeze. "Feel free to pick some flowers to take home with you."

What an excellent idea.

I could hardly wait to get home to Rosie. I had a gut feeling that things between us would be better from now on.

If she would listen and *if* we both worked on it.

When I opened the garage door I was glad to see her car inside. That, in itself, was a miracle.

Stop that. It would do no good to expect the worst, be a pessimist, or act snarky. Rosie had spent time with Elsie too. As God worked through Elsie to help me, He most likely worked through Elsie to help my wife.

I gathered the mums and asters I'd picked from Elsie's garden and headed inside. I paused at the kitchen door to check in with *our* God: *Bless us, Lord. Help us.*

I went inside. "Rosie?"

"In here."

I walked through the back hall into the kitchen. She was dunking a tea bag in a mug. "I'm making tea. Do you want —?" She saw the flowers.

"For you." I handed her the bouquet and kissed her cheek.

"They're beautiful. What's the occasion?"

I'd thought about how to answer this question on the way home. "The flowers are to celebrate the successful completion of our treasure hunts."

She chuckled. "We made it out alive."

"We did." I got a vase out of the cupboard.

Rosie filled it with water and began plucking off extra leaves as she arranged the flowers. "You seem happy."

"More than that. I am inspired."

Her gray eyebrows rose. "Really?"

I was surprised by her reaction. "Aren't you?"

She paused with a gold aster in her hand. "I'm . . . thinking."

"That's not all bad."

"It's too early to say."

It was time for a talk. "Finish that up and I'll bring our tea out to the garden."

We finished our tasks at the same time and went outside to the lawn chairs that gave us a great view of the flowers we'd planted over the span of many decades.

As soon as we sat, Rosie shivered. "It's warm in the sun, but here in the shade . . ."

"I'll get your jacket." I gathered one for myself, along with an afghan for her legs. Rosie was always cold.

"Why thank you, sir," she said, giving me a rare lingering smile. Soon she was settled. "So. Tell me," she said. "What treasure did Mom help you discover?"

I would have preferred she go first, but went ahead. "I definitely want to dig out my old woodworking tools and set up shop where your dad had a space. For real. To make things again."

Her eyes grew large. "How did the treasure hunt lead you to that?"

I told her the story about Elsie's fashion hopes taking decades to come about in a simpler form. "I used to make wood things but when my grandpa died and making a living took over, I let it go. Now that I'm retired I can get back to it again." I thought of the song again. "'To every thing, turn, turn, turn, there is a season...'"

"'Turn, turn, turn,'" she sang.

Together we finished the verse. "'And a time to every purpose under heaven.'" Just like with Elsie.

We laughed. It felt good to laugh.

I set my tea on the ground beside me. "So. What do you think about me working in the shop?"

"I think it's marvelous."

"Good."

"But . . ."

I braced myself for something negative.

"But what kind of stuff are you going to make? More boxes? Wooden toys? What?"

My defenses rose. "I'm not sure. I know you don't like the box I made you, but —"

"How many times do I have to apologize for that? I'm sorry I gave it away. I'd forgotten you made it."

Which shows how I rate. But I didn't say it out loud. It was amazing how old arguments rose so quickly. We needed to change that habit immediately. "It's not about selling things or even showing them off. It's about being creative, using my hands. It's about the process." I looked out over the domes of mum bushes. "Some of my best memories are about working with Grandpa in his shop."

We sat in silence a moment. "A few days ago you mentioned teaching Baylor?"

"If he's willing, I'd love to. I'll ask him."

"That would be nice. I think Baylor could use some extra attention."

"Couldn't we all."

She looked in my direction. "What's that supposed to mean?"

She knew exactly what it meant but I said it again. "It means that I want to spend more time with you."

She blinked, then looked away. "You're going to be busy in your workshop."

"Rosie . . . come on. You know what I mean."

She sighed deeply and I braced myself for her to get defensive. Instead, she said, "I do know what you mean. In fact, I've decided I'm not going to accept the state position with Beautify Kansas."

Where did that come from? "What? Why? You said it's an honor."

"It is. But . . ." With difficulty she pushed herself forward to sit on the edge of the seat. "My treasure hunt was about letting other people shine."

"Which other people?"

"Sandra Carhart."

I pointed at her shoulders. "You actually shuddered when you said her name. Is she that bad?"

"Yes. I . . . I mean no. She's not that *bad*. She can do it. There's just a hint of desperation in her that makes me cringe."

"Desperation for what? Power?"

She shook her head. "I don't think it's that. It's more a desperation for acceptance."

I understood that one. "Everybody wants to feel like they belong and are appreciated." I purposely leveled her with a look. "Don't you agree?"

"Point made and point taken."

I took a sip of my forgotten tea. It was cold. "Maybe Sandra needs the position more than you."

"You sound like my mother."

"That's not a bad thing."

She didn't answer but drank her tea.

I could see how hard this was for her. "I'm proud of you, Rosie. And I appreciate your sacrifice."

"Thanks." But she wasn't smiling. "I think we each have a phone call to make."

I wasn't sure what she was talking about.

"You can call Baylor about the shop. And I'll call the nominating committee. In fact, I was thinking of quitting the entire organization."

"Rosie, no." I sat forward so I could touch her arm. "You don't have to do that."

She sighed deeply. "The truth is, I want to spend more time with you too."

My heart swelled like a boy getting his first kiss. "Well, I'll be. That's good to hear."

She gave me a gentle look beneath her lashes. "You know I love you."

"I believe I do." I stood and pulled her into my arms. "We'll find a new way, Rosie. A better way."

She nodded against my shoulder. "It's crazy we have my mother to thank for all this."

I had the feeling I'd be thanking Elsie a lot in the coming days.

Chapter 30

Holly & Baylor

"A gentle answer turns away wrath,
but a harsh word stirs up anger."
Proverbs 15: 1

I sat at the island and looked at my phone to check new house listings. Not that I had any clients that were looking at the moment. It was a problem. Ever since the Livermores dropped me I hadn't had any prospective buyers. I only had one listing but it was turning into a time-zapping loser. My career was in the pits.

Baylor came in the kitchen, his hair tousled from sleep. "Hey."

"Hey yourself." I thought about continuing to work, but remembered my promise to try to be more . . . motherly. I shut off my phone and turned it face down on the counter. "What do you have planned for this fine Saturday?"

"Grandpa wants me to come over." He opened the freezer and got out a Hot Pocket.

My dad wanted him to come over? I pushed away a twinge of jealousy. "Why did he ask you?"

He chuckled. "I don't think that came out the way you wanted it to."

Mother of the year over here. I got up to top off my coffee and poured Baylor a cup. He usually drowned it in sugar and creamer, but so be it. "Let me rephrase that. Any special reason for the invitation?"

He put his breakfast in the microwave. "Something about his shop."

"He doesn't have a shop."

"That's what I said. Apparently, he's going to set one up and wants me to help. He said we were going to make a molehill out of a mountain—whatever that means. What are you doing today?"

"Not much."

"You want to come along?"

"And work with tools and stuff? I don't think so."

"You could visit with Grandma."

It was not on my top ten for a Saturday.

My phone rang and vibrated noisily against the counter. I picked it up, hoping it was a client, and nearly refused the call when I saw it was *my* grandmother.

"Aren't you going to answer it?" Baylor asked.

I smiled sheepishly as guilt won out. "Hi, Nana. How you doing?"

"I'm doing quite dandy, but I need you to come over. It's time for your treasure hunt — past time."

I tried to think of a good excuse. "Sorry but I'm busy today. I'm going over to help Dad set up some sort of shop."

"That's good. You do that. Encourage him, Holly. He's a man of many talents."

I cringed at the thought of being gifted some homemade creation in the future. "I'll talk to you later." I hung up, relieved that I'd avoided the hunt yet again.

Baylor sat on the stool next to me and blew on the steaming Hot Pocket. "I'm glad you changed your mind about coming with me."

Just because I'd said it didn't mean I wanted to do it. "We'll see." I started scrolling on my phone again.

"So much for trying not to work all the time, Mom."

Shoot. This was going to be a hard habit to break. I shut it off. Again.

He licked his fingers noisily. "Have you seen Paige's podcasts?"

"What are you talking about?"

"Here." He took my phone and swiped to another page. "Fun with Food. Watch."

I watched Paige give a cooking demonstration on how to make macarons. She was totally at ease. Friendly yet professional. "When did this happen?"

He took the phone back and checked. "Almost two weeks ago. She's made three so far: a chocolate mousse, a baked ziti, and this one. It's cross-posted on two different sites. Look how many views she has."

I rounded down. "Twenty-six thousand?"

"It's gone viral. Kind of."

"You've talked to her about these videos?"

"Well, yeah. We talk almost every day."

I scowled. Sure. Shame me, boy. I hadn't talked to Paige since . . .

?

Never mind.

"Isn't it cool? She asked me to come over and watch the next time she made one. And bonus, I get to eat whatever she makes."

She didn't ask me. She didn't even tell me.

Or did she try to tell me? I remembered some phone message about cooking but thought it was more job drama so I hadn't called back.

Vernon came in the kitchen dressed in golf gear. He headed to the coffee pot. "What are you two talking about?"

"Paige's amazing podcasts," I bragged.

"How many views is she up to now?" he asked.

Vernon knew about it?

Baylor showed him the latest numbers and they chatted about her success.

"Can I have my phone back please?" I held out my hand.

Baylor set it in my palm. "Don't you think it's awesome?"

"Of course it is. She is." I got an idea. "What if I made a podcast of me, giving a tour of a house?"

Vernon and Baylor shared a look of disgust.

Why were they acting like that? I got off the stool. "What's wrong with that idea? If Paige can do it, I can do —"

Baylor rolled his eyes. "It's not always about you, Mom."

Low blow. "I'm not saying it is."

Vernon stirred sweetener in his travel mug. "You could let Paige keep a little glory to herself before you commandeer her idea."

Now they were being mean. "So Paige is the only one allowed to make a video of herself?"

"Of course not," Vernon said. "But your timing . . ."

Whatever. I poured the rest of my coffee into the sink. "You're right. Timing is everything. It's late. I need to get to work."

"What happened to coming with me to help Grandpa?" Baylor asked.

"Plans change. Ta ta."

I hadn't planned to go into work, but they hadn't given me much choice. Nana wanted to teach me a lesson and my family wanted to one-up me.

I hated when they ganged up on me.

I walked to Grandpa and Grandma's house. My stomach had butterflies. I hadn't spent any time with them since that stupid night when I'd run away.

The night in the pool house seemed like a lifetime ago. I'd been so mad at everybody. Nana's treasure hunt had helped me sort through it, and I was trying to take her advice to "take a chill pill." Just thinking of her saying those words made me smile. She was one cool lady.

She'd also told me we needed to appreciate each other. Love each other, no matter what. I wished Mom and Dad would do that with each other. Was she still mad at Dad about Brianna? I hated everything about it though Dad was making a real effort to do all the right things. He'd apologized to everybody and promised he wasn't hanging out with Brianna anymore. He'd been wrong but if he'd needed someone to talk to because Mom wouldn't talk? I got it. He and I had spent three evenings together this week. We'd even watched a ball game. He'd taught me about penalties like pass interference and roughing the kicker. Score.

Mom hadn't joined us. I could tell she was trying to pay more attention to me, but it was hard for her. I don't know why. She pretended to care and tried to be interested, but it always seemed more of a should-do than a want-to-do. It was like me in biology class. I put on a good show for the teacher, nodding and taking notes while the whole time I was thinking about my new video game or the superhero movies that were coming out.

Mom was always doing two things at once, being there but not. She'd told me it was a gift, but it felt more like an excuse.

She was full of excuses. I thought about Nana's phone call where she'd invited Mom to have her treasure hunt. Mom had lied to get out of it. What was she so afraid of?

I cut across the grass to the front door. The best thing about Grandpa and Grandma is that I always knew where I stood with them. *They* appreciated me and loved me no matter what.

Grandpa was waiting for me on the porch. "Come in, my boy. I've been waiting for you as long as June is to December."

It was nice to be wanted.

Grandpa and I lifted some tubs of tools into the bed of his pickup and he closed the tailgate. "Now then. Let's get to the shop and we can get set up."

As we drove, Grandpa turned the radio to the oldies station. I didn't mind a bit. There was something about old music that made me feel calm. Homey even.

"What kind of stuff are you going to make, Grandpa?"

"We, Bayo. We."

I liked the sounds of that.

He chuckled. "Honestly, I have no idea. What do you think we should make?"

"I have no idea either. Does it matter?"

"Nope," Grandpa said. "Not a bit."

"I heard you and Grandma both had your treasure hunts. How was it?"

"Enlightening. Want to hear a story about Nana and sewing?"

"Sewing?" I didn't want to hear about sewing. We were going to a manly woodworking shop.

"Sewing. *And* woodworking," he added.

"Sure. I guess."

Grandpa retold the story and laid it all out there. He was a great storyteller and I liked the story. Now, him asking me to the shop made sense.

We arrived at a warehouse kind of building and went inside. There were dozens of workbenches along the sides, with lockers and sawdust everywhere, and power tools in the middle for everybody to use.

"This is awesome."

"I thought so too. This was Papa's space. Now it's mine — and yours."

"Double awesome."

There were a few men working on their projects. Grandpa said, "Ours is at the end, down there. But I want you to meet someone." He held up a hand. "Hey Doug!"

An old man looked up, but I barely saw him as I was distracted by the guy standing next to him . . . "Colton?"

Colton blinked at me. "Baylor. What are you doing here?"

"Well, I'll be," Grandpa said. "You boys know each other?"

"We do. From school," I said. Although Colton and Clark hadn't bullied me since the test, I was still wary.

Colton brushed some sawdust from the workbench to the floor. "Baylor helped me study for a test."

Doug's old face brightened. "The one you knocked out of the park?"

"I got a B."

Doug clapped him on the shoulder. "I am so proud of this boy. He's working hard on his schoolwork so he can grab himself a proper future."

I remembered Colton mentioning a grandpa who encouraged him.

Doug continued. "His cousin, Clark, could follow his example."

From the look on Colton's face, I guessed that Clark had flunked the test. He seemed uncomfortable with the conversation and said, "Want to see what we're making?"

They showed us an end table. I liked the fancy legs. "How do you make them curve like this?"

They ended up showing us how to use the lathe, the scroll-saw, the chisels, and the router. The tools made me want to make something. Anything. I tried to make a leg with a scrap piece. Turns out I loved the smell of cut wood and using my hands to create something.

Grandpa and Doug found lots to talk about. And Colton and I . . . we did okay too.

After we'd been there awhile I asked, "Does Clark come here too?"

Colton shrugged. "Not much. He's come once or twice, but I like it better when it's just me." He was helping me sort nails and screws into jars. "I saved you yesterday."

"Saved me?"

"From Clark. We saw you walking home and he wanted to go after you, but I told him not to. I told him I was done with crud like that."

"Wow. And he listened."

Colton scoffed. "He tripped *me* instead. It may take a while for him to . . . you know . . . move on."

"Thanks. I mean it. Thanks."

By the time we packed up to go home, Colton and I were square and Grandpa and I had ourselves a shop. I couldn't have asked for a better day.

Chapter 31

Paige

"The Lord is my light and my salvation —
whom shall I fear?
The Lord is the stronghold of my life —
of whom shall I be afraid?"
Psalm 27: 1

Before my neighbor Carlos, I had never met a man who liked to shop. It had been his idea to buy some bright-colored mixing bowls and measuring cups for my podcasts. "You're all about making cooking fun, and bright colors are fun."

Of course, Camille had agreed, and so our Sunday afternoon was spent shopping.

We walked the mall, having already checked the two department stores. There'd been some royal blue and red bowls, but those weren't my colors.

"There!" I spotted a set in a store window. Orange, yellow and lime green.

"Perfect!" Carlos took my hand and pulled me inside.

Camille quickly found some matching measuring cups and spoons. "Voila!"

I felt giddy, especially when Carlos found matching cutting boards. And knives.

I dismissed the latter. "Each chef has their own knives. Good ones. Not just pretty ones."

He pretended to pout. "You're no fun."

"Actually, I'm a lot of fun — I'm having a lot of . . . fun." I'd spotted someone I knew. Or sort of knew.

My friends looked where I was looking. "Who's that?" Camille asked.

I kept my voice low. "That's Drew's ex, Barbie."

"Her name is actually Barbie?" Carlos asked. "Poor thing."

Barbie must have heard her name, for she turned in our direction.

I wanted to turn away, but it was too late.

Barbie walked toward me. "Hi, Paige. Nice to see you."

Not really. It was awkward. We'd met each other before Drew dumped her for me. "Nice to see you too."

Barbie saw the bowls and cups. "I saw your podcasts."

"You did?"

"I made the mousse for my husband the other night and he loved it."

I smiled, then hesitated. "Great. Wait . . . you got married?"

"I did."

"Congratulations."

Barbie adjusted her purse on her shoulder. "Things are going really good. Brent is the greatest guy. *He* supports my talents and dreams as much as I support his."

She seemed to be overly sharing considering we hadn't seen each other in a few years. Plus, there seemed to be a dig in there, but I didn't have time to dissect it.

"I'm going to be a nurse now," she added out of the blue.

Okay . . . "That's impressive. Again, congratulations."

She nodded once. "I'm surprised Drew is allowing you to make the videos. That's not like him. He doesn't like anything that bites into *his* time." She eyed me up and down. "But you know that."

I knew that. But I didn't have to worry about that anymore. "Actually, we're not together anymore."

Her eyebrows rose. "Really? Good for you."

Carlos stepped forward. "Hi. I'm her producer." He turned to Camille. "And this is her production designer."

"Glad to meet you." Barbie glanced toward the door. "I have to get going, but kudos on your podcasts. Keep them up." She took a few steps, then turned back, her face softening. "I'm so glad neither of us settled."

"Wow," Camille said after she walked away. "She does *not* like Drew."

"I don't like Drew," Carlos said. "And if you're honest, you don't either, Cam."

Camille's eyes flit from her brother to me and back. "I never said that."

"Yes, you did," he said. "Remember the time you told me —"

Camille stopped his words with a poke to his side.

"It's okay, guys. I knew how you felt. No worries." For any of us. Any more.

Camille changed the subject. "That's pretty cool to hear from one of your fans."

"Imagine all the other people you might hear from," Carlos said, checking his phone. "All twenty-one thousand four hundred and twenty-one fans."

How sweet he'd kept track.

I pushed all thoughts of Barbie and Drew aside. I wanted to go back to the fun we were having choosing bowls, cups, and cutting boards. And . . . "Let's check out," I said. "Then I want to buy some new tops to coordinate with my gear."

The Lopez twins were all-in.

That evening I carried a stainless steel pan of julienned zucchini to the vegetable station at Rolly's.

Chef Barry looked up. "Thanks, Paige. You're the first porter who's ever kept up with my needs without me asking."

"No problem, Chef." I moved to the dessert station and saw they needed more strawberries hulled and sliced. "I'll get right on it."

Chef Helen thanked me. "That's our Paige. Always on top of things. Thanks."

The thank-yous were nice, but a part of me wondered if being too indispensable at this lower-level job would be a good career move.

For a moment I watched my replacement being schooled under the head chef. I hated that he seemed to be a nice guy. I'd heard people say good things about him. Why couldn't he be horrible so they'd fire him and need me?

Suddenly the head chef looked at me, and motioned me over. "You need something, Chef?" I asked.

He talked to me as he seared a pork chop. "I saw one of your cooking podcasts."

"You did?"

"They're quite good. You make your directions clear enough for anyone to follow."

"Thanks. I appreciate that."

He nodded toward a near-empty pan. "Get me more mushrooms, please."

"Of course, Chef."

It was the least I could do.

As usual, after work my entire body ached. I knew my legs would throb and make it hard to get to sleep, but I couldn't wait to try.

"Paige!"

I'd been so intent on getting to my car that I hadn't noticed Drew's car parked in the alley. I was not up to talking with him.

I suddenly thought of Nana's story of her boyfriend waiting outside her rehearsals and work. It made me shiver.

Drew stood beside his car, making me walk toward him.

"What are you doing here?" I asked.

"You're always working."

"I can't do this, Drew. I'm beat." I turned toward my car.

He grabbed my arm. "All worn out from being a go-fer? Did you wash many dishes? Or did you learn how to slice a potato?"

How had he found out about my demotion? "Don't be mean. My title is 'kitchen porter' and people compliment me on how well I do my job."

He snickered. Then his face hardened. "Since when are you making podcasts?"

I shook his arm away. "You saw them?"

"My boss did. You made me feel like a fool for not knowing about it. Doing it behind my back."

"It has absolutely nothing to do with you, Drew."

He took a step toward me, his eyes glistening in the glow of a security floodlight. "Here's the thing. I want to get back together. And so do you. I know it."

I was stunned by his words. And then I felt sorry for him. Although it had only been three days I'd happily moved on, yet he . . . hadn't. I'd enjoyed three days of happiness and freedom. He was clearly miserable.

He drug a shoe through some gravel. "Come on, Paige. Give me another chance."

With difficulty I pushed aside my pity and tapped into my strength. "I can't do it, Drew. I know God has other plans for me and for you. For both of us."

"So God's making you break up with me?"

I hesitated. But then I said, "In a way, yes." I dared him to argue the point.

I heard the back door of Rolly's open. "Paige?"

It was Chef Bernard. "Yes, Chef."

"Everything all right?"

I glanced at Drew, the man I'd thought about marrying. "Yes, everything is fine."

"See you tomorrow then." Chef locked up and went to his car. But he didn't drive off. I appreciated that.

"I need to go," I told Drew.

He shook his head vigorously. "You'll be back."

"I won't."

"This isn't over, Paige."

I didn't argue with him, but walked to my car without saying a word.

Sometimes the right words were no words at all.

I waited in my car until Drew drove off. Chef Bernard waited for me to leave first. Now *there* was a gentleman.

As I drove home I felt my emotions settle. Surprisingly, the adrenaline had calmed. In its place was the peace that had become a part of my life

I sat taller and pressed my shoulders against the seat. The air in the car seemed lighter, the dark unimposing. And I wasn't alone at all. Would never be alone. With God I was free indeed.

Chapter 32

Holly

"One thing I do know.
I was blind but now I see!"
John 9: 25

I put on my best smile to visit a possible new listing. I had met the Crandells when they'd come in the office. I needed to see their house one more time to finalize the deal. Upon driving up I made a quick assessment that it was worth about $350,000. Of course I would have loved for it to be a million-dollar mansion, but at this point I'd take what I could get. And if I listed it *and* sold it I'd make the full commission.

I was counting the thousands to be made as I rang the doorbell.

Mrs. Crandell opened the door and smiled. She had gray hair cropped too short, but had a nice smile that made her cheeks rise up enough to move her glasses. She invited me inside. "We're so eager to show you our home."

Her husband joined us in the foyer. "We're eager for you to sell our home."

"I will do my best, Mr. Crandell."

"Saul. Please."

"And call me Val," Mrs. Crandell said.

"I certainly will. And I'm Holly." Being on a first-name basis was always a plus. "Why don't you give me a tour?"

It was clear they were proud of their house—which *was* a nice house if you liked living in the Eighties. There were huge expanses of floral wallpaper and borders in mauve and blue. The oak trim and cabinets had an orangey cast. There was even a wooden goose with a clothespin beak to hold recipe cards, along with swagged valances and mauve Formica countertops. Unfortunately, everything looked familiar. I'd grown up in a house like this.

"We know it's a little stuck in the past," Val said, "but then, so are we." She exchanged a sweet smile with her husband.

There was no denying they were a cute couple. But their house was too cute, too full of homey bonnets and bows. It was a flipper, for sure. If I could find the right buyer who was willing to gut the place and remodel to sell for a profit . . .

The first floor was quickly seen and we descended into the basement. It had a scattering of old furniture, a sewing machine, and some shop tools, each assigned to a corner. A white washer and dryer sat beneath a tiny window. The walls weren't even drywalled. And with all the ducts and wires overhead many of the ceilings were less than eight-foot tall.

Again it brought back memories of the unfinished basement of my childhood where I'd had dozens of slumber parties. We'd watch Creature Feature, giggle about boys, eat popcorn, and drink grape pop. I'd ruined a rug by spilling my Fanta.

"I know it's not much," Val said. "But with only the two of us . . ."

"It's a very usable space," I said, though in its current state the basement didn't add to the value of the house.

I followed them to the second floor, noting all the baby pictures on the stair wall. An inordinate number. Usually people hung a variety of kid pictures, not just babies. I'd have to tell them to remove the family photos.

There were three bedrooms and two baths. The master broke the mauve and blue trend and was steeped in hunter green and rust. Three kinds of floral wallpaper vied for attention. The next bedroom suffered from quilt-overload, and the third was set up as a nursery.

Which was odd. The Crandell's were in their early sixties. Surely their children were long-ago grown.

"Do you have grandchildren come visit often?"

Saul put a hand on his wife's shoulder. "We had three children, but sadly, we lost them all when they were babies."

The wife went to the crib and moved a stuffed lamb just so.

Now the stair photos made sense. But losing three babies?

My memories slid back to my own loss, a miscarriage between Paige and Baylor. I'd nearly drowned from the sorrow of could-have-beens. Only Baylor's birth had pulled me out of my ocean of tears. The Crandells had never experienced the joy of seeing their children grow up. How horribly unfair.

I was appalled to feel tears threaten. I pressed a hand to my forehead, trying to keep my professional composure. "I'm so sorry for your losses."

"Thank you." Val tipped a mobile, making the farm animals dance. "Obviously, it was years ago, and we've since made a good life for ourselves. A happy life." She looked to her husband.

"Gracious sakes we have. We both teach Sunday school and volunteer at the children's hospital." He winked at her. "We get our kid-fix in many ways. All the fun and none of the fuss."

How could they be so accepting? So gracious?

I tried to regain my self-control by thinking of the task at hand. But I wondered if keeping the nursery intact was . . . healthy. Being reminded every day of what could—

"Holly?"

I must have zoned out for a moment. "Sorry." I put on my agent hat. "I thought of an idea that might help sell the house. With so many people working from home would you ever consider staging this room as an office?"

Val looked at me, aghast. I might as well have slapped her. "Change it?"

Immediately, I felt bad for mentioning it, even though I knew I was right. "Your house doesn't really have an area for a computer or desk. For Zoom calls and the like." Did they know what Zoom was?

Val pointed downstairs. "We have that little desk in the kitchen, where the phone is."

The space was barely big enough to sit and copy a recipe card.

"We don't need a computer," Saul said. "Our fancy phones are enough."

At least they had those.

I had seen enough. "Why don't we go downstairs. I'll show you some comps in the area and we can talk about how best to get your house ready to sell."

We sat at the dining room table. On the wall was a Holly Hobbie cross-stitch with the profile of a little girl in a blue bonnet and patchwork dress.

"Are you familiar with Holly Hobbie?" Val asked, following my gaze.

Too much so. "My mom named me after her."

"How adorable," Val gushed.

I wasn't sure about that, but I remembered having more than one picture of this fictional girl in my bedroom.

"Do you like to cross-stitch?" Val asked.

Crafts were not my thing. "I never learned how."

"It's very relaxing."

I remembered Mom making all sorts of pillows and wall hangings. Pretty then, but tacky now.

I shook the memory away and forced myself into the present. Why couldn't I get the easy listings? This was going to be a difficult conversation.

I set my portfolio on the table and took out some comp sheets for the area that I'd prepared. I went through each one, knowing their prices were higher than what the Crandell's house should be listed for.

Saul noted the prices. "That much?" he said. "We never dreamed our house would be worth —"

"Actually . . ." Now came the hard part. "These homes have been completely remodeled and modernized. So we'll have to take that into account when listing your home."

He pulled his hand back from the listings. "What number are you talking about?"

"I think we should list it for $275,000."

Mrs. Crandell fingered the buttons of her blouse. "We need more than that to buy the one-level house we're eyeing."

Eyeing or buying? "You've already bought a new place?"

"Not yet. We have to sell this one first."

"I'd be happy to help you find a house when the time comes." I said.

"One step at a time," Saul said. He picked up the other listings and flipped through the pages but didn't stop and read anything. Then he tapped the stack on the table and set them aside. "I don't know about all this. I'm not sure we're up to it."

The tension in the room was heavy. I needed to tread lightly or I'd blow the whole thing. It was difficult to deal with price issues with a normal couple, but with the Crandells . . .

They were so sincere, so delightfully befuddled, so . . . needy. They touched me. Saul reminded me of my dad: down-home and caring. I really wanted them to succeed so they could move on. "Perhaps if you made a few of the simpler updates, we could up the price."

"Update what?"

My mental ought-to-do list was long. "A good first step would be removing the wallpaper and painting the walls a nice white or ivory."

Val gazed at the rose-embellished paper in the dining room. "I like flowers. Flowers make me happy."

Saul touched her hand. "I know they do, dear. You have exquisite taste. But not everybody appreciates it like we do. Maybe if we took some of it down . . ."

I jumped at the breakthrough but kept my voice even. "The hard part about making changes to sell is understanding that you're making your house more neutral so buyers can see themselves living in it. The florals are beautiful but very personal to your taste. As Saul said, not everyone will appreciate them."

Val looked at her husband. He nodded. "Holly's right. We love this place but with your bad hip and my knees we need to get a different house, one that has bedrooms and a laundry on the main floor. To do that we need to let go of *this* place."

Val bit her lip and glanced toward the stairs, toward the photo parade of babies who'd lived here for such a short time. I wasn't sure that logic would win out over love.

But then Val nodded once. "How much will these changes cost?"

I wanted to do a fist-pump in the air. "I have a man who can do the work and—" I paused. I knew my man was good but he was pricey. I read the concern in the Crandell's faces. They weren't choosing to move on a whim. They needed to move. More than anything, I wanted them to succeed.

That's when I heard myself saying something I'd never said before. "I'll come over and help you do the work. We can do it together."

Their eyes grew wide. "You'd do that for us? How much do you charge?"

The words came out before I could stop them. "Nothing. I'd do it for free." Why had I just volunteered? I didn't do manual labor at my own house, much less at a client's.

"Free?" Saul said. "Really?"

I wanted to take it back but it was too late. I pasted on a smile. "I'd be happy to."

"That's really nice of you, Holly."

Saul slapped a palm on the table. "When can we start?"

Gracious sakes. What had I done?

After a trip to a paint store where I bought paint and supplies for removing wallpaper, I stopped home and found an empty house. It wasn't surprising. Vernon was at work. Baylor was at school — though he would be home soon.

I had the tools for the job, but now I had to dress the part. I dug through drawers and found some old comfy jeans and a faded tee-shirt that said, *Go to the Bahamas and Forget the Dramas.* Vernon had bought it for me as a "joke" and at first I'd taken offense, but I *had* worn it. I knew I was a drama queen who — to use Baylor's words — needed to chill.

But chilling would have to happen another day. This afternoon I was going to work.

For free.

Doing manual labor.

I chuckled at the thought as I tied my old white tennies that had holes in them. I looked in the mirror. My $80 Michael Kors gold earrings looked strange with a tee-shirt. I took them off and pulled my hair into a high ponytail. The style made me look younger. I'd have to remember that.

Once I was dressed for the part I felt excited — which was bizarre. I was *not* a DIY person. Ever. I even had someone clean our house, and whenever I could get Baylor or Vernon to cook, I did.

So why was my stomach doing a happy dance?

I was just leaving the house when Baylor came in. He gave me a once over. "What's going on? You never look . . . like that."

Suddenly, I got an idea. "I'm helping a nice couple spruce up their house to sell. We're taking down some old wallpaper."

"Why?"

"Because they need to take it down in order to get a good price."

"No, I get that. Why are *you* doing it?"

I put my weight on the other foot. "I'm not sure. They're so sweet and just so clueless about the process that . . ." I shrugged. "They don't have a lot of extra money and . . . I don't know why, but I volunteered. Honestly, I don't know what I was thinking. It was silly to think I could help."

His smile was actually tender. "That's really cool, Mom."

Baylor said I was cool? This was quickly turning into a stellar day.

He put his backpack on a chair. "I don't have any homework. Want some help?"

Wow. I mean, wow.

At the Crandell's we quickly discovered that Saul and Baylor shared an interest in pirates — a subject I knew little about. Yet I did remember multiple pirate-themed birthday parties I'd put together, and at least two Halloweens when Baylor had insisted on being a buccaneer. One year, he'd wanted Paige to dress up as a damsel in distress, but she'd wisely refused.

Val's cheeks were rosy as she took on the job of helper, cleaning up the discarded strips of wallpaper, refilling glasses with lemonade, and keeping a plate of freshly-baked chocolate chip cookies fully stocked. Baylor had already eaten three.

Saul was more help than I expected. Apparently, it wasn't that he couldn't do the work, he just needed to be shown how. We got the dining room stripped pretty fast, but the kitchen was a pain with all the paper around the cabinets.

I finished a long strip by the fridge, then arched my back. "I'm going to feel this tomorrow."

"It's good for you, Mom," Baylor said.

"We really do appreciate your help," Val said.

Saul sprayed adhesive remover on the wall above the tiny desk. "We never thought about taking all this down."

"That's not exactly correct," Val said. "Remember when I talked about sprucing things up after Teddy passed?"

Saul stopped working and nodded. "You thought change would be a good way to start fresh."

"Who's Teddy?" Baylor asked.

I quickly glanced between the couple. I should have warned Baylor about their babies.

"He was our son, our third child," Saul said. "God blessed us with three babies before He loved them into His everlasting arms."

Baylor looked aghast. "They died?"

"They did." Saul looked at his wife and they shared a moment. "I should have let you redecorate, Val. Maybe it would have made things easier then. And now."

Val waved her hands in front of her face. "No, no, no. You stop that, mister. It took a long while, but you and I came to understand that God's choices are beyond us. We don't know His mind and His ways, but we trust Him."

"That's a lot of trust," Baylor said. "I mean . . . they died."

My son was as subtle as the Crandell's wallpaper.

Val took a deep breath and let it out. I could tell she'd used the action to calm herself many times before. "If we trust God with the good things we have to trust Him with the bad." Saul exchanged a nod with his wife. She picked up the latest pieces of paper on the floor. "And while things were certainly bad, God knew exactly how we felt. After all, His Son died too."

Saul held the sprayer against his hip. "Died for *us*. To save us. So He knows about pain. He let Jesus die because He loves us that much."

It was something Nana would say. The Crandell's faith was so strong. So open. So deeply ingrained in who they were.

Mine . . . was not.

Baylor pulled off another long piece of paper. "It's cool you thought of it that way."

Saul nodded. "We didn't always. We went through plenty of sad times, angry times, even dark times." He looked at his wife. "I threw a few things—there's still a dent in the wall of our bedroom from a lamp. And I did a bang-up job of closing myself off to anything that might be the slightest bit enjoyable."

Val nodded. "And I spent way too much time hidden away from the world, not leaving our house, not eating, not sleeping, not wanting to talk to anybody."

"Not even me." Saul sighed wistfully. "But God didn't give up on us. He didn't leave us in that awful place. Little by little He pulled us out of the pit."

Val put a hand on his arm. "He pulled us into a place where we could breathe again." She slipped her arms around her husband's waist and rested her head against his shoulder. "This wonderful man . . ." She looked up at him with a smile filled with love. "I miss our babies every day. There were years when I blamed God, blamed doctors, blamed myself, but Saul here, he helped me see that God doesn't make mistakes. We got to love three babies. And while I miss them, I am so thankful for the joy they gave us. A lot of people never get that at all."

He kissed her forehead. "I love you too, hon." There was a moment of silence as they took a deep breath, together. "Now then," Saul said with a smile. "Let's get back to work so we can move on to the next part of our journey."

I was overcome by what they'd said. What they'd gone through. What they'd done. I was moved by their ability to survive their emotions, leaning on God to get them through. I was amazed by their certainty and their strong beliefs. I mean, I believed in Jesus too. Nana and Papa had taught me about Him, as had Mom and Dad. But simply knowing about faith was a lot different than embracing it like the Crandells did.

Val gathered more of the wallpaper mess at my feet. "Are you okay, Holly?"

I put a hand to my face, hating that my inner commotion showed. "I'm . . ." My breath caught in my throat and suddenly I couldn't say the word I was about to say. I faced her. "Actually, I'm not okay. I'm emotional and confused and disgusted."

Baylor looked at me like I was crazy. "About what, Mom?"

At that moment something cracked inside. A dam broke, emotions overflowed, and words rushed through the breach. "You two lost so much, yet you're strong. It didn't break your faith or your love or ruin your life. I lost a baby too, but . . ." My voice cracked. I closed my eyes as I recalled that awful day. The memory of the pain consumed me.

"Oh . . ." Val pulled me into her arms. "My dear girl. I'm so sorry."

I saw Baylor staring at me. We'd told him about the lost baby — in passing. But we'd never discussed it.

He stepped closer, his voice gentle. "That was before me, right?"

I nodded. "Two years before you. You were our miracle."

"I'm really sorry, Mom."

I shook my head and touched his cheek. "Yes, I lost a child, but I have so many blessings with you and Paige." I studied my son: his lovely dark eyes, his tousled hair, his strong shoulders that showed he wasn't a boy anymore. "When you were young I appreciated all the little wonders because the pain was so raw. But somehow, somewhere, I stopped seeing those special moments and lost my way. I forgot to appreciate what I have."

"Ah, Mom." He put an arm around my shoulder. "It's okay. Things are better now. And they'll keep getting better."

"I believe that too." I hated that I needed comforting. I tried to turn the moment back to normal by smiling at the Crandells. "Sorry about that. It just hit me. I'm fine, I really am." I picked up the scraper to move toward the next spot on the wall.

Baylor took the tool out of my hands and drew me into an awkward hug. "It's all right, Mom. I know you love me. And I love you too."

Then, horror of horrors, I started to cry!

At first it was just a few tears that could be flicked away But as Baylor hugged me and I hugged him, the floodgates opened. There I was, in front of brand new friends, bawling like a baby. I stepped back, making space between me and them like I was contagious. "Sorry again. This is ridiculous. I don't cry like this. Ever. I don't know what's gotten into me."

Val handed me a tissue and touched my arm. Then she began to sing. "'All to Jesus, I surrender, all to thee I freely give . . .'"

Saul joined in. "'I will ever love and trust Him. In His presence daily live.'"

Together they sang the chorus. "'I surrender all. I surrender all. All to Thee, my precious Savior, I surrender all.'"

"That's all it takes, Holly," Saul said. "Give it up and let Him love you."

The whole thing was surreal. How did all these deep feelings about love and God and Jesus come to me while I was standing in a messed up kitchen belonging to a couple I'd just met? Surely change couldn't be that simple. Saying yes?

But then I heard myself saying just that, "Okay. I get it. I'm done with me. I'm done. Yes. I . . . I surrender."

The words lingered in the air between us.

"Wow, Mom."

I wiped my nose with the tissue, "I know it's drastic and weird, but—"

He shook his head. "Yeah. It is. But . . . I'll surrender too." He blinked a few times. "I want to do it too."

What was happening?

Somehow God was happening.

Right there, in the middle of the chaos my son and I surrendered ourselves to another Son. The Son of man.

It was totally and utterly remarkable.

Chapter 33

Paige & Holly

"For the sake of my family and friends, I will say,
'Peace be within you.'"
Psalm 122: 8

With Drew out of my life, plus having a night off from work, I decided to visit my family. "Hello? Anybody home?"

"Back here."

I followed Dad's voice to the kitchen. He handed me a piece of paper. "What do you think this means?"

I read it: *Bay and I are together. Back later.* I wasn't sure what the fuss was about. "So they went out? Why are you acting worried?"

"Because they never go out together. Ever."

I sighed. "I thought things were better."

Dad opened the fridge and got each of us a can of Diet Coke. We went into the family room.

"Mom's still sleeping in the guest room." He put his feet up on the leather ottoman in front of his favorite chair.

I knew that. Baylor had kept me in the loop. "I'm sorry to hear that." I wasn't sure how to ask the next question. "How are you . . . I mean, are you . . . ?"

He nodded, as if understanding what I was trying to ask. "I've tried to make things right with your mom but she's been pretty unrelenting. She's a pro at holding a grudge."

"I know."

He popped open the can and took a sip. "My parents always said, 'Do not let the sun go down while you are still angry.' Holly and I used to be good at that, but recently, well . . ." He brushed the conversation away. "Enough about me and Mom. To what do I owe the pleasure of your visit?"

Since my parents were still having issues, I wasn't sure it was the right time to tell him about Drew.

But he knew me too well. "Your face says you're worried about something. Spill it."

I tried to relax my face and put up the mask, but remembered it was Dad. Maybe it would be better to deal with it one parent at a time. "I broke up with Drew last Thursday."

Dad sat up straighter in his chair. "That was five days ago."

"I know. I thought about telling everybody but . . ." Why had I delayed telling them? "I guess I wanted to make sure it stuck."

He moved from his chair to the place beside me on the couch. "I want to say 'good for you', but I won't."

He just did. "It wasn't easy." I pressed a finger between my brows.

"I'm sure it wasn't," he said. "You've been together a long time. How's he taking it?"

I slipped off my shoes and tucked my feet beneath me. "At first he called and texted a lot." I decided not to mention Drew stalking me at work. "But I think he finally gets that we're over for good."

"That's a relief. If you need manpower to keep him away, let me know."

Dad reminded me of Nana's brave father. I loved him for offering. "I think it will be okay now. Breaking up was hard yet it also feels really . . . right."

He smiled. "That's a good sign."

"Nana would say so. She says if you feel peace it means you've made the right decision."

Dad cocked his head. "Then I guess my decision to unfriend Brianna was right too."

I was glad he'd brought it up. "You feel peace about that?"

"I do. And relief. Having secrets is exhausting."

Somehow breaking up with Drew made me feel more grown up, which led me to say something I hadn't said. "I hate the idea of you sneaking around, Dad—even if you were just talking with Brianna. Honestly, it really blew the image of you being my perfect dad."

His eyebrows touched in the middle. "I'm far from perfect. Far, far from perfect. I know I really let you and Baylor down—not to mention your mother. I let myself down too." He waved his hands in front of his face. "What a mess. If I could go back . . ." He sighed deeply. "I'm so sorry."

"I know." I put a hand on his knee. "I've missed our talks."

He let out a breath he'd been saving. "Me too. When you first said you were moving out I wondered if we'd lose . . . you know."

"I do know. And I worried about it too. I want us to stay close, no matter what."

He nodded. "Just because you moved out and are all grown up doesn't mean things have to change — that much." He got up to get his Coke and returned to the couch. "I've always been upfront about my feelings for Drew, but what made you call it quits?"

I'd thought about it a lot. There were big issues and mini ones that I'd swept aside, refusing to see. Until . . . "Four people helped me see things more clearly."

"Excellent. Who's number one?"

"Nana. She shared a story from when she was a teenager and had a possessive boyfriend."

"Like Drew."

"Like Drew. Did you know Nana played viola?"

"I didn't."

"She was in a special orchestra and quit because of her boyfriend."

He nodded, getting it. "Just like you quit your dream job."

"I did."

"Because of Drew."

I nodded. "Me going back but being demoted happened to Nana too."

"Did she tell you to break up with Drew?"

"Not exactly. But she made me see the truth of things."

"Sounds like Nana. She did the same for me."

I thought of something. "Has Mom had her treasure hunt yet?"

"I don't think so."

"Everybody else has."

Dad nodded. "I wish Holly would go. If anyone can help her find some peace, it's Nana." He sipped his drink. "You said there were four people who helped you make the decision to leave Drew. Who's number two?"

"Actually two and three go together. You've heard me mention Carlos and Camille from across the hall?"

"The twins. So how did they help?"

"By being totally supportive, and encouraging my talents. Carlos is the one who first taped my cooking videos."

"Baylor showed me a few of those. I'm not surprised you're so good at it."

Dad's praise filled me up. "It helps when I'm doing something I love."

"Always. And the fourth person?"

"Barbie. Drew's ex."

Dad's eyebrows rose. "How did she help you?"

"By telling me to follow my dreams and not settle."

He clapped his hands once. "Touchdown! Give the girl a sparkle star! Those are exactly the reasons I never liked Drew. He didn't appreciate how special you were and was far too impressed with himself."

"I see all that now, but it makes me mad that I didn't see it before. All that time wasted." We heard the garage door open.

Dad talked fast. "The time wasn't wasted because . . ." He spread his arms as if presenting me to the world, "look at who you are now." He drew me into a hug.

"You always make me feel better, Dad."

"That's my job."

We heard voices at the back door. They were back.

I was thrilled to see Paige's car outside. Now I could tell the rest of my family about the amazing thing that had happened at the Crandell's.

"Hi, you two," I said, coming into the family room. I fell into a chair. "I'm exhausted."

"Where were you?" Vernon asked. "Your note didn't say." He looked at me head to toe. "I don't think I've ever seen you dressed like that in public."

I pulled at my tee-shirt. "We were working. Hard."

Baylor sat on the ottoman. "We've been stripping wallpaper for one of Mom's clients."

"You?" Paige asked. "I didn't know you could, or would…"

I chuckled. "I know it's not like me, but there's something about the Crandells that made me want to help. Personally." I smiled at my son. "Baylor got swept up in it too."

"I liked it," he said. "Saul knows a ton about pirates."

"Okay . . ." Vernon drew out the word.

I wanted to move on to the most important part of our afternoon. "Beyond the work, something amazing happened."

Paige looked at me, then Baylor. "What?"

I wasn't sure how to explain it. "The Crandells are remarkable people. They're really sweet. Very giving."

"They volunteer at church and at the hospital," Baylor added.

"They sound like nice people," Paige said.

"They are, but it goes beyond *nice*. They're special because of something awful that happened to them." I took a fresh breath. "Years ago they lost three babies. They still have a nursery set up, decades after losing their children."

"Wow," Vernon said. "How tragic. Though still having the room is a bit strange."

I came to the Crandell's defense even though I'd felt the same way. "It was obviously hard for them. I even suggested they change the nursery into an office. Talk about insensitive." The honesty poured out.

"It's a logical idea," Vernon said. "Most people need an—"

I held up a hand, stopping him from saying more. "While spending time with them something switched over in me, and instead of coldly looking at their house as a property to list I felt this compassion well up in me." I put my fists against my gut. "I felt so badly about their loss then and their hope for a new future now. It made me remember losing our baby."

Vernon's eyebrows rose. "I still think about her."

"Me too. And our loss coupled with their losses . . . I didn't just want to sell the place, I wanted to help *them*, no matter how much it took." They were all staring at me. "I know me being generous and helpful is crazy. But then it got crazier."

Baylor nodded. "We were working on the wallpaper and Saul and Val started telling us how they were mad and sad after losing the babies, but then they got through those bad times because of God. They just said it blatant like that. It was kind of weird." He looked at me. "But also pretty cool. Tell 'em what happened next, Mom."

Paige and Vernon's expressions were wary. I was wary too. Me, who rarely said the G-word and who never said the J-word was going to have to say it now.

"What happened, Hol?" Vernon asked.

I sat straighter in the chair. "I think it's one of those 'you had to be there' moments." I looked to Baylor.

"Yeah. You definitely had to be there," he said. "But we both felt it. We both did it."

"Did what exactly?" Paige asked.

I had to just say it. "We surrendered to Jesus." I held up my hands to fend off their reaction. "I know it sounds hokey but it wasn't. It was real and sincere and—"

Vernon raised a hand. "I'm not doubting you, it's just sudden. And sorry, but . . . it's not like either of you."

I huffed and nodded. "Right on both counts." I rubbed my hands on my jeans and saw that the wallpaper stripping had completely ruined my manicure.

"I know what Nana would say happened," Paige said. "She'd say God opened the eyes of your heart and changed you. He arranged for you to meet the Crandells, then nudged you into helping them just so you would surrender to Jesus."

I was stunned by her mentioning God-stuff because we never talked about Him. But I liked her words. "So God arranged all this?"

"Do you think *you* did it?" Paige asked.

It was unnerving to realize I hadn't arranged any of it.

"We *did* surrender," Baylor said. "I think it's awesome to think that God would take the time to put us in the right place at the right time for it to happen."

"Very awesome," Vernon said.

Being so all-in like this was new to me. I was overwhelmed by what had happened to Baylor and I but also . . . "I'm surprised you two are accepting our God moment. You didn't pooh-pooh it or try to explain it away."

"It can't be explained away," Baylor said. "It happened, just like we said."

"I don't doubt it," Vernon said. "I'm really happy for both of you." He looked in my direction and gave me a special wink. "For all of us actually." Then he nodded toward Paige. "Paige has some good news to share too."

"Not now, Dad. It can wait."

"Normally, I would agree. But their good news needs to feed your good news. Tell them."

She looked at each of our faces. "I broke up with Drew."

A slew of emotions rained down on me. Relief drowned out the rest. "Tell us what happened."

As Paige told her story a strange thing happened.

I listened.

Paige had gone home, and Baylor was in his room getting ready for bed. I stood in the doorway of Paige's old bedroom where I'd been sleeping. A lot had changed today. Everything had changed. I wasn't the same Holly who had left for work this morning. I had surrendered to Jesus and He had welcomed me in. I had no idea exactly how that would change my life, but I knew it would. It already had.

One thing was for sure. I couldn't go back to sleeping apart from my husband.

I walked through the master bedroom and found Vernon in the bathroom. He spit out his toothpaste, then noticed I was there. "Hi," I said.

"Hi." He took a drink, then looked at my reflection in the mirror. "I'm really happy for what happened to you and Bay today."

"Thanks. I'm happy too."

He wiped his mouth with a towel, then turned his back on the sink and leaned against it. He had a little smile on his face and looked just like the day I met him. My Vernon. "You've changed, Hol. I can see it."

Really? It showed? "I am changed, in so many ways that it doesn't make sense."

"I know you and I don't talk about our faith much, but you should feel honored God went to all that trouble to get your attention."

It was a nice way to look at it.

But as to my reason for seeking him out . . . "Can you and I talk about . . . us?"

His genuine smile warmed me as God had warmed me. "I'd like that," he said.

It was a very good start.

Chapter 34

Elsie & Holly

"Do not be wise in your own eyes;
fear the Lord and shun evil."
Proverbs 3: 7

I made our bed the same way I'd done it for sixty-nine years.
Our bed. Now mine.

Last night I'd moved back into the master bedroom. In the early
days after Willis died, the memories had been so raw that I'd wanted
to hide from them. But now when I thought of him, the pain had
changed from despair to a kind of bittersweet pleasure in
remembering the joy of our life together.

Last night I'd only awakened twice — both times reaching across
the bed to touch him. Both times I'd withdrawn my hand when the
touch had been denied. The grogginess of sleep made me cry in a way
that I usually could avoid during the waking hours. So be it.

I'd survived. It was odd to find out that my survival — the very
opposite of death — was also the result of death. The victory over
death. I *had* to survive. *That* was my quest. It was my job.

I held onto the back of the chair in the corner where Willis had
sat every day to put on his shoes. But I wasn't going to sit. Instead I
arched my free arm over my head, feeling the stretch of the muscles in
my side.

" . . . twenty-eight, twenty-nine, thirty."

I turned around and stretched the other side. I completed a few
more stretches — as I had done nearly every morning for the past ten
years. Willis had teased me about exercising. "You trying to be a
swimsuit model, Els?" I'd asked him to join me, but he'd said no
thanks. I knew the routine might not make me stronger, but I liked the
feel of my muscles stretching. They were alive and so was I.

So there.

As I got dressed, I thought about my day. It was up in the air. I'd invited Holly to come over, but I doubted she would show up.

"She's hopeless," I told the room.

I immediately put a hand to my mouth. What an awful thing to say about my granddaughter—about anyone.

I can reach her.

I nodded to the voice inside, the voice of the One who *was* hope, who gave hope, who invented hope.

I sank onto the edge of the bed, bowed my head, and offered a daily prayer for my granddaughter. "Forgive my doubt, Father. You want Holly to know You even more than I do. Make us a miracle. Make Holly Yours."

A feeling of peace came over me. I knew He had heard and I knew He would make a miracle. If not today, some day.

But maybe today . . . and so I went to whip up some muffins to serve Holly just in case today was the day her life would change.

For the first time in too-long-to-remember, I, Holly Lindstrom, woke up fully rested and refreshed. My mind usually dove headfirst into the crowded pool of my thoughts but today was different.

I was different.

I turned on my side and saw that Vernon wasn't in bed. I didn't hear him in the bathroom or closet either.

But then I smelled bacon.

What a guy.

I glanced at the clock. It wasn't even seven yet. I'd already told the office I wasn't coming in because I was helping Val and Saul. So I had some time to savor the moment.

I lay back against the pillows and grinned at the ceiling. A song from my childhood Sunday school came to mind. "'This is the day, this is the day that the Lord has made, that the Lord has made. I will rejoice, I will rejoice and be glad in—'"

"You're chipper." Vernon stood in the doorway with a tray of food.

"More chipper now. I smell bacon." I sat up in bed, arranging the pillows. I hadn't had breakfast in bed since the kids used to surprise me on Mother's Day.

He set the tray neatly around my legs. "Voila! Eggs over medium, three strips of bacon, and two slices of toast—one with Kerrygold butter and one with peanut butter. Coffee with sweetener and spicy V-8. Bon appétit."

I was blown away. "This is amazing. Thank you. Are you joining me?"

"Of course." He left the room and brought back a tray for himself. He got settled then lifted his glass. "To both of us changing for the better—all of us. Together."

I clinked my glass into his and we began to eat.

Our discussion last night had been a good one. Somehow we'd both kept our cool and actually talked. And listened. He was sorry. I was sorry. He'd try harder. I'd try harder. Somehow I knew the words weren't empty this time. It's like we both realized we'd been standing on the edge of a cliff, and we both chose to step back and walk away from the precipice.

Of course time would tell, but the hope I felt in my gut had made me leave the guest room behind. With the morning light it still felt right and good.

"What's on your agenda today?" he asked.

I enjoyed the zing of the spicy juice. "I'm going to help the Crandells again."

"I could help after work."

The offer surprised me. "That would be great. Thank you." I had a new thought. "I never told them a specific time so I think I'll go over to Nana's this morning. She's been after me to have my treasure hunt and I've put her off more than once. Maybe it's time."

With a smile Vernon carefully leaned over so as not to spill anything and kissed my cheek. "That's a marvelous idea."

I called Nana and was told to come right over. She greeted me at the door with a hug and a kiss. "I've been waiting for you ever so long."

I couldn't even remember the excuses I'd given. "I know. I'm sorry. I should have come, but . . ."

"But?"

Why not just let it out? "Honestly, I didn't want you to tell me something I didn't want to hear."

Nana put a hand to her chest. "I'm not here to judge you, dear girl. Everything I've shared with the family shows *my* faults, *my* mistakes, and *my* life lessons. Of course I want to help where I can, but my reasons for doing the treasure hunts are quite selfish."

I was shocked. "You are never selfish."

"There, you are wrong." Nana slid her hand around my arm and led me to the couch. She leaned her cane against the cushion beside her. "I created the treasure hunts because I want my family to remember me — all of me."

Great. I knew I hadn't spent much time with her since Papa died. In fact, I'd avoided her. "I'm sorry I haven't — "

"No," Nana said adamantly. "This isn't about guilt trips or duty. It's about sincere interest and love — on both our parts."

I wasn't sure what she was getting at. "I *am* interested in you, Nana."

She shook her head. "You're interested in me as your grandmother — which is lovely." She bumped her arm against mine. "But that's just one slice of me. What about the rest? Not just the grandmother, but the musician, the seamstress, the volunteer, the corporate wife, the child of God . . . Papa helped me see that all of you might benefit if I helped you see how I was in my . . . he called them my *before* years."

"Your *before* years," I repeated. "That's so . . . eloquent."

"Papa could be very eloquent." She grinned. "You should see the love letters he sent me from the war." She put a hand to her chest and made it pulse against her heart. "Hubba, hubba."

I laughed. "I'd like to see those some time."

"I have them all." She patted my knee. "But those are for another day. Before we get started I need to ask how you're doing. I know your family has gone through some trying times lately."

For once in my life I set my own issues aside. "I'll tell you everything, but first . . . how are *you* doing? Being without Papa must be horribly hard."

"It's beyond comprehension."

Oh dear. And I'd ignored her and avoided her calls. "I'm so — "

She held up a hand. "I'm getting through it. The memories are sweet now. The grief took me through the despair of what is, but blessedly it's led me to the joy of what was." She nodded once. "I'm okay. Thanks for asking." She clasped her hands in her lap. "Now. Tell me about your troubles."

My troubles were improving because of Nana. It was strange to know that Vernon, Baylor, and Paige had already had their treasure hunts and they'd all come out better for it.

Would I?

And though I wanted to share my come-to-Jesus moment with Nana — for I knew it would please her — I wanted to wait until after the treasure hunt. Let the morning be about her for a while.

Was I actually being unselfish?

Huh. Would wonders never cease.

"We're doing okay now," I said. "We can talk more about it later, after the hunt." I gave her my most enthusiastic smile even though I was nervous. "Let's do this thing."

She slapped her legs, giving me a classic Grandma side eye. "All righty then. Clue number one is at the church."

Church. I instantly felt guilty because we hadn't been going very often. "What happens there?"

"Go to the office and ask for Betty. I've already called her and told her you're coming. She nudged my leg. "Go on now. Betty's waiting."

I paused at the door and winked at her. "This isn't going to hurt, is it?"

"Pain before gain, Holly-girl."

I entered the church tentatively. It was the church I'd gone to my entire life, the church Vernon and I were married in, and the kids baptized in. I'm not sure why we stopped going. There always seemed to be something to do on Sunday mornings: soccer, busyness, sleeping in, cleaning out the garage. Lame excuses.

When I entered the office I saw a woman sitting at a desk with a BETTY nameplate. I recognized her big Texas hair and perfect makeup, but had never known her name. "Hi, I am — "

"Holly. I know who you are."

Was that good or bad? "I came to — "

She finally smiled. "And I know why you're here. Well, I don't exactly *know* because Elsie didn't tell me the whys of it, but I know what I'm supposed to show you. Come with me."

Betty led me into a meeting room and offered me a seat. On the table was a large 3-ring notebook. "Here are the church bulletins for the year 1998, as well as lists of the Bible study groups." She fingered the notebook with a well-manicured hand. "Any questions?"

"What am I looking for?"

"Elsie said you might ask that."

"And . . . ?"

"You're supposed to 'peruse' — that's Elsie's word — peruse the bulletins, but also pay attention to a picture that has a young blonde woman in the front row, wearing a pink sweater." She leaned forward confidentially. "I peeked and didn't know her, but maybe you do."

1998? Nana would have been in her sixties. But I was supposed to pay attention to someone else wearing a pink sweater?

"Want some coffee?" Betty asked.

"I'm good. Thanks."

"Once you get the woman's name, come see me. Good luck." Betty left me alone.

I opened the notebook and found each program and bulletin in an acetate sleeve. Someone had been busy. Surely Nana didn't want me to go through them all.

I removed the first one from January 4th. I skipped the worship itinerary and turned back to the announcements. I saw Nana's name: *Start the New Year right! If you are interested in joining a Bible study, contact Elsie Masterson.*

I looked at a few more bulletins and found similar announcements. And then an announcement for a church dinner: *We need volunteers to serve! Call Elsie Masterson.*

A White Breakfast before Easter, a Mother's Day supper, volunteering to work for Habitat for Humanity, a gardening day at church, quilting club, and a women's retreat. Nana's name was mentioned with all of them. Her busyness back then reminded me of my mom's busyness now. Like mother, like daughter.

"I had no idea," I told the room. I quickly forgave myself for being ignorant. In1998 I was a college student with classes to think about. And boys — or one boy. Vernon and I started dating that year. Being independent and away from Carson Creek for the first time meant I'd pretty much ignored all things "home" except when I wanted to do my laundry, get a home-cooked meal, or needed money. It was only natural.

I scanned group pictures, looking for a pretty blonde in the front row, wearing a pink sweater.

Deep into October, I found her in a photo of a Bible study group. The picture was dated October 26, 1998. "There you are." And there was Nana in the back row.

I looked at the list of names and counted off people in the row. "Hello, Janet Agnew." She was twenty-something with a heavily layered "Rachel" cut. I'd had a similar cut, thinking I was cool because it was named after Rachel from the sitcom "Friends." But Janet's wasn't styled well, like she hadn't had time to make it smooth. Her expression stood out among the other happy women. She wasn't smiling and her eyes were sad. I took a picture of the photo with my phone.

To make sure I didn't miss anything—and to score extra points with Nana—I scanned through the rest of the year and saw Nana's name five more times. I closed the notebook with a pat to its cover. "Well done, Nana. You made yourself useful and known. Kind of what I'm working toward with real estate."

I stopped at Betty's desk on the way out. "All done. Do you want me to put the notebook somewhere?"

"No need," Betty said with a wave. "Did you find the pink sweater-girl?"

"I did. Her name was Janet Agnew."

"I saw that, but like I said, I'm not familiar." She pulled an envelope from a drawer. "Your prize for learning her name is receiving your next clue."

Written on the front in Nana's shaky cursive were the words, "Clue #2."

"What exactly are you searching for?" Betty asked.

"I have no idea."

Betty nodded. "It's nice she's doing it for you—no matter what the treasure turns out to be."

That remained to be seen.

I waited until I was in my car to open the envelope. A note said: *Find Janet Agnew at Woodlawn.*

Woodlawn cemetery? Where Papa was buried?

I wasn't aware of any other local place with that name. I drove off, wondering about the details of Janet's death—Janet who looked to be about the same age I was in 1998.

Ten minutes later I pulled into the parking lot of the cemetery and parked in front of a little building that had a sign saying OFFICE above the door. Maybe someone inside could help me find Janet. Otherwise I was in for a long search.

Inside was a very elderly man shakily pouring himself coffee from a thermos. Two Oreos sat on top of an opened Baggie. His work shirt had *Abe* embroidered on the pocket.

"Good morning," I said.

He stood, but his shoulders were permanently slumped forward. "Hello, miss. How can I help you?"

"I'm looking for someone, for their grave? Do you have some sort of map or a database or something?"

"We have *something*," he said. He nodded toward a large office file drawer that was sized for index cards. "I don't do computers. We have cards, but they're pretty impersonal." He tapped his head. "But I've been the keeper here for fifty-two years. I know *everybody*."

His pride was charming. "I'm looking for Janet Agnew."

He touched the edge of his desk as if needing support. "Oh."

"You knew her?"

"In life? No. But her death . . . such a sad story. You probably already know that."

"I don't know that. I don't know anything about her."

He cocked his head. "Then why you lookin'?"

"My grandmother, Elsie—"

He slapped a hand on his head. "Mrs. Masterson. I'm so sorry about the mister's passing. Let her know we're doing right by him."

"I'm sure you are."

"But as far as Mrs. Masterson? She called a week ago saying someone might be coming. She didn't say about who—at least that I remember." He bit his lip. "My mind isn't as sharp in some things as it is with others, but Janet Agnew . . . give me a minute to think." In a few moments he stood taller and blinked once. "Section twenty, plot twelve. I'll take you there, Miss . . . ?"

"Holly."

"Nice to meet you. I'm Abe."

As he headed to the door I wasn't sure if his frail body could make it. "Just point me in the right direction."

"No, Miss Holly. I won't do that. Miss Janet could use a proper visitor and have someone new hear her story."

His compassion and kind manners were touching. He seemed to be the perfect man for his job. "I'd like to hear all about her."

Abe led me to a golf cart, which made me feel better about our trek. He offered me his hand as I got in. Then he walked around to the driver's side and we were off. He drove slowly up the winding path that curved under the sprawling branches of ancient oaks.

"When did she die?" I asked.

"Ninety-eight, I believe."

The same year as the Bible study. "I saw a picture of her. She was pretty." I remembered the photo on my phone. "Want to see?"

"Sure." He stopped the cart to look.

Abe squinted his eyes and adjusted his glasses. I blew up the photo so Janet's face could be seen more easily.

"You're right. She's pretty, but kinda sad." He drove on. "Actually, I remember seeing a photo of her in the newspapers. And at the funeral. There wasn't an open casket for that one."

Really. "Was she in an accident?"

He shook his head. "Her death weren't no accident. It was murder. Her husband killed her."

I sucked in a breath. "That's horrible."

"He beat her to death. Never heard why." Abe paused and looked up at the sky before letting out a deep sigh. "There's never a good reason for such evil. People said afterwards that he'd been beating on her for years."

"She was abused. That's awful."

Abe offered a disgusted laugh. "Abused? Yeah, I think death is abuse."

How stupid of me.

I tried to reconcile the pretty woman in the pink sweater with a battered woman who lost her life a short time after. No wonder her eyes had looked sad. No wonder she hadn't been smiling.

"As far as I know the husband's rotting in jail," the caretaker said. "But life's life. He's breathing and she's not. Sometimes life ain't fair." He parked the cart and got out. "Miss Janet's up here a few."

He led me thirty feet off the path to a simple headstone: *Janet Lynn Agnew. B. February 23, 1977 D. October 26, 1998. Rest and find peace.*

I was immediately struck by two dates. Firstly, 1977. "I was born in 1977. She was my age."

He nodded once. "Just starting her life."

There was more. "The date she died . . . I know that date."

"What happened on that day?"

I pulled up the photo on my phone again. It included the caption. "See here? This Bible study photo was dated October 26, 1998."

"Whoa."

It was incredible. Awful and incredible. "She must have been murdered that same day."

He clasped his hands in front of himself and bowed his head. "'Deliver us from evil . . .'"

I shuddered. "Thank you for bringing me here, Abe. Can I have a minute alone with her?" He hesitated, looking between the cart and the gatehouse. "Don't worry about me. I'll walk back."

"If you're sure. Thank you Miss Holly, that's right nice of you to make time for her. You two have a nice visit."

I waited until Abe had driven away. His words lingered. *A nice visit?* I had never visited anyone's grave. I'd recently been at Papa's funeral, but I'd never even thought of going to *visit* him.

Yet here I was, standing in front of a stranger's grave.

What now?

I noticed other graves were studded with fake flower arrangements. Janet had none.

Did anyone ever come to visit her? Siblings? Parents? Friends?

"You're so alone." I sank to my knees on the grass. "I'm so sorry you're here. I was born the same year as you. When you were married and suffering, I was having a grand old time at college."

I thought about all the milestones Janet had missed: children, a career, vacations, friends, holidays, birthdays, anniversaries . . .

As Abe had said, "Life's life." Her husband was still breathing and she was not. Life was absolutely *not* fair.

I reached forward and brushed a stray leaf that teetered on the top of the headstone. I closed my eyes and remembered the woman in the photo. A woman who was in a Bible study, trying to know God better. She hadn't looked happy on the day of her death. Had she told anyone about her abuse? Or had she suffered in silence?

Silence was a killer too.

Suddenly, I thought of Baylor. He'd suffered his teenage pain in silence.

And Vernon. He'd suffered our marital pain in silence.

And most recently, Paige, who'd suffered Drew's emotional abuse, in silence.

An odd thought came to me. Was I suffering in silence?

I shook my head, banishing the thought. I was a budding agent, a strong, independent woman. My family had gone through a few tough times, but things were better. Getting better. I wasn't suffering.

My chest tightened in disagreement.

Yet my recent mistakes made me wonder what was going on with me. In many ways I'd abandoned my family. I'd tried to get Brianna fired. I'd been overly pushy and arrogant at the Chamber meeting. I'd badmouthed a business owner in front of a newbie. I'd belittled clients for their lack of money.

And I'd avoided spending time with my grandmother — my recently widowed grandmother who would do anything for me.

I hadn't suffered, but others had suffered because of me.

It was damning. Pitiful. Embarrassing. I moaned. "Oh, Janet . . . I've had the years you didn't get, the opportunities you didn't have, and I've made bad use of them all. I don't deserve any of it."

The sound of my voice echoed back into my ears. I looked around the cemetery in hopes no one had overheard. Luckily only the dead had witnessed my flaws and selfishness and sins.

It was like a heavy yoke had been placed across my shoulders. I leaned forward on the grass, cupping my forehead in my hands. It was an unnatural position, one that I'd seen in movies when someone was penitent.

And praying.

There'd been far too little of that.

And yet, just yesterday I'd surrendered my life to Jesus. It couldn't be a one-time event. It had to be constant, a repeated decision, day to day, moment to moment.

I had to do it again.

I took a deep breath. "I'm sorry, Lord. You've been so generous with me, so loving, even though I've been neither to anyone or to You. Please forgive me and help me do better. Be better. I surrender. Again."

A sudden breeze swept around me as if drawing me upwards. I sat on my heels. A stray sprig of plastic daisies tumbled toward me, stopping at my knees. *How strange.*

Not strange. Wonderful.

I twirled it between my fingers, my heartbeat steadying. "Thank You, Lord."

Then I stuck the flower in the ground by Janet's headstone. I'd bring her something nicer next time.

I returned to Nana's house, feeling cleansed but exhausted. I knew the treasure hunt wasn't over, yet I'd already won a prize. Although I'd never been one for self-analysis or introspection, I did feel better for the experience. The world didn't publish a zillion self-help books for nothing.

I found Nana in her chair, dozing, so I closed the front door with a gentle click.

Nana roused. "You're back."

"I'm back." I sat nearby.

"You met Janet Agnew?"

"I did. It was kind of disturbing to see her in your group photo and then find out what happened to her on that same day. Her death was such a tragedy."

Nana rubbed the back of her neck as if it had a crick in it. "A tragedy I caused."

I sat upright. "How did you cause her death?"

Nana took a Kleenex from her pocket, blew her nose, then set it on the end table. "I'm your last clue."

"You?"

"I'm going to tell you a story I've never told anyone. No one."

I was intrigued. "Not even Papa?"

Nana shook her head. "Not even him."

"I'm honored, but . . . I'm not sure I want to hear it."

"You need to hear it, Holly-girl. You, more than anyone else in our family, needs to hear it."

Her words made me more apprehensive than ever. Yet at this point I *had* to hear it. "Tell me. Good or bad, I want to know."

Nana pulled her cane close, not because she was going to stand, but as a post to lean her hands upon. "I need to take you back to that particular day in our Bible study . . ."

Chapter 35

Elsie - 1998

"Do not let any unwholesome talk
come out of your mouths,
but only what is helpful for building others up
according to their needs,
that it may benefit those who listen."
Ephesians 4: 29

My daughter came by to pick me up for Bible study. Rosemary had to move a jacket, a notebook, and a cup from the passenger seat before I could get in.

"Sorry," she said. She held up the mug. "Do you like my newfangled travel mug? It has a lid and everything."

It was a great invention. "Your father will never allow me to drink anything in the car."

She pulled away from the curb. "What *I* really want is one of those new cars with cup holders built right in. My friend just got one of those. But Everett doesn't want to get rid of our Oldsmobile until we hit a hundred-thousand miles."

"He's thrifty. Nothing wrong with that."

She sighed. "He's old fashioned. Speaking of . . . are you ready to give the lesson today?"

I wasn't sure why she'd think I wasn't. "Of course I'm ready."

"I know you're going to talk about the Proverbs thirty-one woman, but I hope you aren't going to be too old-fashioned about it."

I wasn't sure what she meant. "*I'm* old-fashioned. The lesson is timeless. It's Scripture."

Rosemary turned right at a stoplight, heading toward church. "I'm afraid you're going to have a mutiny on your hands if you start talking about how we're supposed to be perfect wives and mothers like the chapter talks about."

"It's something to strive for."

"Maybe eons ago—though I doubt that. You don't want to turn people off, Mom."

I didn't like her attitude. Yet I wasn't naïve. The biblical standard *was* high. I patted the Bible in my lap. "It will be all right. I promise."

We pulled into the parking lot and headed inside. Rosemary and I set the chairs in a semi-circle with a podium at one end. The twenty ladies in our Bible study started to file in. I let them chit-chat for a few minutes, then asked them to take their seats. It was my turn to talk.

"Morning, ladies. I'm so glad to be here this morning to teach you about the Proverbs 31 woman."

I'd expected their groans. "Now, now. Give her a chance," I said.

"Give *me* a chance," my best friend, Mary, said. "I read the chapter, and let me tell you, I have little in common with *her*."

"Me neither," Barb said.

We were off track before I even got started "How about we go through verses ten through thirty-one and identify some of the attributes. Mary, you start."

Everyone looked at their Bible. Then Mary said, "It says she's noble." She shook her head. "I can honestly say I have *never* been called noble or called anyone noble."

It was probably true, but I kept things going. "It says 'She is worth far more than rubies.'"

"When Frank gives me a ruby, I'll be noble," Cassie said, rolling her eyes.

Their laughter was unfortunate. I looked to the next woman. "Connie? Continue for us."

She glanced at her Bible. "It says her husband has confidence in her."

"Good. Janet?"

Janet was our shy one. She rarely spoke but always seemed to soak in the lesson. Today when she lifted the Bible close to her eyes I noticed something.

"Where are your glasses?" I asked.

She touched her temple. "They broke. It's okay. I can still read it." She took a moment to read to herself. When she looked up her forehead was furrowed. "I don't know what this means: 'She brings him good, not harm, all the days of her life.' Brings him good?"

"She gives in," Tammy said.

"I hate that verse," Barb said. "I am not giving in to Karl. He doesn't deserve it."

I knew Karl and agreed with her, but that was beside the point. I needed to get them to focus. Maybe if I shared a story . . . "I've learned to always be there for Willis. I know what he likes and I give it to him."

"Oh really," Sandy said, with innuendo in her voice.

Leave it to Sandy. I continued. "The main reason our marriage has lasted forty-six years is that I learned to . . . acquiesce to him."

Tammy cupped a hand around her mouth and whispered loudly. "She means 'submit.'"

They all groaned.

I'd purposely not used that word because I knew the reaction it would get. "Submission is not a bad word. I've learned to give-in when a situation warrants it. Let Willis be boss."

"Let him *think* he's boss," Audrey said.

She was partially right, but I didn't want to get into the intricacies of *that*. As the oldest one in our group I wanted the ladies to look up to me. "When Willis and I argue, I've learned it's best to do whatever it takes to keep the peace."

Tammy shook her head. "Not me. I fight."

"I don't like fighting," Janet said.

"Nor should you." I skimmed ahead to verse twenty-eight and nine: "'Her children arise and call her blessed; her husband also, and he praises her.' He says, 'Many women do noble things, but you surpass them all.'" I looked at the ladies. "Don't we all want our husbands to give us a compliment like that?"

Rosemary laughed aloud. "I can*not* imagine Everett saying anything like that. I'd faint dead away if he did."

Thanks for your support, Rosemary.

More than one woman nodded their agreement. "My kids will never say such things about me," Mary said. "And Connor won't because he doesn't appreciate me."

Were their marriages really so bad? "I work very hard on our marriage."

"Does Willis work hard on it?" Tammy asked.

I wasn't sure how to answer, but decided to go for the fluffy version over the factual. "Of course he does. We've created a good marriage through hard work and persistence. We have risen above our trials and have dedicated ourselves to each other. Over and over."

Sandy crossed her arms. "Then you're a better woman than me, Elsie Masterson."

The lesson had digressed. I decided to offer them an example of something that had worked for Willis and me. Maybe they'd see what we'd done and it would help their own situations. I left the verses behind and tried to think of a verse-affirming story.

Rosemary interrupted my thoughts. "I remember the time you and Dad had an argument about your cooking. Dad didn't like whatever you'd made and said so. You got mad and he got madder and then *you* threw the plate of food against the wall."

How dare she bring that up? It was one of my weakest moments. "That's not fair, Rosemary. I apologized for that. The meal *wasn't* cooked very well. But I'd had a hard day and was tired, and when he complained . . . I overreacted." I made a throwing motion.

"You were human," Connie said. "Don't women have a right to be human and make mistakes?"

Janet partially raised her hand. "I make a *lot* of mistakes."

I wanted to ask what she meant, but Tammy said, "And don't we have the right to overreact occasionally?" She tapped the opened pages of the Bible. "I can't be *this* woman."

Rosemary huffed. "Nobody can."

I wasn't sure what to say. "I admit in that particular situation I didn't handle his complaint well. It would have been better if I'd admitted the food wasn't good and fixed it."

"Sure," Mary said. "If you were a saint."

Rosemary closed her Bible. "Admit it, Mom. Didn't it feel good to throw that plate? I remember I was proud of you for finally standing up to him. Dad can be really nit-picky. And when you constantly give in to him, you're letting him get away with it."

"Isn't that being an enabler?" Audrey said. "I was that way when we were first married, but I quickly found out I had to set the boundaries and—"

"*Enabler.* You sound like one of those talk shows," Connie said.

"But it's true."

One by one the ladies told their stories of strength and confrontation. Except Janet. She just listened and watched. Her face was pulled and she looked confused. I hated that *these* were the lessons she might be learning. Yet every time I tried to intervene and go back to the Bible, the women veered away again.

And then . . . I gave up and gave in. "Fine. I'll tell you about a time when I stood up for myself."

Rosemary clapped. "Go, Mom!"

The memory was vivid. "I had a community meeting scheduled where I was on the board. But Willis came home and said he needed me to go over to some client's house with him for appetizers. We had a big argument about it, and I said I wouldn't go with him. I went to my meeting."

"I'm sure Willis wasn't happy," Mary said.

My memory flipped from my victory to the tension I endured for three days afterward. "No. He wasn't."

"But weren't you happy?" Tammy asked. "Didn't standing strong feel better than blindly submitting?"

It had. Briefly.

But even more than enjoying that moment way back when, I enjoyed getting their kudos and encouragement now. I was *not* a confrontational person, so even if the study had started off rough, it felt better now that we all were all on the same page—even if we'd skipped a lot of pages in between.

Even so I was glad when our time was up. Most of the ladies lingered and chatted with each other on their way out. I gathered my mostly-unused notes and accepted their nice comments about how good it was to have a place to honestly share experiences.

"This was great, Elsie," Tammy said.

"Good lesson," Connie said.

I said *thanks* but I knew the lesson had been lacking.

The last one in the room was Janet. I needed to apologize to her. "Sorry if we got carried away," I said. "The ladies can be quite opinionated."

Janet clutched her Bible to her chest. "No, it was good. When you first started talking I was overwhelmed. I mean, my husband is constantly telling me I do everything wrong. So reading those verses that tell us to be noble and hard-working and creative and generous and . . ." She sighed deeply. "I try to be that kind of person, but I'm not. But after hearing the ladies talk, it's nice to know that I'm not expected to be all that, and that it's okay to stand up to my husband when he's too demanding. I mean, I can't imagine throwing a plate against the wall and yet I know that had to feel good. Right?"

I had never heard her talk so much. "Yes, it did feel good but—"

She shook her head enthusiastically. "I am *not* going to be a doormat anymore."

She'd gone from point A to B in a flash. "No, you shouldn't be a doormat, but—"

She hugged me. "Thank you for being so wise, Mrs. Masterson. I'll let you know how it goes."

But . . .

As soon as she left the room I felt the urge to go after her. I'd led her astray. I should have kept control of the Bible study and got it back on track. Instead, I'd given in to the influence of the other ladies.

But before I could catch up with Janet in the parking lot, Rosemary intercepted me. "We have to go, Mom. I have another meeting right after lunch."

I watched Janet drive away. When I got in the car I felt awful. "I really blew it."

"No, you didn't. We had a rousing discussion."

"A rousing complaint session." I rubbed my eyes. "It wasn't productive. And it wasn't biblical at all."

Rosemary raised a finger. "But it *was* modern and life-applicable."

I felt a heavy pit in my stomach. "Maybe according to the world, but not according to the Bible." I thought of a verse I should have quoted to the ladies. "'You were taught, with regard to your former way of life, to put off your old self, which is being corrupted by its deceitful desires.'"

"Wanting to feel good about ourselves isn't a deceitful desire."

"Putting our husbands down isn't virtuous." I looked out the window. "I should have been stronger and kept the lesson more focused."

"It was focused — just not how you wanted it to be focused. Don't be so hard on yourself. We all know we're supposed to be virtuous women, but shouldn't there be a way to be virtuous and God-fearing while remaining strong? We don't have to be a doormat to our husbands."

Doormat. My thoughts turned to Janet. "I'm afraid I may have misled one of the women."

Rosemary jerked her head to look at me. "Who?"

"Janet."

"In what way? And how do you know? She barely said a word. In fact, she seemed kind of down."

"I saw that. She never talks much, but today she seemed distracted — until after it was over."

"So how was she misled?" Rosemary asked.

"She came up afterwards and thanked me. She talked more than I've ever heard her talk. She implied she's going to stand up to her husband."

"That's not a bad thing."

"During the discussion she said she'd made a lot of mistakes, but I didn't have a chance to ask her about them."

"She probably left the butter on the counter or didn't iron the crease in his pants sharp enough. She's too hard on herself."

"Or maybe it's her husband who *thinks* she makes so many mistakes. Maybe she's been beaten down so much that—"

Rosemary pointed a finger in the air. "To him I'd say, 'Ease up, bucko!'"

It wasn't a joking matter. "Do you know him? Because I don't."

"I don't either. I don't think he comes to church."

I got an uneasy feeling. "Oh dear."

Rosemary gave me a double-take. "You're worried about her?"

"I am." My insides were tight.

She touched my arm. "Don't sweat it, Mom. She'll be fine."

Willis and I had a daily routine: every evening we watched TV together, ate a bowl of ice cream, and stayed up until after the evening news.

And sometimes we dozed.

I woke up first and nudged the footrest of his recliner. "We're sleeping. Let's go to bed."

He nodded and put down the footrest with a clatter. I was just about to turn off the news when I saw a picture of Janet flash on the screen. "I know her! She goes to my bible study. That's Janet Agnew."

"Who?"

I shushed him and turned up the volume. "*…Mrs. Agnew managed to call 911 but was pronounced dead at the scene by paramedics.*"

A cold wave swept over me. "She's dead?"

The news flashed to a video of a man being led away in handcuffs.

"*The husband, Bert Agnew, has been taken into custody and will be charged.*"

"Her husband killed her?" I said. "No. No. No!"

"It appears that way."

I pressed my hands against my face, trying to unsee what I was seeing. What I was feeling.

"Did you know her well?" Willis asked.

"She's in my Bible study." One thing was certain: I had *not* known her well enough to give her marriage advice.

He got up. "Sorry to hear that, Els. I'm going to bed. You coming?"

"In a minute."

He turned off the TV and left the room. My mind couldn't process what I'd seen. I thought of our one-on-one time at church, and Janet's eager declaration that she was going to stand up to her husband.

The phone rang, making me jump. It was Mary.

"Did you see the news?" she asked.

"I did. It's terrible."

"It looks like her husband killed her. Poor thing."

"Did you know he had a temper?" There was silence on the line. "Mary? Did you know?"

"Maybe. I'm not sure. Janet wasn't one to share. But I have seen her be kind of skittish, and I saw bruises on her forearms once. And today I did wonder about her glasses."

"Her broken glasses?"

There was silence on the line.

"I was sitting next to her and she had a little cut on the bridge of her nose. What if Bert socked her and broke them?"

I thought about Janet standing before me. I hadn't noticed a cut. Of course not. I'd been too caught up in her praise. "There's no way to know for sure."

"You're probably right. But I feel bad. If I'd said something when I saw the bruises . . . I suppose there's no way to know exactly what happened in their house tonight either. Bert killed the only witness."

The only physical witness. But I knew what had happened. And I was a part of it.

I felt sick to my stomach.

Chapter 36

Holly

"He comforts us in all our troubles,
so that we can comfort those in any trouble
with the comfort we ourselves receive from God."
2 Corinthians 1: 4

"I felt sick to my stomach." Nana looked totally dejected.

I moved to the ottoman and touched her hand. "It's not your fault. You didn't kill Janet."

Nana shrugged. "Not directly. But I was the one who gave her bad advice about confronting her husband. Not being a doormat."

"Isn't that good advice? At least in general?"

"To most people, yes, but not to a battered, frightened, vulnerable woman."

I wished I could think of something to make Nana feel better, but nothing came to me. I partially changed the subject. "Can I ask you something, Nana? Why did you tell *me* this story? I don't think I've ever given an abused woman any advice."

"The moral of the story isn't about me veering off from the Bible lesson I *should* have been giving. It's about the way I handled Janet." Nana sat a moment, then asked me, "Holly, what do you think I could have done differently?"

"To stop her husband from killing her? Probably nothing. If it hadn't happened that night, it probably would have happened eventually. *That's* not your fault."

Nana bobbled her head back and forth. "Perhaps. But what did I do wrong in regard to Janet?"

I tried to think back to the story. I couldn't think of anything. "I don't know."

She sighed deeply. "I could have listened to her. Fully listened."

"But you did listen. She told you she was inspired by what you said."

"At the end, yes." Nana shook her head. "But she also said she didn't like to fight, and amid the heat of the ladies' complaints, she said she'd made a lot of mistakes."

I didn't get it. "So? The ladies were saying we're human. We're allowed."

"There was something deeper in her words. I remember it bothered me at the time and I wanted to ask about it, but the discussion continued — and I let the moment slip away. She mentioned it when it was just her and me too. And I could see she wasn't herself that day. I could tell she was upset about something. Pensive. Troubled. During the lesson she was like a puppy peering out from a corner while the other dogs were wrestling. How might things have been different if I would have stopped the gripe session and listened to what was going on in her life?"

I hated that Nana felt so guilty. "It might not have made a difference."

"But it might have made *the* difference."

"How so?"

Nana sat back in her chair and looked beyond me into her memories. "What if I'd asked, 'What mistakes, Janet?' and she'd told us about petty mistakes she shouldn't feel bad about?"

"You could have told her those types of mistakes aren't that important."

Nana held up a finger. "But in her world they were. What if we'd given her a chance to tell us how her husband was berating her for 'lots of mistakes'. And her saying she didn't like to fight? That's a red flag if I've ever saw one."

It was.

Nana continued. "If I'd taken time to let Janet share we might have realized how unhealthy her situation was. And Mary could have asked her about the bruises she'd seen."

I nodded. I got it. "And her broken glasses."

"Exactly." Nana reached for my hands and held them on top of her legs. "Holly, my darling girl, you are a whirlwind. When you enter a room people notice."

I didn't understand the segue. "Is that a good thing or a bad —?"

"Like me, you are eager to do your best and be liked. But in the hectic pursuit of your goals, amid the tasks at hand . . . do you take time to truly listen?"

I felt my defenses rise. "I try."

"No, you don't. Although you love your family, I think you often consider them an annoyance. An interruption."

"No, not at—"

She held up a hand. "Let me continue . . . You may even pretend to be in the moment when they try to talk to you about something, but your mind doesn't stop *or* listen. It's already thinking about your to-do list. If it even sees the hurting puppy in the corner it doesn't take the time to stop everything, ask questions, and *hear*."

Ouch. "That's harsh, Nana." But I didn't like that it was right on the money.

She sighed. "It is harsh. And I usually don't like to be so blunt. I prefer to tell my story and let things evolve on their own."

I sat back. "So no one else got a lecture?" I thought of my husband. "Surely you told Vernon how wrong *he* was."

Nana pressed her fingers against her forehead. Was I giving her a headache?

When she spoke her voice was soft. "The treasure hunt isn't a battle to win or a game to beat, Holly. It's a time to share what was, what is. And what could be."

I was overcome. I knew I was competitive, always looking for an edge, relentlessly pushing toward my goals no matter what got in my way.

And I wasn't a good listener. Both my family and my co-workers could attest to that.

And yet . . .

The image of Val and Saul came to mind.

"I know you're right, Nana. I do. I guess I never pin-pointed it so well. I try but I know I don't listen well."

Nana nodded once. "Acknowledging the problem is an important step."

I craved her approval—which was probably another weakness. It was time to share a few things I'd done right.

"Actually, I did listen to some clients recently. I really listened to what they were saying."

"Good for you."

"Their names are Val and Saul, and they've gone through a lot of heartbreak that kept them stuck in the past. They wanted to move on and sell their house, and . . ." I took a fresh breath. "Baylor and I have been helping them take down wallpaper so their house will sell better."

"That's nice of you. And it sounds like you did listen."

"I did. But it's more than the house-stuff." I put a hand against my heart. It was time to share our surrender story. "They have a really strong faith that got them through their grief. They ended up telling us about it, and Jesus, and . . ." My voice broke and I took a moment to compose myself.

Nana reached for my hand. "What happened?"

"I wanted what they had — and so did Baylor. So we . . . we kind of . . . asked God in."

Her eyes got big. "In?"

"Into our lives. We surrendered."

Nana clapped her hands together. "Why didn't you tell me that first thing?"

"I was going to, but then . . . I wanted you to go first."

She cupped my face with her hand. "Now there's the sweet Holly I love."

Funny thing is, I kind of loved that Holly too.

I drove home from Nana's with hope as my fuel. Things could change. Unfortunately, I couldn't change the past with all its tuned-out conversations. But from now on . . .

I felt a wave of doubt. Old habits died hard. How could I undo a lifetime of being selfish? I wanted to listen to others, but would I?

I'll help.

I put a hand to my heart, needing to keep the inner thought in place. Maybe I could do it. Together, we could do it.

I got dressed in my work clothes and heard Baylor come in from school. I stepped into the hall. "What are you doing home? School's not out yet, is it?"

"I'm at lunch. I forgot my history report. I gotta get back." He noticed my clothes. "You going over to the Crandell's?"

"I am."

"I'll come help after school."

What a great kid. "Dad said he'd come too."

His eyebrows rose. "Wow. Cool." He grinned. "I like being over there. I know it sounds weird, but it's fun."

I agreed. "Want me to fix you a sandwich to take back to school?"

His eyes lit up, just the smallest bit. "Sure."

While I made him a sandwich with double mustard and double ham and put it in a Baggie, I did something I rarely did. I asked a question about *him*. "What are you studying in history?"

He dug through the pantry and came out with a bag of Cheetos. "We're studying the time right after the Revolutionary War ended. It was crazy. The country had to figure out *everything* from scratch. Think about how hard that would have been. All these colonies stretched from Georgia to Maine, and there weren't phones or emails or cars or even trains. Everybody had a different opinion about how to do it and Washington . . ."

I put an apple in the lunch bag, and started to wash some dishes, then stopped. I turned toward him and held out my hand for a Cheeto. I hadn't had one in ages. "When did Washington get elected?"

"Not until 1789. They argued about what to call him too. Some wanted to crown him as a king but he didn't like that. And then . . ."

Baylor continued and I listened. Actually, all the trivia was really interesting. But more than that, I loved seeing his excitement.

Using a Baylor word, I realized this listening stuff was kinda cool.

The time at the Crandells was exhausting but delightful. Vernon fit right in and even praised Val's spaghetti after she whipped us up a quick supper. I loved the spontaneity of it. There was no big to-do. No stress. Just an eager and willing effort to spend more time together.

Nana had been right. Too often I'd looked at my family's efforts to connect as an annoyance and intrusion, something keeping me from my work. This was work, but it was completely different from anything I'd done before.

As we had a bowl of chocolate chip ice cream for dessert, I sat back and let the chatter and laughter wrap me in a cozy cocoon. I looked at the newly painted walls of the dining room, and didn't condemn the room for not being open-concept. I heard the mellow sounds of Nat King Cole coming from an LP playing in the living room, bringing me back to simpler times. I smelled garlic and cheese and the pure sweet scent of happiness that wove around every person in the room.

And I teared up. Again. What was with me and tears lately?

Vernon noticed and leaned toward me. "Hol? What's wrong?"

My tears turned to nervous laughter. My eyes met his. "Not a thing." I lifted my glass of tea. "A toast."

Everyone lifted their glasses. "To family and friends and the merging of the two."

"Amen to that!" Saul said.

When we came home from the Crandells, we all fell onto the chairs in the family room.

I kicked off my shoes. "I can't believe we got it all done — thanks to you guys."

Vernon picked at paint on his arm. "Their house looks good now. It's homey. Inviting."

I looked around our show-home. The white walls, the light wood floor, the white cabinets. I was suddenly struck by how much it was a white box with white furniture.

Baylor noticed my gaze. "Their house feels like a real home."

I was a bit insulted but couldn't argue with his words. "It's the company. You're feeling the aftereffects of the nice time we had together."

"Sure," he said. "But it's more than that." He looked from me to his dad. "I know this will sound really weird, but I like their house better than ours."

Vernon untied his shoes and shuffled them off. "Weirdly, I do too."

They said it so simply, as if all my hard work making our house a stunning home didn't count. I sat upright and began counting off points on my fingers. "They have a tiny kitchen without an island, there's carpet in the bathroom, no soaker tub or big shower, eight-foot ceilings, and — "

"So what?" Vernon asked.

"Yeah," Baylor said. "So what?"

I eyed them suspiciously. "You're kidding, right?"

The men looked at each other, then both shook their heads.

I had a sudden notion of where they were going with all this. "Do you actually want us to buy their house? For us?"

"I hadn't thought of going that far," Vernon said. "But . . . why not? We could fix it up how we wanted."

"I like the feel of the dining room," Baylor said. "I can imagine us being there at Thanksgiving and Christmas."

In spite of myself, images danced in my head: Paige cooking a special dinner with me in the kitchen, and Bay and Vernon watching a movie in the family room. Mom and Dad and Nana coming to visit.

I pushed the images away as nonsense. I was being a traitor to myself. *This* was my perfect house. New, clean, and pristine.

Baylor shared more ideas, his imagination going a mile a minute. "I'd take the spare bedroom upstairs and we could make the nursery into an office. But I get first dibs on the basement. I want to set up a couch and a big TV so I can have friends over to play video games."

"It's an unfinished basement with ductwork hanging all over. And there's no bathroom," I said.

"I don't care, but if you want, I'll help fix it up. You know Grandpa would help too. He's got his own tools and there are big tools at the workshop."

I stood and began to pace, needing movement to counteract my thoughts that were swirling like a pinwheel. Buy the Crandells' house? It was absurd. Actually, the whole thought of buying, selling, and moving made me dizzy.

But I didn't toss the idea away.

Why didn't I toss the idea away?

"This house is worth three times what their house is worth," Vernon said.

"The extra money could go toward fixing it up," Baylor said.

"Or a family vacation." Vernon said. "Paige could come too. Speaking of . . . since this is such a big deal, I want to call Paige and run it by her." He got out his phone.

They were both running a mile ahead. I stopped pacing when I heard Vernon talking to her.

"Hey, Paige. A weird situation has come up and we were wondering what you might think about . . ."

He strolled into the entry, but we could hear his part of the conversation. "I realize you're already on your own, but . . . well good. I know we don't need your approval, but I'm glad we have it. I'll let you know what happens." He was grinning when he hung up. "She said to go for it."

I drew in a deep breath. It was three against one.

There were a few things I needed to bring up. "The house needs new heating and air. And probably a new roof."

Vernon and Baylor looked at each other, then both said, "So fix it."

Baylor sat forward, leaning his elbows on his knees. "It's a home, Mom. I want us to have a home."

It was such a simple, complicated statement. After all I'd been through in the past few days with him, Vernon, Paige, Nana, the Crandells, and God . . .

Suddenly, I felt a tightening in my chest. And then a swelling as though *more* had been poured in.

"Plus . . ." Baylor seemed hesitant.

"Plus what?" I asked.

"It's special because it's where you and I found *Him*."

Now I understood the *more*. I stared at our amazing, sensitive, beloved son and knew with a deep inner knowing that we should buy the house. It made little sense — especially to the outside world — and yet I was at a point where choosing something outside the box seemed preferable to our status quo.

They were waiting for me to answer. *God? What do You think?*

What I felt next wasn't a push or even a nudge. It was more the feeling of a gentle hand on my shoulder. An *I'm here* feeling that gave me courage. "All right then. Let's buy ourselves a house."

I filled out the paperwork, but putting together the offer was a family affair. Vernon and Baylor gave their input about how much, closing dates, and contingencies. Within an hour, we were ready to go.

I had my phone in hand, ready to call Saul. "Are you sure we shouldn't wait until morning? It's already after nine and it would give us time to think about it."

Vernon waved a hand. "I'm done thinking. I know I'm more a facts-guy, but this feels right."

"Really really right," Baylor said.

Vernon met my eyes and seemed to sense my anxiety. "Are *you* okay with it, Hol? We don't want you to feel like we pressured you — "

"Even though we did," Baylor said.

Even though they did. Yet their pressure was only part of it. I couldn't ignore the soft pressure of heavenly encouragement. And the fact that nothing had happened this evening that spoke against the idea.

Except common sense.

But besides that . . .

Baylor played with a pen, clearly nervous. "I know I'm just a kid and this is big-money stuff, but no matter how it turns out, I won't forget any of this. Ever."

Neither would I.

Suddenly, he tossed the pen aside and got up. "Wait just a minute."

He ran out of the room and came back with a spiral notebook. He flipped through the pages, then found what he was looking for. "Look at this quote my English teacher gave us today."

I took the notebook and read aloud: "'Twenty years from now you will be more disappointed by the things you didn't do than by the ones you did.' It's by Mark Twain."

Vernon spread his hands. "Thank you, Mr. Twain."

I looked down at the words. Logically, if we bought the house and didn't like it, I could sell it again. But emotionally and spiritually it wasn't just about a house.

I was done with me. It was time for us.

I signed the offer and pushed it toward Vernon for his signature. "Let's do this."

The three of us went to the Crandell's together, offer in hand.

Although I'd called, I hadn't told them why we were coming.

They looked confused by our late-evening visit. Val offered us cookies but we declined. "Can we sit at the table again?" I asked.

We all took the same seats we'd had at dinner.

I saw Val glance at the glossy folder in my hand. She looked nervous. "You three worked incredibly hard today. I thought you'd be early to bed by now. We didn't expect your call." She quickly added, "But we're always glad to see you."

I put the folder in front of them. "We came because . . . I have an offer on your house."

Saul's eyebrows dipped. "How? We haven't even put it on the market yet."

"Now you won't need to," Baylor said.

"Won't . . what?"

"*We* want to buy it," I said.

Val and Saul just sat there and I watched their expressions change from surprise to confusion and finally, to awe.

Saul finally said, "Are you sure?"

It was one last chance to back out. I looked at Baylor and Vernon and when they nodded I nodded. "We are."

Val chuckled. "Well I'll be."

I pointed at the folder. "Open it."

As they began to scan the document, I explained the details. The bottom line was this: "We'll pay you $360,000."

Val's eyes were large. "That's ten thousand over what you said it *could* be worth if it was all redone."

From a business standpoint, the offer was too high. Yet it seemed right. "I just want to make sure you don't sell to anyone else."

"Are you going to flip it?" Saul asked.

I shook my head, loving the grinning faces of my men. "No flipping. We want to move in, as a family. It would be our personal home."

Val put a hand on her mouth and shook her head. "Your family, here? Making it yours?" Her eyes glistened with emotion. "Of course, we accept." She got out of her chair and pulled me up into a hug. "This is beyond wonderful. To have you three living here . . ." She glanced at Saul. "I can't imagine anything more perfect."

"Neither can I," Saul said. "But why do you want this place? It still needs a lot of work."

"Some work, sure," Vernon said. "It will be a family project."

Baylor raised a hand. "My grandpa and I have a shop now. We have lots of tools."

Vernon chimed in. "Holly's great at decorating and I'm . . . I'm good at hiring someone else to fix what we mess up."

We all laughed. Vernon was *not* a handyman.

"I want to make the basement into a game room," Baylor said.

Saul's eyebrows rose. "I have a ping pong table set aside down there. You want it?"

"Sure. Can I see it?"

The men went downstairs, all smiles and laughs, leaving Val and me alone. "He wasn't talking about that kind of games, was he?" Val asked.

"No, but ping pong is timeless."

Val reached over and squeezed my hand. "And you're priceless. Thank you for your offer, your help, your generosity, and your friendship."

My throat tightened but I managed a smile. "It goes both ways. I'm so glad I met you and Saul. You . . . changed me. Changed us."

"And you changed us."

I looked around the house — our house. The heavenly hand on my shoulder turned into a pat on the back.

I couldn't sleep.

I slipped into the family room and took out my laptop, keying in a market search for properties like ours.

A few minutes later Vernon came out of the bedroom, squinting at the light. "What are you doing up?"

"I'm selling our house."

He sat beside me on the couch and I adjusted the screen so he could see it too. "I'm checking comps to see how much it's worth."

"And . . .?"

"I was thinking one million, ninety-five thousand."

"Wow."

"I know. The market's hot right now."

"I never, ever, ever thought I'd live in a house worth that much."

I looked at him, slightly surprised. "I did."

He spread his hands to encompass the room. "And so, here we are."

"This wasn't all my fault."

He held up a hand. "No fault involved, Hol. I was a willing participant. But you're the one who wanted the house as a way to tell the world you'd arrived." He put a hand on my knee. "You have to admit that's true."

Totally true. "Is that all bad?"

He shrugged. "I'm not sure we should care about what other people think. And buying this house *was* a stretch on our finances. *Is* a stretch."

His salary was pretty constant. But mine . . . we were struggling because of me. "I'm sorry I don't bring in more. I thought I'd be better at my job by now."

He bumped his shoulder against mine. "You're still learning and you're getting better with every client. Look at the smash-up job you did with Val and Saul. You should be proud of that."

"I am. This whole thing with us finding each other is kind of surreal. When they were assigned to me, I was less than thrilled. I mean their house . . ."

"Our house."

Touché. "Like I said, surreal."

"The good thing is, we can definitely afford to buy their house. With no mortgage."

I nodded. I was excited but still wary.

"Are you having second thoughts?" he asked.

I hesitated. "Not really. I like thinking about the projects we'll do together. I love Baylor's excitement about the basement. But moving there . . . it might be hard to explain to people at work."

His voice softened. "Is it important they understand? Do we need their approval?"

"I don't want to need it."

He put a hand on my knee. "Then don't. I know there's a verse somewhere about not trying to win the approval of man because the focus is wrong. You and Baylor had a big moment with God. I think it's more important to wonder what He thinks about what we're doing."

It was strange to hear Vernon mention God. "You and I don't talk about God and faith and all that."

"A deficiency we should remedy."

His words sounded lofty, which made me smile. "A deficiency we should remedy?"

He didn't smile back. "You and I have lots of deficiencies, Hol. And we need to work on them." He shrugged. "But, I sure wouldn't mind some extra help. Maybe we've neglected God long enough."

I was stunned by the suggestion coming from him. I knew he believed in God and Jesus but for him to bring it up — bring Him up — and want to be closer to Him? "Did Nana do this to you?"

He chuckled. "Actually, I think God did this to me *through* Nana. She gave me a verse to memorize. Want to hear it?"

Now he knew a verse? "Shoot."

"'Come near to God and he will come near to you.' I think it's time we moved closer to Him."

My thoughts floated around as if they were searching for their proper place, like puzzle pieces fitting together. But yes, I wanted God to be a part of our *now*, part of our future. "I want to be closer to Him too."

The words hung in the air.

"Wow. That was easy," he said.

I scoffed. "Hardly. But Nana has helped me see that the solution to our marriage problems, Baylor's problems, Paige's problems, and my multitude of character and career problems stem from one big hole in our lives."

"A lack of faith?"

Partially. "It's not about believing *in* Him, it's more about *believing* Him."

Vernon cocked his head, deep in thought. Then he said, "I like that. I *get* that. And I think you're right. It's like we've kept Him standing just outside the door."

Yes! "We need to invite Him in. That's what Baylor and I did at the Crandell's."

Vernon laughed. "Seems like that house is Ground Zero."

I laughed with him.

He reached for my hand, squeezing it. "What did Nana teach *you*?"

I remembered all the emotions that had popped up during my time with her. Up emotions, down emotions, and everything in between. But it came down to this: "She made me realize I need to work on loving my family the way they deserve to be loved. And be in the moment so I can listen. Really listen."

"I agree."

I swatted his arm. "Hey!"

He rested our clasped hands on his leg. "All I know is that when I'd want to talk to you about something, I always felt as if I had about twenty seconds to let loose with the gist of it. After that your eyes would cloud over. I'd lose you."

Wow. "I wasn't *that* bad. Was I?"

He reached forward and touched my cheek. "You *were* that bad. But I can already see a change in you." He tweaked the tip of my nose. "Look at us, sitting here having a real conversation about important, serious, grown-up things."

It *was* kind of amazing. And I *had* changed. I *was* listening.

I leaned toward him, stopping inches from his face. "I don't deserve you, husband. Thank you for being so patient with me. So loving. And forgiving. I know I'm not an easy person —"

He put his fingers on my lips. "Shh. Enough of that. As the Crandells are starting fresh, so are we."

I could think of nothing better.

To seal the deal, my darling, long-suffering husband kissed me like he hadn't kissed me in a long time, and pulled me into his glorious arms.

Chapter 37

Holly

"And now these three remain:
faith, hope and love.
But the greatest of these is love."
1 Corinthians 13:13

I peeked at the Thanksgiving turkey in the roaster. Another half-hour and it would be perfection. I was pleased the small desk area of the kitchen of our new house was just the right size for the roaster.

I turned back to Paige and her friends who'd brought along goodies to make their own recipe. "What are you making again?" I asked.

Camille answered, "*Camote Enmielado.*"

"Candied sweet potatoes," Carlos said. "It's a recipe from our Lita, our grandmother. The smell alone is worth the work."

Camille started peeling sweet potatoes, and Paige took an odd-looking cone wrapped in cellophane out of their bag.

"What's that?" I asked.

Paige handed the cone to Carlos and got out a Dutch oven. "I defer to the expert."

Carlos answered. "It's a piloncillo cone. Mexican brown sugar."

Camille said, "You can use dark brown sugar —"

"If you must," Carlos said. "But we wanted everyone to taste it as if Lita made it."

Paige took a few more ingredients out of a sack. "Star anise, cinnamon, and cloves."

"Mmm." I started to drool thinking about the upcoming aroma. "What can I do to help?"

"Nothing right now, Mom," Paige said. "Let us do this for you."

I loved how the three friends worked together. No wonder Paige's cooking videos looked so seamless. They were a finely tuned machine.

Even though Vernon and I had only met the Lopez twins a few times in the past two months, they already seemed like family. Sometimes that's just how it was with people. There was an instant connection as if we'd always known each other.

Paige kept insisting that she and Carlos were just friends but I saw a certain spark between them. And I wouldn't object if he and his sister became actual family. I liked him a lot, and I loved the way he treated Paige. He was a keeper.

I enjoyed listening to their easy banter, and soon the smells of autumn spices filled the kitchen. The candle-makers of the world needed to capture the fragrance and create a scented candle called HOME.

I had just taken the turkey out to rest before carving when the front door opened. Mom and Dad swept in with a *whoosh* of November air.

Dad carried a crockpot. "Cheesy corn," he said. "Where do you want me to put it?"

I looked around the busy kitchen. "I'm not quite sure. This is our first party." In the other house, I'd had a huge serving area for pot-lucks. I'd had an island. I'd had two ovens . . .

It didn't matter. That was then, this was now.

I pointed to the small drop-leaf dinette table. "Pull up the leaves. We can put all the food there."

Vernon took coats. "Where's Nana?"

"Oops!" Everett said with a grin. "I'm as forgetful as a kid without his homework." He winked. "One Nana, coming up."

But when he opened the door Val and Saul were standing there, each holding a pie. "Happy Thanksgiving!" they said.

There was a flurry of activity as they were welcomed inside. Introductions were made to Paige and her friends.

Then the doorbell rang.

I answered it. Baylor stood there with Nana on his arm. His friends Nate and Aimee giggled behind them, holding Nana's familiar breadbasket full of home-made rolls.

"Excuse me, ma'am," Baylor said in a deep voice. "We found this woman wandering around outside. Do you know her?"

"Very funny." There was a second flurry of introductions and laughter. Coats were tossed on a bed and spiced cider was poured. The teenagers disappeared to the basement game room, the men to the living room, and the women to the kitchen. It was comfortable. Natural.

Nana and Val sat on the dinette chairs while Mom stirred the corn.

I noticed Val looking around the kitchen. "Coming back to your house must be odd," I said.

She hesitated for just a moment. "A bit. I'm surprised you haven't remodeled it."

"Not yet. We've only been in three weeks. We want to get a feel for the home as-is first. Then, we'll make changes."

"How do you like *your* new place, Mrs. Crandell?" Paige asked. "Mom said it was real nice. All one floor."

"Call me Val." Her eyes lit up. "And it's perfect. It definitely was the right move for us. We have great neighbors — other couples our age." She smiled and pulled a wrapped gift from behind her chair. She handed it to me. "I've brought you a house-warming gift."

I unwrapped it. When I saw what it was I laughed and turned it around so everyone could see. "It's your Holly Hobbie cross-stitch."

Mom's eyes brightened. "We named you after Holly — "

"I know, I know."

"Who's Holly Hobbie?" Paige asked.

Camille shrugged. "I don't know either."

We explained the character. And though I found the picture completely un-fashionable and even a bit tacky, I set it on the table. "Thank you. I will cherish it forever."

"As I will cherish you, dear lady." Val kissed my cheek.

I put a hand to my mouth, overcome with emotion.

"Mom?" Paige asked.

We heard the men laughing from the other room, as well as the sound of a ping-pong game coming from the basement. "I just love having everyone here."

"We have much to be thankful for," Nana said with a nod.

It was the first time she'd spoken since she'd arrived. "Indeed we do," I said. I looked around the small kitchen with its golden oak cabinets, patterned sheet vinyl floors, and pink laminate countertops. And loved it. "This kitchen, this house, makes me feel . . . whole."

There was a chorus of *Ahhhs*.

"It's not just the house," Nana said. "It's the people. The family and friends."

"The laughter," Paige said.

"The hope," Val said.

"And the love," Nana said. She leaned forward in her chair, her hands on her cane. "'And God saw that it was good.'"

I just *had* to hug her. "It is good, Nana. I'm good. We're all good because of the stories you shared with us."

Camille slipped her arm around Paige's arm. "Paige told me all about the treasure hunts. You've given your family an amazing legacy."

"*You* are the treasure, Nana," Mom said. "I vow to never take you for granted again."

"Oh, you," Nana said, brushing the compliment away.

I would have none of it. "I loved learning about your *before* years. It changed me." I looked at the special people in this house. "It changed all of us."

"Here, here!" Paige said.

"Here, here?" Vernon asked as he came in the kitchen.

"We're thanking Nana for sharing her life with us."

"Then I second the 'here, here!'"

The other men streamed in the kitchen. "What are we missing?" Dad asked.

I heard the heavy footfalls of the teenagers coming up from their kid-cave.

"We're getting hungry," Baylor said.

"It's smelling really good, Mrs. Lindstrom," Aimee said. She nodded at the pumpkin pies. "My mom always makes pecan, but I like pumpkin best."

"Me too," Nate said.

Everybody talked at once, until Nana lifted her cane into the air.

"Shh, everyone!" I said. "Nana? You have something to say?"

"I do." She started to stand and Dad helped her up. She looked over the gathering and smiled. "If you'll allow an old woman a bit of a speech."

"Of course," I said. Everyone encouraged her.

She began by looking at every face. "All of you are my treasure. Pure treasure. I want to thank you for letting me share my *before* and my *now* life with you. If you take anything from my stories, realize that life is more than the hats you wear—it's about connecting with each other, having empathy for one another, and striving to do it all with God's purpose in mind."

"That's really nice, Nana," I said.

She raised a hand. "Before Papa died he urged me to share my undiscovered life with the family. I did that. But don't let it stop there." She waved her cane over all of us. "We all have undiscovered lives. Share them. Listen to each other's stories. Learn from each other, and love each other, no matter what. Your lives will be richer for it."

"God bless us every one," Dad said, grinning.

"Amen and amen," Nana said. "Now let's get this dinner on the table. I'm famished."

As the kitchen bustled with activity, Vernon took my hand and led me into the quiet foyer.

"I have work to do, Vernon."

"It can wait, but this can't." He faced me and took my hands in his. "You are *my* treasure, Holly."

I was surprised and smiled up at him. "And you are mine."

"Are you happy?" he asked.

I felt a smile spread across my lips as I realized the truth. "More than I ever thought possible."

Baylor came out of the kitchen. "Dad? We're waiting for you to carve the turkey."

Vernon kissed my cheek and went to do his duty.

I took a short moment alone in the foyer and let the sights and sounds of my discovered life wrap around me. *Thank You for Your many blessings, Lord.*

Then I let my family's laughter draw me into their warm and loving embrace.

THE END

"God saw all that he had made,
and it was very good."
Genesis 1: 31

Letter to the Reader

It all started with my mom . . .

Marguerite Swenson Young passed away on May 16, 2020 at age 99. While going through her belongings I thought about all the roles she'd played in her long life as a wife, mother, entrepreneur, teacher, saleswoman, activist, fashion designer, dreamer . . . Discovering her undiscovered life inspired me to write this novel.

Elsie Masterson is *not* my mom, but many of the events Elsie shares in her treasure hunts were inspired by events in Mom's life. And mine. I'll detail some of those later. And we did grow up having treasure hunts on Easter with clues that led to a basket of goodies. I passed that tradition onto our kids, and tried to do it with the grandkids until they numbered seven. My brain can't handle making multiple clues for seven different hunts! So now we just hide color-coded eggs with candy inside.

Like Elsie, Mom made sure we knew everything about our dad (Lyle). She bragged him up all the time — especially after he died in 2012. We had to point out what an amazing person *she* was. "Don't forget about you, Mom."

After Dad's death she never did figure out how to say "I". It was always "we" as in, "We'd really like you to come for a visit." Or "We had a busy day today." Eventually we stopped correcting her. After 70 years of being "we", she was entitled.

Just like Willis, Mom died alone. She broke her hip Mother's Day weekend 2020 and lingered a week. After the first day she was unconscious. Her home healthcare ladies (especially Vicki and DeEtte) were so important to her, so dear and loyal, even after she'd been moved to hospice — where other ladies took care of her with love. Our family made sure someone was with her the entire week. But then, the evening before we had to disperse and drive home — the one time she was alone — she passed away. The hospice workers told us that many people like to make the final journey alone. It suits Mom. She would have thought it was impolite to die while she had company.

A note about what the dying hear . . . in the final day of her life, my two sisters and I held her hands and stroked her hair. We stood around Mom and talked to her. We told her it was okay to go, that Dad and other family were waiting for her. We sang hymns over her. And though she had not made a sound for nearly a week, suddenly she made a little groan of pleasure at hearing us sing. I will never forget that. So talk to your loved ones. They hear you.

On a lighter note, Rosemary brought her mother some donuts. I don't remember my mother ever eating a donut. She made breakfast for Dad for 70 years and adjusted her own eating habits to match the diabetic menu that was best for him. I regret never bringing Mom a donut with sprinkles.

In Chapter 33, Elsie says Willis could be eloquent and mentions love letters. My parents got married in 1942, during World War II. Dad was soon shipped off "for the duration" which ended up being over two years. They sent the most amazing love letters to each other. We still have most of them and Mom compiled some of Dad's into a book, *Dearest Marguerite: Letters from a Soldier to the Wife He Left Behind.* Dad didn't see my oldest sister Lois until she was two! I encourage you to read this book, as Mom interspersed history with the personal.

Mom was a chronicler (I get it from her.) She wrote essays about her life. Whether she wrote about a big tree on the family farm in Minnesota, to matter-of-fact accounts of surviving breast cancer, or starting up their many entrepreneurial businesses, to essays about the state of the world and faith and marriage, she *had* to write. We urged her to share more of her emotions in these writings, but it was not her way. Perhaps it's her Swedish, first-born nature, or being married to a facts-centered engineer. But I think it's also because of the era when she was born. Just think about what's happened in 99 years: the Great Depression, World War II, the Korean War, Vietnam, Afghanistan and Iraq. No indoor plumbing, telephones, or central heat and air. A man on the moon, space stations, television, computers, cell phones, the Internet, (yes, Mom learned how to use email.) The list goes on. Mom's Grand Generation was all about learning to adapt, and the best way to do that was not emotionally, but by being very pragmatic. Solve the problem. I commend her and all those who lived through such changes.

By the way, the woman and child swinging on the cover are Mom and me in 1955. She looks so happy. I look a little scared!

Here are a few of the similarities in Elsie's stories and my mother's:

- In Chapter 3, Elsie talks about Willis taking up golf. That's what my dad did when he retired, and Mom went along (even though she never liked it.) And yes, like Elsie, she got a hole in one. Yay, Mom.
- Mom was very involved in church, Faculty Women's Club (University of Nebraska), bridge clubs, and . . . the League of Women Voters. Like Elsie she was asked to be on the state board,

but like Willis, my dad told her no. He wanted her home to travel with him. In later life Mom told me it was one of her few regrets.

- Elsie's story of the overly-possessive boyfriend and quitting the orchestra came from my life. I quit Lincoln Youth Symphony because of a boyfriend. And like Elsie, when I found out they were going on a special trip (mine was to Europe) I asked to come back. I too went from first chair viola to last. And the telephone *was* put in the refrigerator when the boyfriend kept calling. Plus—like Elsie—Mom and Dad finally confronted him when he wouldn't leave me alone. Only now as a grandparent do I see how brave they were.

- Elsie's dormant talent is inspired by my mother. They both were expert seamstresses and I have the very-heavy wool coat that Mom made in a tailoring class. Mom went on to sew our wedding dresses, prom and bridesmaid dresses, school clothes, suits, and coats. Swimsuits too. My sister tells the story of a date coming to pick her up for a dance and he had to wait because Mom was finishing up her dress! I didn't have a store-bought dress until I was a senior in high school. Mom loved to sew pockets in the side seams of dresses.

- Elsie's trip to the Jeanne's fabric store: Jeanne's Fashion Fabrics was my first job and I also worked at Herberger's for years. The pattern that Neda chooses for her wedding dress (Simplicity 6343) was the pattern for my wedding dress. We've been married for 46 years now, and like Neda, my attendants wore lime green and

yellow.

- Mom made me a gorgeous yellow wool coatdress (that had gray flecks) and a pink wool suit like I mention in the book.

- In Chapter 6 Elsie describes her first house as being so small she could vacuum it from one outlet, and they had to choose between ice cream and meat in the freezer. That's a good description of our first apartment. We married when we were 20, with two years of college left. So young!

- In Chapter 6 Paige makes a 3-ingredient chocolate mousse for her neighbor. Want the recipe? https://kitchencents.com/easy-3-ingredient-chocolate-mousse/

- Chapter 11: Here is the painting of Mrs. Cecil Wade that Elsie saw in the museum. She looks so pensive and unhappy. Elegant and resigned.

- I am a huge admirer of John Singer Sargent's paintings. In fact I used 2 of his portraits on the covers for my Manor House Series (on Bride and Rise).

- In Chapter 13 Elsie has Baylor count the "Castleton Rose" china for her dinner party. Here it is, out of my own cupboard.

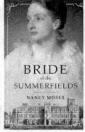

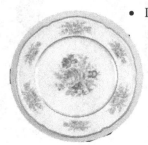

- In Chapter 16 Baylor mentions his teacher Mrs. Williams who didn't abide by small talk. I had a teacher like that: Mrs. June Williams, at East High in Lincoln, Nebraska. She taught Greco-Roman history and was tough. Yet we all loved her and learned a ton from her. *Euge, Mrs. Williams!*

- Chapter 17: Vernon notices that Willis logged in the high and low temperatures for the day at the top of each calendar page. My husband's Grandpa Hays used to do that.

- Chapter 18: When Elsie is in the hospital after a ruptured appendix Willis tells her, "Don't you ever leave me, you hear?" When I was in the hospital with extensive blood clots, my husband said those same words to me. Obviously, they meant a lot because I've remembered them. And I'm still here.
- At the Crandell's, Holly sees a Holly Hobbie cross-stitch. In case you don't know who "she" was, here she is. And Saul and Val's blue and mauve colors, and the green and rust in the bedroom? That's our house in the early 1980s. I think I had a goose recipe holder too.

As you can see, everything in a writer's life is fair game. We can't write our stories or create the characters we create without our own experiences, acquaintances, and family influencing us. As Mom would say, "So be it."

I need to give a huge thank you to my editor, Laurel Conrad — who happens to be my daughter. Her insight and honesty helped me slow down and let the characters "feel the feels." It wouldn't be the same book without her. Thank you, honey.

The other night I watched "Field of Dreams." A man magically gets to meet his father when the father was his own age. The son says, "The last time I'd seen him he was old and used up by life." Meeting him as a peer was very moving. It gave him a different perspective.

This is one of the big takeaways I want you to get from *An Undiscovered Life*: a desire to discover the lives of your elders. Walk in their shoes and get to know them in their *before* years, not just in their current role.

Then cherish them *now*.

Nancy Moser

Verses in *An Undiscovered Life*

Discussion Questions:

An Undiscovered Life

1. Elsie mentions the comfort she and Willis felt in knowing he was going to heaven where they would see each other again. She wonders how unbelievers faced death. Do you have any experience with this? Share.

2. Chapter 7: Holly wants Nana to be on her side. But Nana says, "That is not in the grandmother's handbook. I will give you unconditional love, but not unconditional validation." Was there anyone in your life like Nana? Was their way of doing things helpful or not?

3. Chapter 12: Elsie said her life was missing something more important than freedom: affirmation. Which do you think is more important?

4. Chapter 12: Elsie told her story about running away from her life. She said, "Finding the lesson makes the pain bearable." How does this apply to your life?

5. Chapter 16: Baylor is dealing with bullies. What do you think about his plan to give Colton the wrong answers? What about his decision *not* to follow through? Have you ever had to deal with bullies? What helped you get through it? What didn't?

6. Chapter 19: Elsie tells how she finally forgave Willis his affair — after 17 years. She says, "It's never too late to confess and come to grips with a bad situation." Do you agree with her? Is there a late-coming forgiveness issue in your own life?

7. Chapter 19: In regards to Elsie telling Willis she knew of the affair, she says, "God tends to reward truth, repentance, and forgiveness." Do you agree? How?

8. Chapter 22: Elsie tells Paige that "Weariness is always a threat to courage." How have you found this to be true in your own life?

9. Chapter 22: Elsie tells Paige to "be assertive not aggressive." What is the difference?

10. Chapter 24: Rosemary sees an old birthday card she made for her dad — that he criticized. She finds out her mom stood up for her. "You were my parents but I never really stopped to think of you as just people." Name a time when you discovered something new about your family that surprised you.

11. Chapter 26: Elsie tells Rosemary that sometimes we need to step back to let other people shine. Have you ever been given this choice to step back? What did you do?

12. Chapter 28: Elsie's friend Neda wanted her parents to change. Elsie tells her, "It's not your job to change your parents' minds or actions. You showed your concern, you wanted them to be honest, you wanted to talk about the Burton's genuine faith, and since they rejected you? You're allowed to move on." Do you agree with that advice?

13. Chapter 30: Newly retired Everett is inspired to revamp an old interest into a new hobby. Who in your life has a dormant talent that could be rekindled? Is it you?

14. Chapter 31: Paige has broken up with Drew but he comes to work, wanting back together. God gives Paige the right words — meaning silence. "Sometimes the right words were no words." Name a time when God told you to be silent. Was it the right thing to do?

15. Chapter 32: Changes stir in Holly as she helps the Crandells. Why do you think that couple touched her so deeply? Who have you met in your life — seemingly by chance — that changed your life in some important way?

16. Chapter 32: Holly and Baylor have a come-to-Jesus moment while they're in a very ordinary, unlikely situation. How did you come to Him? If you haven't, why not right now?

17. Chapter 35: In 1998 Rosemary warns her mother not to be old fashioned while teaching Proverbs 31 in Bible study. "You don't want to turn people off, Mom." What do you think about modernizing Scripture for today's society? Have you ever been influenced by what the "world" wants you to think instead of standing up for God's way? And what do you think about a real-life application of the Proverbs 31 woman?

18. Chapter 36: Elsie shares her lesson about listening to others. Holly is moved and convicted and wants to change. How is listening an issue in your life?

19. Chapter 36: Meeting the Crandells changed Holly in a myriad of ways — including her family's decision to buy their house. What do you think about their decision? Do you understand their reasoning? Are you happy for them?

Painting by Leonid Baranov

An Old Lady's Poem

Anonymous

What do you see, nurses, what do you see?
What are you thinking when you're looking at me?
A crabby old woman, not very wise,
Uncertain of habit, with faraway eyes?
Who dribbles her food and makes no reply
When you say in a loud voice, "I do wish you'd try!"
Who seems not to notice the things that you do,
And forever is losing a stocking or shoe.
Who, resisting or not, lets you do as you will,
With bathing and feeding, the long day to fill.
Is that what you're thinking? Is that what you see?
Then open your eyes, nurse; you're not looking at me.

I'll tell you who I am as I sit here so still,
As I do at your bidding, as I eat at your will.
I'm a small child of ten, with a father and mother,
Brothers and sisters, who love one another.
A young girl of sixteen, with wings on her feet,
Dreaming that soon now a lover she'll meet.
A bride soon at twenty – my heart gives a leap,
Remembering the vows that I promised to keep.
At twenty-five now, I have young of my own,
Who need me to guide and a secure happy home.
A woman of thirty, my young now grown fast,
Bound to each other with ties that should last.
At forty, my young sons have grown and are gone,
But my man's beside me to see I don't mourn.
At fifty once more, babies play round my knee,
Again we know children, my loved one and me.
Dark days are upon me, my husband is dead;
I look at the future, I shudder with dread.
For my young are all rearing young of their own,
And I think of the years and the love that I've known.

I'm now an old woman, and nature is cruel;
'Tis jest to make old age look like a fool.
The body, it crumbles, grace and vigor depart,
There is now a stone where I once had a heart.
But inside this old carcass a young girl still dwells,
And now and again my battered heart swells.
I remember the joys, I remember the pain,
And I'm loving and living life over again.
I think of the years, all too few, gone too fast,
And accept the stark fact that nothing can last.

So open your eyes, nurses, open and see,
Not a crabby old woman; look closer . . . see ME!

About the Author

NANCY MOSER is the best-selling author of over 40 novels, novellas, and children's books, including Christy Award winner *Time Lottery* and Christy finalist *Washington's Lady*. She's written seventeen historical novels including *Love of the Summerfields, Masquerade, Where Time Will Take Me,* and *Just Jane*. *An Unlikely Suitor* was named to Booklist's "Top 100 Romance Novels of the Decade." *The Pattern Artist* was a finalist in the Romantic Times Reviewers Choice award. Some of her contemporary novels are: *An Undiscovered Life, The Invitation, Solemnly Swear, The Good Nearby, John 3:16, Crossroads, The Seat Beside Me,* and the Sister Circle series. *Eyes of Our Heart* was a finalist in the Faith, Hope, and Love Readers' Choice Awards. Nancy has been married for over 45 years—to the same man. She and her husband have three grown children, seven grandchildren, and live in the Midwest. She's been blessed with a varied life. She's earned a degree in architecture, run a business with her husband, traveled extensively in Europe, and has performed in various theaters, symphonies, and choirs. She knits voraciously, kills all her houseplants, and can wire an electrical fixture without getting shocked. She is a fan of anything antique—humans included.

Website: www.nancymoser.com
Blogs: Author blog: www.authornancymoser.blogspot.com
History blog: www.footnotesfromhistory.blogspot.com
Facebook: www.facebook.com/nancymoser.author
Bookbub: www.bookbub.com/authors/nancy-moser?list=author_ books
Goodreads:
www.goodreads.com/author/show/117288.Nancy_Moser
Pinterest: www.pinterest.com/nancymoser1/_saved/
Instagram: www.instagram.com/nmoser33/

Excerpt from *Eyes of Our Heart*

Five ordinary people are given an opportunity
to see how God is working in their lives.
Are they willing to merge their journey with His?

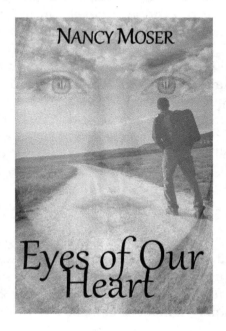

"Surrender" was the word Claire Adams used to describe her obedience to the Almighty. It sounded better than "submission" though the effect was the same.

Claire always prayed before she went to sleep, and hoped she got credit for praying off and on during the day too. As a successful middle-aged woman she didn't pray out of need for a material this or that, or even an emotional that or this, but prayed to be a better person, a better child of God.

It wasn't that she considered herself holy (heaven forbid) but she'd had enough God-moments in her life to want to know Him on a deeper level and make Him proud. Long ago she'd given up the notion of getting her own way, or even wanting her own way. From experience — having had equal moments of saying yes and no to the God of the universe — she knew that His way was the best way and it was easier and far more beneficial to just give in. Surrender.

But on this particular summer night, as Claire went through her bedtime ritual of removing her makeup and slathering on three types of wrinkle cream, she knelt at the side of her bed and offered prayers out of need.

She needed money.

Claire prefaced her request by thanking God for His many gifts: her charming three-bedroom home in a tree-lined neighborhood in Kansas City; her good health (ignoring her aching knees as they were an expected part of getting older); her status as a single, independent woman; and her ability to create mosaic artwork that provided a modicum of fame and financial stability.

Until recently.

Business had been slow. There were fewer customers willing to shell out thousands for a large wall piece when they could buy a wrapped canvas made from their own photo of a waterfall they'd seen on vacation, or purchase a framed landscape for fifty-percent off from their local craft store. The lack of business was the main reason she'd succumbed to covering bowls, lamps, and boxes with tile because they could be sold at a price the masses would accept. She had a gallery, but online sales and seasonal art shows were the new way to reach customers. Yet mosaics were heavy and hard to ship.

She rested her forehead on her clasped hands. "Father? As You know, business is slow. I need to sell more art or I'm going to have to close the gallery, let Darla go, or . . ." She hated to say the next because she really didn't want to offer God the alternative, but since He knew all the details of her life anyway… "Or sell the house and move to a smaller place. I know You have a plan and You'll do what's best, so I'll leave You to work out the details. I trust You. In Jesus' name, amen."

With a nod at the heavenly transaction, and a grunt as she pushed herself to her feet, Claire slipped into bed, leaving God to do His stuff.

CPSIA information can be obtained
at www.ICGtesting.com
Printed in the USA
LVHW022345050922
727595LV00008B/206